CHINESE IMPERIAL POST
HALF CENT
2.00
भारत
INDIA

tiger's quest

tiger's quest

by COLLEEN HOUCK

SPLINTER
New York

An Imprint of Sterling Publishing
387 Park Avenue South
New York, NY 10016

www.sterlingpublishing.com

ISBN 978-1-4027-8404-0 (print format)
ISBN 978-1-4027-8486-6 (ebook)

Designed by Katrina Damkoehler.

Library of Congress Cataloging-in-Publication Data
Houck, Colleen.
Tiger's quest / by Colleen Houck.
p. cm. -- (Tiger's curse)
Summary: Kelsey returns home to Oregon, where Mr. Kadam has enrolled her in college, but danger sends her back to India to begin another quest, this time with Kishan, to try to break the curse that forces Kishan and his brother Ren to live as tigers.
ISBN 978-1-4027-8404-0
[1. Tigers--Fiction. 2. Blessing and cursing--Fiction. 3. Colleges and universities--Fiction. 4. Dating (Social customs)--Fiction. 5. Immortality--Fiction. 6. Orphans--Fiction. 7. Oregon--Fiction. 8. India--Fiction.] I. Title.
PZ7.H81143Tiq 2011
[Fic]--dc22

2010049270

Distributed in Canada by Sterling Publishing
c/o Canadian Manda Group, 165 Dufferin Street
Toronto, Ontario, Canada M6K 3H6
Distributed in the United Kingdom by GMC Distribution Services
Castle Place, 166 High Street, Lewes, East Sussex, England BN7 1XU
Distributed in Australia by Capricorn Link (Australia) Pty. Ltd.
P.O. Box 704, Windsor, NSW 2756, Australia

For information about custom editions, special sales, and premium and corporate purchases, please contact Sterling Special Sales at 800-805-5489 or specialsales@sterlingpublishing.com.

Manufactured in Canada
Lot #:
2 4 6 8 10 9 7 5 3 1
04/11

For my husband, Brad—proof that there really are guys like that out there.

contents

the loom of time

Author Unknown

Man's life is laid in the loom of time
To a pattern he does not see,
While the weavers work and the shuttles fly
Till the dawn of eternity.

Some shuttles are filled with silver threads
And some with threads of gold,
While often but the darker hues
Are all that they may hold.

But the weaver watches with skillful eye
Each shuttle fly to and fro,
And sees the pattern so deftly wrought
As the loom moves sure and slow.

God surely planned the pattern:
Each thread, the dark and fair,
Is chosen by His master skill
And placed in the web with care.

He only knows its beauty,
And guides the shuttles which hold
The threads so unattractive,
As well as the threads of gold.

Not till each loom is silent,
And the shuttles cease to fly,
Shall God reveal the pattern
And explain the reason why

The dark threads were as needful
In the weaver's skillful hand
As the threads of gold and silver
For the pattern which He planned.

PROLOGUE

going home

I clung to the leather seat and felt my heart fall as the private plane rose into the sky, streaking away from India. If I took off my seatbelt, I was sure I would sink right through the floor and drop thousands of feet, freefalling to the jungles below. Only then would I feel right again. I had left my heart in India; I could feel it missing. All that was left of me was a hollowed-out shell, numb and empty.

The worst part was . . . I did this to myself.

How was it possible that I had fallen in love? And with someone so . . . complicated? The past few months had flown by. Somehow, I had gone from working at a circus to traveling to India with a tiger—who turned out to be an Indian prince—to battling immortal creatures to trying to piece together a lost prophecy. Now, my adventure was all over, and I was alone.

It was hard to believe just a few minutes ago I had said good-bye to Mr. Kadam. He hadn't said much. He had just gently patted my back as I'd hugged him hard, not letting go. Finally, Mr. Kadam pried my arms from the vise I'd locked him in, muttered some reassurances, and turned me over to his great-great-great granddaughter, Nilima.

Thankfully, Nilima left me alone on the plane. I didn't want anyone's company. She brought lunch, but I couldn't even think about eating. I'm sure it was delicious, but I felt like I was skirting the edge of a pit of quicksand. Any second, I could be sucked down into an abyss of despair. The last thing I wanted was food. I felt spent and lifeless, like crumpled-up wrapping paper after Christmas.

Nilima removed the meal and tried to tempt me with my favorite drink—ice-cold lemon water, but I left it on the table. I stared at the glass for who knows how long, watching the moisture bead on the outside and slowly dribble down, pooling around the bottom.

I tried to sleep, to forget about everything for at least a few hours—but the dark, peaceful oblivion eluded me. Thoughts of my white tiger and the centuries-old curse that trapped him raced through my mind as I stared into space. I looked at Mr. Kadam's empty seat across from me, glanced out the window, or watched a blinking light on the wall. I gazed at my hand now and then, tracing over the spot where Phet's henna design lay unseen.

Nilima returned with an MP3 player full of thousands of songs. Several were by Indian musicians, but most of them were by Americans. I scrolled through to find the saddest breakup songs on it. Putting the plugs in my ears, I selected PLAY.

I unzipped my backpack to retrieve my grandmother's quilt, only then remembering that I had wrapped Fanindra inside it. Pulling back the edges of the quilt, I spied the golden serpent, a gift from the goddess Durga herself, and set it next to me on the armrest. The enchanted piece of jewelry was in a coil, resting: or at least I assumed she was. Rubbing her smooth, golden head, I whispered, "You're all I've got now."

Spreading the quilt over my legs, I leaned back in the reclined chair, stared at the ceiling of the airplane, and listened to a song called "One Last Cry." Keeping the volume soft and low, I placed Fanindra on my lap and stroked her gleaming coils. The green glow of the snake's jeweled eyes softly illuminated the plane's cabin and comforted me as the music filled the empty place in my soul.

Home

The plane finally landed several mind-numbing hours later at the airport in Portland, Oregon. When my feet hit the tarmac, I shifted my gaze from the terminal to the gray, overcast sky. I closed my eyes and let the cool breeze blow over me. It carried the smell of the forest. A soft, dewy sprinkle settled on my bare arms from what must have been a recent rain. It felt good to be home.

Taking a deep breath, I felt Oregon center me. I was a part of this place, and it was a part of me. I belonged here. It was where I grew up and spent my whole life. My roots were here. My parents and grandma were buried here. Oregon welcomed me like a beloved child, enfolded me in her cool arms, shushed my turbulent thoughts, and promised peace through her whispering pines.

Nilima had followed me down the steps and waited quietly while I absorbed the familiar environment. I heard the hum of a fast engine, and a cobalt blue convertible pulled around the corner. The sleek sports car was the exact color of *his* eyes.

Mr. Kadam must have arranged for the car. I rolled my eyes at his expensive taste. Mr. Kadam thought of every last detail—and he always did it in style. *At least the car's a rental,* I mused.

I stowed my bags in the trunk and read the name on the back:

Porsche Boxster RS 60 Spyder. I shook my head and muttered, "Holy cow, Mr. Kadam, I would have been just as happy to take the shuttle back to Salem."

"What?" Nilima asked politely.

"Nothing. I'm just glad to be home."

I closed the trunk and sank down into the two-toned blue and gray leather seat. We drove in silence. Nilima knew exactly where she was going, so I didn't even bother giving her directions. I just leaned my head back and watched the sky and the green landscape zip by.

Cars full of teenage boys passed us. They whistled, admiring either Nilima's exotic beauty and long, dark hair flying in the wind or the nice car. I'm not sure which inspired the catcalls, but I knew they weren't for me. I wore my standard T-shirt, tennis shoes, and jeans. Wisps of my golden-brown hair tangled about my loose braid and whipped at my brown, red-rimmed eyes and tear-streaked face. Older men cruised past us slowly too. They didn't whistle, but they definitely enjoyed the view. Nilima just ignored them, and I tuned them out, thinking, *I must look as awful as I feel.*

When we entered downtown Salem, we passed the Marion Street Bridge that would have taken us over the Willamette River and onto Highway 22 heading for the farmlands of Monmouth and Dallas. I tried to tell Nilima she missed a turn, but she merely shrugged and said we were taking a short cut.

"Sure," I said sarcastically, "what's another few minutes on a trip that has lasted for days?"

Nilima tossed her beautiful hair, smiled at me, and kept driving, maneuvering into the traffic headed for South Salem. I'd never been this way before. It was definitely the long way to Dallas.

Nilima drove toward a large hill that was covered with forest. We wound our way slowly up the beautiful tree-lined road for several miles.

I saw dirt roads leading into the trees. Houses poked through the forest here and there, but the area was largely untouched. I was surprised that the city hadn't annexed it and started building there. It was quite lovely.

Slowing down, Nilima turned onto a private road and followed it even higher up the hill. Although we passed a few other winding driveways, I didn't see any houses. At the end of the road, we stopped in front of a duplex that was nestled in the middle of the pine forest.

Both sides of the duplex were mirror images of each other. Each had two floors with a garage and a small, shared courtyard. Each had a large bay window that looked out over the trees. The wood siding was painted cedar brown and midnight green, and the roof was covered with grayish-green shingles. In a way, it resembled a ski cabin.

Nilima glided smoothly into the garage and stopped the car. "We're home," she announced.

"Home? What do you mean? Aren't we going to my foster parents' house?" I asked, even more confused than I already was.

Nilima smiled understandingly. She told me gently, "No. This is your house."

"My house? What are you talking about? I live in Dallas. Who lives here?"

"You do. Come inside and I'll explain."

We walked through a laundry room into the kitchen, which was small but had lemon-yellow curtains, brand new stainless-steel appliances, and walls decorated with lemon stencils. Nilima grabbed a couple of bottles of diet cola from the fridge.

I plopped my backpack down and said, "Okay, Nilima, now tell me what's going on."

She ignored my question. Instead, she offered me a soda, which I declined, and then told me to follow her.

Sighing, I slipped off my tennis shoes so I wouldn't mess up the duplex's plush carpeting and followed her to the small but cute living room. We sat on a beautiful chestnut leather sofa. A tall library cabinet full of classic hardbound books that probably cost a fortune beckoned invitingly from the corner, while a sunny window and a large, flat-screen television mounted above a polished cabinet also vied for my attention.

Nilima began rifling through papers left on a coffee table.

"Kelsey," she began. "This house is yours. It's part of the payment for your work in India this summer."

"It's not like I was really working, Nilima."

"What you did was the most vital work of all. You accomplished much more than any of us even hoped. We all owe you a great debt, and this is a small way to reward your efforts. You've overcome tremendous obstacles and almost lost your life. We are all very grateful."

Embarrassed, I teased, "Well, now that you put it that way—wait! You said this house is *part* of my payment? You mean there's more?"

With a nod of her head, Nilima said, "Yes."

"No. I really can't accept this gift. An entire house is way too much—never mind anything else. It's much more than we agreed on. I just wanted some money to pay for books for school. He shouldn't do this."

"Kelsey, he insisted."

"Well, he will have to un-insist. This is too much, Nilima. *Really*."

She sighed and looked at my face, which was set with steely determination. "He really wants you to have it, Kelsey. It will make him happy."

"Well, it's impractical! How does he expect me to catch the bus to school from here? I plan to enroll in college now that I'm back home, and this location isn't exactly close to any bus routes."

Nilima gave me a puzzled expression. "What do you mean catch the bus? I guess if you really want to ride the bus, you could drive down to the bus station."

"Drive down to the bus station? That doesn't make any sense."

"Well, *you* aren't making any sense. Why don't you just drive your car to school?"

"My car? What car?"

"The one in the garage, of course."

"The one in the. . . . *Oh, no*. You have *got* to be kidding me!"

"No. I'm not kidding. The Porsche is for you."

"*Oh, no, it's not!* Do you know how much that car costs? No way!"

I pulled out my cell phone and searched for Mr. Kadam's phone number. Right before I pressed SEND, I thought of something that stopped me in my tracks. "Is there anything else I should know?"

Nilima winced. "Well . . . he also took the liberty of signing you up at Western Oregon University. Your classes and books have already been paid for. Your books are on the counter next to your list of classes, a Western Wolf sweatshirt, and a map of the campus."

"He signed me up for WOU?" I asked, incredulous. "I'd been planning on attending the local community college and working—not attending WOU."

"He must have thought a university would be more to your liking. You start classes next week. As far as working goes, you may if you wish, but it will be unnecessary. He has also set up a bank account for you. Your new bank card is on the counter. Don't forget to endorse it on the back."

I swallowed. "And . . . uh . . . exactly how much money is in that bank account?"

Nilima shrugged. "I have no idea, but I'm sure it's enough to cover your living expenses. Of course, none of your bills will be sent here. Everything will be mailed straight to an accountant. The house and the car are paid for, as well as all of your college expenses."

She slid a whole bunch of paperwork my way and then sat back and sipped her diet soda.

Shocked, I sat motionless for a minute and then remembered my resolve to call Mr. Kadam. I opened my phone and searched for his number.

Nilima interrupted, "Are you sure you want to give everything back, Miss Kelsey? I know that he feels very strongly about this. He wants you to have these things."

"Well, Mr. Kadam should know that I don't need his charity. I'll just explain that community college is more than adequate, and I really don't mind staying in the dorm and taking the bus."

Nilima leaned forward. "But, Kelsey, it wasn't Mr. Kadam who arranged all of this."

"What? If it wasn't Mr. Kadam, then who. . . . *Oh!*" I snapped my phone shut. There was no way I was going to call *him*, no matter what. "So *he* feels strongly about this, does he?"

Nilima's arched eyebrows drew together in pretty confusion, "Yes, I would say he does."

It almost tore my heart to shreds to leave him. He was 7,196.25 miles away in India, and yet somehow he still manages to have a hold on me.

Under my breath, I grumbled, "Fine. He always gets what he wants anyway. There is no point in trying to give it back. He'll just engineer some other over the top gift that will only serve to complicate our relationship even further."

A car honked outside in the driveway.

"Well, that's my ride back to the airport," Nilima rose and said. "Oh! I almost forgot. This is for you too." She pressed a brand-new cell phone in my hand, deftly switching it with my old phone, and hugged me quickly before walking to the front door.

"But, wait! Nilima!"

"Don't worry, Miss Kelsey. Everything will be fine. The paperwork you need for school is on the kitchen counter. There's food in the fridge, and all of your belongings are upstairs. You can take the car and visit your foster family later today if you wish. They are expecting your call."

She turned, gracefully walked out the door, and climbed into the private car. She waved gaily from the passenger seat. I waved back morosely and watched until the sleek black sedan drove out of sight. Suddenly, I was all alone in a strange house, surrounded by quiet forest.

Once Nilima had gone, I decided to explore the place that I was now going to call home. Opening the fridge, I saw that the shelves were indeed fully stocked. Twisting a bottle cap off, I sipped a soda and peeked into the cupboards. There were glasses and plates, as well as cooking utensils, silverware, and pots and pans. On a hunch, I opened the bottom drawer of the refrigerator—and found it full of lemons. Clearly, this part was Mr. Kadam's doing. The thoughtful man knew drinking lemon water would be a comfort to me.

Mr. Kadam's interior design touch didn't end in the kitchen, though. The downstairs half bath was decorated in sage green and lemon. Even the soap in the dispenser was lemon-scented.

I placed my shoes in a wicker basket on the tiled floor of the laundry room beside a new front-loading washer and dryer set and continued on to a small office.

My old computer sat in the middle of the desk, but right next to it was a brand new laptop. A leather chair, file drawers, and a shelf with paper and other supplies completed the office.

Grabbing my backpack, I headed upstairs to see my new bedroom. A lovely queen-sized bed with a thick ivory down comforter and peach accent pillows was nestled against the wall, and an old wooden trunk sat at the foot. Cozy peach-colored reading chairs were arranged in the corner, facing the window overlooking the forest.

There was a note on the bed that lifted my spirits right up:

> Hi, Kelsey!
> Welcome home. Call us ASAP—
> we want to hear all about your trip.
> All of your things are stored away.
> We love your new home!
> Love,
> Mike and Sarah

Reading Mike and Sarah's note in addition to being back in Oregon grounded me. Their lives were normal. My life with them was normal, and it would be nice to be around a normal family and act like a normal human being for a change. Sleeping on jungle floors, talking to Indian goddesses, falling in love with a . . . tiger—none of that was normal. Not by a long shot.

I opened my closet and saw that my hair ribbon collection and clothes had indeed been moved from Mike and Sarah's. I fingered through some things I hadn't seen in a few months. When I opened the other side of the closet, I found all the clothes that had been purchased for me in India as well as several new items still in garment bags.

How on earth did Mr. Kadam get this stuff here before me? I left all this in India. I closed the door on the clothes and my memories, determined not to open that side of the closet again.

Moving to the dresser, I pulled open my top drawer. Sarah had arranged my socks exactly the way I liked them. Each pair of black, white, and assorted colored socks was wound into a neat ball and placed

in a row. Opening the next drawer wiped the smile right off my face. I found the silky pajamas I had purposely left in India.

My chest burned as I ran my hand over the soft cloth and then resolutely shut the drawer. Turning to leave the bright, airy room, a detail suddenly hit me, causing my face to flush scarlet red. My bedroom was peaches and cream.

He *must have picked these colors*, I surmised. *He'd once said that I smelled like peaches and cream. Figures he'd find a way to remind me of him even from a continent away. As if I could forget . . .*

I threw my backpack on the bed and instantly regretted it, realizing that Fanindra was still inside. After taking her out carefully and apologizing, I stroked her golden head and then put her on a pillow. I took my new cell phone out of my jeans pocket. Like everything else, the phone was expensive and totally unnecessary. It was designed by Prada. I turned the phone on and expected *his* number to show up first, but it didn't. There weren't any messages either. In fact, the only numbers stored on the phone were Mr. Kadam's and my foster parents'.

Various emotions raced through my head. At first, I was relieved. Then I was puzzled. Then I was disappointed. A part of me pondered, *It would have been nice of him to call. Just to see if I arrived okay.*

Annoyed with myself, I called my foster parents and told them I was home, tired from the flight, and that I would come over for dinner the next night. Hanging up, I grimaced, wondering what kind of tofu surprise would be in store for me. Whatever the health food meal turned out to be, I would be happy to sit through it as long as I got a chance to see them.

I wandered downstairs, turned on the stereo, made myself a snack of apple slices with peanut butter, and started rifling through the college papers on the counter. Mr. Kadam had chosen international studies as my major, with a minor in art history.

I looked through my schedule. Mr. Kadam had managed somehow to get me, a freshman, into 300- and 400-level classes. Not only that, but he had also booked my classes for both the fall *and* the winter terms—even though winter registration wasn't available yet.

WOU probably received a big, fat donation from India, I thought, smirking to myself. *I wouldn't be surprised to see a new building going up on campus this year.*

KELSEY HAYES, STUDENT ID 69428L7
WESTERN OREGON UNIVERSITY

FALL TERM

College Writing 115 (4 credits). *Introduction to thesis writing.*

First Year Latin 101 (4 credits). *Introduction to Latin.*

Anthropology 476 D Religion and Ritual (4 credits). *A study of the religious practices around the world. Delineates religious observance as seen through anthropology, while focusing on particular topics including spirit possession, mysticism, witchcraft, animism, sorcery, ancestor worship, and magic. Examines the blending of major world religions with local beliefs and traditions.*

Geography 315 The Indian Subcontinent (4 credits). *An examination of South Asia and its geography, with emphasis on India. Evaluates the economic relationship between India and other nations; studies patterns, issues, and challenges specifically related to geography; and explores the ethnic, religious, and linguistic diversity of its people, historic and modern.*

WINTER TERM

Art History 204 A Prehistoric through Romanesque (4 credits). *A study of all art forms of that period with specific emphasis on historical and cultural relevance.*

History 470 Women in Indian Society (4 credits). *An examination of women in India, their belief systems, their cultural place in society, and associated mythology, past and present.*

College Writing II 135 (4 credits). *Second-year class expanding research-based document writing and skills.*

Political Science 203 D International Relations (3 credits). *A comparison of global issues and the policies of world groups with similar and/or competing interests.*

It was official. I was a college student now. *Well, a college student and part time ancient Indian curse breaker,* I thought, remembering Mr. Kadam's continuing research in India. It was going to be difficult to focus on classes, teachers, and papers after everything that happened in India. It was especially odd knowing that I was supposed to carry on and go back to my old life in Oregon just like that. Somehow my old life didn't seem to fit anymore.

Luckily, my WOU courses sounded interesting, especially religion and magic. Mr. Kadam's selections were subjects I probably would have picked for myself—other than Latin. I wrinkled my nose. I'd never been too good with languages. Too bad WOU didn't offer an Indian language. It would be nice to learn Hindi, especially if I'm going back to India at some point to tackle the remaining three tasks outlined on Durga's prophecy that will break the tiger's curse. Maybe . . .

Just then, "I Told You So" by Carrie Underwood came on the radio. Listening to the lyrics made me cry. Brushing a tear away, I considered that *he* probably *would* find somebody new very soon. I wouldn't take me back if I were him. Letting myself think about him for even a minute was too painful. I tucked away my memories and folded them into a tiny wedge of my heart. Then, I shoved a whole bunch of new thoughts in place of the painful ones. I thought about school, my foster family, and being back in Oregon. I stacked those thoughts like books, one on top of the other, to try to suppress everything else.

For now, thinking about other things and other people was an effective distraction. But I could still feel his ghost hovering in the quiet, dark recesses of my heart, waiting for me to be lonely or to let my guard down, so that he could fill my mind again with thoughts of him.

I'll just have to stay busy, I decided. *That will be my salvation. I'll study like mad and visit people and . . . and date other guys. Yes! That's what I can do. I'll go out with other people and stay active and then I'll be too tired to think about him. Life will go on. It has to.*

By the time I headed for bed, it was late and I was tired. Patting Fanindra, I slipped under the sheets and slept.

The next day, my new cell phone rang. It was Mr. Kadam, which was both exciting and disappointing at the same time.

"Hello, Miss Kelsey," he said cheerfully. "I am so glad to hear that you have arrived back home safely. I trust everything is in order and to your satisfaction?"

"I didn't expect any of this," I replied. "I feel supremely guilty about the house, the car, the credit card, and school."

"Don't give it a moment's thought. I was happy to arrange it for you."

Curiosity getting the better of me, I asked, "What's going on with the prophecy? Have you figured it out yet?"

"I am attempting to translate the rest of the monolith you found. I sent someone back to Durga's temple and had pictures taken of the other pillars. It appears each pillar features one of the four elements: earth, air, water, and fire."

"That makes sense," I said, remembering Durga's prophecy. "The original pillar we found must have been related to earth since it showed farmers offering fruits and grains. Also, Kishkindha was underground and the first object Durga asked us to find was the Golden Fruit."

"Yes, well it turns out that there was also a fifth pillar that was

destroyed a long time ago. It represented the element of space, which is common in the Hindu faith."

"Well, if anyone can figure out what's next, it's you. Thank you for checking in on me," I added before we both promised to speak again and hung up.

I studied my new textbooks for five hours and then headed to a toy store to buy orange-and-black stuffed animal tigers for Rebecca and Sammy since I'd completely forgotten to bring them back something from India. Against my better judgment, I also ended up buying an expensive, large, white stuffed tiger.

Back at home, I grabbed the tiger around the middle and buried my face in the fur. It was soft but didn't smell right. *He* smelled wonderful, like sandalwood and waterfalls. This stuffed animal was just a replica. Its stripes were different, and its eyes were glassy—a lifeless, dull blue. *His* eyes were bright cobalt.

What on earth is wrong with me? I shouldn't have bought it. It was just going to make forgetting him that much harder.

Shaking off the emotion, I pulled out a change of clothes and got ready to visit my foster family.

As I drove through town, I went the long way around so I could avoid the Polk County Fairgrounds and more painful memories. When I pulled in front of Mike and Sarah's house, the door opened wide. Mike hurried toward me . . . but couldn't resist getting a better look at the Porsche and ran past me to the car.

"Kelsey! May I?" he asked sweetly.

"Knock yourself out," I said and laughed. *Same old Mike*, I thought and tossed him the keys so he could drive himself around the block a few times.

Sarah put her arm around my waist and guided me toward the house. "We're so glad to see you! Both of us are!" She yelled and frowned at Mike who waved happily before backing out of the driveway.

"We were worried when you first left for India because we didn't receive too many calls from you, but Mr. Kadam phoned every other day and explained what you were doing and told us how busy you were."

"Oh? And what did he say, exactly?" I asked, curious to know what story he had made up.

"Well, it's all very exciting, isn't it? Let's see. He talked about your new job and about how you will be interning every summer and working with him on various projects from time to time. I had no idea that you were interested in international studies. That is a wonderful major. Very fascinating. He also said that when you graduate, you can work for his company full time. It's a fantastic opportunity!"

I smiled at her. "Yes, Mr. Kadam's great. I couldn't ask for a better boss. He treats me more like a granddaughter than like an employee, and he spoils me terribly. I mean, you saw the house and the car, and then there's school too."

"He did speak very fondly of you over the phone. He even admitted to us that he's come to depend on you. He's a very nice man. He also insists that you are . . . how did he say it . . . 'an investment that will have a big payoff in the future.'"

I shot Sarah a dubious look. "Well, I hope he's right about that."

She laughed and then sobered. "*We* know you're special, Kelsey, and you deserve great things. Maybe this is the universe's way of balancing the loss of your parents. Though I know nothing will ever take the place of them."

I nodded. She was happy for me. And, knowing that I would be financially secure enough to live comfortably on my own was probably a big relief to them.

Sarah hugged me and pulled a strange-smelling dish out of the oven. She placed it on the table, and said, "Now, let's eat!"

Feigning enthusiasm, I asked, "So . . . what's for dinner?"

"Tofu and spinach whole wheat organic lasagna with soy cheese and flax seed."

"Yum, I can't wait," I said and wrestled a half-smile to my face. I thought fondly of the magical Golden Fruit that I had left behind in India. The divine object could make the most delicious food appear instantly. In Sarah's hands, maybe even a healthy meal would taste good. I snuck a bite. *Then again . . .*

Rebecca, six years old, and Samuel, four years old, ran into the room and bounced up and down trying to get my attention. I hugged them both and directed them to the table. Then I went to the window to see if Mike was back yet. He had just parked the Porsche and was walking backward to the front door, staring at the car.

I opened the door. "Umm, Mike, it's time for dinner."

He replied over his shoulder, never taking his eyes off the car, "Sure, sure. Be right there."

Sitting between the kids, I scooped up a wedge of lasagna for each of them and took a tiny piece for myself. Sarah raised her eyebrow, and I rationalized my small portion by saying that I'd had a big lunch. Mike finally came in and started chatting animatedly about the Porsche. He asked if he could take Sarah on a date and borrow the car some Friday night.

"Sure. I'll even come over and babysit for you."

He beamed while Sarah rolled her eyes. "Who are you planning on taking out, me or the car?" she asked.

"You, of course, my dear. The car is just a vehicle to showcase the beautiful woman sitting at my side."

Sarah and I looked at each other and snickered.

"Good one, Mike," I said.

After dinner, we retired to the living room where I gave the kids their orange tigers. They squealed in delight and ran around growling at each other. Sarah and Mike asked me all kinds of questions about India, and

I talked about the ruins of Hampi and Mr. Kadam's house. Technically, it wasn't his, but they didn't need to know that. Then they asked me about how Mr. Maurizio's circus tiger was adapting to his new home.

I froze, but only for an instant, and told them that he was doing fine and that he seemed very happy there. Thankfully, Mr. Kadam had explained that we were often out exploring Indian ruins and cataloging artifacts. He'd said my job was to be his assistant, keeping records of his findings, and taking notes, which wasn't too far from the truth. It also explained why I was going to minor in art history.

Being with them was fun, but it also wore me out because I had to make sure I didn't slip and tell them anything too weird. They'd never believe all the things that had happened to me. Sometimes I had a hard time believing it myself.

Knowing they went to bed early, I gathered my things and said goodnight. I hugged them all good-bye and promised to visit again the next week.

When I got home, I spent a couple of hours studying and then took a hot shower. Climbing into bed in my dark room, I gasped quietly as my hand brushed against fur. Then I remembered my purchase, shoved the stuffed tiger to the edge of the bed, and tucked my hand under my cheek.

I couldn't stop thinking about *him*. I wondered what he was doing right now and if he was thinking of me or if he even missed me at all. Was he pacing in the steamy jungle? Were he and Kishan fighting? Would I ever get back to India—and did I really want to? I felt like I was playing whack-a-mole with my thoughts. Every time I punched one thought down, another one would surface in a different place. I couldn't win; they kept popping up from my subconscious. Sighing, I reached over, grabbed the leg of the stuffed tiger, and pulled it back onto the bed. Wrapping my arms around its middle, I buried my nose in its fur and fell asleep on its paw.

2

Wushu

The next few days spun past quickly and uneventfully, and then it was time to start school. I collected my term assignments from each class and realized that my experiences in India would come in handy. I could write about Hampi for my research paper on an Indian metropolis, discuss the lotus flower as a religious symbol in anthropology, and theme my world religion final around Durga. The only class that seemed overly challenging was Latin.

Soon I had settled into a comfortable routine. I saw Sarah and Mike often, went to class, and I spoke to Mr. Kadam every Friday. The first week he helped me with an oral report on the SUV versus the Nano and between his vast knowledge of cars and my hair-raising description of actually driving in India, I got the best grade in the class. My mind was so full of assignments that I had very little time to worry about anything else—or to think about anyone else.

One Friday phone call brought an interesting surprise. After chatting about school and my latest paper about the weather patterns in the Himalayas, Mr. Kadam broached a new topic.

"I've signed you up for another class," Mr. Kadam began. "One that I think you will enjoy, but it will take up more of your time. If you are too busy, I'll understand."

"Actually, another class would probably be a good idea," I replied, curious to know what he had planned for me next.

"Wonderful! I have signed you up for a wushu class in Salem," Mr. Kadam explained. "The class is on Mondays, Wednesdays, and Thursdays from 6:30 to 8:00 p.m."

"Wushu? What's that? Is it some kind of Indian language?" I asked, hoping that wasn't the case.

Mr. Kadam laughed. "Oh, I do miss having you around. No, wushu is a type of Chinese martial arts. You mentioned once that you were interested in trying martial arts, correct?"

I breathed out a sigh of relief. "Oh! Yes, that sounds like fun. Yes, I can fit it into my schedule. When do classes start?"

"Next Monday. I anticipated that you would say yes, and I have sent a package with the necessary materials. You can expect it to arrive tomorrow."

"Mr. Kadam, you really don't have to do all this for me. You need to restrain yourself from piling on more gifts, or I'll never be able to pay back this debt."

He chided, "Miss Kelsey, there is nothing I could *ever* do that would come even close to paying the debt I owe you. Please accept these things. It makes an old man's heart very happy."

I laughed. "Okay, Mr. Kadam, don't get all dramatic about it. I'll accept if it makes you happy. But, the jury's still out on the car."

"We'll see about that. By the way, I have deciphered a bit of the second pillar. It may have something to do with air, but it's too soon to draw any conclusions just yet. That's one of the reasons I'd like you to learn wushu. It will help you develop a better balance of mind and body, which may prove to be helpful if your next adventure takes place off the ground."

"Well, I certainly don't mind learning how to fight and defend

myself too. Wushu would have come in handy against the Kappa." I joked and continued, "Are the translations difficult?"

"They're very . . . challenging. The geographical markers that I have translated are not found on the Indian continent. At this point, I worry that the other three objects we're looking for could be anywhere in the world. Either that, or my brain is too tired."

"Did you stay up all night again? You need your sleep. Make yourself some chamomile tea and go rest for a while."

"Perhaps you are right. Maybe I will have some tea and do some light reading on the Himalayas for your paper."

"You do that. The resting part, I mean. I miss you."

"I miss you too, Miss Kelsey. Good-bye."

"Bye."

For the first time since being home, I felt a surge of adrenaline rush through my body. But, as soon as I hung up the phone, depression kicked in again. I looked forward to our weekly phone calls and always felt sad when they were over. It was the same kind of feeling I would get after Christmas. Holiday anticipation would build up for the whole month. Then, when the presents were opened, the food was eaten, and the people left to go their separate ways, I always experienced a gloomy feeling of loss.

Deep down, I knew that the real reason I was sad was because there was only one present that I wished for. I wished *he* would call. He never did, though. And each week that passed without hearing his voice destroyed my hope. I knew I was the one who left India so he could start a life with someone else. I should have been happy for him. I was, in a way, but I was also devastated for myself.

I had the-vacation-is-over-now-it's-time-to-go-back-to-school blues. He was my ultimate present, my own personal miracle, and I'd blown it. I'd given him away. It was like winning backstage passes to meet the rock star of your dreams and donating the tickets to charity. It sucked. Big time.

Saturday, my mysterious martial arts package arrived via courier. It was large and heavy. I pushed it into the living room and grabbed my office scissors to cut through the tape. Inside, I found black and red workout pants and T-shirts, each bearing the Shing Martial Arts Studio logo which showed one man throwing a punch to the face, and another kicking a foot toward his opponent's abdomen.

I also pulled out two pairs of shoes and a silky red jacket and pants set. The jacket had black frog clasps in the front and a black sash. I had no idea when or how I would ever have need to wear this, but it was pretty.

What made the box heavy was the assortment of weapons I found inside. There were a couple of swords, some hooks, chains, a three-section staff, and several other things that I'd never seen before.

If Mr. Kadam is trying to turn me into a ninja, he'll be very disappointed, I thought, remembering how I froze during the panther attack. *I wonder if Mr. Kadam is right and I'll need these skills. I guess they'd come in handy if I return to India and have to fight whatever stands in the way of obtaining Durga's second gift.* The idea made the hair on the back of my neck stand straight up.

Monday, I walked into my Latin class early, and my happy routine hit a snag when Artie, the lab assistant, approached my desk. He stood very close to me. Too close. I looked up at him hoping the conversation would be quick so he could move out of my personal space.

Artie was the only guy I'd seen in a long time brave enough to wear a sweater-vest with a bow tie. The sad thing was the sweater-vest was too small. He had to keep pulling it down over his rather large stomach. He looked like the kind of guy who belonged in a musty old college.

"Hi, Artie. How are you?" I asked impatiently.

Artie pushed his thick glasses up the bridge of his nose with his middle finger and popped open his day planner. He got right to the point. "Hey, are you free at 5:00 p.m. on Wednesday?"

He stood with his pencil raised and his double chin tucked up against his neck. His brown watery eyes bore into mine as he waited expectantly for my reply.

"Umm . . . sure, I guess. Does the professor need to see me for something?"

Artie scratched busily in his planner, shifting some things and erasing others. He ignored my question. Then, he closed his planner with a POP, tucked it under his arm, and yanked his brown sweater-vest down to his belt buckle. I tried not to notice when the material inched back up.

He smiled weakly at me. "Not at all. That's when I'll be picking you up for our date." Without another word, Artie stepped around me and headed toward the door.

Did I hear him right? What just happened?

"Artie, wait. What do you mean?"

Class was getting started, and the sweater vest turned the corner and was gone. I plopped down in my seat and puzzled through our cryptic conversation. *Maybe he doesn't mean a date-date*, I reasoned. *Maybe his definition of a date and mine are different. That must be it. Better check to make sure, though.*

I tried unsuccessfully to catch Artie in the lab all day. Clarification on the date would have to wait.

That night was my first wushu class. I dressed in the black pants, a T-shirt, and the white slippers. I left the top down on the convertible as I drove through the forest into Salem. My whole body relaxed as the cool evening breeze moved around me. The just-setting sun was turning the clouds purple, pink, and orange.

The martial arts studio was large and took up half the building. I wandered into the back. An open area was surrounded by mirrors and large blue mats that covered the floor. There were five other people already there. Three young men and one fit young woman were warming up off to one side. Stretching on the floor in another corner was a middle-aged woman who reminded me of my mom. She smiled up at me, and I could tell she was a little scared, but she also had a determined gleam in her eye. I sat down by her and bent over my legs. "Hi, I'm Kelsey."

"Jennifer." She blew her bangs out of her face. "Nice to meet you."

Our teacher wandered into the studio, accompanied by a young man. The white-haired instructor seemed old but very spry and tough. In a thick accent, he introduced himself as Chu . . . something, but said we should call him Chuck. The young man next to him was his grandson, Li. Li was a younger version of his grandfather. His black hair was cropped short, and he had a tall, wiry, muscular frame and a nice smile.

Chuck started the lesson with a short speech: "Wushu is Chinese martial arts. You know about the Shaolin monks? They do wushu. My studio's name is *Shing*, which means 'victory.' You will all have a chance to feel victory as you master wushu. Do you know the name kung fu?"

We all nodded.

"*Kung fu* means 'skill.' Kung fu is not a style of martial arts. It just means you have skill. Maybe the skill is riding horses or swimming. Wushu is a style. Wushu is kicks, stretching, gymnastics, and weapons. Now, who are famous people that use wushu?"

Nobody answered.

"Jet Li, Bruce Lee, and Jackie Chan all use wushu. First, I will teach you greetings. This is how you greet your teacher each class. I say, '*Ni hao ma?*' And you say, '*Wo hen hao.*' This means 'How are you?' And 'I am fine.'"

"Ni hao ma?"

We responded with a stuttered, *"Woo hena how."*

"Wo . . . hen . . . hao."

"Wo hen hao."

Chuck grinned at us. "Very good, class! Now let's start with some stretching."

He guided us through calf and arm stretching and then encouraged us to sit on the floor and reach for our toes. He said he wanted us to stretch several times a day to increase our flexibility. Then he had us do splits. Four of my classmates were doing fine, but I felt bad for Jennifer. She was already huffing and puffing just from the stretching, and she was making a very determined effort to sink down into splits.

Chuck smiled at all of us, including his struggling student, encouraging her on. Next, he brought his grandson forward to demonstrate the first stance he wanted us to work on. It was called a horse stance, which looked like it sounded. From there, we moved into bow stance, which killed my calf muscles, and the cat stance. The flat stance was the hardest. The feet stay parallel, but the body has to twist awkwardly to the side. The last one we learned was the rest stance, which didn't turn out to be restful at all.

For the remainder of the class, we practiced the five different stances. Li helped me position my feet properly and spent some time demonstrating the flat stance, but I still couldn't get it. He was very encouraging and smiled at me often.

Jennifer was red-faced but seemed happy when our class was over. The time flew by very quickly. The exercise felt good, and I looked forward to my next class—which was the same night as my date with Artie.

I looked for Artie in the language lab three times on Tuesday to clear things up and hopefully cancel. When we finally connected, Artie made a big show of rescheduling our date and kept flipping pages in his day planner until I ran out of excuses. I started to feel guilty and decided that it wouldn't kill me to go out with the guy just once. Even though I had zero romantic interest in Artie, he could end up being a friend. So I accepted an invitation later in the month.

The next couple of weeks passed without incident, but I soon found myself in another unusual situation. My anthropology partner, Jason, asked me to the homecoming football game.

His request totally surprised me. Then something snapped in my brain, and I realized I'd missed all the clues that he'd been sending. I'd been looking at the world through a film of plastic wrap. My mind was so focused on schoolwork that I had assumed he just wanted to work too.

Jason seemed like a nice guy, but he didn't hold a candle to the man I left behind in India. I quickly made a mental list of each, and Jason's side came out short. I knew it wasn't fair to compare the two. *Nobody* could compete with *him*. Still, Jason didn't make me feel excited or scared, happy, or nervous. My heart didn't race with anticipation. I couldn't even tell if we had any chemistry. I just felt numb.

I have to get over him someday. I have to move on, and try to date, I told myself. I bit my lip. *He's probably ruined my chances of being happy with someone else. How could I ever like other men when they couldn't possibly compare with him?*

Disgusted with my circular argument, I told Jason I would love to go with him to the football game. He seemed delighted at the prospect, but I worried that he mistook my enthusiasm to forget the past with my interest in him.

That night in wushu class, we learned kicks. There were several types: the front stretch-kick, the side stretch-kick, inside and outside circle-kicks, and heel-palm-kicks. My favorite was toe-fist-kick. It made me finally feel like I could punch something.

We practiced kicks all evening until Chuck started randomly calling out kicks to see how fast we could remember them. During the last part of the class, we teamed up in pairs, and I worked with Jennifer. Li asked me to demonstrate the kicks and helped position my arms properly, guiding me through the stance, before moving on. Soon, Li announced that class was over. I thanked him and practiced some more on my own.

"Li likes you," Jennifer whispered conspiratorially when I had finished. "I don't know if he'll muster up the courage to do anything about it, but it's obvious. He watches you all the time. How do you feel about him?"

"I don't have any feelings about him. He's a nice guy, but I never thought of him that way."

"*Oh.* There's someone else."

I frowned at the thought. "*No.* Not anymore."

"Oh, honey, you can't just let life pass you by while you nurse a broken heart. You have to get back up on that horse and try again. Life is too short not to have love in it."

I knew she'd been happily married for fifteen years. Her husband was a sweet, balding man who obviously adored her. Every night after class he told her that she looked amazing and was getting so thin that he couldn't see her from the side anymore. Then he'd kiss her damp curly brown hair and open her car door. If anyone was an expert on love, it was probably Jennifer.

I thought about what she'd said. I knew she was right. *But how do you change your heart?*

Jennifer smiled sympathetically, gathered her things, and squeezed my shoulder. "See you next week, Kelsey."

I waved as they drove away and stared out at the black, empty street for a few minutes, lost in thought. When I turned back to gather my things, I noticed that everyone had left already. Li was standing by the front door, waiting patiently for me to go so he could lock up.

"Sorry, Li. I guess I just lost track of time."

He grinned at me. "No problem."

I scooped up my towel, car keys, and water bottle and headed for the door.

Just as I got into my car, Li called out, "Hey, Kelsey. Wait." He ran over to my door as I rolled down the window. "I wanted to invite you to a game night. A bunch of my friends are getting together on Halloween to play Settlers of Catan. It's a build-up-your-empire type of game, and there will be good eats. My grandma loves to cook. Would you like to come? I can teach you to play."

"Umm." I didn't have any plans for Halloween. I knew kids wouldn't come up to my house because it was way too far off the beaten path. Going over to Mike and Sarah's didn't seem like a good option either. All the neighborhood kids avoided their house because they gave out sugarless treats and lectured the parents on the evils of too many sweets.

Li was still standing there waiting for an answer; so I gave him one. "Sure, it sounds like fun."

He smiled. "Great! See ya!"

I drove home feeling weird. When I walked in the door, I threw my bag on the couch and pulled a bottle of water out of the fridge. I went upstairs, opened the door to my bedroom balcony, and sat on a deck chair. Leaning my head back, I stared up at the stars.

Three dates. I had three dates in two weeks, and I wasn't looking forward to any of them. Something was definitely wrong with me.

3

dating

DATE 1

I couldn't believe the time for my date with Artie had arrived so quickly. I drove to campus, parked, and sat in the car, stalling. I really didn't want to go out with Artie. His persistence had paid off, and I suspected it wasn't the first time he had used the same tactic.

Resigned to get the date over with, I made my way to the language lab. Artie was standing there staring at his watch with a brown package tucked under his arm. I wandered over to him and slid my hands into my jean pockets.

"Hi, Kelsey. Come on. We're running late," he said and walked briskly down the hall. "I have to drop a package off at the post office first for an old *friend*."

He wasn't only big. He was tall, and his stride was much longer than mine. I had to almost jog to keep up with him. Artie strode right through the parking lot, turned onto a sidewalk, and started heading for town.

"Uh, shouldn't we take your car?" I asked. "The post office is a mile-and-a-half away."

"Oh, no. I don't own a car. They're much too expensive."

Good thing I wore my tennis shoes, I thought.

Artie was walking silently and stiffly ahead. I decided it was probably up to me to get the conversation going. "So . . . who's the package for?"

"It's for my old high school girlfriend. She goes to another school, and I like to keep in touch. She dates lots of people on and off, the same as me," Artie boasted. "I date lots of girls. You should see my day planner. I've got dates lined up for years."

It was the longest walk of my life. I tried to pretend I was walking in the Indian jungle, but it was too cold. The sky was dark and overcast, and a stiff wind was blowing. It wasn't walking-outside weather. I shivered in my jacket and passed the time half-listening to Artie and half-admiring the houses that were decorated for Halloween.

We finally reached the post office, where Artie mailed his package. I looked around at the different tiny restaurants on Main Street and wondered which one we would be dining at. I was starving. I'd forgotten to eat lunch because I was too wrapped up in studying. The smell of Chinese food wafting from next door was mouthwatering.

By the time Artie finally stepped outside, I was really cold. I clapped my hands and rubbed them together for warmth. If I had known we'd be outside this long, I would have brought gloves. It turned out Artie had a pair of leather gloves in his pocket, but he put them on his own hands.

My glutton-for-punishment brain insisted that *he* would have given me his gloves. Heck, *he* would have given me the shirt off his back if he thought I might have need of it.

"So, where to next?" I asked. My eyes darted hopefully over to the Chinese restaurant.

"Back to campus. I have a real treat in store for you."

I tried to plaster an enthusiastic smile on my face. "That's . . . great."

On the long walk back to campus, Artie talked about himself. He spoke about his childhood and family. He described all the awards he had won and mentioned that he was president of five clubs, including the chess club. He never asked one question about me. I would have been shocked if he even knew my last name.

My mind wandered to a conversation with a very different man.

I heard *his* warm, hypnotic voice very clearly. Suddenly, I was standing under a tree. The tree where I'd said good-bye. The tree where I'd last gazed into his cobalt blue eyes. The cold, chafing wind of Oregon dropped far away, and I felt a balmy Indian summer breeze blow softly through my hair. The gray overcast evening faded, and I was looking up at twinkling stars in a night sky. He touched my face and spoke.

"Kelsey, the fact is . . . I'm in love with you. And I have been for some time. I don't want you to leave. Please . . . please . . . please . . . tell me you'll stay with me."

He was so beautiful, like a warrior-angel sent from heaven. How could I have denied him anything, especially when all he wanted was me?

"I want to give you something. It's an anklet. They're very popular here, and I got this one so we'd never have to search for a bell again."

My ankle tingled as I remembered his fingers brushing against it.

"Kells, please. I need you."

How could I leave him?

My mind snapped back to the present, and I struggled to contain the strong emotions that surfaced when I allowed myself to think about *him*. As Artie droned on about how he'd won the debate championship single-handedly, I berated myself for allowing my thoughts to take me to a dangerous place. The fact was, even if I *was* having second thoughts about my choice to leave, *he* hadn't called. That proved that I made the right decision, didn't it? If he really loved me as much as he said he did, he would have tried to contact me. He would have pursued me. He would have come for me. He needed space. I was right to leave him. Maybe now I could start healing and let him go.

I wrenched my attention back to Artie and made a real effort to listen to his conversation. There was absolutely no way Artie was the right guy for me—or for any girl for that matter, but that didn't mean I was out of options. I still had a date with Jason tomorrow and one with Li next week.

When Artie and I arrived back on campus, my stomach was growling so loudly that it could be heard within a three-block radius. I seriously hoped that we would be eating at the campus café soon.

He led me to the Hamersly Library media center, asked for two headsets, and gave the lady a paper. Then, he pushed two wooden chairs in front of a six-inch, black-and-white television in the corner of the media section.

"Isn't this a great idea? We can watch a movie, and I don't have to spend a dime!" He grinned while my mouth dropped open. "It's very clever, don't you think?"

I pursed my lips. "Oh, it's clever alright."

I quickly shut my mouth after that and bit back a sarcastic reply. Did he think girls actually liked to be treated this way? It wasn't that a date had to be expensive or that any money had to be spent at all. What annoyed me was that Artie was smug about everything and he didn't think his dates were important enough to listen to. I felt disgusted and hungry. As the movie started, he slipped giant gray earphones over his ears and pointed to mine.

I dusted mine off with my shirt, plugged in the cord, and slammed the headphones over my ears, very irritated that I would be sitting there for *two more hours*. The opening credits of the movie *Brigadoon* flashed across the screen, and I mentally sent messages to Gene Kelly to dance faster.

An hour into the movie, Artie made a move. He was still staring straight ahead at the tiny movie screen when he picked up his heavy arm and settled it on the back of my wooden chair.

I peeked at him out of the corner of my eye. He had a slight smirk on his face. I imagined he was mentally checking off a task in his planner.

- ☑ Seduce date by talking about other girls
- ☑ Impress date with number of awards you have received
- ☑ Do not spend money on date
- ☑ Make date watch corny movie in media center
- ☑ Sneak in comments about your frugality
- ☑ Put arm around date at exactly the halfway mark of the movie

I leaned forward and sat uncomfortably on the edge of my seat for the entire second half of the movie. Making the excuse that I needed to use the restroom, I stood up. He did too and walked over to the lady at the desk. As I walked by, I overheard him asking her to stop the movie and rewind it just a bit so we would remember where we left off.

Great! That adds five more minutes to this fantastic experience! I hurried as fast as I could because I was worried that he might try to start the whole thing over again. I considered the idea of running madly out of the building, but he could see the bathroom door from where we were sitting, and it would be rude. I was determined to just suffer through the last part of the movie, and *then* run home.

Finally, *finally*, the movie was over, and I jumped up like someone had just pulled the fire alarm.

"Okay, Artie. Well, this was great. My car is parked just outside, so I'll see you on Monday, okay? Thanks for the date."

Unfortunately, he didn't take a hint and insisted on walking me to my car. I opened the door and quickly wedged my body behind it.

He put his hand on the car door and leaned his corpulent body toward me. His bow tie was a few inches from my nose. He forced an awkward unnatural smile to his face.

"Well, I had a great time and want to go out with you again next week," Artie said. "How about next Friday?"

Better nip this one in the bud.

"Can't. I have another date planned already."

He pressed forward undeterred. "Oh." He didn't even blink. "What about Saturday?"

I searched my brain frantically for an escape. "Uh . . . I didn't bring my planner with me, so I don't know my schedule that far ahead."

He nodded as if that made perfect sense.

"Look, I have a terrible headache, Artie. I'll see you in lab next week, okay?"

"Okay, sure. I'll call you later."

I quickly slipped into my car and shut the door. Grinning, because I knew I'd never given him my phone number, I drove through the quiet streets of Monmouth and up the mountain to my peaceful home.

DATE 2

For my next date, I was better prepared for the weather. I wore my red WOU sweatshirt and also brought a thicker coat and a red cashmere scarf and gloves that I had found tucked in a drawer. Normally, I would have shunned anything *he* had bought for me, but I didn't have time to buy new ones, and even if I did I'd be using his money anyway.

I met Jason in the stadium parking lot and immediately began cataloging his good qualities. He was cute, a little on the skinny side and shorter than average, but he dressed decently and was smart. Leaning up against his old Corolla, he raised his eyebrows in shock when he saw me emerge from the Porsche.

"Wow, Kelsey! Nice wheels!"

"Thanks."

"Are you ready?"

"Yep. Lead the way."

We shuffled into the crowd of people heading over to the football field. Most were wearing red or Western Wolf shirts, but there were also the navy-blue-and-white colors of the opponent, Western Washington University, scattered here and there. Even a couple of Viking hats were bobbing up and down in the crowd. Jason led me to a truck surrounded by couples having a tailgate party. A small grill was full of smoking sausages and hamburgers.

"Hey, guys! I want to introduce you to Kelsey. We met in our anthro class."

Several faces peered over and around their neighbors to get a good glimpse. I waved shyly back at them. "Hi."

I heard a couple of "Hey, there's," and "Nice to meet you's," and then they went back to their conversations, forgetting we were there.

Jason filled up a plate for me and then popped open a cooler. "Hey, Kelsey, want a beer?"

I shook my head. "Soda, please. Diet, if you have it." He handed me an icy diet soda, grabbed a beer for himself, and pointed to two empty lawn chairs.

Sitting down, he immediately rammed half his hot dog in his mouth and chewed loudly. It was almost as bad as watching a tiger eat. Lucky for me, it was a little less bloody.

Ugh. What's with me? Am I intentionally looking for things that annoy me? I really have to chill out or Jennifer's right: I'm going to miss out on life. I looked away from him and started picking at my food.

"So, you aren't a drinker, eh, Kelsey?"

"Umm, I guess not. I'm underage first of all. Secondly, alcohol lost all appeal for me when my parents were killed by a drunk driver a few years back."

"Oh. *Sorry*." He grimaced and scooted his beer out of sight under the chair.

I mentally groaned. *What am I doing?* Immediately, I apologized,

"It's okay, Jason. Sorry to be such a downer. I promise I'll be much more perky at the game."

"No problem. Don't give it a second thought." He went back to scarfing down his food and laughing with his friends.

The problem was that I did give it a second thought. I knew my parents' death wasn't something you should normally bring up on a first date, but . . . I knew that *he* would have reacted very differently from the way Jason did. Maybe it was because he was older, more than three hundred years older. Or maybe it was because he wasn't American. Maybe it was because he'd lost his parents too. Or maybe it was because he was just . . . perfect.

I tried to shut it down, but I couldn't help myself. I flashed back to a time when I woke up from a nightmare featuring my parents' death, and he was there to comfort me. I could still feel his hand wiping the tears from my cheeks as he pulled me onto his lap.

"Shh, Kelsey. I'm here. I'm not leaving you, priya. *Hush now.* Mein aapka raksha karunga. *I will watch over you,* priyatama." He'd stroked my hair and whispered soothing words to me until I felt the dream fade.

Since then, I'd had time to look up the words I didn't understand in India. *I'm with you. I'll take care of you. My beloved. My sweetheart.* If he were here with me now, he would've pulled me into a hug or onto his lap, and we would have been sad together. He would have stroked my back and understood how I felt.

I shook myself. *No. No, he wouldn't. He might have once, but now he's moved on. He's gone now, and it doesn't matter anymore what he would have done or how he would have reacted. It's over.*

Jason was filling another plate, and I tried to look interested and involve myself in the conversation. Half an hour later, we all got up to head to the football field.

It was nice being outside in the crisp fall air, but the benches were

cold, and my nose was frozen. The cold didn't seem to bother Jason and his friends. They stood up and cheered a lot. I tried to join in, but I never knew what I was cheering about. The ball was too far away and too small for me to see much. I'd never had much interest in football. I much preferred movies and books.

I glanced up at the scoreboard. The first half clock was running down. Two minutes. One minute. Twenty seconds. BZZZZ! The timer sounded, and both teams ran off the field. The homecoming parade started and several antique cars drove around the outside of the field. Beautiful girls dressed in chiffon and silk were perched up on the top of the backseats, waving at the crowd.

Jason joined all the other guys in wolf whistles and screamed out his appreciation with the frenzied throng. The scent of sandalwood drifted over the bleachers, and a silky soft voice whispered in my ear, *"You are more beautiful than any woman out there."*

I whipped my head around, but *he* wasn't behind me. Jason was still standing up and screaming with his friends. I slumped back in my seat. *Great. Now I'm hallucinating.* I pressed my knuckles to my head and pushed, hoping the pressure would shove *him* back to the recesses of my mind.

When the second half of the game started, I stopped trying to feign enthusiasm. This was the second date that had turned me into a popsicle. My body slowly froze to the bench, and my teeth chattered. After the game, Jason walked me back to my car and awkwardly put an arm around my shoulder, massaging it to try to warm me up, but he rubbed too hard and left my shoulder sore. I didn't even bother to ask who had won.

"Hey, Kelsey, I had a great time getting to know you better tonight."

Did he get to know me at all? "Yeah, me too."

"So, can I call you later?"

I considered that for a minute. Jason wasn't a *bad* guy; he was just a guy. First dates were usually awkward anyway, so I decided to give him another shot.

"Yeah, sure. You know where you can find me." I gave him a half-hearted smile.

"Right. Catch ya in anthro on Monday. See ya."

"Yep, see ya."

He headed back to his wild group of friends, and I wondered if we had anything in common at all.

DATE 3

Before I knew it, it was Halloween—and my date with Li.

There was something about Li that made me feel very comfortable. He was more fun to be around than Jason, and I grudgingly admitted that it was very possible I felt more relaxed around Li because he reminded me a little of the man I was trying to forget.

Reluctantly, I pulled back the door to the closet that I vowed never to open and found a long-sleeved, burnt-orange top designed to look like a short trench coat. It was accented with wooden buttons and a tie belt. To go with it was a pair of dark blue stretch denim jeans. They fit perfectly, like they'd been tailored just for me. A dark pair of boots sat in the bottom of the bag and, slipping those on, I twirled in front of the mirror. The outfit made me look tall and chic and well . . . stylish, which was not my norm.

I left my hair cascading down my back in curly waves for a change. Dabbing on some apricot lip gloss, I drove to the studio, being careful to go slower than usual to avoid any wandering trick-or-treaters.

Li was sitting in his car listening to music and bobbing his head up and down. As soon as he spotted me, he immediately turned off the radio and got out of his car.

He grinned. "Wow, Kelsey! You look great!"

I laughed easily with him. "Thanks, Li. It's very nice of you to say that. If you're ready to go, I can follow you to your grandmother's."

I walked back to my car, but Li raced past me and opened the door.

"Whew, I almost didn't make it!" He grinned at me again. "My grandfather always taught me to open doors for ladies."

"Oh. Well, you are the perfect gentleman."

He bowed his head slightly, laughed, and then walked back to his car. He drove slowly too, and checked his rearview mirror often to make sure I made it through the intersections. We stopped in a nice, older neighborhood.

"This is my grandparents' house," Li explained as we stepped into the foyer. "We always meet here for game night because they have the biggest table. Plus, my grandma is a great cook."

Li took my hand and pulled me into a cute kitchen that smelled better than any Chinese restaurant I'd ever been to. A tiny white-haired woman was peering into a rice cooker. When she looked up, her glasses were steamy.

"Kelsey, this is Grandma Zhi. Grandma Zhi, *huó* Kelsey."

She smiled, nodded, and grasped my fingers in hers. "Hello. Nice to meet you."

I smiled back. "Nice to meet you too."

Li dipped his finger into a simmering pot, and she picked up a wooden spoon and smacked him lightly across the knuckles. Then she chastised him in Mandarin.

He laughed while she clucked her tongue fondly. "See you later, Grandma." I caught her smiling proudly at him as we turned the corner.

I followed him to the dining room. All the furniture had been moved to the side to make space for the large dining table, which had been extended with four leaves. Huddled around the table was a group of

Asian boys who were having a heated discussion about the placement of tiles on the game board. Li walked me over to the group.

"Hey, guys. This is Kelsey. She's going to be playing with us tonight."

One guy waggled his eyebrows, "Alright, Li!"

"No wonder he took so long."

"You're lucky that Wen bought the expansion kit."

There were other various mutterings and some chair shifting. I thought I caught one quiet comment about bringing a girl to the party, but I couldn't tell who was talking. After a few moments, everybody settled down to begin the game.

Li sat next to me and guided me through the game process. At first, I never knew if it was a wise decision to trade wheat for brick or ore for sheep, but I could always look to Li for help. After a few turns, I started to feel confident enough to hold my own. I changed two of my settlements for cities, and all the boys groaned.

Near the end of the game, it was obvious that the final point was going to be a race between a boy named Shen and me. He ribbed me good-naturedly about how he was so close that I'd never make it. I put down a sheep, an ore, and a wheat and bought a development card. It was a bonus point, the last one of the game.

"I win!"

The boys grumbled about beginner's luck and made a big show of counting all my points one more time just to make sure my count was accurate. I was surprised to learn that hours had gone by. My stomach growled to remind me.

Li stood up and stretched. "Time to eat."

His grandmother had set out a delicious buffet for us. The boys piled their plates full of fried rice, pot stickers, steamed pork dumplings, vegetable stir fry, and miniature shrimp egg rolls. Li grabbed sodas for both of us, and we sat down in the living room.

He expertly picked up his pork dumpling with chopsticks, and said,

"So tell me about you, Kelsey. Something besides wushu. What did you do this summer?"

"Oh, that. I umm . . . worked in India as an intern."

"Wow! That's amazing! What did you do?"

"Mostly cataloging and keeping records of ruins, art, and historical stuff. What about you? What did *you* do this summer?" I turned the question on him, eager to get the spotlight off of India.

"I worked for Grandfather in the studio mostly. I'm trying to save up for medical school. I got my undergraduate degree from PSU in biology."

I quickly did the math, which didn't seem to add up. "How old are you, Li?"

He grinned. "Twenty-two. I took a lot of classes and went to summer school too. Actually, all the gamers are in college. Meii is majoring in chemistry, Shen is studying computer engineering, Wen has graduated and is working on his master's in statistical analysis, and then there's me in medicine."

"You guys sure are . . . goal-oriented."

"What about you? What's your major, Kelsey?"

"International studies with a minor in art history. Right now I'm studying India," I said, popping another dumpling in my mouth. "But maybe I should switch to wushu to get rid of all these calories."

Li laughed and took my plate. We wandered back to the game room, and I stopped to look at a picture of Li and his grandfather Chuck. They were holding three trophies each.

"Wow, so the studio won all of those?"

Li peered at the picture and flushed. "No, those are all mine. I won them in a martial arts tournament."

I raised my eyebrows in surprise. "I didn't know you were *that* good. That's quite an accomplishment."

"I'm sure my grandparents will tell you all about it," Li said, steering me back into the kitchen. "There's nothing they like to do more than talk up their posterity. Right, Grandma Zhi?" Li pecked her on the cheek and she fluttered her hands to shoo him away from her dishwater.

The guys had set up a new game that was much easier to learn. I lost, but it was really fun. By the time the game was done, it was past midnight. Li walked me out to my car in the cold, starry evening.

"Thanks for coming, Kelsey. I had a great time with you. Do you think you'd like to do this again? We get together every two weeks."

"Sure. Sounds like fun. So does my winning the first game mean you're going to go easy on me in wushu class?" I bantered.

"Nuh-uh. When you win, I go harder on you."

I laughed. "Remind me to lose next time. What happens when *you* win?"

He grinned. "I'll be giving that question some serious thought."

Li backed away and stood under the porch light, watching me drive off.

I climbed wearily into bed thinking that, given enough time, I might actually learn to like Li. He was fun and sweet. I didn't really feel anything for him other than friendship, but maybe that could change in the future. Normal life was starting to feel . . . normal again. I rolled onto my side, cuddled under my grandmother's quilt, and accidentally knocked my white stuffed tiger off the bed.

For a while, I considered leaving it on the floor or putting it in the closet. I lay still, quietly staring at the ceiling, trying to muster the strength of mind to do it. My resolve lasted only five minutes, and I berated myself for being weak. Leaning over the bed, I cuddled my stuffed tiger to my chest, apologizing profusely for even thinking about it.

a christmas present

Now that Halloween was over, my focus turned to preparing for finals and avoiding Artie. Somehow, he tracked down my cell phone number and called me at exactly 5:00 p.m. every evening. Sometimes, he waited for me after class. The guy would not take a hint.

I also spent time trying to sort out my feelings for Jason. We went on a few more dates, but I always felt like we were communicating on two different wavelengths. He thought Shakespeare, poetry, and books were boring, and I couldn't appreciate the subtle differences between college and pro teams. I don't think he cared much that we weren't compatible. Deep down, I knew that my relationship with Jason was not heading anywhere, but he was a mental diversion, and I still liked to partner with him in class.

Just when I thought I had casual dating figured out, Li decided to make it even more complicated. We were chatting in the studio when he suddenly became quiet. He rolled his water bottle back and forth nervously between his palms.

Finally, he spoke, "Kelsey . . . I wanted to ask you if you'd like to see me. Alone. Like a real date."

My mind started to race with confused thoughts. "Oh. Umm, yeah, sure," I said slowly. "I like hanging out with you. You're a lot of fun and easy to talk to."

He grimaced. "Right, but do you *like me* like me, or do you just *like* me?"

I thought for a minute about what to say next. "Well, to be honest with you, I think you're great, and I like you a lot. In fact, you're at the top of my like list. But, I don't know if I can be serious with anyone right now. I just sort of broke up with someone recently, and it still hurts."

"Oh. It's hard to get over things like that. I understand. I'd still want to see you, though. I mean, if you think you'd like to go out with me and if you're ready to."

I considered a moment. "Okay, I'd like that."

"So, how about we start with a martial arts movie? There's a place that shows old movies at midnight on Friday nights. Want to go?"

"Okay, but only if you promise to teach me one of the cool moves from the movie," I added, happy that we had settled the matter. *Sort of, anyway*, I thought as we parted ways.

Li and I began to see each other outside of game night and in class. He was a gentleman and our dates were always fun and interesting. Despite having all this attention, I felt lonely. It wasn't the kind of loneliness I could cure by being around other people. My soul felt lonely. Nighttime was the hardest because I felt *him*, even an ocean away. An invisible tether was wrapped tightly around my heart, connecting us. Its relentless pull kept trying to tug me back. Maybe someday the cords would wear and finally break.

Wushu class was the perfect outlet for venting some of the frustration I felt with my life. The moves were precise and didn't require any emotions at all, which was a welcome change. I was starting to get pretty good too. My arms and legs had more definition, and I felt much stronger as well. If someone attacked me, I might actually be able to fend them off, which was an empowering thought. Who needed tiger protection? I'd just kick my enemy in the face.

As students, we weren't supposed to have thoughts like that, but most people didn't actually have to face immortal Kappa monkeys that wanted to eat you, like I did. So I allowed myself to visualize my many possible opponents and kicked with intensity. Even Li made a comment that my kicks were getting stronger.

Li made good on his bargain and taught me an offensive move from the movie. He let me practice on him but I kept messing it up, and we fell to the mat in a tangle, laughing.

"Kelsey, are you alright? Did I hurt you?"

I couldn't stop laughing. "No, I'm fine. Great move, huh?"

Li was leaning over me, his face close to mine. "Not bad. Now I've got you right where I want you."

All of a sudden, the happy, light atmosphere blew away and was replaced by thick, expectant tension. He leaned his face a little closer to mine and hesitated, watching my reaction. I froze and felt a wave of sadness wash over me. Turning slightly away, I closed my eyes. I couldn't kiss him. The idea felt nice, but not goose-bumpy nice. It just didn't seem right.

"I'm sorry, Li."

He chucked me lightly under my chin. "Don't worry about it. Let's get a milkshake; what do ya say?" His eyes were a little sad, but he seemed determined to keep things lighthearted between us and quickly diverted my attention to other things.

Mr. Kadam broke through my dating funk with welcome news. He'd figured out a major section of Durga's prophecy and asked me to help with some research, which I was more than willing to do. I pulled out a notepad and asked, "What have you got for me?"

"The tests of the four houses. Specifically, it says a house of gourds, a house of temptresses, and a house of winged creatures of some kind."

"What kind of winged creatures?" I gulped.

"I'm not sure at this point."

"What about the fourth house?"

"It would appear there are two houses with winged animals, I believe one will be a type of bird but later in the prophecy metal or iron is also mentioned. The other winged animal has the symbol for 'large' next to it and the same symbol is found again later in the prophecy. I'd like you to research any myths you can find about passing through houses or a test of houses and let me know what you come up with."

"I'll let you know."

"Good."

The rest of the conversation turned to mundane things and though I was happy he was including me in the research, my stomach churned at the thought of returning to India. I was all set for the danger, the magic, and the strangely supernatural, but going back also meant I'd have to face *him* again. I was good at going through the motions of an ordinary life but underneath the surface, where I could hide my innermost feelings, something churned. I was disconnected, out of place. India called to me, sometimes softly, sometimes with a roar, but the beckoning was constant and I wondered sometimes if I'd ever be able to settle down to a normal life again.

Thanksgiving meant a tofurky feast at Sarah and Mike's. I kept glancing at their festive pumpkins and squash cornucopia during the meal trying to figure out how such friendly-looking gourds might become something dangerous, and I spent the time wondering how they would play into the next quest. It was a cold and rainy day, but my foster parents had the fireplace blazing. Surprisingly, I actually enjoyed some of the vegetable dishes. I couldn't do the sugar-free, gluten-free pie, though. It just seemed wrong.

"So, what's new? Any hot guys you want to tell us about at school?" Sarah teased.

I looked up from the pumpkin pie I was stabbing cautiously with a fork. "Um, well, I am kind of dating," I admitted shyly. "There's this guy named Li and then there's Jason. It's nothing serious. We've only gone out a few times."

Sarah was thrilled, and both she and Mike pestered me with a lot of questions that I didn't really want to answer.

Luckily, Jennifer had also invited both Li and me for Thanksgiving dinner, and I managed to excuse myself from my foster parents' in plenty of time to head to Jennifer's. She lived in a nice house in West Salem. I brought a lemon meringue pie, the first one I'd ever attempted to make, and I was proud of the result. I'd let the meringue toast just a little too long, but other than that, it looked good.

Li lit up when he saw me at the door and said to Jennifer, "See? You break the lucky wishbone, and your wish does come true!"

He confided to me that he'd already stuffed himself at his family's Thanksgiving dinner but that he'd saved his dessert stomach for my pie—and was true to his word. Li ate half of my pie in one sitting.

Jennifer also had made a pumpkin pie, a marionberry pie, and a cheesecake. I took a little sample from each and was in heaven. Li groaned, complaining that his stomach was so full he'd have to sleep over. Jennifer's kids jumped up and down at the thought, accidentally dislodging their pilgrim hats, but settled down immediately when she popped in *A Charlie Brown Thanksgiving* DVD.

I was helping Jennifer clean up in the kitchen when she asked, "*So?* How's it going with," she whispered knowingly, "*Li*?"

"Umm, it's going fine."

"Are you guys, you know, together?"

"It's hard to say. I think it's too early in our relationship to call us together."

She shrunk a little and frowned at the dishwater. "Is it still that other one, the one you never talk about, who's holding you back?"

I paused with my damp towel in mid-swipe of her nice turkey platter.

"I'm sorry if I was rude. Honestly, it's just hard to talk about him. But what do you want to know?"

She picked up another plate, washed it, and dipped it in the rinse water. "Well, who is he? Where is he? Why aren't you together?"

"Well, he's in India. And we aren't *together* because . . ." I whispered, "Because . . . I left him."

"Was he *mean* to you?"

"No, no. Nothing like that. He was . . . *perfect*."

"So he didn't want you to leave?"

"No."

"Didn't he want to come with you?"

The corner of my mouth quirked up in a small smile. "I had to beg him to stay behind."

"Then I don't understand. Why did you leave him?"

"He was too . . . I was too . . ." I sighed. "It's complicated."

"Did you love him?"

I set down the platter that I'd been wiping dry for five minutes and twisted the towel in my hands. Quietly, I answered, "Yes."

"And now?"

"And now . . . when I'm alone . . . I feel like I can't breathe sometimes."

She nodded and washed a few more dishes. The silverware clinked softly in the bubbly water. Angling her head slightly, she asked, "What's his name?"

I stared dully at the kitchen window. It was dark outside, and I could see myself reflected with my slumped shoulders and dead eyes.

"Ren. His name is Ren."

Saying his name bruised my already broken heart. I felt a tear slip down my cheek and looked up at the window again, just in time to see

Li in the reflection standing behind me. He turned and walked out of the room, but not before I saw his expression. I'd hurt his feelings.

Jennifer reached over and squeezed my arm. "Go talk to him. It's better to discuss things quickly. Otherwise, mountains are made of molehills."

This situation already felt like a mountain to me, but she was right. I needed to talk to Li.

He had left the house already. As I gathered up my things and said thanks, Jennifer strolled out of the kitchen and waved me on.

I headed out the door and found him leaning up against his car with his arms folded across his chest. "Li?"

"Yes?"

"I'm sorry you had to hear that."

He sighed deeply. "It's okay. You warned me before we started this that it was going to be hard. I guess I only have one question."

"Okay."

He turned to face me and looked deeply into my eyes. "Are you still in love with him?"

"I . . . I think so."

He visibly deflated.

"But, Li, it doesn't matter. He's gone. He's on another continent. If he wanted to be with me that badly, he could be, and he's not. He's not here. He hasn't even called me, in fact. I just need . . . time. A little bit more time to . . . to put aside these feelings. I want to be able to." I reached out and took his hand. "It's not fair to you, I know. You deserve to date someone who doesn't have this kind of baggage."

"Kelsey, everyone has baggage of some kind." He kicked the tire of his car. "I like you and I want you to like me. Maybe it will work out if we just take it slow. Learn to be friends for a while first."

"Is that enough for you?"

"It'll have to be. I don't have any other options except not seeing you, and that's not a good option for me."

"Okay, then, we'll take it slow."

Li smiled and leaned down to kiss my cheek. "You're worth waiting for, Kelsey. And just for the record, the guy was crazy to let you leave."

Though I had borrowed stacks of books from the library and spent countless hours online, I still hadn't found any useful information about the test of the four houses. I hoped the winged creatures on this part of the quest were going to be harmless butterflies, but somehow I doubted it would be that easy. *At least we now had a clue as to how the air theme was going to fit in,* I thought.

With my head tucked in books most of the time, Thanksgiving led quickly into the Christmas season. Bright Christmas displays could be seen in all the neighborhoods and all the store windows. I continued to date both Li and Jason, and in the middle of December, Li took me to his cousin's wedding.

During the last two weeks, I'd been telling myself repeatedly that I really wanted things to work out with Li, that it would be alright if I opened my heart to him. He looked very handsome when he picked me up. He wore a dark suit, and my heart stirred when I saw him. Maybe not with love, but at least with happiness to be with him.

"Wow, Kelsey. You look great!"

I had dipped into my forbidden closet and come out with a peach princess dress made of satin and organza. The top had a fitted corset that flowed into a peach calf-length petal skirt.

The wedding was held at a country club. When the ceremony was over, lion dancers and musicians appeared, and we followed them parade-style to the reception area. One of the musicians played a mandolin. It looked similar to the guitar that had been hanging on the wall in Mr. Kadam's music room.

Red parasols, golden Chinese fans, and fancy origami decorated the dining room, which Li explained were traditional at Chinese weddings. The bride wore a red dress, and instead of boxed gifts, guests gave the couple red envelopes full of money.

Li gestured toward a group of boys all wearing black suits with sunglasses. My eyes widened, and I had to stifle a giggle when I realized it was our game group. They grinned and waved to me. One of them had a large briefcase handcuffed to his wrist.

"Why are they dressed like that?" I asked. "And what's in the briefcase?"

He laughed. "One thousand dollars in crisp, one dollar bills. They're going to handcuff the case to the groom. It's a joke. My cousin used to be a part of our game group until he got too busy at his job. He's the first to get married so he gets the briefcase."

We made our way through the receiving line, and Li introduced me to his cousin and his new bride. She was petite and very beautiful and seemed a little shy. After that, we found our seats at the dinner table, where we were soon joined by all of Li's friends. They teased him about not wearing his shades too.

The bride and groom performed a candle-lighting ceremony to honor their ancestors, and then dinner was served: fish to symbolize abundance, a whole lobster to represent completeness, Peking duck for joy and happiness, shark fin soup to grant wealth, noodles for long life, and sea cucumber salad for marital harmony. Li tried to get me to taste sweet lotus seed buns that symbolized fertility.

"Umm . . . thanks," I said uncertainly, "but I'll pass for now."

After good wishes from both sides of the family, the couple danced their first dance.

Li squeezed my hand and stood. "Kelsey, may I?"

"Sure."

He spun me around the dance floor once before his friends started to cut in. I never got more than one full dance with Li. A handful of dances later, a three-tiered cake was brought out. The inside was orange, and the outside was decorated with pearly almond-flavored icing and beautiful sugar orchids.

When Li dropped me off that night, I felt happy. I'd really enjoyed being a part of his world. I hugged him and pecked him goodnight on the cheek, and he smiled at me like he'd just won a worldwide martial arts title.

I spent Christmas Day with my foster family. Sipping hot chocolate, I watched the kids open their presents. Sarah and Mike had given me a jogging outfit. They were always trying to get me to embrace the highs of running. The kids gave me gloves and a scarf, which I told them I desperately needed. I planned to hang out with them that morning and then spend the rest of the day with Li who would pick me up for an afternoon date at 2:00 p.m.

His present, a martial arts movie collection, was sitting on my coffee table in the living room. I'd already made up my mind that if he didn't try to kiss me by the end of the date, I would kiss him. I had even hung mistletoe outside my door. An irrational part of my mind said that maybe kissing him was the key to breaking the bond I still felt with the man I left. I knew it probably wouldn't be that easy, but it was the first step.

My thoughts drifted to my date. The kids were playing with their new toys, and the adults were sitting by the Christmas tree, listening to carols, and talking quietly when the doorbell rang.

"Are you expecting anyone, Sarah?" I asked as I got up to answer it.

"It's probably a package from Mr. Kadam. He said to expect a surprise."

I twisted the deadbolt and opened the door.

Standing on the front stoop was the most beautiful man on the planet. My heart stopped and then galloped thunderously in my chest. Anxious cobalt blue eyes explored every feature of my face. Lines of tension and stress faded from his expression, and he breathed deeply like a man who had been underwater too long.

Now content, the warrior-angel smiled softly, sweetly, and reached out tentatively to touch my cheek. I felt the link between us wrap its fingers solidly around my heart and tighten, drawing us closer. Circling his arms around me hesitantly at first, he touched his forehead to mine and then crushed my body to his. He rocked me back and forth gently and stroked my hair. Sighing, he whispered only one word, "*Kelsey.*"

5

return

Wrapped in his arms, I listened to the beat of my heart, which swelled and pounded in my chest. Like the Grinch, my heart had shrunk until it was two sizes too small. When Ren touched me, all the emotions I'd been holding back spilled out and flooded through my body, slowly filling the emptiness.

I felt myself blossom and grow with new vigor. Ren was the sun, and the tenderness he showed me was life-giving water. A dormant part of me burst into pulsing life, stretched deep rooty fingers, opened thick green leaves, and shot curling tendrils outward drawing us closer together.

Sarah called out from the kitchen, reminding me that a world existed outside the two of us. "Kelsey? Kelsey? Who is it?"

Snapping back to reality, I stepped away. He let me go, but slid his hand down my arm and laced his fingers through mine. I was mute. My mouth opened to answer, but I couldn't form a single word.

Ren sensed my plight and announced his arrival. "Excuse me, Mr. and Mrs. Neilson?"

Mike and Sarah both stopped mid-stride when they saw him. Ren smiled in his devastating way and extended his hand.

"Hello. I'm Mr. Kadam's grandson, Ren."

He shook hands warmly with Mike and then extended a hand to Sarah. When Ren turned his smile on her, she flushed, nervous as a schoolgirl. It made me feel better to know that I wasn't the only female to lose all sense of reason around him. He had a mesmerizing effect on women of all ages.

Mike said, "Huh, Ren. That's a coincidence. Hey, Kelsey, wasn't that tiger—"

I rushed forward. "Uh, yeah. Funny thing, huh?" I looked up at Ren and hooked my thumb at him.

"But, *Ren* is actually just his nickname. His given name is . . . Al." I punched him on the arm, "Right, Al?"

His eyebrows drew together in amused puzzlement. "Right, Kelsey." He turned to Mike and Sarah again. "It's actually Alagan, but you can call me Ren. Everyone does."

By this time, Sarah had regained her composure. "Well, Ren. Please come inside and meet the children."

He smiled at her again and said, "I would love to."

Sarah responded by stifling a girlish giggle and patting her hair. Ren stooped to pick up several large packages that he'd stacked by the door while I made a beeline for the family room.

While Mike helped Ren, Sarah found me and whispered, "*Kelsey*, when did you two meet? For a minute there, I thought I was finally meeting Li. What's going on?"

I stared straight at the Christmas tree as I mumbled, "That's what I'd like to know."

The men entered the living room, where Ren removed his charcoal herringbone trench coat and draped it over a chair. He was wearing jeans and a long-sleeved gray zip polo shirt that clung to his chest and arms.

"Who's Li?" Ren asked.

My mouth dropped open. "How did you—" I snapped my mouth shut quickly. I'd forgotten about his tiger hearing. "Li is . . . umm . . . a guy . . . that I know."

Sarah raised her eyebrows but didn't say anything.

Ren watched me closely, politely waited for me to sit, and then sat down on the couch next to me. The minute he sat, the kids were all over him.

"I have presents for the two of you," he said conspiratorially to Rebecca and Sammy. "Can you open them together?"

The kids nodded their heads seriously, and he laughed and shoved a large box over to them. They frantically opened it and pulled out a set of Dr. Seuss books. The books looked strange to me at first. I took one out of the set and figured out why.

I whispered to him, "You got first editions! *For kids*? Those are worth probably thousands of dollars *each*!"

He tucked some hair behind my ear and leaned over to whisper, "I got you a set just like it at home. Don't be jealous."

My face turned bright red. "That's not what I meant."

He laughed and picked up the next gift. Mike kept stealing glances out the window at Ren's car.

"So, Ren, I see you have a Hummer out there."

Ren looked up at Mike. "Yes, I do."

"Do you think you could take me for a ride some time? I mean, I've always wanted to ride in one of those."

Ren rubbed his jaw. "Sure, but I can't do it today. I have to get settled in at my new residence."

"Oh . . . you'll be staying here for a while?"

"That's the plan, at least for the term. I've signed up to take a few classes at Western Oregon University."

"Well, that's great. You'll be going to school with Kelsey."

Ren grinned. "Yes, that's right. Perhaps we'll bump into each other there."

Mike turned his attention to the car again with a big smile on his face. Sarah was watching me closely. I tried to maintain a neutral expression, but, inside, I was a mass of questions.

What is he thinking? Staying here? Where? Going to school with me? What am I going to do? Why is he here?

Ren slid a large gift over to Sarah and Mike. "This is for you two."

Mike helped Sarah open it, and they pulled out a brand new red mixer with every attachment known to mankind. I wouldn't be surprised if she could create an ice sculpture with the thing. Sarah began talking excitedly about all the organic wheat-free baked goods she would now be making.

Ren picked up a smaller package and handed it to me. "This is from Mr. Kadam."

I opened it and found leather-bound copies of *Mahābhārata* from India, *Romance of the Three Kingdoms* from China, and *The Tale of Genji* from Japan, all translated into English. There was also a short letter wishing me a merry Christmas.

I stroked my hand over the leather covers and made a mental note to call him and thank him later.

Ren handed me another gift. "This one's from Kishan."

Sarah looked up from her mixer and asked, "Who's Kishan?"

Ren replied, "Kishan is my younger brother."

Sarah gave me a motherly look of exasperation, to which I shrugged sheepishly in response. I'd never mentioned Ren or Kishan to her, and she was probably wondering how I could fail to remember someone like him. *I'd be wondering why I'd been so close-mouthed too.*

I opened the box and found a small jewelry case from Tiffany's.

Inside was a thin, white-gold necklace. The card was very carefully handwritten:

Hey, Kells,

Miss you.
Come home soon.
I figured you'd like something more girlish to wear with my amulet.
There's also an extra gift in the box, just in case you need it.

Kishan

I set the necklace aside and dug through the box. A small cylinder was wrapped in tissue paper. Unrolling it, a cold, metal canister fell into my palm. It was a can of pepper-spray. On it, Kishan had taped a picture of a tiger with a circle and a slash across its face. At the top were the words "Tiger Repellant" in big black letters.

I giggled, and Ren took it from me. After reading the label, he frowned and tossed the can back in the box. Reaching down, he picked up another package.

"This one's from me."

His words immediately sobered me. I glanced up quickly to measure Mike and Sarah's expression. Mike seemed happily ignorant of the tension I felt, but Sarah was more in tune and was considering me

carefully. I closed my eyes for a second, praying that whatever was in the box wouldn't raise a billion questions that I'd have to answer.

I slipped my fingers under the heavy wrapping paper and opened the packaging. Reaching my hand inside the box, I felt smooth, polished wood. The kids helped me yank the carton off. Inside was a hand-carved jewelry box.

Ren leaned toward me. "Open it."

I ran my hand nervously across the top and carefully tilted open the lid. Rows of tiny drawers were lined with velvet, and inside each little drawer was a coiled-up hair ribbon.

"The segments come out. See?"

He lifted the top section and the next one. There were five sections with about forty ribbons per section.

"Every ribbon is different. No two colors are the same, and there's at least one from every major country in the world."

Stunned, I said, "*Ren* . . . I—"

I looked up. Mike saw nothing wrong at all. He probably thought something like this happened every day. Sarah was looking at Ren with new eyes. Her suspicious and concerned expressions were gone.

With a small approving smile on her face, she said, "Well, Ren. It seems you know Kelsey pretty well. She does love hair ribbons."

Suddenly, Sarah cleared her throat loudly, stood, and asked us to watch the kids while they went for a quick run. They brought us two mugs of steaming hot chocolate and disappeared upstairs to change into jogging clothes. Though they exercised all the time, they usually took a break on Christmas. *Was she trying to give Ren and me some alone time? I wasn't sure if I should hug her or beg her to stay.*

The box was still on my lap, and I was absentmindedly fingering a ribbon when they jogged out the door with a wave.

Ren reached over and touched my hand. "You don't like it?"

I looked up into his blue eyes and said huskily, "It's the best present I've *ever* been given."

He smiled brilliantly, picked up my hand, and pressed a soft kiss on my fingers.

Turning to the kids, he asked, "Now who would like a story?"

Rebecca and Sammy picked out a book and climbed up onto Ren's lap. He wrapped an arm around each of them.

He read in an animated voice, "I am Sam. Sam I am. Do you like green eggs and ham?"

The only word he got stuck on was "anywhere," but the kids helped him sound it out, and he got it every time after that. I was impressed. Mr. Kadam must have taught him how to read English.

Ren convinced Sammy to hold the book for him and pulled me closer with his free arm. He tugged me up against his body so that my head rested on his shoulder and then trailed his fingers teasingly up and down my arm.

When Mike and Sarah returned, I bolted up and started gathering my things like a woman with her shoes on fire. Nervously, I glanced at Ren and found him watching me with a slightly amused, steady gaze. Mike and Sarah thanked us and helped me pack my things into my car. Ren said his good-byes too and waited for me outside.

Sarah gave me a look that clearly meant I had some explaining to do. Then she shut the door and left us in the cold December weather. We were finally alone.

Ren slipped off a glove and traced my face with his warm fingertips.

"Go home, Kells. Don't ask me questions now. This isn't the right place. We'll have plenty of time later. I'll meet you there."

"But—"

"*Later*, rajkumari." He slipped his glove back on and walked over to the Hummer.

When did he learn how to drive? I turned my car around and watched the Hummer in the rearview mirror until I turned onto a side street, and it fell out of view.

Thousands of questions pummeled my brain, and I ran through the list on the drive up the mountain. The road was a little icy. I set aside the burning questions filling my mind to focus on the drive.

When I passed the curve and saw my house, I noticed something was different. It took me a minute to figure out what it was: there were curtains in the window of the connecting duplex. Someone had moved in.

I parked in the garage and walked to the front door of the other home. I knocked but nobody answered. Twisting the knob, I found the door unlocked. The home was furnished almost the same way as mine but in darker, more masculine colors. When I saw the old mandolin resting on the leather couch, my nagging suspicions were confirmed. Ren was moving in.

I walked through the kitchen, found the pantry and refrigerator empty, and saw that the bottom half of the back door had been refitted with a huge swinging flap.

Hmm . . . won't keep burglars out. They can crawl right in. But, I guess they'd get a surprise if they tried to steal something here.

I hurried back to my house, closing the door behind me, not even bothering to look upstairs or check his closet for the designer labels I knew were there. There was no doubt in my mind that Ren was my new neighbor.

In fact, I'd just slipped out of my shoes and coat when I heard what could only be the Hummer making its way up the drive. I watched him from the window. He was a good driver. He somehow managed to maneuver the giant vehicle between the protruding branches that might've scratched the paint. He parked the Hummer in the other

garage, and I heard the crunch of his footsteps on the frozen path as he made his way to my front door.

Leaving it open for him, I walked into the living room, sat down in my recliner with my feet tucked under me, and folded my arms across my chest. I knew that body-language specialists said it was a classic defensive pose, but I didn't care.

I heard him close the door, shrug out of his coat, and hang it in the hall closet. Turning the corner, Ren walked into the living room. He searched my face for a brief moment and then ran a hand through his hair as he sat down across from me. His hair was longer than it had been in India. Silky black strands fell over his forehead, and he brushed them back in annoyance. He looked bigger, brawnier than I remembered. *He must be eating better than he used to.*

We looked at each other silently for several seconds.

Finally, I said, "So . . . you're my new neighbor."

"Yes." He sighed softly. "I couldn't stay away from you anymore."

"I didn't think you were trying to stay away."

"You asked me to. I was trying to honor your wishes. I wanted to give you time to think. To clear your head. To . . . listen to your heart."

I'd definitely had time to think. Unfortunately, my thoughts were about as confused as they possibly could be. I hadn't been able to think clearly since I'd left India. And I hadn't listened to my heart since I woke up next to Ren in Kishkindha. I'd shut myself off from my heart months ago.

"Oh. So then, your feelings haven't . . . changed?"

"My *feelings* are stronger than they ever were."

His blue eyes studied my face. He pushed his hair out of his eyes and leaned forward. "Kelsey, every day you were away from me was *agonizing*. It drove me crazy. If Mr. Kadam hadn't kept me busy every minute, I would have been on a plane the next week. I sat patiently through his instruction every day, but I was only a man for six hours.

As a tiger, I wore a path on my bedroom rug from pacing hour after hour. He almost got out a safari rifle to shoot me with a tranquilizer. I couldn't be appeased. I was restless, a wild animal without . . . without his mate."

I fidgeted and shifted in the chair.

"I told Kishan I needed to train to get my fighting skills back up to par. We fought constantly as both men and beasts. We trained with weapons, claws, teeth, and bare hands. Fighting with him was probably the only thing that kept me sane. I'd fall onto my rug every night bloody, exhausted, and drained. But, still . . . I could feel you.

"You were on the other side of the world, but I often woke with the scent of you surrounding me. I ached for you, Kells. No matter how much Kishan thrashed me, it couldn't diminish the pain of losing you. I'd dream of you and reach out to touch you, but you were always just out of reach. Kadam kept telling me it was for the best and that I had things to learn before I could come to Oregon. He was probably right, but I didn't want to hear it."

"But if you wanted to be with me then . . . why didn't you call?"

"I *wanted* to. It tortured me to hear your voice every week when you called Kadam. I waited nearby each time, hoping that you would ask to speak to me, but you never did. I didn't want to pressure you. I wanted to respect your wishes. I wanted it to be *your* decision."

How ironic. There were so many times I wanted to ask for him, but I couldn't bring myself to do it.

"You listened in on our phone conversations?"

"Yes. I have excellent hearing, remember?"

"Right. So what . . . changed? Why come here now?"

Ren laughed sardonically. "It's Kishan's doing. We were sparring one day, and he was beating me as usual. By that point, I didn't even compete much with him anymore. I *wanted* him to hurt me. It helped.

Suddenly, he stopped. He walked around me and looked me up and down. I stood there and waited for him to resume the fight. Then he pulled back his fist and punched me as hard as he could.

"I just stood there and took it, not even bothering to defend myself. Next, he punched me as hard as he could in the gut. I recovered and stood in front of him again, not even caring. He growled and shouted in my face."

"What did he say?"

"A lot of things, most of which I'd rather not repeat. The gist of it was that I needed to snap out of it and that if I was so miserable . . . why didn't I get up and do something about it?"

"Oh."

"He mocked me, saying that the mighty Prince of the Mujulaain Empire, the High Protector of the People, the champion at the Battle of the Hundred Horses, the heir to the throne, was felled by a young girl. He said there was nothing more pathetic than a cowering tiger licking his wounds.

"At that point, I didn't care what he said. Nothing fazed me until he told me that our parents would be ashamed. That they raised a coward. That's when I made a decision."

"The decision to come here."

"Yes. I decided that I needed to be near you. I decided that, even if all you wanted was friendship, I would be happier here than I was in India without you."

Ren got up, knelt at my feet, and took my hand. "I decided to find you, throw myself at your feet, and beg you to have mercy on me. I'll accept *whatever* you choose. Honestly, Kelsey. Just please don't ask me to live apart from you again. Because . . . I *can't*."

How could I remain unyielding? Ren's words penetrated the flimsy barriers around my heart. I'd meant to set up a barbed wire fence, but the barbs had marshmallow tips. He slipped right through my defenses. Ren touched his forehead to my hand, and my marshmallow heart melted.

I wrapped my arms around his neck, hugged him, and whispered in his ear, "A prince of India should never have to get down on his knees and beg for anything. Alright. You can stay."

He sighed and hugged me close.

I grinned wryly. "After all, I wouldn't want PETA to come after me for tiger abuse."

He laughed softly. "Wait right here," he said and walked out the door that connected both our houses. He came back in with a package tied with a red ribbon.

The box was long, thin, and black. I cracked it open and saw a bracelet. The thin chain had a white-gold oval locket. Inside were two pictures: Ren, the prince, and Ren, the tiger.

I smiled. "You knew I'd want to remember the tiger too."

Ren clasped the locket to my wrist and sighed. "Yes, even though I'm slightly jealous of him. He gets to spend much more time with you than I do."

"Hmm. Well, not as much as he used to. I miss him."

He grimaced. "Believe me, you'll get to see plenty of him in the coming weeks."

His warm fingers brushed my arm, and my pulse hammered. He pulled my arm up to eye level, inspected the charm, and pressed a kiss on the inside of my wrist.

Ren's eyes twinkled with mischief as he said, "So do you like it?"

"Yes. Thank you. But . . ." My face fell. "I didn't get you anything."

He tugged me close and wrapped his arms around my waist. "You got me the best present of all. You gave me today. It's the best present I could have wished for."

I laughed and teased. "Pretty poor wrapping job I did then."

"Hmm, you're right. I'd better wrap you up properly."

Ren grabbed my grandmother's quilt from the back of the recliner and wrapped me up like a mummy. I kicked and squealed as he scooped me up in his arms and onto his lap.

"Let's read something, Kells. I'm ready for another Shakespearean play. I tried to read one on my own, but I had a hard time sounding out the words."

I cleared my throat noisily from within my cocoon. "As you can see, *my captor*, my arms are trapped."

Ren leaned over to nuzzle my ear, and then suddenly stiffened. "Someone is here."

The doorbell rang. Ren jumped up, set me on my feet, and spun me out of the blanket before I could blink. I stood there for a moment dizzy and confused. Then I flushed in embarrassment.

I hissed, "What happened to your tiger hearing?"

He grinned at me. "I was distracted, Kells. You can hardly blame me. Are you expecting someone?"

It suddenly hit me: "Li!"

"Li?"

I grimaced. "We have a . . . *a date*."

Ren's eyes darkened, and he repeated quietly, "You have a *date*?"

"Yes . . ." I said haltingly.

My mind raced with thoughts of the man next to me and the one outside my door. *Ren is back, but what does that mean? And what am I supposed to do now?*

The doorbell rang again. At the very least, I knew I couldn't leave Li standing there.

Turning to Ren, I explained, "I need to go now. Please stay here. There's sandwich stuff in the fridge for dinner. I'll be back later. Please be patient. And *don't . . . get . . . mad*."

Ren folded his arms across his chest and narrowed his eyes. "If that's what you *want* me to do. I will."

I sighed with relief. "Thank you. I'll be back as soon as I can."

Slipping on my shoes, I picked up the wrapped set of DVDs I had bought for Li. Tight-lipped, Ren helped me into my coat and then stalked into the kitchen. He leaned back against the counter with his arms crossed over his chest and a raised eyebrow. I gave him a weak, pleading smile and headed for the front door.

I felt a twinge of guilt at having a gift for Li and not for Ren, but quickly dismissed it and pulled open the door acting as if nothing strange was happening. "Hey, Li."

"Merry Christmas, Kelsey," Li said, completely unaware that everything in my life had changed once again.

My date with Li did not go as originally planned. We were supposed to see a martial arts movie and have Christmas dinner at Grandma Zhi's. I was somber, and my thoughts kept drifting back to Ren. It was hard to focus on Li—or anything for that matter.

"What's wrong, Kelsey? You seem very quiet."

"Li, would you mind if we skipped the movie and just had an early dinner? I need to make some calls when I get home. You know, to say merry Christmas to friends."

Li was disappointed but rebounded cheerfully, as usual. "Oh. Sure. That's not a problem."

It wasn't exactly a lie. I *was* planning on calling Mr. Kadam later. But that didn't make me feel one bit better about changing our plans.

At Grandma Zhi's, the boys were mid-way through an all-day-game marathon. I played, but I was distracted and made bad strategic decisions—so bad that even the guys commented on it.

"What's up with you tonight, Kelsey?" Wen asked. "You never let me get away with a move like that."

I smiled at him. "I don't know. Christmas blues maybe."

I was losing badly, so Li grabbed my hand and led me to the living room to open our presents. Li and I exchanged gifts and opened them at the same time.

We pulled the paper off and laughed long and hard. We had bought each other the exact same present. It felt good to let go of some of the tension I had pent up.

"Apparently, we both like martial arts DVDs," Li chuckled.

"I'm sorry, Li. I should have put some more thought into it."

He was still laughing. "Don't worry about it. It's a good sign. Grandma Zhi would say it's good luck in Chinese culture. It means we're compatible."

"Yeah," I said thoughtfully, "I guess it does."

We went back to the game after eating, and I played robotically while thinking about what he'd said. He was right in many ways. We *were* compatible and probably much more suited for each other than Ren and I were. Like Sarah and Mike, these were normal people, a normal family. And Ren was . . . not. He was immortal and gorgeous. He was too perfect.

I could easily envision making a life with Li. It would be comfortable and safe. He would be a doctor and set up a private practice in the suburbs. We'd have a couple of kids and vacation in Disneyland. The kids would all take wushu and soccer. We'd celebrate holidays with his grandparents and have all his friends and their wives over for barbeques.

A life with Ren was harder to picture. We didn't look as if we belonged together. It was like matching up Ken with Strawberry Shortcake. He needed Barbie. *What would Ren do in Oregon? Would he get a job? What would he put on his résumé? High Protector and former Prince of India? Would we purchase a time-share in a wild animal theme park so he could be the main attraction on weekends?* None of it made sense. But I couldn't deny my feelings for Ren—not anymore.

It was painfully obvious that my rebellious heart yearned for Ren. And, no matter how hard I tried to convince myself to fall for Li, the fact of the matter was that I was always drawn back to Ren. I liked Li. Maybe someday I could even love him. I definitely didn't want to hurt Li. It wasn't fair.

What am I going to do?

After I played badly for another hour, Li drove me home. It was early evening when he pulled into the driveway. I looked at the windows for a familiar shadow but didn't see anything. The house was dark. Li walked me to my door.

"Hey, are my eyes deceiving me or is that mistletoe hanging up there?" Li asked, squeezing my elbow.

I glanced up at the mistletoe and remembered my resolve to kiss Li tonight. It seemed like so long ago. Now everything has changed. *Hasn't it? What about Ren? Could we really just be friends? Should I risk everything and take a chance with Ren? Or go with a sure thing like Li? How do I choose?*

I'd been quiet a long time, and Li was waiting patiently for my answer. Finally, I turned to him and said, "Yeah. It is."

I put my hand on his cheek and kissed him softly on the lips. It was nice. Not the passionate kiss I'd been planning, but he still seemed happy about it. He briefly touched my face and smiled. Li's touch was nice. Safe. But, it wasn't anything at all like what I felt with Ren. Li's kiss was a speck of dust in the universe, a drop of water next to a raging waterfall.

How do you live with something so mediocre when you've had something so exceptional? I guess you just do and learn to treasure your memories.

I twisted the key in the lock and cracked the door open.

Li hollered happily, "Night, Kelsey. See you Monday."

I watched him drive off and then stepped inside the house to face the Indian prince waiting for me within.

6 choices

I stepped through the entryway and closed the door behind me, letting my eyes adjust to the darkness. I wondered if Ren was next door and debated whether or not to sort things out with him tonight.

I stepped into the living room and gasped softly when I spotted the familiar form of my blue-eyed white tiger sprawled out on the leather couch. Ren raised his head and looked straight into my soul.

Tears came to my eyes. I hadn't realized that I'd missed this part of him, my friend, so much. I knelt down in front of the couch, threw my arms around his neck, and cried big alligator tears, letting them spill down my cheeks and into his soft white fur. I petted his head and stroked his back. Ren was here. He was finally with me. I wasn't alone anymore. Suddenly, I understood that he must have felt this way too, being without *me* all these months.

I choked back a sob. "Ren, I . . . I *missed* you so much. I *wanted* to talk to you. You're my best friend. It's just that I didn't want to take away your choices. Can you understand that?"

My arms were still wrapped tightly around his neck when I felt him change. His body morphed and soon his arms were around me and I was sitting on his lap. His white shirt was damp from my tears.

Hugging me close, he said, "I missed you too, *iadala*. More than you know. And I understand your reasons for leaving."

I mumbled against his shirt, "You do?"

"Yes. But I want you to understand something too, Kells. You don't take away my choices. You *are* my choice."

I sniffed wetly. "But, Ren—"

He pulled my head back to his shoulder. "This man, Li. You kissed him?"

I nodded mutely against his chest. There was no point denying it. I knew he must have heard it through the door.

"Do you love him?"

"I feel friendship and respect for him, and I like him a lot, but I'm definitely not head over heels about him.

"Then why did you kiss him?"

"I kissed him to . . . compare, I guess. To explore how I really felt about him."

Ren picked me up and set me on the couch next to him. He was warming to the topic, and I couldn't figure out why. I expected him to be angry, but he wasn't at all.

"So *dating* is how you learn if you like each other?"

"Yes," I answered hesitantly.

"Did you have other dates or is this the first one?"

"You mean with Li?"

He raised an eyebrow. "Were there others?"

"Yes." I frowned.

"How many?"

"Three altogether—Li, Jason, and Artie. If you can count Artie. Ren, why all the questions? What are you getting at?"

"I'm just curious about modern courtship rituals. What did you do on these *dates*?"

"I've been out to see a couple of movies, I went out to dinner, I went with Li to a wedding, and I saw a football game with Jason."

"Did you kiss all these men?"

"No! I've only kissed Li, and this was the first time."

"So Li is the one you favor." Ren started mumbling to himself. Turning to face me, he took my hands in his. "Kelsey, I think you should keep dating."

My mouth dropped open. "*What?*"

"I'm serious. I've been thinking about it while you were gone. You talked about giving me choices. I've made mine, but you still haven't made yours."

"Ren, this is crazy! What are you talking about?"

"Date Li or Jason or whoever you want to, and I promise I won't interfere. But I also want a fair chance. I want you to date *me* too."

"I don't think you understand how dating works, Ren. I can't just date three or four men forever. The point of dating is that you end up becoming exclusive with someone you hit it off with."

He shook his head. "You *date* to find the person you *love*, Kelsey."

I sputtered, "So what am I supposed to tell Li, 'By the way, Ren is back, and he thought it would be great if I dated you both?'"

He shrugged. "If Li can't handle a little honest competition, then it's better for you to know that now."

"That's going to make attending wushu class very awkward."

"Why?"

"He's my teacher."

Ren grinned. "Good. I'll tag along. I want to meet him and I could use a good workout anyway."

"Uh, Ren, it's a beginner's class. You don't belong, and I don't want you fighting with Li. I'd really rather you didn't go."

"I'll be a perfect gentleman." He tilted his head, considering me. "Are you afraid that I'd be the obvious choice?"

"*No,*" I replied testily. "I'm more afraid you'd squash him like a bug!"

"I wouldn't do that, Kelsey. *Presuming* I wanted to, that wouldn't be the way to win your affections. Even *I* know that. So will you date me?"

"Dating you would be . . . *hard*."

"Why is it easier to date other men than me? And don't give me the radish explanation again. It's ridiculous."

"Because," I continued quietly, "if it didn't work out, I could survive without those other men."

Kissing my fingers, Ren looked intently into my eyes and said, "*Iadala*, you will *never* lose me. I'll always be near you. Give me a chance, Kells. Please."

I sighed and looked at his beautiful face. "Okay. We'll try it."

"Thank you." He leaned back against the sofa very pleased with himself. "Just treat me like all the other guys."

Right. No problem there. Just treat the most perfect and beautiful man on Earth, who happens to be an ancient prince of India that was cursed to be a tiger, like he's just a regular, average guy. No girl in her right mind could look at him—even without knowing everything I know—and think he was average.

He leaned over to peck me on the cheek. "Goodnight, *rajkumari*. I'll call you tomorrow."

The next morning, the phone rang way too early. It was Ren, asking me out to dinner, our first official date.

I yawned sleepily. "Where do you want to eat?"

"I have no idea. What do you suggest?"

"Usually, the guy has a place in mind before he calls, but I'll cut you a break this time since you're new to dating and all. I know where we should go. Dress casual and pick me up at five thirty. But you can come over and visit earlier if you like."

"I'll see you at five thirty, Kells."

I puttered around the house most of the day watching our connecting door, but Ren stayed stubbornly on his side. I even made chocolate chip cookies, hoping the smell would entice him over early, but it didn't work.

At exactly five thirty, he knocked on my front door. When I opened it, he handed me a pink rose and offered me his arm. He was dressed ridiculously well, especially for a casual date, wearing a dark gray long-sleeved striped shirt with a designer down jacket vest.

Outside, Ren opened the Hummer door. Warm air blew out of the car's heating vents, as he slid his hands around my waist and lifted me up into my seat. He made sure I was buckled in properly and asked, "Where to?"

"I'm introducing you to the pride of the Northwest. I'm taking you to Burgerville."

On the way, Ren told me about all the things he'd been learning in the last few months, including driving. He shared a funny story about Kishan accidentally crashing the Jeep into the water fountain—after which Mr. Kadam wouldn't let Kishan near the Rolls.

"Kadam has been tutoring me in every subject imaginable," Ren continued. "I've been studying modern politics, world history, finance, and business. Apparently, living for centuries, plus Kadam's wise investments, has paid off. We are quite wealthy."

"How wealthy?"

"Wealthy enough to run our own country."

My mouth fell open.

Ren went on nonchalantly, "Kadam has established contacts all over the world. They are quite valuable resources, and you would be surprised by how many important people owe him favors."

"Important people? Like who?"

"Generals, CEOs, politicians from every major country in the world, royalty, and even religious leaders. He is *very* well connected. Even if I were a man all day and spent every waking hour with him, I couldn't come close to amassing the amount of knowledge he's gained over the years. He was already a brilliant adviser to my father, but now he's nothing short of a genius. There is no reward on Earth that could possibly compensate him for the loyalty he's shown to us. I only wish there was a way to express our thanks aptly."

Once in the parking lot of the restaurant, Ren offered me his arm. I took it and said, "Being immortal has its price. Mr. Kadam seems very lonely, and that's something the three of you share. You're drawn together as a family. No one can understand what you've been through more than Kishan and Mr. Kadam. I think the best thing you can do to repay him is to give him that level of loyalty in return. He considers you and Kishan sons and the best way a son can honor his father is to be the kind of man that would make him proud."

Ren stopped, smiled, and leaned over to kiss my cheek. "You are a very wise woman, *rajkumari*. That is excellent advice."

When we reached the front of the line at Burgerville, Ren let me order first and then asked for seven huge sandwiches, three orders of fries, a large soda, and one large blackberry milkshake. When the lady asked if it was to go, he shook his head, confused, and told her we'd be dining in. I laughed and told the lady he was *very* hungry.

At the soda fountain, Ren tasted several flavors and ended up going with root beer. Watching him discover new tastes and new foods was hugely entertaining.

Over dinner, we talked about school and my unfinished research project for Mr. Kadam on air, winged creatures, and the test of the four houses. I also filled him in on Jason and my horrid date with Artie. Ren frowned and couldn't understand why anyone would willingly date Artie.

"He kind of tricks girls into dating him, like me," I explained. "He's just super judgmental and self-involved."

"Hmm." Ren unwrapped his last sandwich and stared at it, considering.

I laughed. "Are you full, Tiger? It would be a shame to skip your blackberry milkshake. They *are* the best in the country."

He retrieved another straw and popped it in the top of the shake. "Here, share it with me."

I took a sip, and Ren leaned over and sucked down about a third of it in one big slurp. Then he grinned.

"And you said you'd never share a milkshake with me again."

I teased him with mock dismay, "Oh, no! You're right! Well, this one doesn't count. I was talking to your better tiger half. So my promise is still valid."

"No, you definitely reneged on your promise. And my tiger half is definitely not my better half. That just gives me more incentive to prove you wrong."

After dinner, we drove to a nearby park and decided to take a walk. Ren grabbed a blanket from the trunk.

"Am I allowed to hold your hand on a first date?" Ren asked.

"You always hold my hand."

"But not on a date."

I rolled my eyes at him but held out my hand. We strolled in the park for a while, and he asked me lots of questions about America and its history and culture. He was easy to talk to. Everything was new and fascinating for him.

We stopped at a pond. Ren sat down, pulled me back against his chest, and wrapped his arms around me.

"Just trying to keep you warm," he said defensively when I shot him a knowing look.

I sniggered. "That's the oldest trick in the book."

Ren laughed and brushed his lips against my ear. "What are some other tricks I should try out on you?"

"Somehow, I think you'll figure them out all by yourself."

Despite my teasing, being close to him did keep me warm, and we talked and watched the moonlit water for hours.

Ren wanted to know about everything I'd done since I'd left India. He wanted to see Silver Falls, go to the Shakespeare Festival, go out to movies, and try every restaurant in town.

After he'd finished grilling me about things to do and places to go in Oregon, the conversation changed.

He squeezed me tighter and said, "I missed you."

"I missed you too."

"Nothing was the same when you left. The spark of life was gone from the house. Everyone felt it. I wasn't the only one who felt your absence. Even Kadam was subdued. Kishan kept saying that there was nothing the modern world had to offer him and often threatened to leave. But, I caught him on more than one occasion eavesdropping on your phone calls too."

"I didn't mean to make your lives more difficult. I'd hoped to make things easier. Make your acclimation back into the world a little less complicated."

"You don't complicate my life. You simplify it. When you're near, I know exactly where I should be—by your side. When you were gone, I just ran around in confused circles. My life was unbalanced. Out of focus."

"So I'm your Ritalin, huh?"

"What's that?"

"It's a medicine that helps people concentrate better."

"That sounds about right." He stood, scooped me up in his arms, and said, "Don't forget, I need frequent doses."

I laughed and pecked him on the cheek. Ren set me on my feet, folded the blanket, and we walked back to the Hummer with his arm around my shoulders.

I felt good. For the first time in months I felt whole and happy.

When he walked me to my door, he said, "*Shubharatri*, Kells."

"What does that mean?"

He flashed me a brilliant, weak-in-the-knees kind of smile and pressed a lingering kiss on the palm of my hand. "It means 'goodnight.'"

Confused and slightly frustrated, I went to bed.

Confused and slightly frustrated was the standard theme while dating Ren. I wanted him to be around much more often, but he was determined to go through what he called *customary dating practices*. This meant leaving me to my own devices unless we had a planned date. He wouldn't even let me see him as a tiger.

Every day, he'd call to see if I was available. Then, he'd ask me out to a movie, to dinner, to go get hot chocolate, or to check out a bookstore. When he determined the date to be over, he left. He completely disappeared, and I didn't catch a glimpse of his striped self the rest of the day. He also refused to kiss me saying he had a lot of catching up to do. Even though he was on the other side of the wall, I missed my tiger.

We started reading *Othello* together. Until Othello was deceived by Iago, Ren really liked his character.

"Othello destroyed his and Desdemona's love, just like Romeo did. It had nothing to do with Iago," Ren commented thoughtfully. "Othello didn't trust his wife. If he had only asked her what had happened to his handkerchief or how she felt about Cassio, he would have learned the truth."

"Othello and Desdemona hadn't known each other very long," I countered. "Maybe they weren't really *in love* in the first place. Maybe their only real bond was through his storytelling and exciting adventures. Not unlike you, I might add."

Ren was lying with his head on my lap. He played with my fingers thoughtfully for a minute and asked hesitantly, "Is that why you're with *me*, Kelsey? For the adventure? Are you bored sitting here reading with me when we could be hiking in India searching for magical objects and fighting demons?"

I considered that for a moment. "No. I just like being *with* you, even if all we do is eat popcorn and read."

He grunted and kissed my fingers. "Good."

I started reading again, but he jumped up and dragged me into the kitchen with a sudden urge to learn how to make microwave popcorn.

One afternoon I was desperate enough to see my tiger that I decided to seek him out without having an official date planned. I knocked on our connecting door and stepped into Ren's living room when there was no reply. A few unopened packages were stacked on his counter but other than that the house had an empty feeling. I made my way upstairs.

"Ren?" I called, but there was still no answer.

Where could he be? I thought and stuck my head into Ren's office. His laptop was on and the screen had three open windows.

Settling in his comfortable leather office chair, I realized the first web page was a very expensive designer clothing store and the second was a link to courtship rituals through the ages.

The third window was an email chain from Mr. Kadam. I felt a bit guilty reading Ren's messages, but they were so short that before I knew it I'd already read the entire thing.

From: masteratarms@rajaramcorp.com
To: whttgr@rajaramcorp.com
Subject: Documents
Ren,
The issue of the documents is resolved.
Kadam

From: masteratarms@rajaramcorp.com

To: whttgr@rajaramcorp.com

Subject: Relocation

Ren,

Per your request, I've attached a file in case of emergency.

Kadam

Documents? Relocation? What are they up to? I maneuvered the mouse cursor over the attachment. With my finger on the button, I hesitated, debating how far I was willing to let curiosity take me, when a voice made me jump.

"It's appropriate to ask for permission before snooping into personal documents, don't you think?" Ren asked casually.

I minimized the window and stood up abruptly. He filled the office doorway, leaning against it on one shoulder while his arms were crossed over his chest.

"I . . . I was looking for you and got sidetracked," I mumbled.

"I see." He softly closed his laptop and propped his hip against the desk, considering me. "I'd say you found more than you were looking for."

I stared at my shoelaces for a few seconds but quickly found a spark of annoyance to assuage the guilt and lifted my head. "Have you been hiding things from me?"

"No."

"Well is there something important going on here that you're not telling me?"

"No," he repeated.

"Promise me," I said quietly, "promise me with a royal oath."

He took my hands in his, looked me in the eyes, and said, "As the prince of the Mujulaain Empire, I promise you that there is nothing to worry about here. If you are concerned, ask Kadam." He leaned his

head a little bit closer. "But what I really want is your trust. I won't abuse it, Kelsey."

"You'd better not," I emphasized by poking him in the chest.

He brought my fingers to his lips, distracting me enough that the subject became suddenly very unimportant.

"I won't," he vowed softly and guided me back home.

The romantic daze dissipated soon after he left, and I found myself angry at the ease with which he bent me to his will with just a casual touch.

On the Monday after Christmas, wushu classes started again, and I had absolutely no idea what I was going to say to Li. Ren agreed to bow out this time so I could talk to Li first. I couldn't concentrate through the whole session and made a halfhearted effort in learning the hand forms. I couldn't keep the names straight. The only ones I could remember were eagle's claw and monkey.

After class, it was time to face the music. *What am I going to say? He's going to hate me.*

"Li, I was hoping we could talk."

"Sure." He grinned.

He was happy and carefree, and I was the complete opposite. I felt so nervous that I had to sit on my hands to stop them from shaking.

Li stretched out his long legs on the mat and propped himself up against the wall next to me.

Taking a long drink of water, he wiped his mouth and asked, "So what's up, Kelsey?"

"Umm . . . I'm not really sure how to say this, so I guess I'll just spit it out. Ren is back."

"Oh. I wondered when he'd show up. I figured he wouldn't stay away from you forever. So, you're breaking up with me then," he said matter-of-factly.

"Well, no, not exactly. See, Ren would like me to keep dating you, but he wants to date me too."

"What? What kind of a guy would . . . wait . . . so you're not breaking up with me?"

I hurried to explain, "No. But I'd understand if you didn't want to see me anymore. He feels that I should date both of you and then choose."

"Well, how . . . sporting of him. And what do you think about that?"

I put my hand on his arm. "I agreed to give it a try, but I told him that dating two guys at the same time isn't the way things usually go and that you'd never agree to it."

"What did he say then?"

I sighed. "He said that if you couldn't handle a little honest competition then it's better for me to know now."

Li's hands closed into fists. "If he thinks I'll just give up and walk away then he's wrong! Honest competition it is."

"Are you joking? You're pulling my leg, aren't you?"

"My grandfather taught me to set goals and then fight for what I want and there's no way I'm letting you go without a fight. A young man who doesn't have the foresight to seek out the girl he wants to be with and actively pursue her, doesn't deserve her."

I blinked. Li and Ren were cut from the same cloth, even though they were centuries apart.

He continued, "So is he here in town?"

"Not exactly," I sighed, "he's my new neighbor."

"Right. He already has a proximity advantage then."

I mumbled wryly, "Sounds like you guys are planning to storm the castle."

He either ignored my comment or didn't hear it. He pulled me up distractedly and walked me to my car.

As Li leaned in my open door, I added, "Oh, and he also wants to come to a wushu class."

Li rubbed his hands together and laughed. "Excellent! We'll see exactly what the man's made of then. Bring him tomorrow! Tell him as a special courtesy, I'll even waive the class fee."

"But, Li, he's not at my level."

"Even better! The beginner needs to learn a thing or two!"

"No. You misunderstood. He's—"

Li kissed me hard on the lips, which effectively shut me up. He grinned and closed the door before I could finish my reply. Waving, he disappeared into the darkness of the studio.

The next day, I found a carefully written note taped to the orange juice inside the refrigerator.

Of all forms of caution, caution in love is perhaps the most fatal to true happiness.
—Bertrand Russell

I sighed, peeled it off the bottle of orange juice, and pressed it into my journal. I called Ren, since he didn't seem to want to see me other than planned dates, and told him that he was invited to the wushu class. Then I told him flat out what I thought about that idea. He shrugged off my reaction and declared that Li would be an excellent rival and that he was looking forward to meeting him.

Exasperated, I gave up trying to talk him out of it and hung up on him abruptly. He called back several times that day, but I ignored the phone and took a long bubble bath.

That evening, Ren pulled the Hummer out of the garage and came

over to pick me up. I really, really, *really* didn't want to be in the same room with Li and Ren and couldn't help feeling grateful that we hadn't advanced enough yet in wushu to use weapons.

His body filled the doorframe. "Ready? I can't wait for my first class."

My sullen silence didn't seem to faze him at all, and he talked about starting classes at WOU for the entire car ride.

We arrived a few minutes late. Class had already begun, and Jennifer was running through the warm-ups in our corner. Ren walked confidently by my side. Keeping my eyes down, I hurried in, plopped my bag on the floor, and shrugged out of my coat.

I glanced over at Jennifer, who was on the floor stretching her legs. She'd paused in mid-stretch to stare at Ren. Her eyes were practically popping out of their sockets. Li's stare bored over my head to Ren who returned his gaze boldly and studied Li as if assessing for weaknesses.

Ren took off his jacket, which solicited a squeak from Jennifer who was now totally focused on Ren's golden-bronze biceps. His perfectly fitted muscle shirt showed off his extremely well-developed arms and chest.

I hissed at him quietly, "For *heaven's sake*, Ren! You're going to give the women heart palpitations!"

His eyebrows lifted up in confusion. "Kells, what are you talking about?"

"You! You're too—" I gave up in disgust. "Never mind."

I cleared my throat. "Sorry to interrupt the class, Li. Hey, everybody, this is my guest, Ren. He's visiting from India."

Jennifer's mouth dropped open with a big silent, *"Oh!"*

Li gave me a questioning look for a moment before he got back to business. He ran us through kicks and forms and seemed thoroughly irritated when he saw that Ren knew every move. Li ordered us to pair up and decided that Ren would partner with Jennifer while he worked with me.

Ren turned toward Jennifer good-naturedly, and she blushed from her feet to the roots of her hair. We were practicing take-downs. Li demonstrated one on me and then asked us all to give it a try. Ren was already talking comfortably with Jennifer, gently guiding her through the move and giving her tips and pointers. Somehow, he'd quickly put her completely at ease. He was very charming and sweet. When she tried to take him down, he fell dramatically and rubbed his neck, causing her to erupt into giggles.

I smiled and thought, *Yeah, he has that effect on me too.* I was happy that he was being nice to my friend. Suddenly, I found myself flat on my back, staring at fluorescent lights. While I was busy watching Ren and Jennifer, Li had flipped me over hard. I wasn't really hurt, just a bit surprised. Li's determined expression immediately changed to regret.

"I'm so sorry, Kelsey. Did I hurt you? I didn't mean to—"

Before he could finish apologizing, Li was thrown to the mat a few feet away. Ren kneeled over me.

"Did he hurt you, Kells? Are you alright?"

Angry and embarrassed, I hissed, "Ren! I'm *fine*! Li didn't hurt me. I just wasn't paying enough attention. It happens."

Ren growled, "He should have been more careful."

I whispered quietly, "I'm fine. And *really*! Did you have to throw him *halfway* across the room?"

He grunted and helped me stand up.

Li hustled back over, pointedly ignoring Ren. "Are you okay, Kelsey?"

I put my hand on his arm. "I'm fine. Don't worry about it. It was my fault for being distracted."

"Yes. *Distracted.*" His eyes shifted to Ren briefly. "Good throw, but I'd like to see you try to do *that* again."

Ren grinned widely. "*Anytime.*"

Li smiled back subtly and narrowed his eyes. "*Later*, then."

I stood by Jennifer, who was quivering with excitement. She opened her mouth to ask the first of what I was sure were hundreds of questions, and I stuck a finger in the air.

"Hold that thought. I just want to get through class. Then I promise I'll tell you what's going on."

She mouthed, "Promise?"

I nodded.

Jennifer spent the rest of the hour vigilantly watching Ren, Li, and me. I could see the wheels turning in her brain as she listened carefully to every remark and probably categorized every look and casual touch. Li guided us through simple hand forms for the rest of the hour and then abruptly dismissed class. He and Ren seemed to be locked in a staring contest. Both of them had their arms folded across their chests, coldly assessing one another. I walked Jen to the door.

She squeezed my arm. "Your Ren is wonderful. *And* absolutely yummy. I can see why you had a hard time letting him go. If I were a couple of years younger and wasn't happily married, I'd lock him up with me and swallow the key. What are you going to do?"

"Ren wants me to date both of them."

Jennifer's mouth fell open and I hurried to add, "But I'm not making any decisions yet."

"This is so exciting! It's better than my favorite soap opera. Good luck, Kelsey. See you Monday."

When we were driving home, I asked Ren, "What did you and Li say to each other?"

"Nothing much. I'm going to attend wushu classes, but I have to pay Li's fee, which he purposely set at an exorbitant amount, thinking that I couldn't afford it."

"I don't like this. I feel like the child in a hostile joint-custody battle."

He replied softly, "You can date us both or you can break up with Li now. But to be fair, you should give Li at least a week."

"Ha! What makes you think I'd choose you? Li's a good guy too!"

Ren rubbed his jaw and said quietly, "Yes. I think he is."

That comment surprised me, and I quietly thought about it as we drove home. Ren dropped me off, helped me out of the car, and disappeared as usual.

Dating Li, Ren, and Jason at the same time was absolutely ridiculous. It almost felt like I was surrounded by knights jousting for a girl's favor. As they stomped around in battle armor, sharpened lances, and prepared to mount their horses, I pondered my options. I still had a choice at the end of the day. I could choose the winner, the loser, or none of them. The good news was that it would buy me some time.

I could understand the idea of a romantic rivalry from Ren's point of view, at least a little. During his century, men probably did battle for females. Surely Ren's tiger instinct told him to drive off the other males. What I hadn't expected was Li's reaction. *Who knew that he cared this much?* I thought. *If Li had just broken up with me, it would have made my part in this little production much easier. Maybe they'd both kill each other in the process, and everybody would die in the end, like in* Hamlet.

When we walked into wushu on Monday, Li and Ren seemed to have an unspoken agreement not to look at each other. The class warily watched them, but eventually everyone settled down when nothing happened. Neither Li nor Ren paired up with me anymore.

Li went out of his way to take me to nice dinners and plan elaborate picnics. Ren was content to come over and read with me or watch movies indoors. Kettle corn became his favorite snack, and Ren was an expert at making it. We watched old movies, and afterwards he asked tons of questions. He enjoyed a variety of films, especially *Star Wars*. He liked Luke and thought that Han Solo was too much of a bad boy.

"He's not worthy of Princess Leia," said Ren, which gave me a deeper understanding of his knight-in-shining-armor persona.

On Friday night, Ren and I were about to watch another movie when I remembered I had scheduled a date with Jason. I told Ren he could watch the movie without me. Ren grumbled, then picked up his bag of popcorn, and headed to the microwave.

When I came downstairs in a dark blue dress with strappy shoes and my hair straightened, Ren stood up abruptly and dropped his bowl of popcorn on the floor.

"Why are you dressed like that? Where are you going?"

"Jason's taking me to a play in Portland. Besides, I thought you had some kind of a chivalrous noninterference policy regarding my dating anyway."

"When you dress like that, I get to interfere all I want to."

The doorbell rang, and when I opened it, Ren suddenly moved up behind me to help me into my coat. Jason shifted back and forth very uncomfortably. His eyes darted up to Ren.

"Uh, Jason, this is my friend Ren. He's visiting from India."

Ren stuck out his hand and smiled abrasively. "Take good care of *my girl*, Jason."

There was a very definite implied "or else" attached to the end of the sentence. Jason gulped.

"Uh-huh. Sure thing."

I pushed Ren back in the house and shut the door in his face. It was actually a relief being with Jason. I didn't feel the intense pressure that I now felt with Li and Ren. Not that they were pressuring me. Ren in particular seemed to have infinite patience. I guess that came from his tiger half.

Jason took me to see *The Lion King*. The costumes and props were amazing, and I caught myself wishing Ren were there with me instead of Jason. Ren would have loved to see how all the animals were portrayed.

After the show, the crowd spilled out onto the sidewalk. People strolled leisurely every which way across the street, forcing cars to edge forward in dangerous spurts as they tried to nudge the patrons along. An elderly lady dropped her playbill in the street and was bending over to pick it up when a car turned the corner.

Without thinking, I ran up in front of the woman and motioned for the car to stop. The driver hit the brakes, but not fast enough. My strappy shoes got caught on a crack in the pavement as I tried to move out of the way. The car bumped me slightly, and I fell over.

Jason ran to help me, and the driver got out. I wasn't hurt badly. My dress and my pride were damaged, but, other than that, I only had a few scrapes and bruises. A theater photographer ran over to snap some pictures. Jason posed with me in my torn dress and smudged face and provided my name, saying that I was a hero for saving the elderly woman.

Pulling off my broken, strappy shoe in disgust, I made my way to the car. Jason talked excitedly about the accident and thought my picture had a good chance of getting into the theater's magazine.

He chatted the whole way home about the next term and about the last party he'd gone to. When he pulled up to my house, he didn't open the door for me. I sighed, thinking, *Chivalry is mostly dead in this generation.* Jason kept looking at my torn dress and then at the windows. He was probably terrified that Ren would come after him for not taking care of me. I turned in my seat to face him.

"Jason, we need to talk."

"Sure. What's up?"

I sighed softly and said, "I think we should stop dating. We don't have a lot in common. But I'd like to still be friends."

"Is there someone else?" His eyes darted to the front door again.

"Sort of."

"Uh-huh. Well, if you change your mind, I'll be around."

"Thanks, Jason. You're a great guy." *A little gutless but still nice.*

I kissed him good-bye on the cheek, and he drove off in a pretty good mood.

That wasn't too bad. I know I won't get off so easily next time.

I stepped into the house and found another note lying on the kitchen counter next to a small bowl full of kettle corn.

You never lose by loving.
You always lose by holding back.
—Barbara DeAngelis

I'm sensing a theme here. Grabbing a diet cola and the popcorn, I slowly climbed up the stairs carrying my broken, strappy shoes.

One down. And one to go.

back to school

The next morning Ren called to see if we could have breakfast together and watch a movie. I said yes and hung up the phone. My body was a bit sore from my fall, so I popped some aspirin and took a hot shower.

The smell of burnt pancakes wafted up the stairs. I joined Ren in the kitchen. He had bacon sizzling on the stove and was scrambling eggs in a large bowl. My frilly apron was tied around his waist. It was quite a sight.

"I would have come down to help you, Ren," I said and removed his burnt pancake from the griddle.

"I wanted to surprise you."

"This is a surprise alright," I laughed and took over the stove. "What is the peanut butter for?"

"Peanut butter and banana pancakes, of course."

I laughed. "Really? And how did you come up with that creation?"

"Trial and error."

"Okay," I acquiesced. "But you also have to try some pancakes my way, with chocolate chips."

"Deal."

When I had a stack of pancakes sufficiently high enough to please Ren, we sat down to eat. He took a big bite of his.

"Well? What do you think?"

"Excellent. But they would be even better with peanut butter and banana."

I reached out to get the syrup, revealing a long, purple bruise on my arm. Ren immediately noticed and touched my arm gingerly.

"What's this? What happened to you?"

"What? Oh . . . that. I was trying to prevent an old lady from being hit by an oncoming car that bumped me instead. I fell down."

Ren jumped off his stool and poked and prodded me, carefully feeling my bones and rotating my joints. "Where does it hurt?"

"*Ren!* Really, I'm fine. Just some cuts and scrapes. Ow! Don't push on that!" I slapped him away. "Cut it out! You aren't my doctor. It's only a few simple bumps and bruises. Besides, Jason was right there with me."

"Was he hit by the car too?"

"No."

"Then he wasn't right there with you. Next time I see him, he's going to get some matching bumps and bruises so that he can truly empathize."

"Ren, stop making threats. It doesn't matter anyway because I told him I didn't want to see him anymore."

Ren cracked a self-satisfied smile. "Good. The boy still needs to learn a few things, though."

"Well, you aren't the *man* who needs to teach him and just for that I get to pick the movie and I'll warn you right now, I plan on picking the girliest movie I can find."

He grunted, mumbled something about rivals, bruises, and girls, and went back to his pancakes.

After breakfast, Ren helped me clean up, but mister likes-to-tell-me-what-to-do wasn't out of the doghouse yet. I inserted the movie, sat next to him with a big grin on my face, and waited for him to squirm. The swelling opening theme for *The Sound of Music* began and I giggled knowing he'd suffer for the next few hours. The problem was . . . Ren loved it. He put his arm around my shoulders and toyed with the ribbon at the end of my braid. He hummed along to "My Favorite Things" and "Edelweiss."

He paused the movie in the middle, retrieved his mandolin, and started picking through the song. The mandolin had a more exotic sound than the guitar in the movie.

"It's beautiful!" I exclaimed. "How long have you played?"

"I took it up again after you left. I always had a good ear for music, and my mother often asked me to play for her."

"But you picked up "Edelweiss" very quickly. Have you heard it before?"

"No. I've just always been able to hear the notes and know how to play them."

He started playing "My Favorite Things," and then the song changed and became a sad but lovely tune. I closed my eyes, leaned my head against the couch, and felt the music take me on a journey. The song started out somber, bleak, and lonely then moved to something hopeful and sweet. My heart felt like it was beating along with the song. Emotions swept over and through me as the song told its story. The end was melancholy and sad. I felt like my heart was breaking. And, that's where he stopped.

I blinked my eyes open. "What *was* that? I've never heard anything like it before."

Ren sighed and set the mandolin carefully down on the table. "I wrote it after you left."

"You *wrote* that?"

"Yes. It's called 'Kelsey.' It's about you . . . us. It's our story together."

"But it ended sadly."

He ran a hand through his hair. "That's the way I felt when you left."

"Oh. Well, our story isn't quite over yet now, is it?" I slid over to Ren and wrapped my arms around his neck.

He squeezed me, pressed his face against my neck, whispered my name, and said, "No. It's *definitely* not over yet."

I brushed his hair away from his forehead and said quietly, "It's beautiful, Ren."

He held me very close. My heart began to beat faster. I looked into his vivid blue eyes, then at his perfectly sculpted lips, and willed him to kiss me. He dipped his head closer but stopped just short of contact. He studied my expression, raised an eyebrow, and turned away.

"What is it?" I asked.

He sighed and tucked a lock of hair behind my ear. "I'm not going to kiss you while we're dating." His eyes studied my face as he went on, "I want you to have a clear head when you choose me. You get all weak-kneed when I touch you, let alone kiss you. I refuse to take advantage of that. A pledge made in a moment of passion isn't lasting and I don't want you to have any doubts or any regrets about having a life with me."

"Wait a minute," I gasped incredulously. "Let me get this straight. You won't kiss me because you think your kisses make me too drunk to think straight? That I'd be incapable of making an informed decision if I was swooning with passion for you?"

He nodded cautiously.

"Is this all coming from your antiquated studies of courtship? Because a lot of those dating suggestions are outdated."

"I know that, Kelsey." He ran a hand through his hair. "I just don't want to pressure you to choose me in any way."

Angrily, I jumped off the couch and walked in a circle. "This is the craziest thing I've ever heard!" I went to the kitchen to get a soda and realized that I wasn't just shocked, I was mad and that part of my anger stemmed from the fact that he wasn't too far off from the truth. I did get weak-kneed every time he touched me.

I suddenly felt like a pawn in one of Li's board games. *Well, two can play at that game.* I decided to retaliate. *If there was going to be a war for my affection then why couldn't I be a fighter too? Girls have an entirely unique arsenal of weapons*, I mused as I planned my battle strategy. From that point on, I decided that I would test Ren's resistance. I would get *Ren* to kiss *me*.

I immediately put my plan into action. We returned to the movie, and I tucked my head against Ren's shoulder, my lips just inches from his, and traced little circles on the back of his hand. My aggressiveness made him nervous. He kept twitching and shifting his position, but he didn't let go or move farther away.

After the movie, Ren suddenly announced that our date was over. *I liked this. The balance of power had shifted.* I trailed my fingers over his muscular bicep then traced little hearts on his forearm and pouted.

"Your hours as a man are so short. Don't you want to be with me?"

He touched my face. "More than I want to breathe."

I couldn't help it; I swayed into him.

He caught me and shook me gently, "I'm not going to kiss you, Kelsey. I don't want you to be confused about who you want. Of course if you chose to kiss *me*, I wouldn't put up much of a fight."

Pushing away from him, I groused, "Ha! Well, you'll be waiting a long time for that, Mister." I put my fists on my hips and smirked. "That news must be shocking for a man who always gets what he wants."

He snuck his hands around my waist and pulled me up against his chest then ducked his lips to within inches of mine. "*Not . . . what I want . . . the most.*"

He hesitated for a minute, waiting for me to make a move, but I didn't. I was determined to get him to kiss me first. Instead, I smiled and waited. We were locked in a silent struggle of wills.

Finally, he broke away. "You are entirely too tempting, Kelsey. Date's over."

Suddenly, nothing in the world was as important to me as winning this war of wills with Ren. Leaning in closer, I batted my eyes innocently, and, in the most seductive voice I could manage, asked coyly, "Are you *absolutely* sure you have to leave?"

I felt his arm muscles tighten and his pulse quicken. He cupped my cheek with his hand. Hoping to push him over the edge, I placed my hand on top of his and pressed a warm kiss on his palm. Teasing his palm with my lips, I heard him hitch a breath. *I had no idea he reacted this way to me. This will be easier than I thought.*

I squeezed his arm lightly and walked toward the stairs, feeling his eyes on me. Doing my best Scarlett O'Hara impersonation, I turned one last time and said, "Well . . . *Tiger*, if you change your mind, you know where to find me." I trailed my fingers along the railing and continued up the stairs.

Unfortunately, he didn't follow me. I'd envisioned Ren playing the role of Rhett Butler and, not being able to help himself, he'd sweep me into his arms and carry me up the stairs in a dramatic show of passion. But Ren shot me an amused look and left, closing the door quietly behind him.

Drat! He has more self-control than I thought.

It didn't matter. It was just a minor setback. I spent the rest of that day brainstorming. *How do you catch a very old, very alert tiger by surprise? Use his weaknesses: food, feminine wiles, poetry, and overprotectiveness. The poor guy didn't stand a chance.*

The next morning, I opened the once-forbidden side of the closet, picked out a navy cable cardigan and a printed skirt, a thin belt, and tall brown boots. I straightened my hair and paid special attention to my makeup, especially the peach lip gloss.

Next, I made Ren a giant Dagwood sandwich—and slipped a love note on top. *Two can play the poetry game*, I thought smugly.

The soul that can speak through the eyes
can also kiss with a gaze.

—Gustavo Adolfo Becquer

When he came over to pick me up for class, he looked me up and down, and said, "You look beautiful, Kells, but it's not going to work. I'm on to you."

He helped me into my coat, and I replied innocently, "I don't know what you're talking about. What's not going to work?"

"You're trying to get me to kiss you."

I smiled up at him and said demurely, "A girl shouldn't give away *all* her secrets now, should she?"

He leaned in close, pressed his lips to my ear, and whispered in a velvety voice, "Fine, Kells. Keep your secrets. But, I'm watching you. Whatever it is you think you're trying to do isn't going to work. I still have a few *tricks* up *my* sleeve too."

Ren left me alone all afternoon. I tucked another note in his gym bag as he was getting out of the car before wushu.

Soul meets soul on lovers' lips.

—Percy Bysshe Shelley

I was sitting on the floor stretching when I saw him pull the note out of his bag. He read it through a couple of times and then looked up and caught my look. I met his hot gaze with an innocent grin and waved happily to Jennifer as she crossed the room.

Back at home inside our garage, Ren opened the door for me. Instead of helping me out, he leaned over and growled softly. His lips brushed against the sensitive skin under my ear. His voice was seductive, dangerous.

"I'm warning you, Kelsey. I'm an *extremely* patient man. I've had extensive practice in waiting out the enemy. My life as a tiger has taught me that persistence and diligence *always* pay off. Consider yourself forewarned, *priyatama*. I'm on the hunt. I've caught your scent, and I *won't* be thwarted in my course."

He stepped away and extended a hand to help me out. I ignored it and walked to my door with a stiff back and wobbly legs. I heard his soft laugh on the breeze as he disappeared into his own part of the house.

He was driving me crazy. I was tempted to break down the door and throw myself at him, but I refused to give in. *I* was going to entice *him* this time. He would be the one begging for mercy, not me.

Soon, I discovered that the battle of wills between Ren and me had pushed Li to the furthest corner of my mind. Every time I was with Li, my mind drifted far away, planning ways to seduce Ren. It was so obvious that even Li noticed.

"Earth to Kelsey. Are you going to acknowledge my existence now?" Li asked tensely one evening during one of his favorite martial arts movies.

"What do you mean?"

"Kelsey, you've just been going through the motions for the last week. You haven't been here at all."

"Well . . . I'm back in school now, and homework is distracting."

"It's not your homework, Kelsey. It's *him*."

In an instant, I felt remorse. Li had done nothing wrong, and the least I could do was to pay attention to him. "I'm sorry, Li. I didn't realize that I'd been ignoring you. You're absolutely right. I'm here with you now, 100 percent. Tell me again why this martial arts movie is a classic."

Li studied my face for a minute and then began explaining about *Snake in the Eagle's Shadow*, Jackie Chan's debut movie. I really was interested, and he seemed appeased by that.

The rest of the evening went smoothly, but I felt guilty about Li. I wasn't giving him the attention he deserved. What was worse was that I wished Ren had been watching the movie with us.

When I got home late that night from my date, I taped a note onto Ren's side of our connecting door.

> Once he drew
>
> With one long kiss my whole soul thro'
>
> My lips, as sunlight drinketh dew.
>
> —Alfred Lord Tennyson

Ren hadn't kissed me in three weeks, and I thought I was weakening more than he was. I'd tried everything I could think of and still hadn't gotten so much as a nibble on my baited lip. I had nothing to show for my weeks of effort. I now owned an entire collection of lipsticks and glosses and had tried every single one of them to no effect.

In wushu, he pulled another note out of his bag, read through it, and raised an eyebrow in my direction. This one was the most over-the-top one that I'd given him, and I'd purposely saved it for last. It was my last-ditch effort.

Give me a kiss, and to that kiss a score;
Then to that twenty, add a hundred more:
A thousand to that hundred: so kiss on,
To make that thousand up a million.
Treble that million, and when that is done,
Let's kiss afresh, as when we first begun.
—Robert Herrick

Ren didn't say anything, but he looked at me with smoldering, intense eyes. I boldly returned his gaze and felt a hot, sizzling link spark up between us. It connected us and burned a hole through my middle even though we were on opposite sides of the room. I couldn't tear my eyes away from him, and he appeared to be suffering with the same affliction.

Suddenly, Li announced that we were going to be doing take-downs again, which he had avoided since his first session with Ren. This time, Li and Ren were going to demonstrate the moves to the rest of us. Li instructed us to all sit back against the wall. Ren reluctantly broke eye contact with me and moved up to face his opponent.

The two men circled each other. Li made the first move, a backward roundhouse to show off and move in closer, but Ren gracefully blocked it. Li shifted his weight to one leg and swept behind Ren's knee then threw a punch at Ren's chest. Ren shifted to the right so Li's sweep missed and used his palm to block the punch. Li used an elaborate corkscrew maneuver next, placed one hand on the floor, and attacked with a scissor kick. Ren grabbed Li's foot and twisted, bringing Li down hard on his stomach. Li rolled away angrily and returned a series of punches. Ren blocked him high, low, and even backward, effectively neutralizing Li's attacks.

Li realized he was getting nowhere. He faked a punch to grab Ren's arm and yanked hard so he could do a backward kick to the face, but Ren pulled him off balance, and Li fell to the mat again. He did a kick-up and turned to face Ren, and they circled again.

"Do you really want to continue this?" Ren said. "You've proved you're a good fighter."

"I'm not trying to prove anything." He grinned. "I just wanted to stop you from ogling my girl." He shot off a quick double punch to Ren's chest. Ren simply grabbed Li's wrists and twisted them outward. Li howled and stepped away. He came back with a front kick to Ren's face.

Ren grabbed his heel. "She hasn't decided yet whose girl she is." He lifted his arms and threw Li, flipping him upside down. "But, if I were a betting man, I wouldn't be giving you very good odds."

I gasped in outrage and embarrassment. Ren turned to look at me. Seeing he was distracted, Li grabbed Ren's arms from behind and pushed up, a move that immobilized most people. Without missing a beat, Ren ran up a wall with Li still holding his arms and flipped over him in the air.

When he landed, he flicked his wrists, effectively reversing their positions. Li's elbows were now pointed in the air while Ren pushed down slightly. When Li gasped in pain, Ren quickly let him go. Li spun out and tried sweeping Ren's legs again, but Ren leapt over them, twisted, and pinned Li easily.

Jennifer looked at me nervously and grabbed my hand. Li was enraged. He wiped his mouth and spat out, "You let me worry about my odds." He spun and kicked, making contact with Ren's chest. The impact caused both of them to take a few steps back. Li taunted, "At least I didn't give her up and walk away."

The moves were too fast for me to discern now. I saw punches, arm-blocks, step-back twists, side kicks, foot play, and kick blocks.

At one point, Ren ran at Li and did a complicated aerial somersault in tucked position, double twisted, and flipped over Li entirely in the air. As he was coming down, he placed his hand on Li's back and used his momentum to push Li flat on his face on the mat. The class started clapping and cheering.

Ren pressed his hand against Li's back, holding him immobile, and growled quietly, "No. But you *will*. She's *mine*."

Ren let him up, and Li became a raging bull after that, going after Ren with everything he had. Sweat was pouring down his face, and he was breathing hard. He attacked even more viciously than he had before, and Ren stepped up his game a little too. Li was finally getting in some punches. I was mortified that they were fighting over *me*. *Publicly*. At the same time, I couldn't take my eyes off them.

Li was a force to be reckoned with. He was obviously highly skilled. However, there was still a world of difference between him and Ren. It was almost like they were moving at two different speeds.

I watched Ren fight. In fact, it would have been impossible for me to look away. Each move was a beautiful study in form. I found myself entranced by the calculated control and power he displayed. He was simply magnificent. A fighter worthy of the tiger he often was.

I was furious that he had the audacity to claim me as his in front of everyone. Yet, at the same time, I was secretly thrilled that he wanted me that fiercely. He really was a warrior-angel. *My warrior-angel*, I thought possessively.

After about fifteen minutes of fighting hard and getting nowhere, Li, panting forcefully, dismissed the class.

I tried to talk with him, but he waved me off and grabbed a towel to cover his head.

Li didn't call or ask me out on any dates the next week. After wushu class on Friday, Li asked to speak with me and told Ren he would drive me home. Ren nodded and left quietly. They'd been oddly civil to each other since the fight.

Li sat down and patted the mat next to him. "Kelsey, I need to ask you something, and I want you to answer honestly."

"Okay."

"Why did you leave Ren?"

I shifted uncomfortably. "I left him because . . . we're not right for each other."

"What do you mean?"

I stayed silent for a moment, and then replied, "There are a couple of reasons. The main one is that . . . it's difficult to explain. First of all, he's gorgeous, and I'm . . . not. He's also very wealthy. In fact, he comes from royalty. He's from a different culture and background, and he hasn't dated much and—"

"But, Kelsey, the two of us are also from different cultures and backgrounds, and that didn't bother you. Does his family not like you?"

"No. His parents are gone. His brother likes me." I twisted my hands in my lap. "I guess it boils down to me thinking that he's going to wake up and figure out I'm not a princess. I think he'll be disappointed if he chooses me. It's just a matter of time before he realizes that and leaves me for someone else, someone better."

Li turned toward me, his face incredulous. "So you're telling me that the reason you left him was because you thought *he* was too good for *you*?"

"Basically, yes. He would have trapped himself with me and been unhappy."

"Does he ever *act* unhappy around you?"

"No."

Li said reflectively, "Kelsey, as much as it kills me to say this, Ren strikes me as a very careful, thoughtful person. During our fight, I used every dirty trick and skill at my disposal, and he barely hit me back. He clearly had the advantage. His skills are beyond anything I've seen before. It's like he studied with all of the old masters."

He probably did.

"But, during the fight, he actually *took* hits so that I wouldn't get hurt. That shows not only incredible skill, but amazing forethought."

I shrugged. "I already knew he was a good fighter."

"No, you don't understand my point. To hone skill like that, to fight like that, takes discipline. He could have smashed me into the floor, but he didn't." He laughed ironically. "Half the time, he wasn't even watching me! He was watching you, concerned about your reaction. He wasn't even paying attention to the guy who was seriously trying to kill him."

"What are you trying to say, Li?"

"I'm trying to say that the man is desperately in love with you. It's obvious to me and to everyone else. If *you* love *him*, you have to tell him. Your fears about him leaving you don't fit with his personality. Like I said, he's the type of man who makes decisions and sticks by them. There's nothing about him that makes me think he's anything less than sincere."

"But—"

Li took my hands in his and looked into my eyes. "*Kelsey*. He only sees *you*."

I looked down at my hands.

"And as far as you not being good enough for him, it's actually the opposite. He isn't good enough for you."

"You're just saying that."

"No. No, I'm not. You're amazing and sweet and pretty, and he'd be lucky to have you."

"Li, why are you *doing* this?"

"Because . . . I genuinely like the guy. I respect him. And, because I can see that your feelings for him are much stronger than your feelings for me. You're happier with him."

"I'm happy with you too."

"Yes, but it's not the same. Go home to him, Kelsey. You obviously love him. Tell him that. Give him a chance." He sniggered quietly. "But don't forget to tell him that I was the bigger man who walked away." He reached over and wrapped me in a bear hug. "I'll miss you, Kelsey."

Something in me clicked, and my perspective suddenly changed. It was time to let Li go. It wasn't fair to continue to put him through this. My heart would never belong to him; deep down, I'd known that for a while. I'd been using him as an emotional crutch. My whole relationship with him had become an excuse so I could postpone facing Ren. Whether I ended up with Ren or not, I knew this had to be the end for Li and me.

Emotional, I hugged him back. "I'll miss you too. You've been good to me and good for me. I won't forget you. Tell the guys thanks for teaching me to play."

"Sure thing. Come on." He stood and helped me up, kissing my cheek softly. "Let's get you home. And, Kelsey?"

"Yes?"

"If he ever *does* leave you, tell him I'll come looking for him."

I laughed forlornly. "I'm sorry I put you through this, Li."

He shrugged. "You're worth it. I have a sneaking suspicion that if

I'd forced your hand when he showed up, you would have chosen him anyway. At least this way, I got to hang around a little bit longer."

"It wasn't fair to you."

"Didn't somebody say that all's fair in love and war? This was a little bit of love mixed in with a little bit of war. I wouldn't have missed it for the world."

I took his hand in both of mine and squeezed. "You're going to make some woman very happy someday, Li. And I hope that someday finds you soon."

"Well if you happen to have a twin sister somewhere, send her my way."

I laughed, but I felt like crying.

Li drove me home. We were both silent, and I thought about what he had said. He was right. Ren *was* a careful, thoughtful person. He'd had centuries to think about what he wanted. For some reason, he wanted me. I knew deep down that he loved me and would never leave me. I also knew that if I *had* chosen someone else, he would've always been around to take care of me if I needed him.

My feelings for *him* were never in question. Li was right. I should tell him. Tell him that I'd made my choice.

I'd been deliberately trying to seduce the man for several weeks, and now that I was finally going to get what I wanted . . . I was nervous. My resolve wobbled. I felt suddenly vulnerable, fragile. My thoughts were incoherent and scattered. *What should I say?*

When he stopped the car, Li encouraged me one more time. "Tell him, Kelsey." He hugged me briefly and then drove off.

I stood outside Ren's door for too many minutes thinking about what I was going to say.

The door opened, and Ren came out to stand beside me. His feet were bare, and he was still wearing his muscle shirt and white pants

from wushu. He looked earnestly at my face and sighed unhappily. "Tell me what, Kells?"

In a stilted voice, I said, "Heard that, did you?"

"Yes." His face was tight, cautious. I suddenly realized that he thought I was going to choose *Li*.

He ran a hand through his hair. "What would you like to tell me?"

"I'd like to tell you that I've made my choice."

"I figured that."

I reached up and wrapped my arms around his neck, but he remained stiff and unyielding. I stood up on my tiptoes to get closer. He sighed, reached down to put his arms around me, and picked me up. He held my body snugly against his rock-solid chest while my feet hovered several inches in the air. I spoke softly in his ear, "I choose you."

He froze . . . then drew his head back to look at my face, "So then, Li—"

"Is out of the picture."

He flashed me a brilliant smile that lit up the dark night. "So then we—"

"Can be together."

I pulled his head closer and kissed him softly. He broke away to study my face in surprise and then locked me tightly in his arms and kissed me back. His was no soft, sweet kiss. It was a hot, melty, smoldering one.

There are many different types of kisses. There's a passionate kiss of farewell—like the kind Rhett gave Scarlett when he went off to war. The kiss of I-can't-really-be-with-you-but-I-want-to-be—like with Superman and Lois Lane. There's the first kiss—one that is gentle and hesitant, warm and vulnerable. Then there's the kiss of possession—which was how Ren kissed me now.

It went beyond passion, beyond desire. His kiss was full of longing, need, and love, like all those other kisses. But, it was also filled with promises and pledges, some of which seemed sweet and tender while others seemed dangerous and exciting. Ren was taking me over. Staking a claim.

He seized me as boldly as a tiger captures his prey. There was no escape. And I didn't *want* to. I would have happily died in his clutches. I was his, and he made sure I knew it. My heart burst with a thousand beautiful blooms, all tiger lilies. And I knew with a certainty more powerful than anything I'd ever felt before that we belonged together.

He finally lifted his head and murmured against my lips, "It's about bloody time, woman."

8

jealousy

Ren kissed me again and slid an arm under my knees. He managed to carry me into the house and kick the door closed without ever taking his lips off mine. I'd finally gotten my Rhett Butler moment. He lowered himself into the recliner, snuggled me on his lap, grabbed my quilt, and tucked it around me.

He kissed me everywhere—my hair, my neck, my forehead, my cheeks . . . but always returned to my lips like they were the center of his universe. I sighed softly and basked in the barrage of Ren's kisses—drowning kisses, soft kisses, sultry kisses, kisses that lasted a mere second, and kisses that lasted an eternity. It was easy to believe that my warrior-angel had captured me and had flown me up to heaven.

A deep rumble echoed in his chest.

I pulled back, laughing. "Are you *growling* at me?"

He laughed softly, twisted my hair ribbon around his fingers, and pulled gently, loosening my braid. Biting my ear lightly, he whispered a threat, "*You* have been driving me crazy for *three weeks*. You're *lucky* all I'm doing is growling."

He trailed slow kisses down my neck. "And does this mean you'll be over here more often?"

He spoke, moving his lips against my throat, "Every minute of the day."

"Oh. So . . . you weren't just avoiding me then?"

He put his finger under my chin and turned my face to his. "I would *never* avoid you on purpose, Kells." He stroked the side of my neck and collarbone with his fingertips, distracting me.

"But you did."

"That was regretfully necessary. I didn't want to pressure you, so I stayed away, but I was always near. I could hear you." He pressed his face into my cascading hair and sighed. "And smell your peaches-and-cream scent, which drove me absolutely crazy. But, I wouldn't let myself see you unless you agreed to a date. When you started purposefully tempting me, I thought I'd go insane."

"Ah-hah! So you *were* tempted."

"Yours was the worst kind of *pralobhana*, temptation. I would have had you for a moment, but then I would ultimately lose you. It was all I could do not to grab you and carry you off."

It was strange. Now that I'd admitted aloud that I wanted to be with him, I didn't feel shy or hesitant at all. I felt . . . liberated. Joyful. I planted dozens of kisses across his cheeks, his forehead, his nose, and finally his chiseled lips. He sat immobile while I traced his face with my fingertips. We looked at each other for a long moment, his beautiful cobalt blue eyes locked with my brown ones. Ren smiled, and my heart leapt, knowing he, in all his perfection, belonged to me.

I slid my hands from his shoulders up into his hair, brushed it away from his brow, and said softly, "I *love* you, Ren. I always have."

His smile widened. He snuggled me tighter in his arms and whispered my name. "I love *you*, my *kamana*. If I had known that you were the prize I'd get after being captive for centuries, I would've endured it thankfully."

"What does *kamana* mean?"

"It means 'the beautiful wish I desire above all others.'"

"Hmm." I pressed my lips against his neck and inhaled the warm sandalwood scent of him. "Ren?"

"Yes?" He twisted his fingers through my hair.

"I'm sorry I was such an idiot. It's all my fault. I wasted so much time. Can you forgive me?"

His fingers paused in my hair. "There's nothing to forgive. I pushed you too fast. I didn't court you. I didn't say the right things."

"No. Believe me. You said all the right things. I just think I wasn't prepared to hear them or to believe them."

"I should have known not to rush you. I wasn't patient enough, and a tiger without patience doesn't get his dinner."

I laughed.

"Did you know that I started to have feelings for you before you even knew I was a man? Do you remember when I ran around frantically during a performance at the circus?"

"Yes."

"I thought you were gone. Matt had been talking with his father and had said that one of the new girls had left. I thought they'd meant you. I had to know if you were still there. You didn't come by my cage that day, and I became distraught, despondent. I couldn't settle down until I saw you in the audience."

"Well, I'm here now, and I won't leave you, Tiger."

He growled, squeezed me, and teased, "No, you *won't*. I won't ever let you out of my sight again. Now, about all those poems you gave me . . . I think some of those deserve to be studied in great depth."

"I definitely agree."

He kissed me again. It was lingering and sweet. His hands cupped my face, and I think my heart actually flipped over in my chest. He pulled back, kissed the sides of my mouth, and sighed deeply. We snuggled together until his time was up.

The next night I cooked a special dinner for Ren. When my mom's famous stuffed shells were ready, Ren scooped a giant portion onto his plate, speared a shell, and chewed happily.

"This is one of the best things I have ever eaten. In fact, it's only second to peanut butter, *chittaharini*."

"I'm glad you like my mom's recipe. "Hey, you never told me what *chittaharini* means."

He kissed my fingers. "It means—'one who captivates my mind.'"

"And, *iadala*?"

"'Dear one.'"

"How do you say, 'I love you'?"

"*Mujhe tumse pyarhai.*"

"How do you say, 'I'm *in* love'?"

He laughed. "You can either say, *anurakta*, which means 'you are becoming fond of or attached to.' Or you can say you're *kaamaart*, which means 'you're a young woman intoxicated with love or love-stricken.' I prefer the second."

I smirked. "Yes. I'm sure you'd like to advertise that I'm drunk with love for you. How do you say 'My boyfriend is handsome'?"

"*Mera sakha sundara.*"

I dabbed my lips with a napkin and asked if he'd like to help me make dessert. Ren pulled back my chair and followed me into the kitchen. I was ultra-aware of his nearness, especially as he kept finding reasons to touch me. As he put away the sugar, he stroked my arm. When he reached around me to set the vanilla on the counter, he nuzzled my neck. It got to the point where I started to drop things.

"*Ren*, you're driving me to distraction. Give me a little space so I can finish making the dough."

He did, but stayed close enough that I had to brush up against him when I put away ingredients. I shaped the cookies, dropped them onto the pan, and announced, "We now have fifteen minutes until they're done."

He grabbed my arm and yanked me up against him. The next thing I knew, the timer went off and I jumped. Somehow, I'd ended up on the kitchen counter locked in a passionate embrace. One of my hands was in his hair; his silky locks were twisted around my fingers while my other hand had apparently grabbed a fistful of designer shirt and was slowly mangling it. His freshly pressed shirt was now crumpled terribly. Mortified, I released my unruly grip and stammered, "Sorry about your shirt."

He snatched my hand back, pressed a kiss on my palm, and smiled wickedly. "I'm not."

I shoved him away and hopped down. Pushing my finger against his chest, I said, "You're dangerous, pal."

He grinned. "It's not my fault that you're intoxicated by me."

I gave him a look, but it didn't faze him at all; he was too pleased with himself. I took the cookies out of the oven, and turned to get the milk. When I handed him a glass, Ren had already downed one very hot cookie and was on his second.

"These are delicious! What are they?"

"Double chocolate chip with peanut butter filling."

"They're the second best thing I've ever tasted."

I laughed. "You said the same thing at dinner."

"I recently readjusted the ranking."

"So what ranks first now? Is it still peanut butter pancakes?"

"Nope—you. But it's close." His smiled dimmed. "It's time for me to change, Kells."

I felt a slight tremor go through his arm. He kissed me sweetly one more time and then morphed into his tiger form. He moved over to the stairs, leapt up in two strides, and headed for my bedroom.

Ren made himself comfortable on the throw rug near my bed while I changed into my pajamas in the bathroom. After brushing my teeth, I knelt beside him.

Putting my arms around his neck, I whispered, "*Mujhe tumse pyar-hai*, Ren." He started purring while I pulled my blanket over me. I hadn't seen the tiger half of him since he showed up on Christmas Day and I'd missed him. I wrapped my arms around him and stroked his soft fur. Snuggling next to him, I used his soft paws as a pillow and drifted off feeling at peace for the first time since I'd left India.

On Saturday, I woke up in my bed clutching my stuffed white tiger. Ren was straddling a chair and resting his head on his arms, watching me. I groaned and threw the blanket over my head.

"Good morning, sleepyhead. You know, if you wanted to sleep with a tiger, all you had to do was ask." He picked up the toy tiger. "When did you buy this?"

"The first week I got here."

He grinned. "So you missed me?"

I sighed and smiled. "Like a fish misses water."

"It's nice to know I'm so necessary to your survival." He knelt by the bed and brushed the hair away from my face. "Did I ever tell you, you're the most beautiful in the mornings?"

I laughed. "No way. My hair is a mess and I'm in my pajamas."

"I like watching you wake up. You sigh and start wiggling. You roll back and forth a few times and usually mumble something about me." He grinned.

I leaned up on my elbow. "So I talk in my sleep, huh? Well, that's embarrassing."

"I like it. Then you open your eyes and smile at me, even when I'm a tiger."

"What girl wouldn't smile when you're the first thing she sees? It's like waking up on Christmas morning to the best present ever."

He laughed and kissed my cheek. "I want to go see Silver Falls today, so get your lazy bones out of bed. I'll wait for you downstairs."

On the way to the falls, we stopped at White's in Salem, a little diner that had been in business for decades. Ren ordered a Large Mess, which was their specialty: hash browns, eggs, sausage, bacon, and gravy scrambled together in a big pile. I'd never seen anybody finish it, but Ren polished it off and then stole my toast as well.

"You've got quite the appetite," I commented. "Haven't you been eating?"

He shrugged. "Mr. Kadam set up a grocery service, but I only know how to make popcorn and sandwiches."

"You should have told me. I would've cooked for you more often."

He took my hand and kissed it. "I wanted to keep you otherwise occupied."

The drive was beautiful. Miles and miles of Christmas tree farms on both sides of the winding road led up into hilly, forested country.

We spent the day hiking to South Falls, Winter Falls, and Middle North Falls and were headed to three others. It was cold, and I'd forgotten my gloves. Ren immediately pulled a pair of gloves out of his jacket pocket and slipped them over my hands. They were too big, but they were lined and warm. The gesture brought me back to my awful date with Artie. Ren and Artie were like night and day.

We'd been discussing the difference between the forests of India and the forests of Oregon when I had a thought and interrupted, "Ren, during that whole time I was dating Li, weren't you even a tiny bit jealous?"

"I was extremely jealous. I see red anytime someone else comes near you."

"You didn't really act like it."

"I almost went ballistic. I couldn't think straight. When another guy approaches you, I just want to rip him apart with my claws. Even if I like him—like Li. And especially if I don't—like Jason."

"There's no reason for you to be jealous."

"I'm not, *now*. Jason backed off, and I owe a debt of gratitude to Li for finally getting you to admit your feelings."

"Yes, you do owe him for that. By the way, he said if you ever left me, he'd come looking for you."

He smiled. "It'll never happen."

Passing a clearing, I noticed him stick his nose in the air. "What do you smell?"

"Hmm, I smell bear, mountain lion, deer, several dogs, horses, fish, lots of squirrels, water, plants, trees, flowers, and you."

"Doesn't it bother you to smell everything so powerfully?"

"No. You learn to tune it out and focus on what you want to smell. It's the same with hearing. If I concentrate, I can hear little creatures digging underground, but I just tune it out."

We arrived at the Double Falls, and he led me over to a mossy rock that served as a lookout point. I shivered, my teeth chattering, even in my jacket and gloves. Ren quickly whipped off his jacket and secured it around my body. Then he pulled me back against his chest and wrapped his arms around me. I felt his silky hair brush against my face as he leaned his head down next to my cheek.

"It's almost as beautiful as you, *priya*. This is so much better than having to worry about Kappa chasing us or needle trees puncturing my skin."

I turned my head and kissed his cheek. "There *is* one thing I miss about Kishkindha."

"Really? What's that? Let me guess. You miss the arguing."

"Fighting with you is fun, but making up is better. That's not what I miss though. I miss having you around as a man all the time. Don't get me wrong. I love the tiger part of you, but it would be nice to have a normal relationship."

He sighed and squeezed my waist. "I don't know if we'll ever have a normal relationship." He was quiet for a minute and then confessed, "As much as I enjoy being a man, there's a part of me that wants to run free in the forest."

I laughed from inside the deep layers of his jacket. "I can just picture the look on the park ranger's face when hikers say a white tiger was running through the trees."

Over the next few weeks, we fell into a routine. By mutual decision, we decided to put wushu on hold, and I had to spend a half hour on the phone consoling Jennifer and encouraging her to keep going without me.

Ren wanted to be near me all the time, even when he was a tiger. He liked to stretch out along my legs while I sat on the floor and studied.

In the evenings, he played his mandolin or practiced on the new guitar he'd bought. Sometimes, he sang for me. His voice was quiet and deep with a warm, lilting resonance. His accent was more pronounced when he sang, which I found *very* hypnotic. His voice alone was potent enough, but when he sang, it put me in a trance. He often joked about the beast soothing the savage girl with music.

Sometimes, I would do nothing but sit with Ren's tiger head in my lap and watch him sleep. I stroked his white fur and felt his chest rise and fall. Being a tiger was part of who he was, and I was comfortable with it. But, now that I'd finally accepted that he loved me, I was overcome with a desire to be with *him*.

It was frustrating. I wanted to share every moment with him. I wanted to listen to his voice, feel his hand in mine, and lay my cheek against his chest while he read to me. We were together, but we weren't *together*. Ren spent most of his human hours at school, which left little time for us to develop our relationship. I was starving for him. I could talk to him, but he couldn't reply. I quickly became an expert on reading tiger expressions.

I snuggled with him on the floor every night, and every night he picked me up and put me back in my own bed after I fell asleep. We did homework together, watched movies, finished *Othello*, and moved on to *Hamlet*. We also kept in constant contact with Mr. Kadam. When I answered the phone, he spoke to me about school and Nilima and told me not to worry that my test of the four houses research had proven futile. He was polite and asked about my foster family but then he'd always ask for Ren.

I wasn't trying to eavesdrop but it was obvious that something was going on when they spoke in hushed tones and sometimes switched to Hindi. Every once in a while, I'd hear strange terms mentioned: Yggdrasil, Naval Stone, and Noe's Mountain. I'd ask Ren what they were talking about after he hung up but he'd just smile and tell me not to worry or that they'd been discussing business or that they were in a conference call with others who spoke only Hindi. I remembered the e-mail from Mr. Kadam about documents and had suspicions that Ren was hiding something but afterwards he would be so unguarded and genuinely happy about being with me that I eventually forgot my worries, at least until the next phone call.

Ren started writing little poems and notes and placing them in my bag for me to find during the school day. Some of them were famous poems and some were his own. I pressed them into my journal and kept a copy of my two favorites with me all the time.

You know you are in love
when you see the world in her eyes,
and her eyes everywhere in the world.

—David Levesque

If a king owned a pearl without price
A gem he cherished above all
Would he hide it away
Bury it from sight
Afraid others would take it?
Or would he display it proudly
Set it in a ring or crown
So that all the world could behold its beauty
And see what richness it brings to his life?
You are my pearl without price.

—Ren

Reading his innermost thoughts and feelings almost made up for our non-tiger time together being limited. Not quite. But almost.

After art history one day, Ren surprised me by falling into step behind me.

"How did you know where my class was?"

"I got out early today and tracked you. Easy as peach pie with whipped cream, which you promised to make for me later."

"I remember." I laughed, and we headed toward the language lab to return a long-forgotten video.

Behind the language lab desk was Artie.

"Hey, Artie. Just returning a video."

He shoved his glasses up onto the bridge of his nose. "Ah, yes. I'd wondered where that video was. It's very late, Kelsey."

"Yeah. Sorry about that."

He slipped it into an empty spot that I imagined he'd probably been staring at week after week as it drove him slowly crazy. "I'm glad you had the integrity to return it at least."

"Right, I'm full of integrity. See ya around, Artie."

"Wait, Kelsey. You haven't returned my phone calls, so I assume your answering machine is not working. It's going to be hard to fit you in, but I believe I have next Wednesday available."

He picked up his pencil and his planner and was already scribbling my name down. *How could he ignore the very large man behind me?*

"Look, Artie, I'm seeing someone else now."

"I don't think you've thought this out clearly, Kelsey. The date we had was very special, and I felt a real connection. I'm sure if you reconsidered, you would see that you should be going out with *me*." He glanced at Ren briefly. "I am *clearly* the best option."

Exasperated, I said, "*Artie*!"

He shoved his glasses up again and stared me down, willing me to give in with his eyes.

At that point, Ren stepped between us. Artie reluctantly dragged his eyes away from me and looked at Ren with distaste. The two men were such a contrast that I couldn't help comparing them. Where Artie was soft, jowly, and paunchy in the middle, Ren was lean and big in the chest and arms. *And*, having seen his incredible torso without a shirt on, I could also vouch for him having fantastically chiseled abs, as well. He could easily grind Artie into the ground.

Artie was pasty white and hairy-armed with a red nose and watery eyes. Ren could stop traffic. And *had*. *Literally*. He was a golden-bronzed Adonis come to life. I'd frequently seen girls trip over the sidewalk and bump into trees when he walked by. None of these qualities fazed Artie. He was supremely self-confident. He boldly stood his ground and was completely uncowed by Ren's awesomeness.

Artie droned nasally, "And who might *you* be?"

"I am the man Kelsey's dating."

Artie's expression was incredulous. He peered down at me around Ren's shoulder and said snidely, "You would rather date this *barbarian* than me? Perhaps I've misjudged your character. You obviously make questionable choices based purely on lustful impulses. I thought you were of a higher moral caliber, Kelsey."

"Really, Art—" I started.

Ren stuck his face very close to Artie's and threatened quietly, "Do *not* insult her again. The young lady has made her position clear. If I ever hear that you are hounding her or any other young woman again, I will come back and make your life *very* uncomfortable."

He stabbed Artie's day planner with his finger. "Perhaps you'd better write that down so you don't forget. You should also make a note to yourself that Kelsey will not be available again. *Ever*."

I'd never seen Ren from this perspective before. He was lethal. I would be shaking in my shoes if I were Artie. But, as usual, Artie was oblivious to everything except himself. He didn't see the dangerous predator lurking behind Ren's eyes. Ren's nostrils were flared. His eyes were fixed on his target. His muscles were taut. He was ready to pounce. To mangle. To *kill*.

I put my hand on his arm, and the change was instantaneous. He let out a tense breath, relaxed his stance, and slid a hand on top of mine, covering it with his.

I squeezed his hand. "Come on. Let's go."

He opened my car door for me, and after making sure I was buckled in, he leaned in and said, "How about a kiss?"

"No. You didn't need to act so jealous. You don't deserve a kiss after that."

"Ah, but you do." He grinned and kissed me until I changed my mind.

Ren was quiet on our drive home. "What are you thinking?" I asked.

"I'm thinking that maybe I should buy a bow tie and a sweater-vest since you seem to like them so much."

I laughed and punched him on the arm.

Later that week, I saw Ren engaged in a serious conversation with a pretty Indian girl. Ren seemed a little perturbed. I was wondering who the girl was when I felt a hand on my shoulder. It was Jason.

"Hey, Kelsey." He joined me on the steps and followed my gaze. "Trouble in paradise, huh?"

I laughed. "No. So what's up with you?"

"Not much," he replied, digging into his backpack and handing me a theater magazine. "Here's a copy of that article. The one with your picture in it."

On the magazine cover was a picture of Jason and me standing next to the car. My hand was on the old lady's arm as she thanked me. I looked awful. *Like I'd been hit by a car.*

Jason suddenly stood up. "Uh, you can keep it, Kelsey. Catch ya later," he called over his shoulder as Ren approached.

Ren stared after Jason. "What was that about?"

"Funny, I was about to ask you the same question. Who's the girl?"

He shifted uncomfortably. "Come on. Let's talk about it in the car."

After he pulled out of the parking lot, I folded my arms across my chest and said, "Well, who is she?"

He winced at my tone. "Her name is Amara."

I waited, but he didn't add anything else. "*And* . . . what did she want?"

"She wanted my parents' phone number . . . so her parents could call my parents."

"What for?"

"To arrange marriage."

My mouth fell open. "Are you serious?"

Ren grinned. "Are you *jealous,* Kelsey?"

"Darn right, I'm jealous. You belong to *me*!"

He kissed my fingers. "I like you being jealous. I told her that I'm already taken, so don't worry, my *prema*."

"That's just weird, Ren. How can she want to propose marriage when you don't even know each other?"

"She didn't exactly propose marriage; she proposed the idea of marriage. Usually, the parents handle it, but in America, things have changed slightly. Now, it's more like the parents screen potential mates, and the kids get to pick from their choices."

"Well, you've been through it once already. I mean, you were engaged to marry Yesubai. Did you *want* to marry her? Your parents picked her out especially for you, right?"

He hesitated and spoke carefully. "I . . . *accepted* the match, and I looked forward to having a wife. I hoped to have a happy marriage like my parents had."

"But would *you* have picked *her* for a wife?"

"It wasn't up to me." He smiled, trying to appease me. "But, if it makes you feel better, I *did* pick you, even though I wasn't really looking for someone."

I still didn't feel like letting this go. "So you would have gone through with it, even though you didn't know her from . . . *Eve?*"

He sighed. "Marriage was and still is different in Indian culture. When you marry, you try to make your family happy with someone who shares your cultural background and who embraces and keeps the traditions and customs important to your family. There are a lot of things to consider, such as education, wealth, caste, religion, and where you come from."

"So it's like screening applications for college? Would I have made the cut?"

He laughed. "It's hard to say. Some parents believe that dating an outsider taints you forever."

"So you mean just *dating* an American girl taints you? What would your parents have said about us?"

"My parents lived in a very different time."

"Still . . . they wouldn't approve."

"Mr. Kadam is like a parent in a way, and *he* approves of you."

I groaned. "It's not the same thing."

"Kelsey, my father loved my mother, and she wasn't Indian. They were culturally from different backgrounds and had to merge different traditions, and yet, they were happy. If anyone from that time would have understood us . . . it would have been them. Would your parents have liked *me*?"

"My mother would have adored you; she would have baked you chocolate peanut butter cookies every week and giggled every time she saw you, like Sarah does. My father never thought any man would be good enough for me. He would've had a hard time letting me go, but he would have liked you too."

We pulled into the garage, and I had a sudden vision of the four of us sitting in my parents' library talking about favorite books. Yes, they would have heartily approved of Ren.

I smiled for a moment then frowned. "I don't like the idea that you have other girls chasing after you."

"Now you know how *I* felt. Speaking of which, what did Jason have to say?"

"Oh. He gave me this."

I handed him the article as we walked in the house. Ren sat down and read it quietly while I made us a snack. He came into the kitchen with an expression of worry on his face.

"Kelsey, when was this taken?"

"About a month ago. Why? What's wrong?"

"Maybe nothing. I need to call Kadam."

He got on the phone and spoke quickly in Hindi. I sat on the couch and held his hand. He was talking fast, and Ren looked very worried. The last thing he mentioned before he hung up was something about Kishan.

"Ren, tell me. What's going on?"

"Your name and picture are in this magazine. It's a pretty obscure publication, so we might get lucky."

"What are you saying?"

"We're afraid that Lokesh can trace you back to here."

I responded, confused, "*Oh*. But what about my student ID and my driver's license?"

"We had them all changed. Mr. Kadam has connections. He arranged it so your records don't match your name with your photo. Did you really think he could arrange a passport in a week for you to go to India last summer?"

"I guess I didn't think about it." My mind reeled with the new information, and the vision I had seen in India of the power-hungry wizard flashed back to me. Suddenly worried, I said, "But, Ren, I'm registered at school under my name, and there are records of me in the foster care system that could lead back to Sarah and Mike. What if he finds them?"

"Mr. Kadam changed those too. The state records officially say you were emancipated at fifteen, and this house and all of the bills for it go to a hidden account. Even *my* driver's license is a fake, and I'm registered under a different name. Kelsey Hayes officially goes to WOU, but your picture was switched out so he couldn't find you. We left no records of your name tied to your picture. Those were the documents mentioned in the e-mail you saw on my computer."

"What about my high school yearbook?"

"Taken care of. We wiped you out of the official records. If somebody contacted an old high school classmate with an old yearbook they could match you up, but the odds of that happening aren't likely. They would have to check every high school in the country, assuming they knew which country to look in."

"So, you think this article means—"

"That there is a record he could find you with."

"Why didn't you two tell me all this before?"

"We didn't want to worry you unnecessarily. We wanted you to live as normal a life as possible."

"So, what are we going to do now?"

"Hopefully, finish out the term, but, just in case, I've sent for Kishan."

"Kishan's coming here?"

"He's a good hunter and can help me keep watch on things. He'd also be less *distracted* than I am."

"Oh."

Ren pulled me close and rubbed my back. "I won't let anything happen to you. I promise."

"But what if something happens to *you*? What can *I* do about it?"

"Kishan will watch my back so I can watch yours."

Kishan

With no word of Lokesh, and thankfully, nothing out of the ordinary happening, I loosened up enough to enjoy the annual Valentine's dance. The night would be fun, and all the proceeds would go toward funding the Jensen Arctic Museum.

Ren pulled a garment bag out of my closet and hung it on the bathroom door.

"What's this, Tiger? You think you can choose what I'm going to wear now, huh?"

"I like you in anything you wear." He pulled me into a tight hug. "But, I've wanted to see you in *this* dress. Will you wear it tonight?"

I snorted. "You probably want me to wear it because I haven't worn it on a date with anyone else. You can't stand the peach dress now because you say it smells like Li even after it's been dry-cleaned."

"The peach dress is lovely on you, and I picked it out especially for you. But, you're right. It reminds me of Li, and I want tonight to be only about us." He kissed my cheek. "I'll pick you up for dinner in two hours. Don't make me wait too long."

"I won't."

He touched his forehead to mine and added softly, "I hate to be apart from you."

After he left, I took a hot shower, wrapped a towel around my head and a robe around my body. Unzipping the garment bag, I found a claret-red chiffon dress with a trumpet skirt and double flutter sleeves. It was a wrap-dress style that tied at the side of my waist. A box on the floor contained strappy red shoes.

I sighed. *What is the obsession that men have with strappy shoes?*

Now that I had a billion lipsticks, I easily found one that matched my dress. I spent a long time with a curling iron twisting my hair into long ringlets that I swept up with jewel-studded combs, leaving a few loose to curl around my ears. I applied makeup and even had time to paint my fingers and toes with red polish to match.

Ren rang the doorbell, trying to be formal. I opened it and gasped softly. My warrior-archangel wore a brilliant white shirt with a gray vest and a red satin tie with a four-in-hand knot that matched my dress. His black tuxedo jacket was thrown casually over his shoulder, and his hair fell appealingly over one eye. He looked like a supermodel that had just stepped off the pages of GQ.

I suddenly felt like a little girl playing dress-up compared to him. I could imagine every girl at the dance wanting to reach up and brush his hair off his forehead.

Ren smiled, and my heart dropped down into my shoes where it flopped like a fish out of water. From behind his back, he brought out a bouquet of two dozen red roses. He stepped inside and put them in a vase of water he'd already prepared.

"*Ren!* You can't expect me to go to a dance with you looking like that! You're bad enough when you dress *normal!*"

"I have no idea what you're talking about, Kelsey." He reached up and pulled lightly on one of my spiral curls, tucking it delicately behind my ear. "Nobody will even notice me when I'm standing next to you. You look absolutely lovely. Now can I give you your Valentine's present?"

"You didn't need to get me anything else, Ren. Believe me, *you* are present enough."

He pulled a jewelry box out of his pocket and opened it for me. Inside was a pair of diamond and ruby drop earrings set in gold starbursts.

I whispered, "They're *beautiful!*"

He helped me take them out of the box. I liked the feel of them dangling from my ears and tapping against my face when I turned my head.

I stood on my tiptoes and kissed him. "Thank you. I love them."

"Why do I see a 'but' in your expression?"

"The 'but' is that you really don't need to buy me expensive things. I'm perfectly happy with normal, average things like . . . socks."

He scoffed, "*Socks* are hardly a romantic present. This is a *special* occasion. Don't spoil my night, Kells. Just tell me that you love me and that you love the earrings."

I reached up, wrapped my arms around his neck, and smiled at him. "I *love* you. *And* . . . I love my earrings."

His face lit up in an achingly beautiful smile, and my heart flopped around again.

I picked up his gift from the desk and handed it to him.

"It's pretty lousy when you compare it with earrings and roses. It turns out rich tigers are hard to shop for."

He tore through the paper, and there was my lame present, a book.

I explained, "It's called *The Count of Monte Cristo*. It's about a man who was falsely accused and put in prison for a long time, and then he escapes and seeks revenge against his accusers. It's a very good story that made me think of you being in captivity for hundreds of years. I thought we could take a break from Shakespeare and maybe read it together."

"It's a perfect gift. Not only are you offering me a new piece of literature, which you know I appreciate, but you're also offering me hours and hours of reading with you, which is the best gift you could give me."

With scissors, I clipped a rosebud from the bouquet and tucked it into his lapel. Then we were off to dinner, which had been arranged in a private dining room.

After we were seated and waited on by no less than three personal servers, I whispered, "A normal restaurant would have been perfectly fine for me."

"A normal restaurant is where hundreds of men are taking their hundreds of dates tonight. It's not special or private. I wanted to have you all to myself."

Ren captured my hand and kissed it. "It's my first Valentine's date with the girl I love. I wanted to see you sparkle in the candlelight. Speaking of which . . ." He pulled a sheet of paper from the lapel of his jacket and handed it to me.

"What's this?" I opened it and recognized his handwriting. "You wrote me a poem?"

He grinned. "I did."

"Will you read it to me?"

He nodded and took the page. He began speaking, and the timbre of his voice warmed me. He read . . .

I lit a candle and watched the flame.
It danced and twisted
Wild and unfettered.
It captured me and flickered in my eyes.
When I passed my hand over it

It stirred.
The flame rose higher, burned hotter.
When I pulled my hand away the heat diminished,
Grew fainter, and extinguished.
I stretched out my hand again to savor the burn.
Would it singe and scald? Blister and blaze?
No! It tingled and warmed,
Smoldered and glowed,
Setting me ablaze, body and soul.
It was glimmering, luminous, radiant,
The fiery blush of her cheek.

—Ren

He ducked his head as if embarrassed at the beautiful words. I stood up and walked around to his side of the table. I twisted my way onto his lap and put my arms around his neck. "It's beautiful."

"You're beautiful."

"I'd kiss you, but I'd get lipstick all over you and then what would the waitress say?"

"She can say whatever she wants."

"I'm fighting a losing battle, aren't I?"

"Yes. I plan on kissing you . . . a lot, before this night is over."

"I see. So I might as well get on with it then. Wouldn't you say?"

"I would definitely say you should."

We kissed, and I became so oblivious to everything except Ren that I didn't hear the waitress come back in. My face burned bright red.

Ren laughed quietly. "Don't worry. I'll leave her a big tip."

The waitress approached our table as I awkwardly removed myself from Ren's lap. To my horror, the bottom half of his face was smeared with red lipstick. I could only imagine what *my* face looked like. Ren didn't care at all.

I sped off to fix my face and asked him to order dinner. By the time I returned, the food was waiting. Ren rose to hold out my chair as I sat and leaned over to press his cheek against mine.

I played with my new earrings distractedly. Ren noticed.

"You don't like them?"

"I think they're lovely, but I feel really guilty about you spending this kind of money on me. I think you should take them back to the store tomorrow. Maybe they'll let you just pay a rental fee."

"We'll talk about it later. For now, I just want to enjoy seeing you wear them."

After dinner, we drove to the dance. Ren swept me out on the floor and twirled me around. Holding me close, he never took his eyes off me as he spun me to the music. He was so distractingly handsome that I couldn't tear my eyes away from him either.

He hummed along to a song called "My Confession."

Smiling, I admitted, "This song describes how I feel about you. It took a long time for me to confess how I feel about you, even to myself."

He listened more carefully to the words then smiled. "I've known how you felt about me since that kiss before we left Kishkindha. The one you got really mad about."

"Oh, the one you thought was *enlightening*?"

"It was *enlightening* because that's when I *knew*. I knew that you felt as strongly about me as I did about you. You can't kiss a man like that and not be in love with him, Kells."

I reached up to play with the hair at the nape of his neck. "So that's why you were so cocky and self-assured after that."

"Yes. But all that bluster went away after you left."

His expression became serious. He kissed my fingers, pressed my hand to his chest, and said intently, "*Promise me* you'll never leave me like that again, Kelsey."

I looked up into his cobalt blue eyes and said, "I promise. I'll *never* leave you again."

His lips brushed against mine lightly. Suddenly, he smiled mischievously, twirled me away, and then yanked me tightly against his chest. He slid his arm behind my back and lowered me slowly in a circular dip. Snapping me up quickly, we began moving to the tango music, and Ren maneuvered me smoothly along with the Latin rhythm of the song.

I knew people were probably watching us, but at that point, I didn't care. He was able to sweep through the moves expertly, even though I didn't know what I was doing. The dance was fiery and passionate, and I was quickly overwhelmed by him and the cadence of the melody. He wrapped me up in a blanket of mental and physical sensations, orchestrating the perfect seduction.

When the song was over, he had to hold me up because my legs had turned to gelatin. He laughed and nuzzled my neck, happy with my reaction.

The song changed back to a normal, slow one. After I had recovered enough from his tantalizing onslaught against my senses to speak, I said, "I thought that kind of dancing only happened in the movies. *Where* did you learn to dance like that?"

"My mother taught me several traditional forms of dancing, and then I picked up a lot of moves over the years by watching. Mr. Kadam hooked me up with Nilima, who became my practice partner."

I frowned. "I don't really like the idea of you dancing with Nilima. If you want to practice, teach me."

"Nilima is like a sister to me."

"Still."

"Alright, I promise to never dance with another woman." He smiled. "Though, I still like it when you're jealous."

We started slow dancing again, and I put my head on his shoulder, closed my eyes, and just let myself enjoy the feeling of being held by him. The song was only halfway over when I felt him stiffen and saw him look behind me.

"Well . . . well . . . well," a silky, familiar voice interrupted. "The shoe's on the other foot this time. I believe this is *my* dance."

I spun around. "Kishan? I'm so happy to see you!" I threw my arms around him.

The golden-eyed prince folded me in his arms, pressed his cheek against mine, and said, "I'm happy to see you too, *bilauta*."

10

hired guns

Kishan pulled back to have a good look at me. "I missed you. Has my idiot brother been treating you well?" In a stage whisper, he asked, "Did you have to use the tiger repellant?"

I laughed. "Ren's been treating me very well despite my giving *him* a pretty lame Valentine's gift."

"Ah. He doesn't deserve one anyway. What did he give you?"

I reached up to finger an earring. "These. But, they're much too extravagant for me."

Kishan stretched out his hand and touched an earring lightly. His rakish pirate about-to-make-off-with-your-woman-and-what-do-you-think-you're-gonna-do-about look melted away to a soft smile that turned up the corner of his mouth. He said quietly, "Mother would have approved."

"Do you mean these belonged to your mother?" I asked Ren, who nodded briefly. "Ren, why didn't you *tell* me?"

He responded lightly, "I didn't want you to feel pressured to wear them if you didn't like them. They're a bit out of date now."

"You should have told me they were your mother's." I slipped my arms around his neck and kissed him softly. "Thank you for giving me something so precious to you."

Ren hugged me close and kissed my cheek.

I heard a dramatic sigh behind us. "Ugh, I think I preferred him whiny and despondent. This is just sickening."

Ren growled softly, "Who invited you here anyway?"

"You did."

"Yes, but I didn't invite you *here*. How did you find us?"

"We flew into Salem, and I found the invitation for the dance at the house. I thought if there was a party, I should be here. Figures that all the pretty girls would already be taken. Perhaps . . . I can borrow *yours*."

Kishan held out a hand, but Ren stepped in front of me and threatened, "Over my dead body."

Kishan pushed up the sleeves of his sweater. "Anytime, bro. Let's see what you've got, Mr. Romance."

Intervention time. In my sweetest voice, I said, "*Kishan*, we're kind of in the middle of a date and, though I'm *very* happy to see you, I wonder if you'd mind heading home for now? As you can see, it's not so much a party as it is a couple's thing. We won't be gone long, and there's sandwich stuff and a giant plate of cookies back home. Do you mind? *Please?*"

"Fine. I'll go. But only because *you're* asking."

Ren retorted, "And *you're* asking *for it*."

Kishan flicked Ren on the ear and mocked, "That's right. And we'll see if you can *bring it* to me later. Bye, Kelsey."

I had a very strong feeling that my hand on his arm was the only thing holding Ren back from going after his brother. He watched until Kishan was out of sight, but even afterward, he couldn't seem to relax. I tried to pull his attention back to me.

"*Ren*."

"He takes too many liberties. Maybe it was a mistake to ask him here."

"Do you trust him?"

"It depends. I trust him with most things. Except—"

"Except?"

"Except *you*."

"Oh. Well, you don't have to trust *him* with me. You just have to trust *me*."

He scoffed, "*Kells*—"

"I'm serious." I put my hands on the sides of his face so he would look at me. "I want you to understand something. Perhaps Yesubai chose him, but *I* chose *you*. You are the one I want. Not Kishan."

I sighed. "I feel kind of sorry for Kishan, actually. He lost the person that he loved. That's why we should make the most of our time. You never know when someone you love will be taken from you."

He held me close for a minute and pressed his cheek to mine as we slow danced, knowing that I was no longer talking about Kishan.

"That won't happen to us. I won't leave you. I'm immortal, remember?"

I smiled halfheartedly. "That's not what I meant."

"I know what you meant." He teased. "But I had to fight off three men to win your affection, and I don't want to have to take on my brother too."

I laughed. "You're exaggerating, Tarzan. You didn't really have to fight off anyone, well, except Li. You had my heart all along anyway, and you probably knew it."

"*Me* knowing it and *you* knowing it are two different things. I was a lonely tiger for too long. I deserve to be happy with the woman I love. And I won't let anyone take her from me, least of all Kishan."

I gave him a look. He sighed and twirled me around. "I'll try to be more patient with Kishan, but he knows how to push all my buttons. It's extremely difficult to control myself around him, especially when he flirts with you."

"Please try. For my sake?"

"For your sake, I'd undergo excruciating torture, but I can't tolerate him flirting with you."

"I love *you*. I'll tell him to knock it off. But, try not to beat each other up while he's in town, okay? No tiger fights. Don't forget you need him here, remember?"

"Fine, but if he continues to throw himself at your feet, all bets are off."

After a moment, I said softly, "You didn't say it back . . . that you love me too."

"Kelsey, 'I am constant as the northern star, of whose true-fix'd and resting quality there is no fellow in the firmament.'"

"Caesar died, you know."

"I was hoping you didn't know that one."

"I know them all, Shakespeare."

"Okay, then I'll just say I love you. There is nothing in this world more important to me than you. I'm only content when you're near. My whole purpose is to be what you need me to be. It's not poetry, but it's from my heart. Will that do?"

I smiled lopsidedly. "I think so."

We didn't stay at the dance much longer because Ren's mood had changed despite my teasing, kisses, and pronouncements of love. He danced with me, but his mind was elsewhere, and when I told him I'd like to head home, he didn't protest.

When we pulled up the drive, I noticed that the lights were on in my house. Before we went in, Ren enfolded me in a soft embrace and kissed me tenderly.

He put his forehead against mine and said, "This is not exactly the ending to our romantic date that I had planned."

"You still have another hour." I grinned and put my arms around his neck. "What did you have in mind?"

He laughed softly. "Actually, I was planning to ad lib the rest, but that's not going to happen with Kishan around."

Ren kissed me again, and we heard a muffled comment too faint to understand. He ripped his lips away from mine and growled quietly, muttered something in Hindi, and opened the door with a scowl.

Kishan was watching television while scarfing down an incredible amount of snacks. Six different bags of pretzels, popcorn, cookies, chips, and assorted other goodies were strewn about the coffee table, all half-eaten.

"Just sickening," Kishan groused. "Couldn't you guys have finished kissing at the dance so I didn't have to hear it?"

Ren helped me out of my coat with an irritated growl, before I headed upstairs. He said he'd be up as soon as he got Kishan settled in. The *settled in* part sounded ominous to me, but I nodded, hopeful that they would at least attempt to be civil to each other.

I was just slipping my pajama top over my head when I heard Ren bellow, "*You* ate *all* of my peanut . . . butter . . . *cookies*?"

I shook my head. *Two tigers living this close to one another is going to be a major headache.*

Not hearing Kishan's reply, I decided to let them work it out for themselves. I carefully nestled the ruby earrings in my ribbon box for safekeeping and wondered about Ren and Kishan's mother. I scrubbed off the makeup and pulled the jeweled combs out of my hair, letting the soft curls cascade down my back.

I found Ren resting on my bed, scooted against the headboard. His tuxedo jacket was thrown across a chair, and his tie was undone and hanging around his neck.

I climbed onto his lap and kissed his cheek. His arms wrapped around me, pulling me close, but he kept his eyes closed.

"I'm trying to deal with Kishan, Kelsey, but it's going to be very, very hard."

"I know. Where's he going to sleep?"

"In my bed, in the other house."

"And where are you going to sleep?"

He opened his eyes. "Here. With you. Like I always do."

"Umm, Ren, don't you think that Kishan will make assumptions about . . . *you know*, us being together. *Together*?"

"Well. Don't worry. He knows we're not."

"*Ren*. Are you blushing?" I laughed.

"No. I just didn't expect this topic of conversation."

"You are definitely from a different time, Prince Charming. It's kind of an important conversation to have."

"What if I'm not ready to have this conversation yet?"

"Really? Three-hundred fifty years go by, and you aren't *ready* to have that conversation?"

He growled softly. "Don't misunderstand me, Kells. I'm more than *ready* to have *that* conversation, but *we* aren't going to. At least, not until the curse has been broken."

My mouth dropped open. "Are you saying what I think you're saying? That we can't be *together* until we get chased by immortal monkeys and demons at least three more times, which could take *years*!"

"I'm really hoping it doesn't take that long. But, yes. That's what I'm saying."

"And you aren't going to budge on this, are you?"

"No."

"Fantastic! So I *am* going to be an old maid living with two very large cats!"

"You're *not* going to be an old maid."

"By the time you decide to be with me, I will be."

"*Kelsey*, are you saying you're ready for all that now?"

"Probably not, but what about a year from now? Or two years? Eventually, I'll go crazy."

"It won't be easy for me either, Kells. Mr. Kadam agrees that it's just too dangerous. His descendants live exceptionally long lives, and he feels that the amulet is responsible for that. It was an awkward conversation, but he told us both that it would be best if we didn't take any . . . unnecessary chances. We don't know how the amulet or curse works, and, until we're men again, complete and whole, I can't risk anything happening to you."

I remarked dryly, "It's not like Mr. Kadam killed his wife, Ren."

"No. But he wasn't a tiger, either."

"Afraid we'd have kittens?" I teased.

"Don't even joke about that," Ren said stone-faced.

"Well then, what are you afraid of? Do you want to take a class?" I couldn't help it. Mom's sarcastic humor made an appearance.

"*No!*" he said with great consternation. I laughed. "Kelsey! You aren't taking this seriously."

"Sure I am. I just happen to be talking about something that makes me nervous, and I usually respond to nerves with humor and sarcasm. Seriously, Ren, you're talking about *years* when I am almost to the point of attacking your rather attractive self *now*." I sighed. "Do you really think it would be dangerous?"

"The truth is I don't know. I don't know how the curse will affect us. And, I won't put you at risk. So can we delay having this conversation . . . at least for a while?"

I grumbled, "Yes. But you should know that I have a . . . difficult time thinking straight around you."

"Hmm," he pressed his lips against my neck.

"That doesn't help by the way." I sighed. "I guess a lot of very cold showers loom in my future."

Ren mumbled against my throat, "You and me both. Did you have difficulty thinking straight around your other boyfriends?"

"What boyfriends?"

"Jason or Li?"

"I don't really think of Jason as more than a friend. Li was a good friend with potential. Mmm . . . that feels nice. They were people who were interesting and who I wanted to know better. But, not boyfriends. I didn't love them like I love you, and they didn't make me feel this way." I groaned softly. "Not like this."

He trailed kisses along the line of my jaw. "What about before them?"

"No. There was no one. You are my first . . . everything."

He lifted his head and smiled his devastating smile. "I am exceptionally delighted and deliriously happy to hear you say that." He gathered my hair over my shoulder and pressed kisses along the arch of my neck. "Just for the record, Kells, you're my first everything too."

I shivered. Sighing, he kissed me sweetly and snuggled me against his chest.

I played with the buttons on his shirt and spoke quietly, "You know, my mother talked with me about this right before she died. She and Dad really hoped that I would wait until marriage like they did."

"For me, it was assumed. In my time, in my country, casual relationships didn't exist."

"Ah," I teased, "so you think our relationship is casual?"

"No. Not for me, it isn't." He tilted his head and watched my expression carefully, "What about you?"

"Me neither."

"That's good to know." He reached over, grabbed my blanket, and tucked it around us.

"Ren?"

"Hmm?"

"What would you say if I said I *wanted* to wait, you know, until."

A smile lit his handsome face. "Until . . . *what?*"

I bit my lip nervously. "Until . . . *you know.*"

He grinned even wider. "Is this a proposal? Do you want Mr. Kadam's phone number so you can ask for his approval?"

I snorted, "You wish, Romeo! But seriously, Ren, if I wanted to wait, would it . . . *bother* you?"

He put his hands on both sides of my face, looked into my eyes, and said simply, "I would wait for you forever, Kelsey."

I sighed. "You always say the right thing."

I was enjoying snuggling with him when a dormant thought popped in my head that made me sit up. "Wait a minute! Your first everything, huh? That's not *exactly* true, is it? Mr. Kadam once told me that he broke into the Queen's Bath in Hampi, which was a rite of passage for young men. Didn't *you* accompany him to Hampi on several occasions?"

Ren froze. "Well, *technically speaking*—"

I smiled and raised an eyebrow mockingly. "*Yes*, Ren? My *love?* You were saying?"

"I was saying that, technically speaking, yes, Kadam, Kishan, and I broke in. But, we only made it to the front door, and everyone was sleeping. We didn't see a thing."

I poked him in the chest. "Are you telling me the truth, Lancelot?"

"I am absolutely, 100 percent, telling you the truth."

"So, if I ask Kishan tomorrow, he will corroborate your story?"

"Of course he will." He mumbled quietly, "And if he doesn't, I'll punch him in the face."

"I heard that. You better be telling me the truth, Ren, and you will *not* punch Kishan in the face."

"I'm just teasing you, Kells. I *promise*. I have never looked at anyone but you since the day you first read to me by my circus cage. You're a swan among swallows."

"Nice line, but I think you should consult your field guide again."

He frowned at me and ignored my comment. "As far as Kishan goes, he deserves to be punched for eating my cookies anyway."

"I'll make you more tomorrow, so don't give him grief over that."

I laughed until he effectively shut me up with his lips.

The next day over Ren's third omelet and Kishan's fourth, Ren announced he wanted to take up wushu again. Kishan clapped his hands together, showing he couldn't wait to clobber Ren.

The brothers rented a small studio where we could be alone, so he and Ren could tutor me. They didn't teach me any fancy moves or forms, but instead gave me a crash course in Disabling Your Opponent 101. We all thought it best if I learn some defensive moves with the possibility of Lokesh hanging about, as well as who-knows-what lurking ahead of us on the next quest. We all stretched for a few minutes, and then Ren began his lessons using Kishan as a test subject.

"Lesson one. If your attacker is running toward you, bend your knees and wait for him to get closer. Then, grab his arm, swing yourself around him, and lock your arms around his throat. If he's a big guy, then pull up into the top of his throat under the jaw."

Kishan ran at Ren and attacked from behind. Then it was my turn. Ren ran toward me, and I grabbed his arm and jumped on his back. I threw my arms around his neck in a brief stranglehold but then pecked him on the cheek before hopping down.

"Good. Lesson two. If the attacker knows more martial arts than you do, don't fight him. Just try to disable him. Go for the stomach or the groin, and punch or kick as hard as you can."

Kishan attacked again and started a complicated martial arts assault. I recognized a jump kick to the face with his knee bent and a round-house, but he also did a lot of complicated moves I'd never seen done before. Ren kept backing away, moving out of Kishan's range until he found an opening and punched Kishan hard in the stomach. Kishan got up right away and came back at him again. This time, he fought harder and threw Ren to the ground, which was when Ren punched upward, stopping just shy of debilitating his brother.

"If you have to pick one or the other, choose the groin. It's much more effective. Lesson three. Go for the sweet spots. These are the eyes, the Adam's apple, the ears, the temple, and the nose. For the eyes—gouge with two fingers, like this. For the ears—use both hands and thump against both ears at once, as hard as you can. Everything else is a flat-handed, hard chop."

Ren demonstrated each one then asked me to practice on him again. He wanted me to actually hurt him because he wanted it to be realistic. I just couldn't bring myself to do it.

Kishan growled and got up, pushing Ren out of the way. "She's never going to learn like this. She needs to feel a real attack."

"No, you're too rough. You'll hurt her."

"What do you think *they'll* do to her?"

I put my arm on Ren's. "He's right. It's okay. Let him try."

Ren reluctantly agreed to stand back against the wall.

I stood nervously with my back to Kishan, waiting for the attack. He came up behind me, grabbed my arm hard, and twisted me around. His hands went around my throat; he was strangling me. I heard a vicious growl before Kishan was thrown against the far wall. Ren stood in front of me tenderly touching the red fingerprints on my throat.

He yelled at Kishan, "I told you! You're too rough! She's going to have bruises on her neck!"

"It needs to be rough to be realistic. She needs to be ready."

"Ren, I'm okay. Let him try again. I need to prepare myself so I can think clearly in an attack. You might need me to save you someday."

He stroked my neck softly and looked at me, undecided. Eventually, he nodded and moved out of the way again.

Kishan ran to the other side and hollered back, "Don't think. Just react."

I turned away to wait for the attack. Kishan was quiet. I listened hard for his footsteps but heard nothing. All of a sudden, his arms were wrapped tightly around me from behind, and he was dragging me. He was too strong. He was choking me. I wiggled, wrestled, and stomped against his feet, all to no avail.

Desperate, I sucked in a breath and popped my head up against his chin. It hurt. Bad. But, he loosened his grip enough that I slipped out of his grasp and to the floor. Then, I stood up suddenly, rammed my shoulder into his groin, and punched him as hard as I could in the stomach.

Kishan fell to the floor, rolling over. Ren barked a loud laugh and thumped his brother on the back before returning to me. "You asked for it! *Don't think. Just react.* Oh, man! I wish I had a camera!"

I was shaking from my effort. I did it, but I seriously didn't think I could handle more than one opponent. How would I be able to protect Ren if I could barely hold my own? "Is Kishan going to be okay?"

"He'll be fine. Just give him a minute."

Ren was thrilled with my small victory. Kishan stood up grimacing. "That was good, Kelsey. If I was a normal man, I would have been down for at least twenty minutes."

I felt a little dizzy. "Uh, guys? Can we stop for today? My head is spinning. I think I need some aspirin. Remember, I don't recover as quickly as you two."

Ren sobered, felt my head, and found a big lump forming. He insisted on carrying me to the car, even though I could walk perfectly well. When we got home, he settled me on the couch, punched Kishan

hard in the gut just to make a point, and went to the kitchen to get a bag full of ice for my head.

As we practiced for the next two weeks, I started to feel confident that I could maintain my composure during an attack. Kishan and Ren also started taking turns circling the grounds at night, making sure that nobody could slip in to surprise us.

I stowed an emergency backpack under the front seat of Kishan's black GMC truck with clothes and other items I would need in a hurry. I put my quilt, traveling papers, the ruby earrings, and Fanindra in the bag. Ren and Kishan filled it with money from several different countries and added a bag of clothing for themselves as well. They parked the truck about a mile down the main road and covered it with branches to camouflage it.

I always wore my amulet and Ren's locket bracelet, but I was worried about my ribbon box. If we had to leave town quickly, I didn't want anything to happen to it. Ren suggested that we mail a package to Mr. Kadam for safekeeping. We shipped my ribbon box and several other irreplaceable personal items to India.

Keeping the mood light was difficult, because we all felt that something bad was coming our way. Kishan joined us now for movie nights and usually ate all the kettle corn, which annoyed Ren. We stayed home most nights and I cooked. Kishan easily ate twice as much as Ren, who ate *a lot*. The Safeway delivery guy probably thought we were running a bed and breakfast with the amount of food we had delivered each week.

One Saturday in March, I suggested a trip to Tillamook and the beach. The weather was supposed to be unseasonably warm and sunny. The likelihood of it actually being that way and staying that way was minimal, but the beaches of Oregon were beautiful, even in the rain. The minute I promised chocolate peanut butter ice cream, Ren became very supportive of the idea.

We packed ingredients for s'mores and a change of clothes in the back of the Hummer. I drove to Lincoln City and then turned right on Highway 101, which ran along the Oregon coast. It was a pretty drive, and both tigers stuck their noses up to smell the ocean when I cracked the windows. Later, I pulled in to the Tillamook Cheese Factory Visitor's Center and parked in the spot farthest away from the crowds.

"Meet you guys inside."

I slipped on a light jacket. Despite the warm weather forecast, the sky was a little overcast, with sunshine peeking through the gray clouds only occasionally. It was a bit windy, but rain didn't seem likely until later that evening. I walked into the store and browsed through the variety of cheeses on display.

Ren slid his fingers through mine. He wore an ice blue hooded sweater with some kind of Asian dragon pattern running from shoulder to shoulder.

I reached up to trace a dragon. "Where did you get this?"

He shrugged. "Off the Internet. I've become an expert Internet shopper."

"Hmm. I like it."

He raised an eyebrow. "*Do* you?"

"Yep," I sighed, "Hmm . . . we'd better keep you away from the ice cream."

He looked offended. "*Why* would you keep me away from the ice cream?"

"Because you're hot enough to melt it, and then Kishan would cry. The ice cream girls are checking you out already."

"Well, perhaps you failed to notice the young gentleman behind the counter. He was very disgruntled when I walked over here."

"You're lying."

"No . . . I'm not."

I peeked at the guy behind the register. He *was* watching us. "He probably just wants to make sure we aren't tasting too many free samples."

"I don't think so, Kelsey."

We wandered to the ice cream counter where I inhaled the scent of freshly made waffle-cones. Kishan ordered a triple cone with blueberry cheesecake, chocolate orange, and root-beer-float flavors.

"That's an interesting combo, Kishan."

He grinned at me over his giant cone and took a huge bite of root-beer-float ice cream. Ren was up next, but he seemed to be having trouble.

"I'm torn."

"Between what?"

"Chocolate peanut butter and peaches and cream."

"You love chocolate peanut butter. It should be an easy choice."

"Ah, true," he leaned down to whisper, "but I love peaches and cream more."

He kissed me on the cheek and ordered a double scoop of peaches and cream.

I ordered a double with chocolate peanut butter on the bottom and my favorite, Tillamook mudslide, on top and promised him he could eat the second half of my cone. I added a large square of chocolate peanut butter fudge to the order then paid the bill.

From there, it was just a short drive to the beach. Because it was overcast and still fairly cool, the beach was deserted. It was just the three of us, the seagulls, and the roar of the cold ocean.

The nippy rock-blue water crested, spilled over the pumice-gray sand, and sprayed the large black rocks. This was the ocean of the Northwest: beautiful, cool, and dark. Very different from the beaches of southern California or Florida. Far out on the water, a fishing boat drifted slowly by.

Ren spread out a large blanket and started building a fire. He soon had a crackling blaze going and joined me on the blanket. We ate, laughed, and talked about various styles of martial arts: karate, wushu, ninjutsu, kendo, aikido, Shaolin, Muay Thai, Tae Kwon Do, and Kempo.

Ren and Kishan argued about which form to use in which situation. Eventually they stopped, and Ren invited me to walk along the beach with him. We kicked off our shoes, held hands, and let the cold water lap over our bare feet as we walked all the way to the black rocks, about a half a mile away.

"Do you like the ocean?" he asked.

"I like to look at it or cruise on it, but swimming in it scares me. Wading is fine, but that's about it."

"Why? I thought you loved stories about the ocean."

"I do. There are some great books about the sea—*Robinson Crusoe*, *Twenty Thousand Leagues Under the Sea*, *Treasure Island*, and *Moby Dick*."

"Then why are you afraid?"

"One word. *Sharks*."

"Sharks?"

"Yes. Apparently, I need to introduce you to the movie *Jaws*." I sighed. "I know, statistically speaking, that most beach swimmers aren't eaten by sharks, but just the fact that I can't see anything in the water freaks me out."

"But swimming pools are fine?"

"Yes. I love swimming, but I've seen too many televised *Shark Week* specials to feel comfortable in the ocean."

"Maybe you'd feel differently about diving."

"Maybe, but I doubt it."

"I'd like to try it sometime."

"Be my guest."

"You know, statistically speaking . . . *you* are much more likely to get eaten by a tiger."

He tried to grab my arms, but I darted out of his range and laughed. "Not if the tiger can't catch me."

I took off running as fast as I could, and he laughed and chased me back across the sand trying to grab my heels.

He let me elude him for a while, even though I knew he could have overtaken me at any time. Eventually, he scooped me up and threw me over his shoulder.

I laughed. "Come on, Tiger, the water's getting higher, and we've left Kishan to his own devices for too long."

He carried me back to the blanket and set me down.

I got out the marshmallows to toast. Ren challenged Kishan to a race, going from the blanket to the rocks and back.

"Come on, Kishan, first one back wins."

"What do I win?"

I suggested, "How about you get the first s'more."

Kishan shook his head. "How about the prize is a kiss from Kelsey?"

Ren's face darkened.

I ventured, "Uh, Kishan. I don't think that's a good idea."

Kishan persisted, "It's fine, Kelsey. It'll give him real motivation to try. *Unless* he thinks he's going to lose."

Ren growled. "I *won't* lose."

Kishan poked Ren's chest. "On your *best* day, you wouldn't even see my tail."

"Fine. Let's do this."

"*Guys*, I don't think—"

"Go!"

They both took off running so fast they became almost a blur on the sand. My marshmallows forgotten, I stood to watch them run. Kishan

was lightning fast, but Ren was quick too. He was right behind Kishan. When they turned at the rock, Ren turned tighter, got a couple of feet ahead of Kishan, and was able to maintain his advantage on the run back. At the halfway mark, Kishan reached out, grabbed the blue hood on Ren's sweater, yanked it hard, and pushed him into the sand.

Ren spun and fell, but quickly got back up and surged forward, running with a vengeance. His legs pumped even faster than seemed possible. Sand flew out from behind him several feet, as he came up neck and neck with Kishan. The race ended with Kishan winning by a foot.

Ren was angry. Kishan laughed and nudged Ren aside so he could claim his prize.

I stood up on my tiptoes and pecked Kishan on the cheek. Ren seemed appeased and started to relax. He picked up a rock and threw it out into the ocean.

He grumbled, "You only won because you cheated."

Kishan said, "I won because I know *how* to win. Cheating is irrelevant. You have to learn to do whatever it takes to win. Speaking of which, *that* was not the prize I had in mind."

He reached over and grabbed my elbow, then he spun me around and dipped me over in a dramatic kiss. It was much more drama than substance, but Ren went ballistic.

"*Let. Her. Go.*"

After Kishan stood me up, I moved back a step and Ren barreled into Kishan's stomach, effectively cutting off his peals of laughter by shoving him into the sand. They rolled across the sand wrestling and growling at each other for the next ten minutes. I decided not to intervene. It seemed like fighting and wrestling with each other was a favorite pastime of theirs.

When they finally broke off fighting, we all ate s'mores. Smoothing

Ren's hair back from his forehead, I said, "You know he didn't really mean anything by it. He's just trying to bother you on purpose."

"Oh, he meant it alright. I told you, if he keeps making plays for you, then all bets are off. Hey, these are really good. Hmm, they could use—"

"Peanut butter?" we both said at the same time.

He started planting sticky kisses all over my face. I laughed, rolled him off my lap, and jumped away. He'd just sprung to his feet to catch me when my phone rang. It was Jason.

"Hey, Jason. What's up?"

"I just thought you'd like to know that there were a couple of guys on campus yesterday asking about you. They said they represent a legal firm, and they have news about your parents' will."

"I see. What did they look like?"

"Tall guys, expensive suits. They seemed legitimate, but I didn't tell them anything. I figured I'd talk with you first."

"Okay. Thanks for telling me, Jason. You were right not to tell them anything."

"Are you in some kind of trouble, Kelsey? Is everything alright?"

"Everything's fine. Don't worry."

"Okay, see ya."

"See ya."

I closed my phone and looked at Ren. He stared back, and we both knew. *Lokesh had found me.* I heard Kishan speaking quietly and turned to see he was on his phone, presumably with Mr. Kadam.

We started packing up immediately. Suddenly, the atmosphere at the beach had changed. It now seemed somber, dark, and sinister, when it once had felt friendly and safe. The sky appeared foreboding and ominous, and I shivered in the suddenly cool breeze.

Ren and Kishan agreed that if Jason hadn't told the men anything, it was unlikely that they had found our home yet. We decided to drive home, tie up a few loose ends, and leave Oregon.

On the drive, I called Sarah and Mike and told them I was returning to India right away. "Mr. Kadam has made an important discovery and needs my help. Ren will be going with me. I'll call as soon as I land."

I called Jennifer and told her the same thing. She kept hinting that if I was eloping with Ren, I should just flat out tell her. Eventually, she believed the story and said she'd pass along the info to Li. I was careful not to mention the city or how long I'd be away. I tried to be as vague as possible.

When I hung up, Ren assured me that my family would be safe. He said that Mr. Kadam had arranged a surprise vacation for Sarah, Mike, and the kids. They were getting a three-week, all-expenses-paid trip to Hawaii, but only if they left immediately. They would be told that the trip was a prize from their favorite running-shoe company.

I kept looking in the mirrors the entire drive home, expecting black sedans to come barreling down on me with shady men shooting at us. To say I was scared was an understatement. I'd faced demons and immortal monkeys, but, somehow, it felt totally different to face modern-world bad guys. I could rationalize that demons weren't real; therefore, even though they were chasing me, they weren't really a threat, but actual men who wanted to kidnap and torture or kill seemed much more menacing.

When we got home, I pulled into the garage and waited in the car until the brothers checked the house. Returning about ten minutes later, Ren put his fingers to his lips and quietly opened my door. He had changed into dark clothing, heavy boots, and a black jacket.

"What's going on?" I mouthed.

Ren whispered back, "Someone's been in the house, both houses actually. Their scents are everywhere, but nothing's been taken. No one's here now, so go upstairs, and quickly change into dark clothing and running shoes. Then meet us downstairs. Kishan's watching the doors. We'll go out the back of the house, take the long way to Kishan's truck, and head for the airport."

I nodded, hurried into the house, and ran up the stairs. I washed my face, pulled on dark jeans, a long-sleeved black sweater, and sneakers. I grabbed my jacket and met them downstairs. Kishan led the way as we crept through my house and into Ren's.

Both Kishan and Ren had armed themselves with weapons from my wushu box. The three-section-staff was folded and threaded through Kishan's belt at his lower back, and Ren had tucked a pair of Sai knives through his belt loop. Ren and I continued to follow Kishan as he led the way outside and into the trees.

He stopped often to smell the air and look at the ground. We had about a mile to hike to the truck. Every noise, every pop and crack in the forest startled me, and I whipped around often, expecting an attack. I felt an itch between my shoulder blades like we were being watched.

After about five minutes, Kishan froze. He gestured for us to get down, and we sank behind some ferns. There was someone in the trees moving quietly, following in our tracks. Even I could hear him, which meant he was close. Kishan whispered, "We need to get out of here. When I say 'now,' go." A few tense seconds passed. "Now," he whispered.

He led us deeper in the forest at a faster pace. I was trying to move as silently as I could, but I was afraid whoever was behind us could hear me. My feet couldn't seem to find the right places to step, and I often cracked branches and skidded on wet spots as I ran. We came upon a clearing, and Kishan froze and hissed back, "Ambush!"

We turned back. The man who was following us caught up and blocked our path. Kishan ran at him, closing the distance quickly. When he was just a few feet away, Kishan pulled out the staff, and whipped it overhead to gain momentum. I'd thought the weapon unwieldy, but in Kishan's hands it spun like the blades of a helicopter. With a snap he swept the man's legs out from under him, and then, he took a giant leap, twirled the weapon, and cracked the staff across the fallen man's back and head. With a flick of his wrist, the weapon folded into his palm and he shoved it back into his belt. The man didn't get up.

Ren grabbed my hand and yanked me behind him as he ran. Stopping at a copse of trees, he pushed me behind a fallen log and told me not to move, then he ran back to join Kishan. He took a ready stance not far from his brother. I saw the flash of Sai knives as he took them out and twirled them skillfully while Kishan once again wielded the staff. Both brothers peered into the forest and waited.

The other men had caught up to us. What happened next was no fight in a dojo. This was battle. *War.* Ren and Kishan looked like two uber-soldiers. Their faces showed no emotion. They moved sharply, efficiently. They wasted no energy. They moved in harmony like a pair of lethal dancers, Ren with the Sai knives and Kishan with the staff. Between them, they took down at least a dozen men, but dozens more shot out from the trees.

Ren punched one man in the neck with his elbow, probably crushing his windpipe. When the man bent over, Ren cartwheeled over his back, flipped around, and kicked the next guy in the face. Kishan was brutal. He broke a guy's arm and then kicked another guy's knee at the same time. I could hear the sickening snap and the scream as both of his opponents slumped to the ground. It was like being in the middle of one of Li's martial arts films, only here the blood and the danger were real.

When none of the men could stand, the brothers ran back to me.

"More are coming," Kishan said flatly.

We ran. Ren picked me up and threw me over his shoulder. Even with my weight slowing him down, he still moved faster than I could. The brothers were running at top speed. Fast, but silent. Somehow, they knew where to step to avoid making noise. Kishan slowed and started running behind us, taking up a flank position. We continued this way for at least ten minutes. I figured we were far away from the men, but, suddenly, I heard pings and pops as something hit the trunks of the trees around us.

Immediately, Ren and Kishan doubled their speed, leapt behind a fallen log, and took cover. "Are they shooting at us?" I whispered.

"No," Kishan whispered back. "Not with bullets anyway. Bullets sound different."

We sat quietly. I was breathing harder than they were, even though they were the ones who had been running. We waited. The brothers were both listening very carefully. I was about to ask a question, but Ren pressed a finger to his lips indicating that I should keep silent. They used some kind of hand signals to communicate with each other. I watched carefully, but I couldn't figure out what they meant. Ren rolled his finger in a circle and Kishan handed Ren his staff, morphed into the black tiger, and slunk off into the trees.

I pointed toward where Kishan had left. Ren pressed his mouth next to my ear and whispered in a barely audible voice, "He's drawing them off."

He positioned me in the hollow of the tree and moved so that his body covered mine.

I sat there, tense, my face pressed against Ren's chest for a long time. I heard a terrible roar. Ren wrapped his arms around me and whispered, "They've followed him. They're about a half mile away now. Let's go."

He took my hand and began leading me toward the hidden truck again. I tried to be as quiet as I could. After several minutes, a dark shape leapt in front of us. It was Kishan. He switched back to a man. "They're everywhere. I led them as far off as I could, but it looks like a whole regiment was sent after us."

Ten minutes later, Kishan froze and sniffed the air. Ren did too. Men jumped down on us from the trees; several of them descended from harnesses and ropes. Two men grabbed me, pulled me away from Ren, and held me tightly, while five men attacked him. He roared in fury and switched to a tiger. The men didn't seem surprised by this. Kishan had already changed to a tiger and had taken down several of his opponents.

Ren stood on his hind legs, thrust his paws on a man's shoulders, and roared in his face. He bit the man's neck and shoulder, pushed him to the ground, and used his body as a jumping off point. He leapt in the air, claws extended, and swiped two men across the chest. His ears lay flat against his head, his fur bristled, and blood dripped from his jaws. His tail raised and lowered like a lever just before he hurtled himself into the air again. He landed on the back of a man attacking Kishan, and the weight of his body alone disabled the attacker.

I struggled but couldn't even move because the men held me so tightly. Kishan roared. One of the men had used a pronged weapon that had some kind of electric Taser attached to the end. The black tiger whirled, knocked the weapon to the ground with a paw, and snapped it in half with the weight of his body.

Quickly, Kishan jumped on top of the man who had fallen to the ground and bit into the man's shoulder. Kishan lifted the man off the ground with his powerful jaws, and jerked his head violently until the man stopped moving. Kishan dragged the limp body several feet, and with a fling of his head, threw the man into the bushes. Then, he raised himself up on his haunches like a bear and swiped at other men who came near. His jaws dripped blood as he snarled viciously.

Ren kept trying to get back to me, but men always stepped between us. I took advantage of the momentary distraction when Ren dropped a man at our feet to kick one of my attackers in the groin as hard as I could and elbow the other one in the stomach. He doubled over but kept a tight grip on my arm. Then, he cuffed me at my temple and my vision got blurry.

I heard Ren's terrible roar. I kept struggling, but I felt dizzy. The man held me in front of him as if I was bait. He taunted the tigers by handling me roughly. I knew it was to distract the brothers, and unfortunately, it worked. Ren and Kishan kept trying to clear a path to me and frequently looked my way, which allowed more men to get behind them.

Other men arrived. Apparently, reinforcements had been called, and these men had more weapons. One of the men pulled out a gun and fired at Ren. A dart hit him in the neck, and he briefly staggered. I saw red and suddenly my vision cleared. I felt power sizzle through my limbs. I popped the back of my head into my captor's nose and gratifyingly felt the cartilage break. The man screamed and loosened his hold enough for me to jump away. I ran to Ren. He changed into a man. Another dart hit. He was still on his feet, but he was moving much slower. I yanked the darts from his body.

He tried to push me behind him, "Kelsey! Move back! Now!"

A third dart hit him in his thigh. He staggered once more and fell to one knee. Men surrounded him, and, knowing I was near, he began fighting again to keep them away from me. Kishan was enraged, mauling man after man while trying to get to us, but more kept coming. He was too busy to help me with Ren. He was barely holding his own ground. I tried to pull the men off Ren, but they were big. They were also professional fighters, maybe military, so they mostly ignored me and focused on the two more dangerous targets. I was just an annoying fly they swatted away. *If only I had a weapon.*

I felt desperate. There had to be something I could do to protect Ren. He finished off the last man near us and fell to his knees panting forcefully. Bodies were piled in groups around us. Some dead, some wounded. But, more men were coming. There were so many! I could see them creeping closer, eyes trained on the weary man at my side.

Fear for Ren's life steeled my resolve. Like a mother bear protecting her young, I stood in front of Ren, determined to somehow stop the men from advancing, or at least give them a different target to shoot at. There were more than a dozen men stalking toward us, most of whom had guns. A fire burned in me, a need to protect the man I loved.

My frame shook with energy, with power. I faced the man closest to me and stared at him darkly. He raised his weapon, and I raised my hand in defense. My body burned hot, and I felt a molten inferno travel down my arm and into my hand. The flames ignited, and the symbols Phet had once drawn on my hand reappeared and blazed crimson. A lightning bolt exploded from my hand to the body of my attacker. It lifted his body into the air and slammed him into a tree hard enough to make it shake. He fell in a crumpled mass at the base.

Not having time to question or figure out what had happened, I turned to face the next attacker and the next. I was overcome with rage; a furious wrath bubbled through me. My mind screamed that no one would hurt those that I loved. Euphoric in my power, I took them down one after another.

A pinprick struck my arm and another one hit my shoulder. They felt like bee stings, but, instead of burning, numbness spread. The fire in my hand sputtered and went out, and I stumbled to the ground in front of Ren. He shoved an attacker back, still fighting, though he had been shot with darts several times. My vision was getting dark, and my eyes were closing.

Ren picked me up, and I heard him yell, "Kishan! Take her!"

"No," I mumbled incoherently.

The whisper of his lips brushed against my cheek, and then I felt iron arms lock around my body.

Ren shouted, "Go! Now!"

I was being carried swiftly through the trees, but Ren wasn't following. He was still fighting, as the attackers closed in on him. He switched to a tiger again. I heard him roar with outrage and pain, and I knew in the soft fuzziness of my mind that it wasn't the physical hurt that caused him to cry out. It couldn't have been, because I felt it too. The horrible, ripping pain was because I had been taken from him. I couldn't keep my eyes open. I reached out a hand and grasped feebly at the air.

I pleaded hazily, "Ren! No!" before falling into darkness.

11
return to india

The deep thrum of an engine stirred me. My head throbbed, and there was a funny taste in my mouth. Something was very wrong; my mind was still fuzzy. I wanted to wake up, but I knew that on the other side of consciousness, a new kind of horror awaited me, so I allowed myself to sink back a little deeper into the murky blackness, and hovered there, like a coward. I needed something to hold onto, a crutch that I could lean on to give me enough strength to face what lay ahead.

I was lying on a bed. I felt the soft sheets and stretched out my hand hesitantly. A furry head butted against my fingers. Ren. He was here. *He* was the motivation I needed to rise above the darkness and step into the light.

I cracked open my eyes. "Ren? Where am I?" Every part of my body hurt.

A pretty face looked down at me. "Kelsey? How are you feeling?"

"Nilima? Oh, we're on the plane."

She pressed a cold wet cloth to my forehead, and I mumbled, "We got away. I'm so glad."

I stroked the tiger's head. Nilima looked at the tiger next to me briefly and then nodded. "Let me get you some water, Kelsey."

She left, and I closed my eyes again, pressing my hand against my throbbing forehead.

I whispered, "I was so afraid you weren't going to make it. I guess it doesn't matter now. We were very lucky. Let's not split up ever again. I'd rather be captured with you than be separated."

I slid my fingers into his fur. Nilima returned with some water. She helped me sit up, and I took a long drink then mashed the wet towel over my eyes and my face.

"Here . . . I brought you some aspirin," she said.

I swallowed the tablets gratefully and tried to open my eyes again. I looked into Nilima's concerned face and smiled. "Thanks. I feel better already. At least we all made it. That's the important thing. Right?"

I looked over at the tiger. *No. No!* I started gasping for air. My lungs locked. "*Kishan?*" I pleaded in a raspy voice, "Where is he? Tell me we didn't leave him behind! Ren?" I yelled. "*Ren? Are you here? Ren? Ren?*"

The black tiger just watched me with sad, golden eyes. I grabbed at Nilima's hand.

"Nilima, tell me! Is he here?"

She shook her head, tears filling her eyes. My vision became blurry, and I realized that I was crying too.

I desperately clutched her hand. "*No!* We *have* to go back! Tell them to turn the plane around. We can't just leave him there! We *can't*!"

Nilima didn't react. I turned to the tiger.

"Kishan! This isn't right! He wouldn't leave *you*. They'll *torture* him. They'll *kill* him! We have to do something! We can't let this happen!"

Kishan changed to a man and sat on the side of my bed. He nodded to Nilima, and she left us alone.

He picked up my hand and spoke quietly, "Kelsey, there was no choice. If he hadn't stayed behind, we wouldn't have made it."

I shook my head in denial. "*No!* We could have waited for him."

"No, we couldn't. They shot me with tranquilizers too. I only got hit once, and I barely made it to the plane despite my ability to heal. He'd been hit at least six times. I was amazed that he could still stand. He fought bravely and well and bought us time to get away."

I grabbed his hand as tears dripped off my chin. "Is he . . . ?" I sobbed, "Did they kill him?"

"I don't think so. None of them had weapons other than Taser sticks and tranquilizer darts. It appeared their instructions were to take us alive."

"We can't let them do this, Kishan. We have to try to help him."

"We will. Mr. Kadam is already working on locating him. It won't be easy, though. He's been searching for Lokesh for centuries, and the man has kept hidden well. There is one thing in our favor. Ren doesn't have the amulet, so Lokesh may be willing to offer a trade: the amulet for Ren."

"*Fine*. We'll give him the amulet if we can get Ren back."

"We'll worry about that when the time comes, Kelsey. For now, you should rest. We'll be in India in a few hours."

"I was asleep that long?"

"You were hit twice and were knocked out for about fifteen hours."

"Did they follow you to the plane?"

"They tried. Luckily, the plane was ready to take off. Jason probably saved our lives."

I thought about Ren being engulfed by enemies while we ran away, and I choked on a sob. Kishan leaned over, wrapped me in a hug, and patted my back.

"I'm sorry, Kelsey. I wish it had been me, not Ren. I wish I'd had the strength to carry both of you out of there."

My tears dripped on his shirt. "It's not your fault. If you hadn't been there, we both would have been captured."

I sat up, sniffed, and wiped my eyes on my sleeve.

He ducked his head to look in my watery eyes. "I promise you,

Kelsey, that I will do everything in my power to save him. He's still alive. I can feel it. We'll find a way, and we *will* defeat Lokesh."

I wished I felt as sure as Kishan that we could save Ren. Nodding, I squeezed his hand and whispered that I'd be all right. He asked if I'd like to eat something, and even though I felt knots twisting my stomach, I said yes. He looked relieved as he rose to look for Nilima.

I wondered if he was right. *Could Ren still be alive?* Since the day I first saw Ren at the circus, there was a strange connection between us. Tentative and wispy at first, it grew stronger. When I went back to Oregon, the link stretched and pulled like a rubber band.

It tugged me and tried to draw me back to him. And, in the last few months as we became closer, the connection solidified and tightened, forming a steel connection. We were part of each other. I felt his absence, but the bond was still there. It was still strong. He was alive. I knew it. My heart was still tied to his. It gave me hope. I resolved that I would find him, at any cost.

Nilima invited me to eat something. She set out a dinner with a glass of lemon water that I sipped slowly while I thought about what I could do to help Ren. Kishan had changed back to his tiger form before resting at my feet. His golden eyes watched me sadly, and I leaned down to pet his head, reassuring him that I would be okay.

By the time we landed, I still didn't have a clue as to how I would find Ren, but I knew that I would never let myself be so unprepared again. The next time something like this happened, I would fight. Now that I knew I had this . . . this lightning bolt power inside me, I would practice it. I would also ask Kishan to continue to train me in martial arts and maybe even in weapons. Perhaps Mr. Kadam would teach me too whenever Kishan was a tiger. Regardless, I would never let someone I loved be taken again. Not while I was still alive.

Mr. Kadam met us at the private airport. He wrapped me in a hug. "Miss Kelsey, I missed you."

"I missed you too." My eyes stung with unshed tears, but I refused to let them spill over.

"Come. Let's get you home. There is much we need to discuss."

When we got home, Kishan took my bag upstairs and left me alone with Mr. Kadam in the peacock room.

Books were piled high on his beautiful mahogany desk; the normally organized and clean top was covered with papers. I picked up a few papers to examine the notes written in his elegant script. "Have you figured out the second prophecy?"

"I'm close. Actually, it's thanks to you that I'm as close as I am. The landmark that puzzled me turned out to be the Himalayas. All this time, I'd been searching for a certain mountain, not realizing that it was a mountain *range* I needed to find. Thanks to your report on the Himalayas and their weather patterns, I was able to open my mind to that possibility, and it led to new discoveries for me."

"Glad to be of help." I set the papers down and asked quietly, "What are we going to do? How are we going to find Ren?"

"We'll find him, Miss Kelsey. Don't worry. There's even a chance he may be able to escape on his own and call us."

A thought occurred to me. "Will he be able to change into a man if he's captured?"

"I don't know. He wasn't able to before, but now you've broken part of the curse. That may make a difference."

I squared my shoulders. "Mr. Kadam, I want you to train me. I want you to work with me on weapons and martial arts. You taught both of the boys, and I want you to coach me too."

He looked at me thoughtfully for a minute. "Alright, Miss Kelsey. It will take discipline and many, many hours of practice to become competent. Don't expect to be able to do what Ren and Kishan can do. They have been trained all their lives, and the tiger within each of them makes them stronger."

"That's okay. I'm prepared for that. I plan to ask Kishan to continue working with me. I can learn faster if I practice with both of you."

He nodded. "Perhaps it is for the best. Not only will you learn new skills, but sometimes it helps to keep your hands busy when they are tied. I still need to focus much of my attention on research, but I will make time to train with you every day. I can also give you routines to practice on your own as well as some things you can learn with Kishan."

"Thank you. I'd like to help you with your research too. I can take notes, and a new set of eyes can't hurt."

"We can start today."

I nodded. He gestured to the leather furniture and we sat down.

"Now, tell me about this new power you seem to have. Kishan explained it to me, but I want to hear what happened from your perspective."

"Well, I needed to protect Ren and was so angry I think I actually saw a red haze around me. He'd been hit with darts, and he was staggering, weakening. I knew that he wouldn't last much longer. I stepped in front of him to face our attackers. I was desperate because there were so many men coming at us. A kind of fire burned in me."

"What did it feel like?"

"It felt like . . . a whoosh of power in my center, like a pilot light in a water heater that suddenly bursts into flame. My stomach tightened as if to push the heat up to my chest. My heart burned, and the blood felt like it was boiling in my veins. I felt a bubbling sensation traveling down my arm. When it reached my hand, the symbols that Phet had painted in henna reappeared and glowed red. I could hear a *snap, crackle, pop* kind of noise and then this power rose and spilled out of me. A lightning bolt shot out of my hand. It picked one guy up in the air and slammed him into a tree."

"And this power worked several times?"

"Yes. I was able to take down several men until I was shot with the tranquilizers. Then, the power sort of fizzled out."

"Did the lightning bolts kill them or just stun them?"

"I hope it just stunned them. To be honest, we didn't stick around long enough to find out. My first target, the man who hit the tree, was pretty hurt I imagine. I was really desperate."

"I'd be curious to see if you can reproduce the effect when you aren't in danger. Perhaps we can practice. It would also be interesting to see if you can widen the band to encompass more than one person at a time and to see how long you can maintain the burst."

"I'd also like to practice the intensity. I'd prefer not to kill people," I added.

"Of course."

"Where do you think it came from?"

"I have . . . a theory."

"Really? Tell me."

"One of the ancient stories of India says that when the gods, Brahma, Vishnu, and Shiva, faced the demon king, Mahishasur, they could not defeat him. They combined their energies, which took the form of light, and the goddess Durga emerged from that light. She was born to fight him."

"So, Durga's made of light, and you think that's why I have this power in me?"

"Yes. There are also several references that say she wears a necklace that flashes like lightning. Perhaps that stream of power resides in you."

"That's . . . I don't even know how to feel about that."

"I imagine it must feel disconcerting."

"You can say that again."

I paused for a moment and twisted my hands together.

"Mr. Kadam, I . . . I'm worried about Ren. I don't think I can do this without him."

He ventured, "The two of you have become closer then?"

"Yes. He's . . . I've . . . We . . . Well, I guess I could just sum it up by saying I love him."

He smiled. "You do know that he loves you, as well, don't you? He didn't think of anything but you for the months you were apart."

I couldn't help but grin. "So he was miserable, huh?"

Mr. Kadam smiled. "Desperately so. Kishan and I never found a moment's peace until he left."

"Mr. Kadam, can I ask you a question?"

"Of course."

"There was a girl, an Indian girl, who was interested in Ren and wanted her parents to match them up. Ren told me that dating outside of his culture is considered inappropriate."

"Ah. What he told you is accurate. Even in modern times, it's a custom that's still followed. Does this bother you?"

"Kind of. I don't want Ren's people to ostracize him."

"Did he express concern about this?"

"No. He didn't seem to care. He said he'd made his choice."

Mr. Kadam stroked his short beard. "Miss Kelsey, Ren hardly needs anyone's approval. If he chooses to be with you, no one will object."

"Maybe not to his face, but there might be . . . cultural ramifications that haven't occurred to him yet."

"Ren is well aware of *all* the possible cultural ramifications. Remember, he was a prince who was highly trained in political protocol."

"But, what if being with me makes his life more difficult?"

He chided softly, "*Miss Kelsey*, I can guarantee that being with you has been the *only* thing in his long life that gives him a modicum of peace. His life before you was fraught with difficulty, and I would venture to say that getting the approval of others has dropped very low on his priority list."

"He told me that his parents were from different cultures. Why were *they* allowed to marry and be together?"

"Hmm, that's an interesting story. To tell it properly, I'd have to tell you about Ren and Kishan's grandfather."

"I'd love to learn more about his family."

He sat back in the leather recliner, and steepled his fingers under his chin. "Ren's grandfather was named Tarak. He was a great warlord who wanted to live in peace in his later years. He'd grown tired of the infighting between kingdoms. Though his empire was the largest and his armies were the most renowned, he sent word to several other warlords governing over smaller territories, inviting them to a summit.

"He offered each one a portion of his land if they would sign a nonaggression pact and cut back their armies. They agreed, as the contract would bring each of them great wealth and properties. The country rejoiced as the king brought his armies home and prepared a grand feast in celebration. That day was considered a holiday throughout the land."

"What happened?"

"About a month later, one of the rulers who signed the pact roused the others, telling them that now was the time to strike and that between them, they could rule all of India. Their plan was to first take Tarak's ancestral lands. Then, from there, they could conquer all of the other smaller kingdoms easily.

"They broke their oath to Tarak and engaged in fierce battle, laying siege to his city. Many of the king's soldiers had retired from active duty and had been given parcels of land in exchange for their years of service. With the armies at half strength, they couldn't defeat the combined armies of the other warlords. Fortunately, Tarak was able to send runners out to enlist aid."

"Where did they go for help?"

"China."

"China?"

"Yes. Specifically they went to Tibet. The Indian/Chinese borders of that time were not as defined as they are today, and trade between the two countries was commonplace. Tarak especially had a good relationship with the Dalai Lama of the time."

"Wait a minute. He enlisted the aid of the Dalai Lama? I thought the Dalai Lama was a religious leader."

"Yes, the Dalai Lama was and is a religious leader, but religion and the military had close ties in Tibet, especially after gaining the attention of the Khan family. Centuries ago, Genghis Khan invaded but was satisfied by the tribute Tibet paid him, so for the most part, he left it alone. After Khan died, though, his grandson, Ögedei Khan, wanted those riches and returned to take over the country."

Nilima came into the library to bring us lemon waters. He thanked her and continued, "Three hundred years after the takeover, Altan Khan built a monastery and invited Buddhist monks to teach the people. Buddhist ideology became widespread, and by the early 1600s, virtually all of the Mongols had become Buddhist. A man named Batu Khan, another descendant of Genghis Khan, who was in charge of the Mongol armies, was sent by the Dalai Lama to help Ren's grandfather when he asked for aid."

I sipped my lemon water. "Then what happened? They won, right?"

"Indeed. The combined Mongol armies in addition to King Tarak's military were able to defeat the upstarts. Tarak and Batu Khan were of the same age. They became friends. Tarak, in gratitude, offered precious jewels and gold to take back to Tibet, and Batu Khan offered his young daughter to be married to Tarak's son when the time was right. Ren's father, Rajaram, would have been around ten years old at the time, and his mother had just been born."

"So, Ren's mother is related to Genghis Khan?"

"I haven't researched the genealogy, but one must assume there is some relation."

I sat back in my chair shocked. "What was his mother's name?"

"Deschen."

"What did she look like?"

"She looked a lot like Ren. She had the same blue eyes, and her hair was long and dark. She was very beautiful. When it was time for the marriage to take place, Batu Khan himself brought his daughter to meet with Tarak and stayed to oversee the wedding. Rajaram was never even allowed to see his bride until they were married."

"Did they have a Hindu or a Buddhist wedding?"

"I believe it was a combination of the two. In a Hindu wedding, there is typically an engagement ceremony, a feast with gifts of jewelry or clothing, and then a wedding in which the groom gives the bride a *mangalsultra*, or marriage necklace, that she wears for the rest of her life. The whole process takes about a week. By comparison, a Buddhist wedding is a personal celebration, not a religious one. Only a few people are invited. Candles and incense are burned, and flowers are offered at a shrine. There are no monks, priests, or assigned marriage vows. I imagine Rajaram and Deschen probably followed the customs of a Hindu wedding, and perhaps also added offerings to the Buddha."

"How long did it take for them to realize they loved each other?"

"That is a question I cannot answer, though I can tell you that their love and respect for each other was truly unique. When I knew them, they were very much in love, and King Rajaram often consulted with his wife on important matters of state, which was highly irregular at the time. They raised their sons to be open-minded and accepting of other cultures and ideas. They were good people and very wise leaders. I miss them. Did Ren speak of them?"

"He told me you watched over them for him until they died."

"That is true." Mr. Kadam's eyes became moist, and he seemed to fix his gaze on something I couldn't see. "I held Deschen when King Rajaram passed out of this world and then later, held her hand when she closed her eyes forever." He cleared his throat, "That's when she entrusted me with the care of her most precious possessions—her sons."

"And you have done more for them than any mother could ever ask. You are a truly wonderful man. A father to them. Ren told me he could never repay you for all you've done for him."

Mr. Kadam shifted uncomfortably. "That is neither here nor there. He does not need to repay me for what I gave him freely."

"And that is *exactly* what makes you so special."

Mr. Kadam smiled and stood to refill my water glass, probably to deflect attention from himself. I changed the subject.

"Did Ren and Kishan's parents ever know they were changed into tigers?"

"As you know, I was the king's military advisor. As such, I was put in charge of the armies. When Ren and Kishan were placed under the spell, they tried to sneak back into the palace at night as tigers. There was no way they could have gotten in to see their parents because Rajaram and Deschen were too well guarded, and Ren and Kishan would have been killed on sight. Even tigers as rare as they were would not have been allowed to enter the palace grounds. Instead, they came to me. I had a small house near the palace so I could be summoned at any time."

"What did you do when you saw them?"

"They scratched at my door. You can imagine my surprise when I opened the door to find a black and a white tiger sitting there staring at me. At first, I grabbed my sword. Military instinct is strong, but they didn't react to me. I lifted my sword above my head ready to strike, but they both sat there calmly, watching, waiting. For a time, I thought I was dreaming. Several minutes passed. I opened my door wider and moved back, keeping my sword at the ready. They entered my house and sat on my rug.

"We watched each other for hours. When I was summoned to attend training, I begged off, telling the servant that I felt ill. I sat in my chair all day and watched the tigers. They seemed to be waiting for something. When evening came, I prepared a meal and offered meat to the animals. They both ate and then lay down to sleep. I stayed awake all night, watching them. I had trained my body to go several days without sleep, so I remained vigilant, though they slept as harmless as kittens."

I sipped my lemon water. "Then what happened?"

"Early in the morning, just before the sun came up, something changed. The white tiger shifted and changed into Prince Dhiren; the black one followed suit and became Kishan. Ren quickly explained what had happened to them, and I immediately requested audience with their parents. I explained that it was imperative that Rajaram and Deschen accompany me to my home without guards. Their private guard took a lot of convincing, and only the king's absolute trust in me led him to comply with my wish.

"I led them back to my home. When I opened the door, Deschen let out a small scream when she saw the tigers. Rajaram moved in front of his wife to protect her. He was very upset with me. I begged them to enter and told them the tigers meant them no harm.

"After I'd finally convinced them to close the door, the two brothers rose to stand before their parents as men. They had very little time left and quickly changed back and allowed me to relate the story. The five of us stayed in counsel all day in my little home. Runners came to say that a vast army led by Lokesh was approaching and that he had already destroyed several villages and was on his way to the palace."

"What did you all decide to do?"

"Rajaram wanted to destroy Lokesh, but Deschen held him back, reminding him that Lokesh may be the only way to save the boys. They gave me a special charge: to take the boys and leave. Deschen couldn't bear to part with her sons, so arrangements were made for her to come with me under the pretense that she would be visiting her homeland.

"In reality, we snuck away to a small summer home near the waterfall where you found Kishan. Despite Rajaram's best efforts, he couldn't capture Lokesh. The armies were pushed back for a while, but Lokesh seemed to gather strength while Rajaram lost it. A few years passed. Without his wife and sons, Rajaram no longer had the will to be the king. Deschen also had become despondent. There seemed to be no hope for her sons, and her beloved husband was far away, taking care of the empire.

"I sent a missive to Rajaram explaining that Deschen was suffering. Reluctantly, he stepped down from the throne and turned over the affairs of the kingdom to a quorum of military advisors. He had told his people the false story of Ren and Kishan's deaths and explained that his wife had fled to China to find solace. He said that he needed to leave for a time to bring her back. He never returned. He joined us in the wilderness, bringing along some of their wealth and most precious things so that the boys would be able to keep their inheritance."

I asked, "Is that when Deschen died?"

"No. Actually, Deschen and Rajaram lived several more years. Reunited, they were happy and cherished every minute they had with the boys. It soon became obvious that Ren and Kishan weren't aging. I became the caretaker for the family. I was the intermediary between them and the outside world. The boys hunted and brought us food, and Deschen gardened and grew vegetables. I often ventured into town to purchase items and to listen to news.

"After several years, Ren's father became ill with what I now suspect was nephritis, or kidney disease. We heard that Lokesh was still fighting with the military, but that the Mujulaain people continued to fight back. Great legends were being told about the royal family. They had passed on into myth. The story I told you when I met you at the circus is the story as it is told today.

"Ren eventually asked me to wear his amulet. At the time, we didn't know what it would do to me. We only knew that it was powerful and important. He was afraid that if a hunter caught him it would be gone forever. Perhaps it was a premonition because he was captured soon after that.

"Kishan tracked him, and I learned that he had been sold to a collector in another part of the country. I returned disheartened. Ren's capture was the final blow to his father, and he died within the week. Deschen lapsed into deep despair and stopped eating. Despite Kishan's and my best efforts, she too, died, not a month after her husband.

"Kishan would not be consoled after his mother's death, and he often stayed in the forest. A few months later, I told him that it was time. I began my search for Ren. He told me to take the money and jewels. To take whatever I needed to find him. I took some, leaving the most precious family heirlooms there for Kishan to watch over, and began my quest.

"As you know, I was not able to rescue Ren. I studied every myth and story about tigers and about the amulets that I could find. Over the years, I invested their money, and it grew. I began with the spice trade and then moved on, buying and selling companies until the boys became wealthy.

"During those years, I married and had a family. After I left them, I followed Ren from place to place and spent many hours in research. For decades I searched for Lokesh and a way to break the curse. Lokesh, after failing to hold the Mujulaain Empire, mysteriously disappeared and never resurfaced, though I suspected he was still alive, like I was. That leads us to you, and you know the rest of the story."

"So, if Ren and Kishan lived in the jungle with their parents, how come they never made up?"

"They tolerated each other for their parents' sake, but they tried to avoid becoming men at the same time. In fact, I never saw them as men together again until you came along. It was a tremendous breakthrough to get Kishan to return and be a part of the family again."

"Well, Ren doesn't exactly make it easy on him. It's weird. I get the sense that they respect and even love each other, but they just can't let the old wounds heal."

"You have gone a long way toward healing all of us, Miss Kelsey. Rajaram would have been delighted by you, and Deschen would have wept at your feet for giving her sons' lives back. Don't let yourself doubt for a moment that you are right for this family or right for Ren."

My mangled heart thumped hollowly in my chest. Even thinking about him hurt, but my hands fisted in determination.

"So what should we start with? Research or sword-fighting?"

"Are you able to begin with some physical training?"

"Yes."

"Alright, get your things put away and then join me in the gym downstairs in half an hour."

"I will. And, Mr. Kadam? It's nice to be home."

He smiled at me, winked, and then set off for his room.

I headed upstairs and found that all the precious things I'd shipped were safe and sound. My ribbon box was in the bathroom. My books and journals had been moved to a library shelf along with newly framed pictures of my family and a vase of fresh pink tiger lilies. My grandmother's quilt rested on the foot of my bed, and my stuffed white tiger sat among the mound of plum-colored pillows.

I unzipped my bag and pulled out Fanindra, apologizing for leaving her out of the battle in the forest. We would be better prepared next time. I set her on the new library shelf on top of a round, silk-covered pillow.

I quickly changed into my wushu clothes and headed downstairs to meet Mr. Kadam. Kishan heard me bustling around and trotted down the stairs behind me. He curled up in a corner of the room on the gym mat, put his head on his paws, and watched sleepily.

Mr. Kadam was already there. The wall was flipped open to showcase his collection of swords. He walked over with two wooden sticks.

"These are called shinais and are used in the practice of kendo, which is the Japanese form of fencing. Use these to practice forms before moving on to the steel weapons. Grip it with both hands. Reach out as if you are shaking hands with someone, then wrap your three bottom fingers around the weapon and leave your thumb and forefinger loose."

I tried to follow his instructions, and before I knew it, Mr. Kadam was moving onto the next step.

"For advancing, walk heel-step, heel-step. For retreating, back up ball-step. This way you are always ready and won't distribute your weight wrong."

"Like this?"

"Yes. Very good, Miss Kelsey."

"Now lunge. When someone attacks, swing this leg back, move your body out of the way, and bring your sword up to defend yourself, like this. If someone comes from the other side, move back this way."

This was complicated. My arms already hurt, and the footwork was hard to remember.

He continued, "Eventually, we'll move on to heavier swords to build up your arms and shoulders, but for now, the footwork is what I want you to practice."

Mr. Kadam had me do footwork drills for an hour while he gave me tips. I began to move in a rhythm and crossed the floor back and forth doing lunges, advance-retreats, and deflecting moves. While I worked, Mr. Kadam watched, correcting my form from time to time and citing sword fighting instructions.

"Draw your sword *before* you engage an opponent. It takes too much time to do it once you're in a fight. And make sure your feet always stay grounded and balanced.

"Don't overextend yourself! Keep your elbows bent and close to your body.

"Fight to win. Search for weaknesses and exploit them. Don't be afraid to use other techniques if they will help you, like lightning power, for example.

"It's better to get out of the way than to block someone. Blocking saps your strength; moving out of the way requires less energy.

"Know the length of your sword and estimate the length of your opponent's weapon. Then, maintain a distance at which he cannot easily reach you.

"Though it's good to practice with bigger, heavier swords, lighter swords can do just as much damage. The big ones tire you out faster in a fight."

By the time I was done, I was sweaty and sore. I'd been holding the shinai up the whole time I was practicing footwork. And, even though it was lightweight, my shoulders were burning.

Mr. Kadam encouraged me to work on the footwork for an hour every day and said that he would teach me more tomorrow.

Kishan changed to a man after I'd sufficiently rested. He practiced wushu kicks and sweeps with me for another two hours. By the time I climbed the stairs to my room, I was exhausted. A hot dinner was left under a warming cover in my room, but I decided to shower first.

Clean and ready for bed, I lifted the lid and found grilled chicken and vegetables. There was also a note from Mr. Kadam inviting me to help with research in the library the next morning. I finished my dinner and walked over to Ren's room.

It was so different from the first time I'd entered his room. A thick carpet covered the floor. Books sat on top of the dresser, including a couple of the first-edition Dr. Seuss books that he'd mentioned buying. A paperback copy of *Romeo and Juliet* in Hindi was dog-eared and worn. A state-of-the-art CD player was set up in the corner with several CDs, and a laptop and writing materials sat on his desk.

I found his Valentine's present, his copy of *The Count of Monte Cristo*, and tucked it under my arm. He must have sent it in the package with my special things. Knowing he treasured it made me smile. One of my old hair ribbons was tied around rolled up parchment. I untied the ribbon and found several poems written by Ren in a language I couldn't read. Rolling up the pages and retying them, I decided to try to translate them.

I opened his closet. The last time I was here it had been empty, but now it was full of designer clothes. Most of them had never been worn. I found a blue sweatshirt that was similar to the one he'd worn to the beach. It smelled like him—waterfalls and sandalwood trees. I threw it over my arm.

When I returned to my room, I set the parchment on my desk and climbed into bed. I had just snuggled under my blanket with the stuffed white tiger and the sweatshirt when I heard a knock at my door.

"Can I come in, Kelsey? It's Kishan."

"Sure."

Kishan stuck his head in the door. "I just wanted to say goodnight."

"Okay, goodnight."

Spying my white tiger, he came in closer to inspect it. He grinned lopsidedly and flicked the tiger on the nose.

"*Hey!* Leave him alone."

"Wonder what he thought of *that*."

"If you *must* know, *he* was flattered."

He smiled for a moment and then grew serious. "We'll find him, Kells. I promise."

I nodded.

"Well, goodnight, *bilauta*."

I propped myself up on my elbow. "What does that mean, Kishan? You never told me."

"It means 'kitten.' I figured if we are the cats, you've got to be the kitten."

"Hmm, well, don't say it around Ren anymore. It makes him mad."

He grinned. "Why do you think I do it? See you in the morning." He turned off the light and closed the door.

That night, I dreamed of Ren.

# of prophecies and practicing

It was the same horrible dream I'd had before. It was dark, and I was seeking something desperately. I entered a room and found Ren tied to an altar with a man in purple robes standing over him. It was Lokesh. He raised the knife and cut into Ren's heart. I jumped on Lokesh and tried to take the knife away, but it was too late. Ren was dying.

Ren whispered to me, "Kelsey, run! Get out of here! I'm doing this for you!"

But I couldn't run. I couldn't do anything to save him. I could only crumple to the floor, knowing life without Ren was meaningless.

Then, the dream changed. Now it was dark, and he was sitting in a cage in his tiger form. Bloody lacerations ran down his back.

I knelt down. "Come on, Ren. Let's get you out of here."

He changed to a man and touched my face. "No, Kelsey. I can't leave. If I do, he'll catch you, and I can't let that happen. You can't be here. Please go."

He kissed me briefly. "Go!" He thrust me away from him and disappeared.

I turned in circles, calling out for him, "Ren? Ren!"

I saw a figure through the fog. It was Ren. He was healthy, strong, and unhurt. He was laughing as he talked with someone.

I touched his arm. "Ren?"

He didn't hear me. I stood in front of him and waved. He couldn't see me. He laughed and put his arm around a pretty girl's shoulder. I grabbed his lapel and shook him, but he couldn't feel my touch.

"Ren!"

He walked away with the girl and pushed me aside as if I was just a useless obstacle. I started crying.

A bird singing outside woke me up. I'd slept deeply, but I didn't feel rested. I'd dreamed of Ren all night, captured, a prisoner. And, whatever situation we were in, he always pushed me away, either to protect me or to get rid of me.

Five weeks. Five short, blissful weeks was all we had together. Even if I counted the time he was there but avoided me except for dates, our time in Oregon was only about two months. It was not enough. Not when you're in love with somebody. Somehow I always seemed to lose the people I loved. *How would I live without him?*

And yet . . . he was here. My parents were too. I could feel them so close I could almost touch them sometimes. It was the same with Ren only . . . stronger. So many weird things had happened to me. I had a pet snake that also functioned as a fashion accessory; I was almost eaten by a sea-horse vampire monkey; I had a boyfriend who was a tiger most of the time; and apparently I could shoot lightning from my hand.

I was so overcome by Ren's capture that I couldn't even begin to process my Thor-like power. *What else could possibly happen to me?* I didn't want to think about it because whatever I imagined, the reality would be much worse.

I got dressed and went downstairs to help Mr. Kadam. He was busy working on the computer.

"Ah, Miss Kelsey. Good morning. If you're ready, I have some maps I'd like you to check for me."

"Sure."

He set out a giant map of India and slid over a paper with the translation of Durga's second prophecy. A sable-furred head bumped against my leg, and I leaned over to pet him. I was happy Kishan was here, but I couldn't help wishing it was a white tiger sitting next to me.

"Good morning, Kishan. Already eat breakfast? I'll make you some cookies later if Mr. Kadam has all the ingredients."

He huffed and settled at our feet. I picked up the prophecy and read it through.

Seek her gifts before all else
For Durga's blessing waits anew.
The place of gods begins your quest
'Neath Noe's glacial mountain blue.
Let Ocean Teacher 'noint your eyes;
Unfold the hoary sacred scrolls.
Teach arrant wisdom and advise
Gates of Spirit he controls.
Paradise awaits; remain steadfast
And find the navel stone
Which leads you to the heart of all
Ancient history's leafy throne.
Atop the world-tree is your airy prize.
Grasp bow and arrow, let fly true.
Discus routs and 'chief's disguise
Can stave off those who would pursue.

Four houses shall your spirit test
Of birds, bats, gourds, and siren's nest.
And last of all look to the sky
As iron guardians round you fly.
India's masses shall be robed
And rise in strength across the globe.

"Hmm," I pondered aloud. "Well, the first two lines are obvious. We have to go to a temple of Durga again. We'd already guessed that much. This time, we'll make sure to bring the proper offering."

"Yes. I have compiled a list of Durga's temples all over India, and some that are in nearby countries as well."

"Kishan, please remind me to wear my bell anklet."

Mr. Kadam nodded and bent over his notes. I bit my lip and thought about when Ren had given me the anklet. He'd begged me to stay with him, but I'd left.

What a waste. We could have shared all those months together if I just hadn't been so stubborn. I would have given anything to turn back time. Now, he was gone, taken prisoner, and there was a good possibility that I'd never set eyes on him again.

Trying to snap out of my sad thoughts, I focused on Durga's prophecy again.

"Noe's mountain? That's the Himalayan mountain range? How do you figure?"

"Noe is short for Noah."

"As in Noah's ark?"

"Yes."

"Umm, wasn't Noah's ark supposed to have landed on Mount Ararat?"

"You have a good memory. That's what I thought at first, but Mount Ararat is in modern Turkey, not India. The location of the ark has been hotly debated regardless."

"Okay, but what led you to the Himalayas?"

"A couple of things led me to that assumption. First, I don't believe the next item would be hidden in a location that far off the Indian continent. The prophecy mentions that the item would help the people of India, so it doesn't make sense that it would be so distant.

"The second reason has to do with the tale of Noe, or Noah. The Bible story is not the only one that describes a great flood. In fact, many dozens of cultures have stories of a great flood that covered Earth. I researched and cross-referenced all of the flood myths. There's Deucalion and Pyrrha of Greece, the Epic Flood story of Gilgamesh, Tapi of the Aztecs, and so on. One similarity among all of them is that, when the rains abated, the people were led to dry ground.

"In India, there is a myth that Manu saved the life of a fish who, in turn, told him the flood was coming. He built a boat, and the fish pulled him to the mountains. Several locations have been suggested as a landing site, but I omitted many of them for not being 'of glacial mountain blue.' The mountain that makes the most sense to me is—"

"Mount Everest."

"Yes. If you take the account literally and assume the entire Earth was flooded, then the land that would appear first would be the Himalayan Mountains. Because the Himalayas 'touch the sky,' one could make the assumption that the second quest we will embark on will be related to air. Birds and other flying creatures are featured heavily in the prophecy as well, *and* the object we are seeking is called an 'airy prize.'"

"Mount Everest? You don't think Kishan and I would have to—"

"No, no. Climbing Mount Everest is something only a brave handful of people have ever done. I wouldn't think of having you attempt that. No, what we are searching for is a city at its base, a city with a wise teacher. I'm hoping that you might be able to make a list of possible cities for me and perhaps think of a place I haven't yet."

"It sounds like you've already given this a lot of thought."

"I have. But, as you mentioned before, sometimes a new set of eyes can help."

Mr. Kadam handed me a list that I went through city by city, checking each one off the map. Sure enough, he had already crossed off every city within a several-hundred-mile radius of Everest. The only site on the map not crossed off was north of Everest and written in Chinese.

"Mr. Kadam? What's this city?" I asked, pointing to the spot.

"That's called Lhasa. It's in Tibet, not India."

"Well, maybe the teacher lives there on the other side of the Himalayas, but the item we're seeking is still hidden in India."

Mr. Kadam froze and then ran to get a book on Tibet. "Wait just a moment . . . a place of the gods." He flipped open the book and looked in the index. Fingering through pages quickly, he began muttering to himself. "Ocean Teacher . . . spirit gates . . . yes . . . yes!"

He slammed the book shut and grabbed me in a brief hug, eyes twinkling. "That's it! You've done it, Miss Kelsey!"

"What did I do?"

"Lhasa is the city ''neath Noe's mountain'! Its name translated means 'city of the gods'!"

"What about the teacher who is supposed to show us things?"

"That's the best part! The Ocean Teacher is probably one of the lamas. Possibly even the Dalai Lama himself!"

"What? Lhasa is nowhere near the ocean."

"Ah. The verse doesn't have to mean the ocean literally. It may mean his wisdom is as deep as the ocean or perhaps his influence is as vast as the sea."

"Okay, so we go to Lhasa and ask to meet with the Dalai Lama." I chucked the black tiger on the shoulder. "Sounds pretty easy to me, right, Kishan?"

He huffed and stretched his head.

Mr. Kadam mumbled, "Yes. That might be a problem."

"You don't happen to have a good relationship with the current Dalai Lama, right? Kind of like Ren's grandfather did?"

"No. And the current Dalai Lama isn't in Tibet. He's living in exile in India. The prophecy clearly indicates we need to go to the city ''neath Noah's mountain' and begin our quest there. It says here that the Ocean Teacher will anoint your eyes, unfold sacred scrolls, teach wisdom, and possibly lead you to the spirit gates."

"What are those?"

"Spirit gates mark entryways into shrines in Japan. They are said to be the doorways between the secular world and the spiritual world. When people pass underneath them, they cleanse themselves and prepare for the spiritual journey that will take place beyond."

"Are there any spirit gates in Tibet?"

"None that I'm familiar with. Perhaps there is a different meaning in the prophecy."

"Okay, what about this navel stone?"

"Ah, I do know what the navel stone is. I believe it means that you are seeking an omphalos stone. They are stones to represent the center, or the navel, of the world, and several were placed in the area of the Mediterranean, the most famous of which is housed at the oracle of Delphi. Some scholars have submitted that gaseous fumes were directed up through the opening of the stone, and when a seer stood over it and breathed in the gas, he or she would have a vision.

"It was supposed to be a way for humankind to communicate with the gods. It's also said that when you hold the stone, you can see into the future. There's a stone in Thailand, one in the Church of the Holy

Sepulchre in Jerusalem, and one is the foundation stone for the Jewish temple in the Dome of the Rock."

"What does it look like?"

"It's shaped somewhat like an egg standing on end with a hole in the top and carved webbing along the outside."

"So we find this omphalos stone and sniff its fumes or hold it, and it will show us to a world tree?"

"Correct."

"And the tree?"

"A world tree is another very common theme in many cultures and myths. There is a wish-fulfilling tree that took care of the needs of the people of India called the Kalpavriksha. It flourished when the people were wise and good, but, when the nature of humankind changed, the tree dimmed.

"In my studies of the Golden Fruit, I found a record of a special tree at the Kamakshi temple in southern India. It's a mango tree that bears four kinds of mangoes believed to represent the four Vedas or castes. In Norse mythology, there is a tale of a world tree named Yggdrasil. In Slavic and Finnish mythology, they selected an oak tree to represent the sacred world tree. In Hindu culture, it's a fig tree called Ashvastha. You might think of it as the Tree of Life. There are such trees mentioned in the cultures of Korea, Mesoamerica, Mongolia, Lithuania, Siberia, Hungary, Greece . . . you get the idea."

"Hmm, yes. I get the idea. So we're looking for a special tree. Do we at least know what type?"

"No. The stories all use examples of trees common to their lands, but most of the myths refer to something very large, with birds resting in the branches. These tests that are mentioned seem like they would fit that theme."

"Gotcha. Bottom line, we don't eat the fruit, right?"

He laughed. "Not all of the myths have fruit, but you are absolutely right. There is a test associated with most of them. Some even mention a giant serpent at the base. The leaves tie Earth to heaven, and the roots are supposed to sink into the underworld."

"Now as for these . . . tests. Do you think there's anything scary that will try to eat me like the Kappa?"

He sobered instantly. "I sincerely hope not, Miss Kelsey. In fact, I'm encouraged by the word paradise. I hope these tests will be more mental exercise than physical."

"Right. I'll just need to keep an eye out for the iron guardians. So, it says we have to ascend to the top to find the prize and pass four tests. I wonder what it means that India's masses shall be robed. Do you think it means clothes?"

"It could be a symbol for royalty, I suppose."

"Well, it sounds like you've got this pretty figured out, or at least as much as you can. It seems the next thing to do is go back to Durga's temple. Do you think it will work without Ren?"

"It won't hurt to try. You said that Ren had to be in tiger form before Durga accepted your offering. Is that correct?"

"Yes. She specifically noted the relationship between me and Ren."

"Then it would be wise to have a tiger accompany you. We will use Kishan instead of Ren, if, of course, you are amenable, Kishan?"

The black tiger huffed in response, which we assumed meant yes. I glanced down and petted his head. "Let's just hope she likes black."

"Meanwhile, I'll make some discreet calls to see if I can arrange to meet someone in Tibet or perhaps even with the Dalai Lama here in India."

"Do you think that will work? Will he agree to meet with us?"

"I have no idea."

"But shouldn't we wait for Ren? Shouldn't we find him first before we head off looking for the next item?"

"Miss Kelsey, I don't think Ren would want us to wait. Honestly, I haven't been successful in locating him, and I was hoping that when you discover the second item—"

"That we would be caught up in a vision again."

"Exactly."

"And that we might be able to figure out where Lokesh is, which could lead us to Ren."

"Yes. I know it's a long shot, but it may be the only clue we get."

"Alright, I'll go."

Kishan growled and changed into a man. "And I'll go with you."

"Don't feel obligated to chaperone me, Kishan."

He hissed, "Of course, I'm obligated. Ren charged me with taking care of you, and that is exactly what I plan to do. I'm no coward."

I put my hand over his. "Kishan, I've *never* considered you a coward. Thank you. I'll feel much safer with you around."

His tight face relaxed and he said, "Good. Now that that's settled, would you like to train for a few hours?"

"That's probably a good idea."

Mr. Kadam waved us off. "I'll work with you a bit this afternoon, Miss Kelsey, perhaps after lunch."

"Okay. We'll see you later."

I met Kishan in the dojo after changing clothes. He worked with me on throwing someone much larger than myself. I had to practice on him several times, and then he put me through a stretching and strengthening circuit. When he finally decided our session was complete, he chucked me under my chin and said he was proud of me.

Just as I was about to head upstairs to have lunch with Mr. Kadam, Kishan ran up behind me and tossed me over his shoulder. He took the stairs two at a time while I pounded on his back. He laughed.

"If you aren't prepared to throw off your attacker, you will have to suffer the consequences." He deposited me in the chair across from Mr. Kadam and grabbed some lunch for himself.

I was sore and tired. "I don't think I'm going to have the energy for another workout in sword fighting today, Mr. Kadam. Kishan really put me through my paces this morning."

"That's okay, Miss Kelsey. We can try a different kind of workout instead. Let's try practicing your lightning ability."

I grimaced. "What if it was just a fluke? Maybe it was a one-time thing."

He countered, "Maybe you've had the power all along and just never had the motive to use it."

"Okay, I'll try. I just hope I don't end up zapping you."

"Yes. Do try to avoid that."

We finished lunch and headed outside. I'd never been out on the grounds before. Patio steps led down to a cleared open area the size of a football field that was surrounded on all sides by jungle. Mr. Kadam had set up bales of hay with target boards at different distances, like the kind in archery tournaments.

"I want to try stationary targets first, and if that is successful, I'd also like to attempt moving targets. Now, you had said that you were angry and needed to protect Ren. It felt like a burning fire that started in your stomach and moved out to your hand, correct? I want you to think back and try to capture that feeling again."

I closed my eyes and pictured myself in front of Ren as he faltered behind me. I let the feelings rush over me again and created a mental image of his captors approaching me. A hot spark nibbled at my stomach. I focused on it and encouraged it to expand.

It burst like a lava bubble, flew up through my body, and shot out my hand. Thick, white, pulsing light surged from my palm toward the first target and hit. The entire target exploded like a fiery bomb, leaving only fragments of smoking hay, which burned themselves out as they floated, peppering the air. All that was left of the target was a black blast mark on the ground. Tiny black curls of smoke lifted, rose into the sky, and then slowly dissipated.

Mr. Kadam grunted and stroked his beard. "Very effective weapon."

"Yeah, but I don't want to do that to a person. It didn't seem as destructive as that on the people."

"Let's not worry about that quite yet. First, let's work on distance. Go for the next target and the next."

I blasted both of those targets in succession without any waning of intensity.

"Kishan, will you be so good as to set out more targets? This time, I'd like you to set them farther back and side by side."

Kishan headed down the field, and Mr. Kadam explained, "I'd like you to try to expand your range to encompass all three targets. Try to imagine something large like an elephant or a dinosaur, and you have to hit the whole length of it."

"Okay, I'll try."

I focused on the targets at the other end of the field while waiting for Kishan to move out of the way. Squinting into the sun, I fired off a shot and only hit the far left target.

"It's okay. Try again, Miss Kelsey."

This time, I focused on sustaining the burst longer and moved my hand in an arc, letting the bolt hit each of the targets.

"Hmm, interesting adaptation. Now we know you can maintain it." He rolled a finger in the air in a giant circle signaling Kishan to set them up again.

"Try again. This time, focus on widening it. Close your eyes for a moment and envision a Chinese fan. You hold the edge, and, as it leaves your hand, spread it out in front of you so the blast spreads like a fan's edges."

"All right, but stand behind me, okay?"

He nodded and moved slightly behind. I held out my hand and let the fire travel up my arm. I imagined holding the edge and lifted my palm toward the targets. The thick white light shot out slower this time. As it traveled, I spread my fingers out like a fan, willing the power to spread. It worked . . . too well. Not only did I obliterate the targets but also the trees on both sides of the field. Kishan had to drop to the ground so it wouldn't hit him.

I hollered out, "Sorry!"

He waved that he was alright.

Mr. Kadam signaled Kishan in and said, "Very good! With a little more practice, I think you will be able to hit exactly what you want when you need to. Tomorrow, we will practice degrees and see if we can lower the strength of the bolt to incapacitate rather than . . . umm—"

"Obliterate?"

He laughed. "Yes. It's all about control. I have high hopes that you will be able to master this, Miss Kelsey."

"I hope your hopes are right."

"I would like you to practice a bit more with Kishan on this for the next few days. Think only of targeting and widening your strike. I will work with you tomorrow on focusing your power levels."

"Okay. Thanks."

The weeks flew by. Before I knew it, a month and a half had passed. I completed my term online. My teachers were fascinated by Mr. Kadam's explanation. He'd told them that he'd found a rare artifact that he needed my help to catalog and promised them that I'd write a paper about it.

I couldn't wait to hear what I'd be writing about. I finished my finals, which gave me something to focus on other than Ren. Mr. Kadam also made excuses at the college for Ren, saying there was a family emergency and he had to return to India. The dean seemed very understanding and willing to do anything he could to help.

After my school work was complete, I helped Mr. Kadam with notes in the early morning and then worked out with Kishan until lunch. The afternoon was set aside for weapons practice. Kishan was teaching me how to take care of the weapons and which to choose in different types of battles. He also taught me hand-to-hand combat and several ways to take down stronger opponents.

I worked with Mr. Kadam in the early evenings on my lightning power. I was now able to control the level so I didn't destroy my targets. I could shoot a black hole through the bull's-eye like an arrow. Or, I could hit them all at the same time and knock them over. I could totally obliterate all or just the one I chose.

It was very empowering but also very scary. With this kind of force, I could be a superhero or a bad guy, and I really didn't want to be either one. All I really wanted was to help Ren and Kishan break the curse . . . and to be with Ren.

In the evenings, I kept to myself and read or wrote in my journal. The house felt different without Ren. I kept expecting to see him standing outside on the balcony. I dreamed about him every night. He was always trapped, either tied to a table or in a cage. Every time I tried to pull him out or rescue him, he stopped me and sent me away.

One night, I woke up from one of my Ren nightmares and got out of bed. I grabbed my quilt and headed out to the veranda. A dark head rested against the rocking loveseat, and, for a minute, my heart stopped. I slid open the door and stepped out onto the veranda. The head moved.

"Kelsey? What are you doing up?"

My poor heart fell back into a dormant state. "Oh. Hey, Kishan. Nightmare. What are you doing out here?"

"I sleep out here often. I like being in the open air and it's easier to keep watch on you."

"I think I'm pretty safe here. I doubt you need to keep watch over me while we're here."

He moved over and invited me to sit beside him. "I'm not going to let anything get to you, Kelsey. It's my fault it happened."

"No, it's not. You couldn't have stopped it."

He leaned his head back against the cushion, pressed his eyes closed, and rubbed his temples. "I should have been more vigilant. Ren thought I would be less distracted than he was. The truth is, I was probably *more* distracted. It would have been better if I'd never gone to America."

Confused, I asked, "What do you mean? Why do you say that?"

He looked at me. Golden eyes pierced mine as if searching for the answer to a question he hadn't asked. He tore his eyes away brusquely, growled, and muttered to himself, "I never learn."

I picked up his hand. "What's the matter?"

He reluctantly met my gaze again. "Everything that's happened to us has been my fault. If I would have left Yesubai alone, nothing would have changed. She would have been Ren's princess, and she wouldn't have died. You wouldn't be in danger now. My parents would have lived normal lives. Because I couldn't control myself, everyone around me suffered."

I put my other hand over his, cradling it between mine. He turned his over and clutched my fingers.

"Kishan, you loved her, which I have learned was a very rare thing during that time. Love makes you do crazy things. Yesubai wanted to be with you despite all of the negative ramifications. I bet that even if she knew her life would be cut short, she'd most likely go through it all over again."

"I'm not entirely sure of that. I've had a long time to think it over, and Yesubai and I barely knew each other. Our secret meetings were very brief, and I would be dishonest if I said that I haven't suspected her of acting as a pawn in her father's game. I don't *really* know if she loved me. Somehow, I think that if I was sure of that, then it would have all been worth it."

"She tried to save the two of you, didn't she?"

He nodded.

"She wouldn't have gone against her father if she didn't at least care for you. I don't see how she could have resisted you anyway. You're as good looking as your brother. You're sweet, and you're very charming when Ren's not around. If she didn't love you, she was crazy.

"It also makes sense because in my mind the only way she could have possibly refused Ren was if she loved you. Besides, my life would have been much sadder without Ren and you in it." I squeezed his fingers. "It's not your fault that these things happened. Lokesh is the one who did these things, not you. He probably would have come after your amulets even if Yesubai hadn't been a part of your lives."

"I made a deal with the devil, Kelsey. When you do that, there are prices to pay."

"You're right. When you make wrong choices or bad decisions, you always have to face the consequences. But, falling in love is not a bad choice."

He laughed self-deprecatingly. "For me it is."

"*No*, agreeing to go behind your brother's back was the bad choice, but, in the end, you chose your family. You chose to protect and stand by Ren and help him escape."

"It was still a mistake. I shouldn't have trusted Lokesh."

We sat and rocked quietly for a moment.

I whispered, "Making mistakes is what makes us human. It's how we learn. My mom always said that making a mistake isn't bad; what's bad is refusing to learn from it so you don't repeat it."

He leaned over and put his head in his hands. He spoke quietly as if mocking himself, "*Right*. You'd think I'd learn. Not to repeat history, I mean."

"*Are* you in danger of repeating history?" I teased, "Been in contact with Lokesh, have you?"

"I'd kill Lokesh if we crossed paths again, without hesitation. But, am I in danger of repeating history? Yes."

"I don't think you're likely to betray your brother again."

"Not in the way you're thinking, anyway."

I sighed. "Kishan, I don't want you spending all your free time watching over me. You're obviously fixating too much on the past. You should be enjoying your new life. Did you date anyone while you were home last fall? Did you go out or take some classes?"

He looked away. "It's not the past I'm fixating on." He sighed. "Classes don't interest me much." He stood and walked over to the rail. He leaned over and stared at the lit pool below. Softly, he said, "And it *seems* that the only girls I'm ever interested in . . . always belong to Ren."

I stared at his back surprised. He turned around and leaned a hip against the railing. He watched my reaction cautiously, his expression vulnerable and solemn.

I stammered, "Are you serious?"

"Yes. I'm serious. I'm a fairly candid, straightforward kind of guy. I don't joke about this kind of thing."

"But I don't get it. Yesubai I understand, what with her violet eyes and long black hair, but surely you—"

"Kells, stop right there. I'm not teasing you or playing any games. It took me a long time to decide if I should even say anything. Look, I know you love him, and I'd never think about trying to take you away from him. At least not when I know there's absolutely no chance you'd have me anyway." He smiled dryly. "I don't handle rejection well."

He folded his arms across his chest. "But, yes. If Ren wasn't with you, I'd do everything in my power to keep you in my life. To win you for myself."

I sat back on the bench, shocked. "*Kishan.* I—"

"Hear me out, Kelsey. You . . . calm me. You heal what's broken and give me hope that I can have a life again. And, despite what you may think, you're as beautiful as Yesubai was. I feel . . ." He looked away from me as if embarrassed, and growled, "What kind of a man *am* I? How could this happen to me? Twice! It serves me right. This time, Ren wins. It's fair. We've come full circle now." He turned back to me. "Please forgive me. I didn't mean to burden you with this."

Kishan was different when Ren wasn't around. He let his vulnerability show and didn't try to cover it with the arrogance and bluster that he always produced to bother Ren. I knew he was speaking sincerely. His heartfelt words affected me deeply. It saddened me. I knew that he needed to recover from the past as much as Ren did. I decided to try to lighten the mood.

I stood and hugged him. I meant it to be brief, but he held on as if I was his only anchor to humanity. I patted his back and broke away. Then I took his hand and pulled him back to the seat. I adopted my mother's no-nonsense approach to difficult situations. She always said that the best thing you can do to support someone is be their friend and be honest.

I said, "Well, Kishan, for the record, if Ren wasn't around, I'd date you in a heartbeat."

Kishan scoffed, "Look, Kells, just forget I even said anything, okay? It's a moot point anyway."

"You know, I never said thank you for punching Ren and making him come after me in Oregon. I would have never been brave enough to go back to him."

"Don't make me out to be the hero, Kells."

"But you *were* my hero. I might not even be with Ren if it wasn't for you."

"Don't remind me. The truth is, I wanted you back probably as much as he did. If he hadn't gone, I would've gone after you to get you for myself, and we might be having an entirely different discussion right now."

For a minute, I let myself imagine what would have happened if Kishan had come for me at Christmas instead of Ren. I punched him lightly in the arm.

"Don't worry; I'm here now. It's probably just my cooking you love anyway. I make a mean double chocolate chip peanut butter cookie."

I heard him mumble softly, "Right . . . cooking."

"Can we be friends?"

"I was always your friend."

"Good. I have a friend *and* a hero. Goodnight, Kishan."

"Goodnight, *bilauta*."

I turned at the door. "And don't worry. Your feelings are probably just temporary. I'm sure the more you get to know me, the more annoying I'll become. I have a grouchy side you haven't even seen yet."

He just raised an eyebrow and said nothing.

Despite my assurances that I would be fine without him watching over me, it felt nice knowing there was a tiger sleeping on the balcony. Sleep came upon me. For once, I didn't have any nightmares.

Vatsala Durga Temple

We kept to our schedule for another couple of weeks. I was getting stronger and felt confident that I could hold my own in a fight. Not because of my physical strength but because of the lightning power. That ability came easily for me. I could take out a weed all the way across the field and not damage the surrounding grass. It was like I had some inner ability to auto-focus, and I just knew where I needed to aim.

Mr. Kadam was spending most of his time trying to find Ren. Since we had discovered that the city we were looking for was Lhasa, the rest of the prophecy fell into place. Mr. Kadam was sure if we began our journey there, we'd find what we were looking for. Before we left, though, we had to make another trip to a temple of Durga.

Boxes started arriving in preparation for our trip. Mr. Kadam had purchased new clothes for me. Hiking boots, a dozen pair of wool socks, wool and fleece sweaters, Gore-Tex jackets, pants, and gloves, thick, long-sleeved T-shirts, a pair of white, insulated snow boots, insulated pants in a variety of styles, and assorted hats soon filled a corner of my closet.

After the latest package had arrived, which included sunglasses, sunscreen, and other various toiletries, I headed downstairs.

"*Mr. Kadam*, it looks like you're having me climb Everest after all. Just how many bags do you expect me to take, anyway?"

He chuckled. "Come in, Miss Kelsey, come in. I have something interesting to show you."

"What is it? A jacket that will keep me warm in an avalanche, maybe?"

"No, no. Here." He handed me a book.

"What's this?"

"It's called *Lost Horizon* by James Hilton. Have you ever read it?"

"No. I've never even heard of it."

"Have you heard the term *Shangri-la*?"

"Well, yeah. As in special nightclubs in old Hollywood movies? I think there might even be a casino in Las Vegas by that name."

"Ah, yes, well, I found a connection between this book and our quest. Do you have some time now to discuss it?"

"Yes. Let me just tell Kishan to come listen too."

When I returned, I made myself comfortable in the chair, and Kishan settled himself on the floor in front of me.

"*Lost Horizon* is a book written in 1933 describing a utopian society in which the inhabitants live exceptionally long lives in perfect harmony with one another. The city was set in the Kunlun Mountains, which is part of the Himalayas.

"What's truly interesting, though, is that Mr. Hilton based his story on the ancient Tibetan Buddhist myth of Shambhala, a mystical city that is isolated from the rest of the world and has many hidden secrets. In the modern world, the term *Shangri-la* has come to mean 'a place of happiness, a utopia, or a *paradise*.'"

"So we'll be searching for Shangri-la through the spirit gates?"

"Yes, that's what I've come to believe. This myth is fascinating. Do you know this book draws upon several famous cities and their stories? There are ties to the Holy Grail, the Fountain of Youth, El Dorado, the City of Enoch, and Hyperborea of the Greeks. All of those accounts are similar to the story of Shangri-la.

"In every story the people are searching for something that will grant immortality or a land that holds a perfect society. Even the Garden of Eden has many comparable themes—the tree, the snake, a paradise, beautiful gardens. Many have searched for such places and have never found them."

"Well, fantastic. The more I learn, the harder the task seems to be. Maybe it would be better not to know all this stuff. It might seem less daunting."

"Would you rather I didn't tell you?"

I sighed. "No, I need to know. It helps to have a frame of reference. So, nobody has ever come close to finding Shangri-la?"

"No. Not that people haven't tried. I came across an interesting piece of information, in fact. It seems that Adolf Hitler believed that Shangri-la held the key to the perfect ancient master race. He even sent a group led by a man named Ernst Schäfer on an expedition to Tibet in search of it in 1938."

"Glad they didn't find it."

"Indeed."

Mr. Kadam gave me *Lost Horizon* to read and warned me that we would most likely leave by the end of the week. We went back to our normal routine for the next few days, but I felt nervous. I'd been through some scary experiences the last time we did this, but I'd always had Ren with me. I fought with him half the time and kissed him the other half, but despite all the emotional turmoil associated with that, I always felt safe. I knew he'd protect me from the evil monkeys and the Kappa.

Now that a new adventure loomed before me, I wanted Ren with me so desperately my insides felt achingly hollow. The only thing that kept me going was knowing I was doing this for him. I wouldn't even allow myself to think he might not live through the next few weeks. He had to. Life without him would be meaningless.

I would still go through to the end for Kishan's sake, though. I couldn't abandon him. It wasn't in my nature. I knew he would protect me the best he could, and I was feeling even more confident of my own abilities. But it wouldn't be the same without Ren.

Each hour that passed produced no leads for finding him. Kishan was melancholy enough on his own, so I didn't bother talking to him about it. It was awkward to talk about Ren with Kishan anyway since his confession. And if I talked to Mr. Kadam about it, he always looked guilty, buried himself in research, and stopped sleeping whenever I mentioned how hard it was for me without Ren.

Kishan and I didn't speak again about his feelings for me. It was a little awkward at first between us, but we both doggedly ignored the subject until our relationship became easier. He continued to practice martial arts with me every day.

I found that I liked him more and more. There were definite similarities between the brothers, but there were several differences too. For example, Kishan seemed more careful than Ren. Kishan was willing to discuss any subject, but he was always slow to answer. His thoughts were insightful. He also was hard on himself and felt immense shame and self-recrimination over our situation.

However, there were things he said, words he chose, that reminded me of Ren. Kishan was easy to talk to, like his brother. Even their voices sounded the same. Sometimes, I forgot who I was speaking to and called him Ren accidentally. He said it was understandable, but I knew it hurt him.

Tension floated through the house the entire week before our trip. Finally, the day arrived for us to leave. The Jeep was loaded with our bags. With Kishan settled in Ren's spot, we headed off. Mr. Kadam had traveling papers for each of us and explained that we would actually be driving through three different countries. I peeked into a bag and saw that my passports and papers now said K. H. Khan and featured an older picture of me from high school. *Talk about a bad hair day.*

Our destination was Nepal, to a city called Bhaktapur. It took two days just to traverse India, and we crossed into Nepal at the Birganj-Raxaul border. Mr. Kadam had to go through a long process of paperwork at the border and said we had to show proof of the *Carnet De Passage En Douane*—a customs document that granted us permission to temporarily import our vehicle into Nepal.

After we settled into a hotel, we left Kishan to nap, while Mr. Kadam took me out in a rickshaw to see the Birganj clock tower.

When we got back to our rooms, Kishan accompanied us to dinner at a restaurant near the hotel. Mr. Kadam ordered *chatamari* for me, a kind of Nepalese pizza with dough made of rice flour. I picked a few toppings that I was familiar with. He ordered *masu*, a curried meat with rice dish, for himself. He picked chicken, but it was also available in mutton or buffalo, which I didn't know they had in Nepal. Kishan got vegetable *pulao*, a fried rice dish with cumin and turmeric, mutton *masu*, and *thuckpa*, a stir-fried egg noodle dish.

The next day, we rose early for the drive to Bhaktapur. Mr. Kadam checked us into our hotel, and then we walked toward the main square. We passed a large market featuring dozens of kinds of pottery. Many of the pieces were colorfully painted over black clay, which seemed to be a common material.

Other stands displayed masks of animals, gods, goddesses, and demons. Vegetables, fruits, and food carts lured us closer. We bought some of the famous honeyed yogurt, called *kuju dhau*. It was full of nuts, raisins, and cinnamon and was made from buffalo milk.

We left the market area and entered the main square. No rickshaws or taxis were allowed in the area. Mr. Kadam said that it kept the square quiet, clean, and peaceful. As we walked, he explained, "This is called

Durbar Square. Ah, there's what we're looking for—the Vatsala Durga Temple."

Two stone lions guarded the entrance to the temple. It was cone-shaped like the Virupaksha Temple in Hampi, but it had a brick patio surrounding it. Two large posts supported a giant bell next to the building.

"Hey, Mr. Kadam, I didn't need to wear my bell anklet after all. There's a giant bell up there."

"Yes. It's called the Taleju Bell. It's made of bronze, and it rests on the temple's plinth. Would you like to hear the story of the bell?"

"Sure."

"Its nickname is the Barking Bell. One of the ancient kings who lived here had a dream. The stories vary, but in his dream, nightmarish, dog-like creatures attacked the people during the night."

"Dog-creatures? Sounds like werewolves."

"That is very possible. In his dream, the only way to frighten the creatures away and save the people was to ring a bell. The peal of the bell was so loud and so strong that the creatures left them alone. When the king awoke, he immediately ordered a special bell to be made. Such was the power of his dream. The bell was cast and used to signal curfew for the townsfolk. As long as the townspeople followed the signal of the bell, they were believed to be safe. Many people still say that dogs will bark and whine each time that bell is rung."

"That's a good story." I elbowed Kishan. "I wonder if it works on were-tigers."

Kishan caught my elbow, pulled me closer, and teased, "Don't bet on it. If a tiger comes after you, you won't be able to easily frighten him off. Tigers are very *focused* creatures."

Something told me he wasn't speaking of the same thing I was. I desperately searched for something I could say to change the subject.

Most of the men walking around wore tall caps on their heads. I asked Mr. Kadam about them, and he launched into a long, detailed recitation of the history of fashion and religious wear.

"Mr. Kadam, you are like a walking encyclopedia on every subject imaginable. You're very handy to have around and more interesting to listen to than any other teacher I've ever had."

He smiled. "Thank you. But, please, feel free to let me know if I ever get carried away on a particular subject. It's one of my personal foibles."

"If I *ever* become bored," I said with a laugh, "I'll let you know."

Kishan grinned and used my comment as an excuse to put his arm around my shoulders and stroke my bare arm. "I can guarantee that I'd never bore you either," he teased.

It felt nice, *too nice*. I guiltily overreacted, squirmed under his heavy arm, and tried to push it off. "Sheesh! Take liberties much? Ever heard of *asking* a girl first?"

Kishan leaned over and spoke softly, "Deal with it."

I scowled at him. Then I concentrated on our tour.

We spent all afternoon familiarizing ourselves with the area and made plans to return to the temple at dusk the next evening. Mr. Kadam had either pulled strings or used his vast pocketbook to get us in alone after closing.

Streaks of color washed over the darkening sky as we arrived back at the temple. Mr. Kadam walked with us to the front steps and handed me a backpack full of various items to be used for an offering. It was filled with different objects related to air: various types of bird feathers, a Chinese fan, a kite's tail, a helium-filled balloon, a wooden flute, a plastic airplane that flew on rubber band power, a tiny barometer, a toy sailboat, and a small prism that transformed light into rainbows. We'd also included a couple pieces of fruit for good luck.

Mr. Kadam handed me Fanindra, who I slid up my arm. She had

twisted into armband position so I could wear her, which I took to be a sign she wanted to come along. Kishan and I climbed the stone steps that led to the center of the temple. We passed between the stone elephant guardians and then the pair of lions. The statue of Durga could be seen from the street in an alcove high above us. I was worried that if she came to life like the last time, someone walking on the brick streets would see her.

Silently, Kishan and I walked behind the building, around the stone porch surrounded by pillars, and found the circular stairs leading to the top of the temple. He reached out for my hand. It was dark and cool inside. The street lanterns from the square eerily lit the hallway leading to the statue. Kishan walked beside me as quiet, dark, and cool as the temple surrounding us. I liked Kishan a lot, but I missed the light and warmth that always seemed to surround Ren.

We entered a small room and stood before a stone wall. I knew the statue of Durga was on the other side, lit up from the streetlights below. The statue was set back about two feet from the outer wall of the temple, and we could stand on either side of it and still be hidden in the shadows.

"Okay, what we did last time was make an offering, ring a bell, ask for wisdom and guidance, and then Ren changed to a tiger. That's what seemed to work."

"I'll follow your lead."

We pulled out all of our air offerings and placed them at the feet of the statue before moving back into the shadows. I lifted my ankle, brushed my fingers across the tinkling bells, and smiled as I thought of Ren.

We moved back from the wall, and Kishan reached for my hand again. I was grateful for his steadiness. Even though I had already seen a stone statue come to life once before, I was still nervous.

"I'll say something first and then it'll be your turn."

He nodded and squeezed my hand.

"Great Goddess Durga, we come seeking your help once again. I ask your blessing as we go in search of the next prize that will help these two princes. Will you grant us your aid and share your wisdom?" I turned to Kishan and nodded my head.

Kishan stood quietly for a moment and then spoke, "I . . . don't deserve a blessing." He glanced at me and sighed unhappily before continuing. "What happened is my fault, but I ask you to help my brother. Keep him safe . . . for *her*. Help me protect her on this journey and keep her out of harm's way."

He looked at me for acceptance. I leaned up on my tiptoes, kissed his cheek, and whispered, "Thank you."

"You're welcome."

"Now, become a tiger."

He changed into his tiger form, his dark fur almost disappearing in the shadowy room. A stiff, cold wind ripped through the building and rushed up the stairs. My long-sleeved shirt billowed around me. I dug my hand into the scruff of Kishan's neck and shouted over the noise of the wind, "This is the scary part!"

The wind swirled dust and sand around us in a cyclone as years of grit blew out of cracks and off the floors. I squinted and covered my mouth and nose with my sleeve. Kishan nudged me back to a corner of the room, sheltering me from the powerful gusts of wind near the open windows of the temple.

I was trapped between him and the wall, which was good because he had to dig his claws in the floor to remain standing. He pressed his body against me. I knelt down and wrapped my arms around Kishan's neck, burying my face in his fur.

Carvings that had been muted with a covering of dust began to

appear. The wind and sand polished the floor until it looked like marble. I put one arm around a pillar to anchor myself and the other around Kishan.

After a while, the wind died down, and I opened my eyes. The room looked dramatically different. Stripped of grime and years of dust, the temple was beautifully glistening. The rising moon cast its light into the room, illuminating it, so that it appeared ethereal and dreamlike. On the back wall behind the statue of Durga, a familiar handprint had appeared. Kishan changed to a man and stood beside me.

He asked, "What happens next?"

"Come on and watch."

I pulled him after me, placed my hand into the print, and let the energy crackle down my arm and into the wall. A rumbling shook the wall, which made us step away. The wall rotated until it had spun 180 degrees. We were now facing the statue of Durga.

This version of Durga was similar to the other statue I had seen. Her many arms were spread out in a fan around her, and her tiger sat at her feet. There was no boar this time. I heard the sweet tinkling of bells and a beautiful voice said, "Greetings, young one. Your offerings have been accepted."

All of the items we had placed at her feet shimmered and then disappeared. Sand-colored stone began to shift as Durga's arms swayed in the air. Stone lips became ruby red and smiled at us. The tiger growled and shook itself. The stone flew away from its form like dust. The creature sneezed and sat at her feet.

Kishan was captivated by the goddess. She shivered delicately, and a small breeze drifted through the building and blew all the dust away from her, uncovering her like a luminous gem buried beneath the sand. Instead of gold, Durga's skin was soft, pale pink. She relaxed her arms and reached up with an empty hand to take off her golden cap. Luxurious black hair tumbled down her back and over her shoulders.

With a tinkling voice, she said, "Kelsey, my daughter, I'm so glad you were successful in finding the Golden Fruit."

She turned to look at Kishan, tilted her head, and raised an eyebrow in beautiful confusion.

Lifting a delicate, pink limb, she gestured to Kishan. "But who is this? Where is your tiger, Kelsey?"

Kishan boldly took a step forward and bowed deeply over her outstretched hand. "Dear lady, I am also a tiger."

He changed into his black tiger form and back. Durga laughed, a happy sound that echoed in the room. Kishan smiled at her. She looked back at me and noticed the snake wrapped around my arm.

"Ah, Fanindra, my pet."

She gestured to come closer, so I took a few steps forward. Fanindra's top half came alive, and she stretched her body out to the goddess's hand. Durga patted the snake's head fondly.

"There is more work for you to do yet, my dear one. I need you to stay with Kelsey for a little while longer."

The snake hissed quietly and then relaxed on my arm and became inanimate again, but her green jeweled eyes glowed softly while we spoke.

Durga turned her attention to me. "I sense you are sad and troubled, daughter. Tell me what causes you pain."

"Ren, the white tiger, has been taken prisoner, and we can't find him. We were hoping you could help us locate him."

She smiled at me sadly. "My power is . . . limited. I can counsel you on finding the next object, but I have little time for anything else."

A tear dropped off my cheek. "But, without him, finding the objects would hold no meaning for me."

She stretched out a soft hand to my cheek and caught a glistening teardrop. I watched as it hardened and became a twinkling diamond sitting on top of her fingertip. She gave it to Kishan, who was delighted with the gift.

"You must remember, Kelsey, that the quest I send you on doesn't help only your tigers. It also helps all of India. It is vital that you retrieve the sacred objects."

I sniffed and wiped my eyes on my sleeve.

She smiled at me sweetly, "Don't fret, dear one. I promise you that I will watch over your white tiger and keep him from harm and . . . oh . . . I see." She blinked and stared straight ahead as if she could see something we couldn't. "Yes . . . the path you take now will help you save your tiger. Guard the object well, and don't let it or the Golden Fruit fall into the wrong hands."

"What should we do with the Golden Fruit?"

"For now, it is to help you on your journey. Take it with you and use it wisely."

"What is the airy prize we seek?"

"To answer that question, there is someone I want you to meet."

She raised a pink limb and pointed behind us to the back of the room. A rhythmic click-clacking noise drew our attention.

In the moonlit corner of the room sat an old, gnarled woman on a wooden stool. Wisps of her gray hair stuck out of a faded red handkerchief. She wore a simple homespun brown dress with a white apron. A small loom was set in front of her. I watched quietly as she pulled beautiful threads out of a large woven basket and twisted them around the shuttle. The shuttle pulled the threads back and forth through the loom.

After a moment, I asked, "Grandmother, what are you weaving?"

She replied in a kind but weary voice, "The world, my young one. I weave the world."

"Your threads are beautiful. I've never seen colors like those before."

She cackled, "I use gossamer to make it light, fairy wings to give it sparkle, rainbows to make it iridescent, and clouds to make it soft. Here. Come and feel the fabric."

I grasped Kishan's hand, pulling him closer, and then stretched out my fingers to touch the material. It tingled and crackled.

"It has power!"

"Yes. There is great power here, but I must teach you two things about weaving."

"What is it, Grandmother?"

"These long, vertical threads are called the warp, and these colorful, horizontal ones are called the weft. The warp threads are thick, strong, and often plain, but, without them, the weft has nothing to cling to. Your tigers cling to you; they need you. Without you, they would blow away in the winds of the world."

I nodded in understanding. "What else do you need to teach me, Grandmother?"

She leaned closer to me and whispered conspiratorially, "Masterful weaving makes exceptional cloth, and I have woven great threads of power into this piece. A good piece of cloth must be versatile. Fulfill many purposes. This one can collect, craft, and cloak. Guard it well."

"Thank you, Grandmother."

"There is one more thing. You must learn to take a step back and visualize the whole piece. If you focus only on the thread given to you, you lose sight of what it can become. Durga has the ability to see the piece from beginning to end. You must trust her.

"Don't allow yourself to become disheartened when the thread doesn't suit or seems unsightly to you. Wait and watch. Be patient and devoted. As the threads twist and turn, you will begin to understand, and you will see the pattern finally materialize in all its splendor."

I let go of Kishan's hand, so I could step closer to the old woman. I kissed her on her soft, wizened cheek and thanked her again. Her eyes twinkled, and the shuttle started moving again. The rhythmic click-clacking noise continued as she slowly faded from sight. Soon, we could hear only the sounds of the loom and then nothing at all.

We turned to face Durga, who was petting her tiger's head and smiling at us.

"Will you trust that I will look after your tiger, Kelsey?"

"Yes. I will."

Durga beamed. "Wonderful! Now, before I send you on your way, I will bestow another gift." She began rotating the weapons in her arms and stopped at the bow and arrow set. She raised the bow, and Kishan stepped forward.

"Patience, my ebony one. I have a gift for you as well, but this . . . is for my daughter."

She handed me a medium-sized golden bow with a quiver of gold-tipped arrows.

I curtsied, "Thank you, Goddess."

She turned to Kishan and smiled. "Now, I will choose something for you."

He bowed deeply and grinned rakishly at her. "I will gladly accept *anything* you offer me, my beautiful goddess."

I rolled my eyes at him. *Sheesh.*

She nodded her head slightly in acknowledgement, and I couldn't be sure, but I thought I saw a little dimple where she twitched her mouth up in a small smile.

I looked at Kishan, who was grinning goofily, bewitched by Durga. *He* was *very handsome. Didn't Zeus have affairs with mortals? Hmm, I'll have to ask Mr. Kadam about that when we get back.*

Durga handed Kishan a golden discus, and he seemed delighted by it. It even made him bold enough to press a warm kiss on the back of her hand. *Overstep boundaries much?* I wasn't *jealous*. I was more shocked that he would act that way with a goddess.

The two stared at each other, so I cleared my throat, "*Ah-hem.* So is there anything else we need to know before we head off? We were thinking of Lhasa and the Himalayas. You know, searching for Noah's ark and Shangri-la."

Durga blinked and got back to business. Her tinkling voice echoed, "Yesss . . ." her voice started fading, and her limbs returned to their former position. "Beware of the four houses. They will test you. Use what you've learned. When you obtain the object, it will help you escape and help you find the one you love. Use it to—"

The goddess froze. Her soft skin hardened into stone.

"Drat! I have to ask her questions *first* the next time we do this!"

Wind blew through the room, and the statue began to move and was soon facing the street outside once more.

"Hello? Earth to Kishan."

He'd stood watching until Durga was gone from sight. "She is . . . exceptional."

I snickered. "Yeah. So what is it with you and unattainable women anyway?"

The light faded from his eyes, and he visibly withdrew into himself. He grimaced. "Yes. You're right, Kelsey." He laughed at himself dryly. "Maybe I can find a support group."

I giggled but then became sad. "I'm sorry, Kishan. That wasn't very nice of me to say."

Smiling ruefully, he held out his hand. "Don't worry about it, Kells. I've still got you. Remember, you're my warp and I'm your weft."

"Yeah. Not too flattering for me, eh?"

"You're a beautiful warp."

"Hmm, I don't think my warp drive is operating within normal parameters."

He tilted his head, confused. "What's a warp drive?"

I winced. "Sorry. Dad was a Trekkie. I couldn't resist."

"A Trekkie?"

"I've got to introduce you to *Star Trek*. It's a television series *and* not one but several movies. You may like it." I mumbled, "Too bad Scotty can't beam us out of this crazy life, huh?"

Kishan's brows knit together in confusion. He had no idea what I was talking about.

"Just ignore me. Someday, when we're not fighting demons, I'll teach you all about science fiction. We'll start easy. Maybe with *E.T.*"

He shrugged his shoulders. "Whatever you say, Kells."

I teased, "Come on, *ebony one*. Let's go find Mr. Kadam."

He grinned. "After you, my lovely."

I rolled my eyes at him again and headed down the stairs. "Didn't get enough flirt time in with the goddess, huh? Well, knock it off. It doesn't work on me, anyway."

He laughed and followed me downstairs. "Then I'll keep trying until I find something that does."

"Don't hold your breath, Casanova."

"Who's Casanova?"

"Never mind."

The moon had disappeared behind the clouds, and the temple walls and floors were covered with the same grime and dust as when we entered. Kishan took my hand again, and together we stepped out into the dark night.

14
the friendship highway

We met Mr. Kadam outside the temple. When we asked if he'd noticed the statue moving, he said that he hadn't. He hadn't felt the wind either. I told him that he should come with us next time. He always took the look-out position and said he had assumed that Durga would appear only for me and the tigers. He thought that his presence might deter us from our course.

I teased, "Of course, if you did come along, you'd probably fall under Durga's spell the way Kishan did, and then I'd have to bring *both* of you out of your love stupor."

Kishan scowled at me while Mr. Kadam's face lit up with delight. "The goddess is beautiful, then?"

I responded, "She's *okay*."

Kishan began gushing, "Her beauty surpasses all other women. Her ruby lips, soft limbs, and long dark hair would be enough to cause any man to lose control of his faculties."

I scoffed, "Oh, *please!* Exaggerate much? *Ren* never reacted that way."

Kishan glared at me. "Perhaps *Ren* had a *reason* to look elsewhere."

Mr. Kadam laughed. "I would very much like to meet her if it will work."

"It can't hurt to try. The worst that could happen is nothing, and then you could always leave, and we'd try it again."

After we returned to the hotel, we showed Mr. Kadam our new weapons. Kishan was going on and on about *the goddess this* and *the goddess that* and was twisting his discus in the light so the gleaming gold reflected on the walls of the hotel room. I listened for a while and heard Mr. Kadam talking about how the discus represented the sun, which was the source of all life and that the circle was a symbol of the cycle of life, death, and rebirth. I stopped listening, so I could tune out Kishan's constant praising of Durga and her lovely feminine features, which practically made me gag.

I leaned in the door frame between their connecting rooms, rolled my eyes, and during a break in Kishan's Durga tribute, mocked, "Are you going to yell like Xena when you throw the discus? No! Even better. We'll buy you a leather kilt."

Kishan's golden eyes turned to me. "I hope your arrows are as sharp as your tongue, Kelsey."

He walked toward me. I stood my ground, blocking his way, but he just picked me up and moved me to the side. Leaving his hands on my arms for a moment, he leaned over and whispered, "*Perhaps* you are jealous, *bilauta*." Then he closed the connecting door behind him, leaving me alone with Mr. Kadam.

Flustered, I flopped into a chair and muttered, "I am *not* jealous."

Mr. Kadam looked at me thoughtfully, "No you're not. At least not in the way he might hope."

I sat up straighter. "What do you mean?"

"You're protecting him."

I snorted. "Protecting him from what? His own delusions?"

He laughed. "No. You clearly care for him. You want him to find happiness. And because Ren isn't here, all of your maternal instincts are focused on Kishan."

"I don't think what I feel for Ren is maternal."

"Of course, it is. Well, a part of it is, anyway. Do you remember what the weaver told you about the different threads?"

"Yes. She said I'm the warp."

"Exactly. Ren's and Kishan's threads weave around you. Without your strength, the fabric couldn't be complete."

"Hmm."

"Miss Kelsey, do you know much about lions?"

"No. Not really."

"A male lion cannot hunt for himself. Without the female, he would die."

"I'm not sure I'm getting the point."

"My point is that a lion without a lioness dies. Kishan needs you. Perhaps even more than Ren does."

"But I can't be all things to both brothers."

"I'm not asking you to. I'm just saying that Kishan needs . . . hope. Something to hold onto."

"I can be his friend. I'll even *hunt* for him. But, I love *Ren*. I won't give up on him."

Mr. Kadam patted my hand. "A friend, someone who cares about him and loves him and won't let him give up on himself, is what Kishan needs."

"But isn't that what *you've* done for him all these years?"

He chuckled. "Oh, yes. Of course. But a young man needs a young *woman* who believes in him. Not a crusty old man."

I got up and hugged him. "*Crusty* and *old* are two words I'd never use to describe you. Goodnight."

"Goodnight, Miss Kelsey. We leave early in the morning, so get some rest."

When I dreamed that night, it was of both brothers. They were standing in front of me, and Lokesh was ordering me to choose which one would live and which one would die. Ren smiled sadly and nodded toward Kishan. Kishan's face tightened, and he looked away from me knowing that I wouldn't pick him. I was still pondering my choice when the courtesy wake-up call startled me.

I packed up my bags and met Mr. Kadam and Kishan in the lobby. We drove in silence about ten miles to Kathmandu, the largest city and capital of Nepal. Kishan and I sat in the Jeep while Mr. Kadam went into a building to finalize paperwork for our trip through the Himalayas.

"Uh, Kishan? I just wanted to say that I'm sorry for acting like a jerk yesterday. If you want to fall in love with a goddess then, by all means, go for it."

He snorted, "I'm not falling in love with a goddess, Kells. Don't worry about me."

"Well, still. I wasn't being very sensitive."

He shrugged. "Women don't like hearing men talk about other women. It was rude of me to go on like that. Honestly, I only praised her beauty so much to get a rise out of *you*."

I turned around in my seat. "What? Why would you do that?"

"I *wanted* you to be jealous, and when you weren't, it . . . bothered me."

"Oh. Kishan, you know I still feel—"

"I know. I know. You don't have to remind me. You still love Ren."

"Yes. But it doesn't mean that I don't care about you. I'm *your* warp too. Remember?"

His face brightened. "That's true."

"Good, don't forget that. We're all going to have happy endings, okay?"

I reached a hand back to him, and he held it in both of his and grinned. "Promise?"

I smiled back at him. "Promise."

"Good. I'll hold you to that. Maybe I should get it in writing. I, *Kelsey*, promise *Kishan* that he will get the happy ending he seeks. Should I define the parameters for you now?"

"Uh, no. I'd like to keep it vague for the time being."

"Fine. Meanwhile, I will create a mental list of what constitutes a happy ending and get back to you."

"You do that." He kissed my fingers brazenly, holding them tightly while I struggled to pull my hand out of his grip.

"Kishan!"

He laughed as he finally let me go and then changed to a tiger before I could verbally chastise him.

"Coward," I muttered as I turned back in my seat. I heard him growl softly but ignored him.

I seriously racked my brain for the next few minutes trying to find a happy ending for Kishan. At this point, my own happy ending wasn't even a guarantee. The best I could come up with was finishing the four tasks, so the brothers didn't have to be tigers anymore. I hoped that by the time we finished them, the happy endings would sort of take care of themselves.

Mr. Kadam returned and said, "We've received permission to take the Friendship Highway tour route to Tibet. It's something of a miracle."

"Wow. How did you manage it?"

"A high government official in China owes me a favor."

"How high?"

"The highest. Still, we have to stick to the tour stops and check in at each place along the way so they can keep tabs on us. We leave immediately. Our first stop is Neyalam, which is about 150 kilometers from here. It should take us about five hours just to hit the Chinese/Nepal border."

"Five hours? Wait a minute, 150 kilometers? That's roughly ninety miles. That's only eighteen miles per hour. Why does it take so long?"

Mr. Kadam chuckled. "You'll see."

He handed me the tour guide, map, and brochures so I could follow along and help him navigate. I thought the Rockies were huge, but comparing the Himalayas with the Rockies was like comparing the Rockies with the Appalachians, literally mountains to molehills. The peaks were thick with snow, even though it was early May.

Stark rocky glaciers rose up before us, and Mr. Kadam told me the landscape becomes tundra and then permanent ice and snow a little higher. Trees were small and scattered. The ground was mostly covered with grasses, dwarf shrubs, and moss. He said there were some conifer forests in other parts of the Himalayas, but we would be passing mostly through the grasslands.

When he said, "you'll see," he wasn't kidding. We were climbing at about ten miles per hour into the mountains. The road wasn't exactly up to standard, and we bumped and weaved around potholes and sometimes herds of yaks and sheep.

To pass the time, I asked Mr. Kadam about the first company he bought into.

"That would be the East India Trading Company. It was started before I was born in the early 1600s, but it became a very big business by the mid–eighteenth century."

"What kinds of things did you trade?"

"Oh, lots of things. Cloth—silk mostly—tea, indigo, spices, saltpeter, and opium."

I teased him, "Mr. Kadam! You were a drug dealer?"

He winced. "Not in the current definition of the word, no. Remember, opium was touted as medicinal then, but I did transport the drug in the beginning. I owned several ships and funded large caravans. When

China banned the opium trade, triggering the Opium Wars, I stopped shipping it and focused most of my business in the spice trade."

"Huh. Is that why you like grinding your own spices so much?"

He smiled. "Yes, I still like to look for the best quality products and enjoy using them in my cooking."

"So you've always been in the cargo business then."

"I guess I have. I never really thought about it that way."

"Okay, I have two questions for you. Do you still have a ship? I know you kept a plane from that company, but do you still have a ship? Because that would be so cool. The second question is what's saltpeter?"

"Saltpeter is also known as potassium nitrate. It was used to make gunpowder and is also, ironically, a food preservative. And, in answer to your other question, the boys *do* own a boat, but not one of my original shipping boats."

"Oh. What kind of a boat?"

"A small yacht."

"Ah. I should've guessed."

We stopped near the China/Nepal border in a city called Zhangmu where we had to fill out paperwork again. Then, after a day of driving and traveling only a total of ninety-six miles, we drove into Neyalam and checked into a small overnight guesthouse.

The next day we climbed even higher. The brochure said that by the end of the day we'd be above thirteen thousand feet. On this section of the drive, we saw six of the major mountains in the Himalayas, including Mount Everest, and stopped to take in the magnificent view of Mount Xixapangma.

On day three, I started feeling a little sick, and Mr. Kadam said he thought I had altitude sickness. He explained that it was common when traveling higher than twelve thousand feet. "It should pass. Most people adjust within a few hours, but for some it can take several days for their body to acclimate to the elevation."

I groaned and tilted my seat back to rest my dizzy head. The rest of the day went by in a blur. I was disappointed that I couldn't appreciate the scenery. We drove to Xigatse, where Mr. Kadam and Kishan saw the Tashilumpo Monastery while I stayed in the small hotel.

When they returned with dinner for me, I rolled over and waved them away. Mr. Kadam left, but Kishan stayed.

"I don't like seeing you sick, Kells. What can I do?"

"Uh, I don't think there's anything you *can* do."

He left me alone for a minute. Soon he was back pressing a damp cloth to my forehead.

"Here, I brought you some lemon water. Mr. Kadam said it helps to hydrate."

Kishan forced me to drink the entire glass and then poured another glassful from the bottled water they'd bought. He finally let me stop after my third glass.

"How are you feeling now?"

"Better, thanks. Except my head is pounding. Do we have any aspirin?"

Kishan found a small bottle. I downed two, sat forward, placing my elbows on my knees, and massaging my temples with my fingers.

He watched me quietly for a moment, and then said, "Here, let me help."

Kishan scooted me forward a little so he could sit behind me. He placed his warm hands on the sides of my head and started massaging my temples. After a few minutes, he moved into my hair and down the back of my neck, kneading away the stiffness that came from sitting immobile in a car for three days.

When he got to my shoulders, I asked, "Where did you and Ren learn to give massages? You're both very good at it."

He stopped for a moment and then slowly began again as he spoke. "I didn't know Ren had given you a massage. Mother taught us. It was something she'd been trained in."

"Oh. Well, it feels fantastic. Your hands are so warm they feel like heating pads. My headache's almost gone now."

"Good. Lie down and relax. I'm going to do your arms and feet."

"You really don't have to. I'm feeling better now."

"Just relax. Close your eyes and let your mind drift. Mother taught us that massage can take away the pains of the body and the spirit." He started working on my left arm and spent a long time on my hand.

"Kishan? What was it like being a tiger for all those years?"

He didn't respond for a long moment. I cracked open an eye and looked at him. He was focusing on the space between my thumb and forefinger. His golden eyes flicked over to my face.

"Quit peeking, Kells. I'm thinking."

I obediently closed my eyes again and waited patiently for his answer.

"It's like the tiger and the man are always battling each other. After my parents died, Ren had been kidnapped, and Mr. Kadam left to search for him. There was no reason to be a man at all. I let the tiger take over. It was almost like I was watching the tiger from a distance. I felt completely detached from my surroundings. The beast ruled, and I didn't care."

He moved to my feet, which tickled at first, but then I let out a deep sigh as he worked on my toes.

"It must have been terribly lonely."

"I was running, hunting . . . and doing everything by instinct. I'm surprised I didn't lose my humanity altogether."

"Ren told me once that being away from me, being on his own, made him feel more like a beast than a man."

"That's true. The tiger's strong, and it's extremely difficult to maintain a balance, especially when I'm a tiger for most of the day."

"Does it feel different now?"

"Yes."

"How?"

"I'm reclaiming my humanity piece by piece. Being a tiger is easy; being a man is difficult. I have to interact with people, learn about the world, and find a way to deal with my past."

"In a way, Ren was more fortunate than you even though you were free."

He tilted his head and moved to my other foot, "Why do you think that?"

"Because he was always with people. He never felt alone like you did. I mean, he was trapped, he was hurt, he had to perform in the circus, but he was still a part of human life. He still had the opportunity to learn, though in a limited way."

He laughed wryly. "You forget, Kelsey, that I could have ended my solitude at any time and chose not to. He was a captive, but I was sitting in a trap of my own design."

"I don't understand how you could do that to yourself. You have so much to offer to the world."

He sighed. "I deserved to be punished."

"You did *not* deserve to be punished. You need to stop thinking that way. I want you to tell yourself you're a good man and you deserve some happiness."

He smiled. "Alright. I'm a good man and I deserve some happiness. There, are you satisfied?"

"For now."

"If it makes you happy, I'll try to change my attitude about it."

"Thank you."

"You're welcome."

He moved over to my other arm and began massaging my palm.

"So what changed for you? Did getting six hours back as a man make enough difference for you to want to live again?"

"No. It wasn't that at all."

"It wasn't?"

"No. What changed my perspective was meeting a beautiful girl by a waterfall who said she knew who I was and knew what I was."

"*Oh*."

"She's the one who rescued me from my tiger skin and pulled me back to the surface. And, no matter what else happens . . . I want her to know that I will be eternally *grateful* for that." He lifted my hand and pressed a warm kiss on my palm. He smiled charmingly and placed my arm back on the bed.

I looked up into his sincere golden eyes and opened my mouth to explain to him again that I loved Ren. His expression changed. He set his face and said, "Shh. Don't say it. No words of protest tonight. I promise you, Kelsey, that I will do everything I can to reunite the two of you and try to be happy for you, but that doesn't mean I can easily set aside my feelings, okay?"

"Okay."

"Goodnight, Kells."

He pressed a kiss to my forehead, turned off the light, stepped through the connecting door, and shut it softly.

I felt better the next day, extremely grateful to have recovered from my altitude sickness. We stopped in Gyantse, which was only two hours away but was on the route, and tourists were expected to spend the day there, so we had to as well. Mr. Kadam said that he'd been there before, that it used to be a major city on the spice trade route. We stopped to see the Kumbum Chörten, which was a school of Tibetan Buddhism, and had a Szechuan-style lunch at a local restaurant. The city was beautiful, and it was nice to get out of the car and walk for a while.

We stayed in a hotel again that night, but Kishan spent most of his time as a tiger while Mr. Kadam tried to teach me how to play chess. I couldn't bend my brain around the game. After he quickly beat me a third time, I said, "Sorry, I guess I'm more of a reactionary player than a think-ahead kind of girl. One of these days, I'll teach you how to play Settlers of Catan."

Smiling, I thought about Li and his friends and Grandma Zhi. I wondered if Li ever tried to contact me. Mr. Kadam had disconnected all our phones and got us new cell phones and numbers right after we arrived in India. He said it was safer not to contact anyone back home.

Once every two weeks or so, I wrote to my foster parents and told them we were out of cell phone range. Mr. Kadam had it mailed from faraway locations so that there was no way to trace where the letters had come from. I never gave them a return address because I told them we were always moving.

They used a post office box to write me back, and Nilima picked up our mail and read the letters to me over the phone. Mr. Kadam dictated what things would be appropriate for me to include in the letters. He also had people discreetly keeping an eye on my foster family. They'd returned from their Hawaiian vacation with nice memories and nicer tans and found nothing amiss at home. Fortunately, it seemed that Lokesh hadn't found them.

On day five of the Friendship Highway tour, we stopped to see Yamdrok Lake. Its nickname was the Turquoise Lake, for obvious reasons. It sparkled like a bright jewel set against the backdrop of the snow-capped mountains that fed it.

Mr. Kadam said it was considered sacred by the Tibetan people who often made pilgrimages to the lake. They believed it was the home of protective deities who watched over the lake and made sure it didn't dry up. They believed that if it did, it would mean the end of Tibet.

Kishan and I waited patiently while Mr. Kadam engaged in an animated conversation with some local fishermen who seemed to be trying to sell him the catch of the day.

When we got back in the car, I asked, "Mr. Kadam, exactly how many languages do you know, anyway?"

"Hmm. I'm not really sure. I know the main ones needed for trade with Europe—Spanish, French, Portuguese, English, and German. I can converse well in most of the languages of Asia. I'm a bit weak on the languages of Russia and the Norse, know nothing of the islands or Africa, and I only know about half of the languages of India."

Puzzled, I asked, "Half? Just how many languages are there in India?"

"There are literally hundreds of languages in India, both modern and classic. Though only around thirty are officially recognized by the Indian government."

I stared at him in amazement.

"Of course, I only know a smattering of most of those. Many are local dialects that I picked up over the years. The most commonly used language is Hindi."

We wound our way through two more mountain passes and finally began our descent toward the Tibetan plateau. Mr. Kadam talked in order to keep my mind busy during the drive down the mountain as I was feeling a bit carsick.

"The Tibetan Plateau is sometimes called the Roof of the World due to its high elevation. It averages around 4,500 meters, or roughly," he worked out some calculations in his mind, "14,750 feet. It's the third least populated place in the world, Antarctica being first and Northern Greenland being second. It's home to several large brackish water lakes."

I groaned and closed my eyes, but that didn't help.

I tried to focus on something else and asked, "Mr. Kadam, what's a brackish lake?"

"Ah, there are four classifications of salinity in bodies of water—fresh; brackish, or brack; saline, or salt; and brine. A brackish lake, for example, the Caspian Sea, is somewhere between saltwater and freshwater. Most brackish water is found in estuaries where a saltwater ocean meets a freshwater river or stream."

Kishan growled softly, and Mr. Kadam stopped his lecture. "Look, Miss Kelsey. We're almost at the bottom."

He was right, and after a few minutes on a normal, flat, only *somewhat* bumpy road, I felt much better. We drove another couple of hours to the city of Lhasa.

15

yin/yang

Mr. Kadam had managed to secure a meeting with the Dalai Lama's Tibetan office since a personal meeting was not possible. Mr. Kadam attempted to keep the reason for the visit vague so as not to reveal more details than were necessary with the staff. It wasn't ideal, but it would have to do. Our appointment was set for Monday, which gave us three days to cool our heels.

To pass the time, Mr. Kadam took us on a whirlwind tour of Tibet. We saw the Rongphu Monastery, the Potala Palace, the Jokhang Temple, the Sera and Drepung monasteries, and also shopped at the Barkhor market.

I enjoyed seeing the tourist attractions and being with Kishan and Mr. Kadam, but underneath, I still felt an undercurrent of sorrow. The dull ache of loneliness swept over me in the evenings. I still dreamed of Ren every night. Although I trusted Durga to keep her promise and watch over him for me, I really wanted to be with him myself.

Mr. Kadam took us out of the city limits on Saturday to practice using our new weapons. He started with Kishan and the discus. The discus was heavy for Mr. Kadam, just like the *gada* had been, but seemed light to both me and Kishan.

When Mr. Kadam turned his attention to me, I was ready. He taught me how to string the bow first.

"The force you use to pull back the string is what determines the power of the bow. It's called the draw weight."

He tried to string my bow and found he couldn't. Kishan was able to string it easily. Mr. Kadam stared at the bow for a minute and had Kishan take over teaching me.

I asked him, "Why are the arrows so small?"

Kishan replied, "Arrow length is determined by the size of the archer. It's called a draw length, and yours is pretty small, so these arrows should fit you perfectly. The length of the bow is also determined by your height. An archer doesn't want a bow that's unwieldy."

I nodded.

Kishan continued his explanation of the various workings of the bow and arrow, including the string notch, the arrow shelf where the arrow rests and is pulled back, and the bowstring. Then it was time to try it out.

"Take your shooting stance by placing your non-dominant foot about five to ten inches ahead," Kishan said. "Keep your legs shoulder width apart."

I followed his instructions. Though it was more difficult for me than for Kishan, I managed to get the job done.

"Good. Nock your arrow and rest it on your thumb with the single fletching pointing out. Hold the bowstring with your first three fingers and tuck the arrow between your first and middle finger.

"Now lock your bow arm and look at your target. Draw back until your thumb touches your ear and your fingertip touches the corner of your mouth. Then release your arrow."

He demonstrated the entire process for me a few times and sunk two arrows into a distant tree. I copied his moves. When I got to the drawing part, my hand shook a little. He stood behind me and guided my hand as I drew back.

When I was in the right position, he said, "Okay, you're ready. Now aim and shoot."

I let go and felt a snap as the bow shot my arrow off with a twang. The arrow sunk into the soft dirt at the foot of the tree.

Mr. Kadam exclaimed, "That was very good! A wonderful first attempt, Miss Kelsey!"

Kishan made me practice again and again. I quickly built up enough skill to hit the tree trunk like Kishan, although not in the exact center. Mr. Kadam was amazed at my progress. He thought it was probably thanks to all my training with the lightning power. We quickly noticed that the arrows never ran out and that they also eventually disappeared from the target.

That will surely come in handy.

Kishan was working on his discus again when I took a break. I sipped some bottled water while watching Kishan practice.

Nodding toward Kishan, I asked Mr. Kadam, "So how's he doing with the discus thing?"

Mr. Kadam laughed. "Technically, Miss Kelsey, it's not a discus. A discus is used in the Olympics. What Kishan is holding is called a *chakram*. It's shaped like a discus, but if you look carefully, the outer edge is razor sharp. It's a throwing weapon. In fact, it's the weapon of choice for the Indian god Vishnu. It's a very valuable weapon when wielded by someone with skill, and Kishan, fortunately, has been trained in its use, though he hasn't practiced in a long time."

Kishan's weapon was made of gold with diamonds embedded in the metal, similar to the *gada*. It had a curved leather handgrip like a yin-yang symbol. The metal edge was about two inches wide and razor sharp. I watched as he practiced, and he never caught it on the razor edge. He either caught it on the handgrip or on the inside of the circle.

"Do they normally return like that? Like a boomerang?"

"No. They don't, Miss Kelsey." Mr. Kadam stroked his beard thoughtfully. "Watch. Do you see? Even if he targets a tree it makes a good jagged slash in the trunk and then spins back to him. I have never seen that before. Normally it can be wielded like a blade in close combat or it can be thrown over a distance to disable an enemy, but it will remain embedded in the target until it's retrieved."

"It looks like it slows down when it approaches him too."

We watched him throw a few more times. "Yes, I believe you are correct. It slows on approach to make it easier for him to catch it. Quite a weapon."

Later that evening, when we returned to our hotel, Kishan placed a board game on the table after dinner. I laughed.

"You got Parcheesi?"

Kishan smiled. "Not exactly. This is called Pachisi, but you play it the same."

We took out the pieces and set up the board. When Mr. Kadam saw the game, he clapped his hands together as his eyes twinkled with a competitive gleam.

"Ah, Kishan, my favorite game. Do you remember when we played with your parents?"

"How could I forget? You beat Father, which he handled fine, but when you beat Mother at the last roll of the dice, I thought she'd have you beheaded."

Mr. Kadam stroked his beard. "Yes. Indeed. She was rather put out."

"Do you mean you guys played this game way back when?"

Kishan chuckled. "Not like this exactly. We played the live version.

Instead of pawns we used people. We constructed a giant game board and set up a home base that everyone had to get to. It was fun. The players would wear our color. Father preferred blue and Mother, green. I think you were red that day, Kadam, and I was yellow."

"Where was Ren?"

Kishan picked up a piece and twirled it thoughtfully. "He was off on a diplomatic trip at that time, so Kadam subbed for him."

Mr. Kadam cleared his throat, "*A-hem*, yes. If the two of you don't mind, I would prefer to be red again, as the color brought me luck last time I played."

Kishan spun the board so the red color was in front of Mr. Kadam. I picked yellow; Kishan, blue. We played for an hour. I'd never seen Kishan so animated. He almost seemed like a young boy again, with all the cares of the world lifted off his shoulders. I could easily envision this proud, handsome, taciturn man as a happy, carefree boy who grew up to stand in the shadow of his older brother, loving and admiring him, but at the same time feeling that he was somehow less important. Somehow less deserving. By the end of the game, Kishan and I had left Mr. Kadam in the dust. There was only one pawn left for each of us, and mine was closer to home.

On the last roll, Kishan could have knocked me out to win the game. He stared at the board for a moment studying it carefully.

Mr. Kadam's steepled fingers were tapping his upper lip, which was turned up in a small smile. Kishan's golden eyes met mine briefly before he picked up his pawn and skipped over mine, moving into a safety zone.

"Kishan, what are you doing? You could have gotten me out and won the game! Didn't you see that?"

He sat back in his chair and shrugged. "Huh, I must've missed that. Your turn, Kelsey."

I muttered, "It's totally impossible that you missed that. Okay. Then too bad for *you*." I rolled a twelve and made it all the way home. "Ha! I beat the two infamous live-version players!"

Mr. Kadam laughed. "Indeed you did, Miss Kelsey. Goodnight."

"Goodnight, Mr. Kadam."

Kishan helped me clean up the game.

I said, "Okay, so 'fess up. Why'd you throw the game? You're not a good bluffer, you know. I could read your expression. You saw the move and deliberately skipped over me. What happened to doing whatever it takes to win?"

"I still do whatever it takes to win. Perhaps by losing the game, I won something better."

I laughed. "Won something better? What do you think you won?"

He pushed the game to the side of the table and stretched his hand across to hold mine. "What I won was seeing you happy, happy like you *were*. I want to see your smile come back. You smile and laugh, but it never reaches your eyes. I haven't seen you *really* happy these last few months."

I squeezed his hand. "It's hard. But, if Kishan, the ultimate competitor, is willing to throw a game, then, for you, I'll try."

"Good." He let go of my hand reluctantly and stood up to stretch.

I set the game on the shelf and said, "Kishan, I keep having nightmares about Ren. I think Lokesh is torturing him."

"I've been dreaming of Ren as well. I've dreamed that he begs me to keep you safe." He grinned. "He also threatens me to keep my hands to myself."

"He'd definitely be saying that. Do you think it's a dream or a true vision?"

He shook his head. "I don't know."

I pressed my hands on top of the game. "Every time I try to save

him or help him escape, he pushes me away as if I'm the one in danger. It feels real, but how do we know?"

Kishan wrapped his arms around me from behind and hugged me. "I'm not sure, but I do feel he's still alive."

"I feel the same." He turned to leave. "Kishan?"

"Yes?"

I grinned. "Thanks for letting me win. *And* for keeping your hands to yourself. *Mostly.*"

"Ah, but you forget, this is just one battle. The war is far from over, and you will find that I make a formidable opponent. In *any* arena."

"Fine," I offered. "Then it's a rematch. Tomorrow."

He bowed slightly. "I look forward to the challenge, *bilauta*. Goodnight."

"Goodnight, Kishan."

The next day at breakfast, I picked Mr. Kadam's brain about the Dalai Lama, Buddhism, karma, and reincarnation. Kishan quietly listened while curled up at my feet as the black tiger.

"You see, Miss Kelsey, karma is the belief that everything you do, everything you say, every choice that you make, affects your present or your future. Those who believe in reincarnation live with the hope that if they make good choices and sacrifices in life *now*, they will have a brighter future or a better position in the next life.

"Dharma is about maintaining order in the universe and following the rules that govern all mankind in civil and religious customs."

"So if you follow your dharma, you'll have good karma?"

Mr. Kadam laughed. "I suppose that is an accurate statement. Moksha is the state of nirvana. When you have passed the tests the mortal world offers and you rise above it to a state of higher consciousness, you reach enlightenment or moksha. For this person, there is no rebirth. You become a spiritual being, and the temporal worldly things are no longer of import. The passions of the flesh become meaningless. You become one with the eternal."

"You're kind of an eternal being *now*. Have you experienced moksha? Do you think it's possible to attain it while you're alive?"

"That's an interesting question." He sat back in his chair and thought for a moment. "I would have to say that, despite my many years on this planet, no. I have *not* experienced total spiritual enlightenment; however, I have not truly sought after it either. My relationship with the divine is perhaps still a quest I have yet to take. That is not one I wish to tackle at this very moment though. Instead, how about a walk to the marketplace?"

I nodded, eager to see something new and focus on the more immediate quest at hand. The market was full of interesting products. We passed stands selling statues of Buddha, incense, jewelry, clothing, books, postcards, and *malas*—similar in purpose to Catholic prayer beads. Other interesting items we saw for sale were singing bowls and bells—which were used to produce sounds that helped focus energies and were also used in certain religious ceremonies and during meditation. I saw prayer flags and woven or painted *thangkas*. Mr. Kadam said the banners taught myths, showed important historical events, or depicted the life of Buddha.

At the appointed time, Kishan, Mr. Kadam, and I were ushered into the business office of the Dalai Lama. It was a testament to Mr. Kadam's resources that we'd even gotten this far since usually only dignitaries made it into this office. We were met by an austere man dressed in a typical business suit who indicated that he would do an initial screening and that if our case proved urgent enough, he would refer us to an upper office.

He invited us to sit, and I was content to let Mr. Kadam wade through the interview. The man asked several questions about our purpose. Mr. Kadam again answered vaguely, hinting that the answers to his questions were not meant for just anyone's ears. The man was intrigued and pressed harder for answers. Mr. Kadam's reply was that the information we needed to share must be heard only by the Ocean Teacher.

At those words, I noticed a slight shift in the man's eyes. The interview ended, and we were led into another room where we were met by a woman who continued the same line of questioning. Mr. Kadam kept to the same answers as before. He responded politely without giving away too much information.

"We are pilgrims seeking an audience on a matter of great import to the people of India."

She waved her hand. "Please explain. What exactly is of great import?"

He smiled and leaned forward. "We are on a quest that has led us to the great country of Tibet. Only within its borders can we find what we are seeking."

"Are you seeking riches? For you won't find any here. We are a humble people and have nothing of worth."

"Money? Treasure? These are not our purpose. We have come to seek the knowledge that only the Ocean Teacher possesses."

Again, when Mr. Kadam mentioned the Ocean Teacher our interviewer abruptly paused. She stood and asked us to wait. Half an hour later, we were guided into an inner sanctum. The accommodations were more humble than the last two rooms. We sat upon old, wobbly wooden chairs. A reticent monk dressed in red robes entered. He looked down on us from his beaked nose for a long moment and then took a seat.

"I understand you wish to speak with the Ocean Teacher."

Mr. Kadam bowed his head in silent acknowledgement.

"You have not shared your reasons with the others. Would you share them with me?"

Mr. Kadam spoke, "The words I would give you would be the same words I gave to the others."

The monk nodded brusquely. "I see. Then I am sorry, but the Ocean Teacher has no time to meet with you, especially as you have been unforthcoming as to your purpose. If the matter you wish to discuss is deemed important enough, your message will be conveyed."

I spoke up, "But it's very important that we speak with him. We would share our reasons, but it's a matter of trusting the right people."

The monk looked thoughtfully at each of us. "Perhaps you would answer one last question."

Mr. Kadam nodded.

The monk pulled a medallion from around his neck, handed it to Mr. Kadam, and said, "Tell me, what do you see?"

Mr. Kadam replied, "I see a design similar in nature to the yin-yang symbol. The yin or dark side represents the female and the yang, which is the light side, represents the male. These two sides are in perfect balance and harmony with one another."

The monk nodded as if he expected that answer and stretched out a hand. His expression was closed. I knew he was going to dismiss us.

I hurried to interject, "May we look at the medallion?"

His hand arrested in midair before handing the medallion to Kishan.

Kishan turned the medallion back and forth for a moment and whispered, "I see two tigers, one black and one white, each chasing the other's tail."

The monk pressed his hands on the desk as I took the medallion and nodded with interest. I quickly glanced at Mr. Kadam, and then at the monk, who was now leaning forward waiting for me to speak.

The medallion *was* similar to a yin-yang symbol, but a line divided the medallion in half. The outline of white and black could be identified as cats, so I could easily see why Kishan had said they were tigers, each with a strategically placed dot for an eye. The tails curled around the center and twisted together around the bisecting line.

I looked up at the monk. "I see part of a *thangka*. A long, central thread, which is female, serves as the warp and the white and black tigers are both male and wrap around her. They are the weft which complete the fabric."

The monk inched closer. "And how is this *thangka* woven?"

"With a divine shuttle."

"What does this *thangka* represent?"

"The *thangka* is the whole world. The fabric is the *story* of the world."

He sat back in his chair and ran a hand over his bald head. I handed him back the medallion. He took it, looked at it thoughtfully for a moment, and then placed it around his neck. He rose.

"Will you excuse me for a moment?"

Mr. Kadam nodded. "Of course."

We didn't wait long. The young woman who had interviewed us earlier instructed us to follow her. We did and were given accommodations in a comfortable suite of rooms. Our bags were packed at the hotel and brought to us.

We took an early dinner together after which Mr. Kadam and Kishan retired to their rooms. Having nothing better to do, I went to mine also. The monks brought me some orange blossom tea. It was an effective soporific, and I soon drifted off to sleep, but I dreamed fitfully of Ren again. In my dream, he was becoming desperate.

This time Ren was even more fiercely protective of me and demanded that I leave him immediately. He kept saying that Lokesh was getting closer, and he needed me to be as far away from him as possible. The dreams felt real, and I woke up crying. There was nothing I could do. I tried to comfort myself with Durga's promise to watch over him.

Kishan joined me at the breakfast buffet the next morning. I was already at the end of the line spooning some yogurt into a bowl when Mr. Kadam entered, stepped behind me, and asked me how I slept.

I fibbed and said I slept well, but he studied the dark circles under my eyes and patted my hand knowingly. Guiltily, I turned away from Mr. Kadam's perusal and waited for the monk in front of me as he finished putting fruit onto his plate.

The monk's hand shook as he lifted a small piece of slippery mango from the bowl. He dropped it onto his plate with a splat and began the slow process of digging for another piece. Without looking at us, the old monk spoke, "I understand you wish to visit with me."

Mr. Kadam immediately clasped his hands together, bowed, and said, "*Namaste*, wise one."

My hand froze in midair—yogurt spoon and all—and I slowly turned to look into the smiling face of the Ocean Teacher.

16

the ocean teacher

The old monk grinned at me while I stared open-mouthed. Fortunately, Mr. Kadam came to my rescue and gently guided me to a table.

Kishan was already eating, not caring that I had caused a scene. *Figures. The tigers only think of two things—food and girls. Usually in that order.*

Mr. Kadam set my bowl down and pulled out a chair for me. I sat and stirred my yogurt while surreptitiously glancing at the wizened old man. He was happily humming as he continued to fill his plate one small item at a time. When he was finished, he sat down across from me and smiled as he dug into his eggs.

Mr. Kadam ate quietly. Kishan returned to the buffet and filled his plate again. I kept silent and sipped my juice. I was too nervous to eat and had no idea if it was proper to talk or ask questions, so I just followed Mr. Kadam's lead.

Long finished with our meal, we watched the Ocean Teacher eat, as he slowly took one bite at a time and chewed methodically. Finally finished, he carefully wiped his mouth and said, "You know, my favorite memories of my mother are winding the threads for her weaving, assisting her in tending the sheep, and helping her stir the breakfast porridge. I always think of my mother when I eat breakfast."

Mr. Kadam sagely nodded. Kishan grunted. The Ocean Teacher looked at me and grinned.

Hoping it was okay to speak, I asked, "Did you grow up on a farm then? I thought Lamas were born to be Lamas."

He cocked his head at me and happily answered, "Yes, is the answer to both questions. My parents were poor farmers who grew enough food to sustain themselves and sell a bit at market. My mother was a weaver who could make beautiful cloth. My parents named me Jigme Karpo. They didn't know who I was at the time. I had to be found."

"You had to be found? Found by whom?"

"The regent is always searching for reincarnations of former Lamas. He usually has a vision showing him where to find the new incarnation of a certain person and sends out a search party. In my case, they knew to look for a farmhouse resting on a hill with a tall, climbing rosebush growing next to our water well.

"After asking around, they found my home and knew it was the right place. Items from previous Lamas were brought in and shown to me. I picked up a book that belonged to the previous Ocean Teacher. The search party felt confident then that I was the reincarnation of that past Lama. At that time, I was two years old."

"What happened to you then?"

Mr. Kadam interrupted and patted my hand, "I am curious as well, Miss Kelsey, but perhaps he has only a short time to spend with us, and we should focus on other matters."

"Right, sorry. I let my curiosity carry me away."

The Ocean Teacher leaned forward and thanked the monks who cleared the table. "I can spare a few minutes to answer your question, young lady. To sum it up, I was taken from my family and began my training with a kind old monk. My mother wove the material for my first maroon robe.

"I began training as a novice monk and had my head shaved. My name was changed, and I received a wonderful education in all subjects including art, medicine, culture, and philosophy. All of these experiences fashioned me into the man sitting before you. Did that answer your question, or did my explanation generate several more questions?"

I laughed. "It generated several more."

"Good!" He smiled. "A mind with questions is a mind open to understanding."

"Your childhood and background are so different from mine."

"I imagine yours is just as interesting."

"What do you do here?"

"I train the Dalai Lamas."

I stared at him. "You teach the teacher?"

He laughed. "Yes. I've trained a couple of them. I'm a very old man, but we are not so dissimilar. I've had the opportunity to meet people from all over the world, and I find that all people are fundamentally alike. We are one human family. Perhaps we have different clothes, our skin is of a different color, or we speak various languages, but that is on the surface only. We all have dreams and seek for the things that will bring true happiness. To know all the world, I just need to learn about myself."

I nodded.

Mr. Kadam interjected, "As you are aware, we have come to seek the wisdom of the Ocean Teacher. We have a task to perform, and we ask for your guidance."

The monk pushed back the sleeves of his robe and stood. "Then come. Let us adjourn to a different room that offers more privacy." He stood up carefully with the support of two monks who quickly maneuvered to walk beside him, but the Ocean Teacher, though slow, walked without assistance.

"You said you taught two of the Dalai Lamas, so that means you must be—"

"One hundred and fifteen."

"What?" I gasped.

"I am one hundred and fifteen years old and proud of it."

"I have never met someone who lived that long." I quickly realized that I indeed knew three men who had lived that long and looked at Mr. Kadam who smiled and winked at me.

The Ocean Teacher didn't notice my strange expression as he went on, "If a man wishes to do a thing and has enough passion to find a way . . . he will achieve it. I wished to live a long life."

Mr. Kadam stared thoughtfully at the monk for a moment, and said, "I am older than I seem as well. I am humbled by you, sir."

The Ocean Teacher turned and clasped Mr. Kadam's hand. His eyes twinkled with mirth. "It's being around monks and monasteries that does that. It keeps me humble too."

The two men laughed. We followed him through winding gray corridors to a large room with a smooth stone floor and a large polished desk. He indicated we should sit as we passed a comfortable lounging area. We all sank into soft upholstered chairs as the Ocean Teacher pulled up a plain wooden chair that had been hidden behind his desk and sat to talk with us.

When I asked if he would prefer a more comfortable chair, he replied, "The more uncomfortable my chair is, the more likely I will get up and keep busy doing things that need doing."

Mr. Kadam nodded and began, "Thank you for agreeing to meet with us."

The monk grinned. "I wouldn't have missed this for the world." He leaned forward conspiratorially. "I must admit, I've been curious to know if the tiger's quest would happen in this lifetime. Now that I think of it, I was born near the city of Taktser, which, translated, means 'roaring tiger.' Perhaps it was my destiny all along to be the one to meet those who are to journey on this quest."

Mr. Kadam asked excitedly, "You know of our quest?"

"Yes. From before the time of the first Dalai Lama, the story of two tigers has been handed down in secret. The strange medallion is the key. When this young man said that he saw two tigers, one black and one white, we knew you were likely the right ones. Others have seen the cats and often identify the white tiger, but no one has identified the black cat as a tiger, and certainly no one has spoken of the line down the middle being linked to the divine weaver. That's how we knew it was you."

I ventured, "So you can help us then?"

"Oh, most definitely, but first, I have one request of you."

Mr. Kadam smiled magnanimously. "Of course, what may we do for you?"

"Can you tell me about the tigers? I know of the place you seek and how to advise you, but . . . the tigers were never explained, and their place in the quest was held in deepest secret. Is this something you know of?"

Kishan, Mr. Kadam, and I looked at each other for a moment. Kishan raised an eyebrow when Mr. Kadam slightly nodded.

Mr. Kadam asked, "Is this room secure?"

"Yes, of course."

Mr. Kadam and I both turned to Kishan. He shrugged his brawny shoulders, stood up, and morphed into his tiger form. The black tiger blinked his golden eyes at the monk and growled softly then sat on the floor beside me. I leaned over to scratch his sooty ears.

The Ocean Teacher sat back in the chair with surprise. Then he rubbed his bald head and laughed with glee. "Thank you for trusting me with this amazing gift!"

Kishan changed back into a man and sat down in the chair again. "I wouldn't exactly call it a gift."

"Ah, and what would you call it?"

"I'd call it a tragedy."

"There is a saying in Tibet, 'Tragedy should be utilized as a source of strength.'" The monk sat back in his chair and touched a finger to his temple. "Instead of wondering *why* this has happened, perhaps you should consider why this has happened to *you*. Remember that *not* getting what you want is sometimes a wonderful stroke of luck."

He turned his attention hopefully to me. "And what of the white tiger?"

I spoke, "The white tiger is Kishan's brother, Ren, who has been captured by an enemy."

He tilted his head, considering, "One's enemy is often the best teacher of tolerance. And what of you, my dear? How do you fit into this quest?"

I raised my hand, turned, and let the power bubble up inside me. It flowed through my hand, and I aimed for the flower sitting in a vase on his desk. My hand sparkled, and a pinpoint of white light surged toward the flower. The bloom glowed for just a moment before disappearing in a soft puff of ash that lightly rained down upon the wooden desk.

"I am the central line of the tiger medallion, the warp. My role is to help free the two tigers." I indicated the quiet man on my right. "And Mr. Kadam is our guide and mentor."

The Ocean Teacher did not seem shocked by my power. Happy as a little boy on Christmas morning, he clapped his hands together. "Good! Wonderful! Now, let me help you with what I can."

He rose, took the tiger medallion from around his neck, where it had laid hidden in his voluminous robe and pushed it into a slot near his bookshelf. A narrow cupboard opened, from which he took out an ancient scroll preserved in glass and a vial filled with a green, oily substance.

He indicated we should step closer. As we circled his desk, he carefully turned the glass containing the ancient scroll to display what was inside.

"This scroll has existed for centuries and lists the signs associated with the tiger medallion and those who come to claim it. Tell me, what do you know of your quest already?"

Mr. Kadam showed him the translation of the prophecy.

"Ah, yes. The beginning of this scroll contains more of the same with only a few differences. Your prophecy says I am to do three things for you, and these I will do. I am to unfold the scrolls of wisdom, anoint your eyes, and lead you to the spirit gates. This ancient document you see before you is the scroll that is said to hold the wisdom of the world."

I asked, "What does that mean?"

"Legend, myth, stories of mankind's origin—all of these are based on eternal truths, and some of those truths are contained here. At least that's what I've been told."

"Haven't you read it?"

"No, not at all. In my philosophy, it is unnecessary to know all truths. Part of the process of enlightenment is to discover truth for yourself through self-introspection. None of the former Dalai Lamas have read these scrolls either. They were not meant for us. They were held in safekeeping to be given to you when the time is right."

Mr. Kadam asked, "If the scroll was handed down and held in secret by the Dalai Lamas, then how was it passed to you?"

"The scrolls and the secret must be held by two men. The Dalai Lama doesn't know who the next Dalai Lama will be, so he entrusts his teacher. When his teacher dies, he entrusts that teacher's reincarnation. When the Dalai Lama dies, the teacher shares the secret with the next Dalai Lama so that the scroll is never lost. With the current Dalai Lama in exile, the duty falls to me."

I said, "Do you mean to say that these scrolls have been held for centuries for . . . *us*?"

"Yes. We have passed down the secret as well as the instructions detailing how we would find the ones to give this to."

Mr. Kadam bent to examine the scroll in the glass. "Amazing! I yearn to examine this."

"You must not. I was told the scroll was not to be read until the fifth sacrifice was complete. It's even been suggested that to open it early would cause a catastrophe of the gravest kind."

I muttered, "The fifth sacrifice? But, Mr. Kadam, we still don't even know what that will be." I turned to the Ocean Teacher. "All we know of so far are the four sacrifices and the four gifts. We won't know the fifth until much later. Are you sure we can be successful in our quest without reading the scroll?"

The monk shrugged. "It is not for me to know. My duty is to place this in your care and fulfill my other two obligations. Come. Sit here, young lady, and let me anoint your eyes."

He pulled a chair over for me, approached me with the green vial, and addressed us, "Tell me, Mr. Kadam, in your studies, have you come across a people called the Chewong?"

Mr. Kadam took a seat. "I confess . . . no, I have not."

I sniggered softly. *That's an amazing fact in and of itself. Mr. Kadam not knowing something? Is it even possible?*

"The Chewong are from Malaysia . . . fascinating people. There is tremendous pressure on them now to convert to Islam and mainstream into Malaysian society; however, there are several who fight for their rights to keep their language and culture. They are a peaceful people, nonviolent. In fact, they have no words for warfare, corruption, conflict, or punishment in their language. They have many interesting beliefs. One noteworthy ideal relates to communal property. They feel it's dangerous and wrong to eat alone, so they always share their meals with one another. But, the belief that applies to you concerns the eyes."

I licked my lips nervously. "Umm, what exactly do they do to the eyes? Serve them for supper?"

He laughed. "No, nothing like that. They say their shamans or religious leaders have *cool eyes* while the average person is considered to have *hot eyes*. A person with cool eyes can see different worlds and can discern things that may be hidden from ordinary view."

Mr. Kadam was intrigued and began asking many questions while my eyes darted to the green, oily liquid that the monk was dripping onto his dry, papery fingers.

"Uh, I have to warn you that I have an eye phobia. My parents had to hold me down to get drops in my eye when I had pinkeye as a child."

"Not to worry," the Ocean Teacher said. "I will anoint your closed eyelids and share a few words of wisdom with you."

I relaxed considerably and obediently closed my eyes. I felt his warm fingers stroke across my closed lids. I expected the gooey stuff to drip down my cheeks, but it was thicker, more like a lotion, and smelled sharp and medicinal. The smell tickled my nose and reminded me of the menthol rub my mother used to put on my chest to help me breathe easier when I was sick. My eyelids tingled and turned icy cold. I kept them closed while he spoke softly.

"My advice for you, young one, is to tell you that the very purpose of life is to be happy. In my own limited experience, I have found that, as we care for others, the greater is our own sense of well-being. It puts the mind at ease. It helps remove whatever fears or insecurities we may have and gives us the strength to cope with any obstacles we encounter. Also, when you need guidance, meditate. I have often found answers through meditation. Lastly, remember the old saying that 'love conquers all' is true. As you give love, you will find it returns to you magnified."

I carefully cracked open my eyes. I felt no pain or discomfort, but they were slightly sensitive. Now it was Kishan's turn. We switched places, and the monk dipped his fingertips once more. Kishan closed his eyes, and the substance was swiped across his closed eyelids.

"Now for you, black tiger. You are young of body but old of soul. Remember, no matter what sort of difficulties you must endure and no matter how painful your experiences, you must not lose hope. Losing faith is the only thing that can truly destroy you. The lamas say, 'To conquer yourself and your weaknesses are a greater triumph than to conquer thousands in battle.'

"You have a responsibility to help lead your family in the right direction. This includes your immediate family as well as your global family. Good intentions are not sufficient to create a positive outcome; you must act. As you take part and become actively engaged, answers to your questions will appear. Lastly, like a great rock is not disturbed by the buffetings of the wind, the mind of a judicious man is steady. He exists as a stanchion, a stalwart support. Others can cling to him, for he will not falter."

The Ocean Teacher put the stopper back in the vial, and Kishan blinked his eyes open. The green substance had disappeared from his lids. He sat next to me and stretched out his hand to touch my arm. The man who was the Ocean Teacher, a great lama of Tibet, held out his hand to shake Mr. Kadam's.

He said, "My friend. I sense that your eyes have already been opened, and you have seen more things that I can imagine. I leave this scroll in your hands and ask that you come to visit with me from time to time. I would like to know how this journey ends."

Mr. Kadam bowed gallantly. "I would consider it a great honor, wise one."

"Good. Now only one thing remains on my agenda, and that is to guide you to the spirit gate." He explained, "Spirit gates mark the boundary between the physical world and the spirit world. As you pass through them, you cleanse yourself of weighty earthy matters and focus on the spiritual. Do not touch the gate until you are ready to enter, for that is forbidden. The known gates are in China and Japan, but there is one in Tibet which has been kept secret. I will show you on the map."

He rang for a fellow monk to bring in a map of Tibet.

"The gate you seek is a simple, humble one. You must travel there on foot and take only basic provisions, for to find the gate you must prove that you walk by faith. The gate is marked with the simple prayer flags of the nomads. The journey will not be easy, and only the two of you may access the gate. Your mentor will have to stay behind."

He showed us a path where we could begin the ascent. I gulped as I recognized the location despite my inability to decipher the language. *Mount Everest*. Fortunately, it seemed that the spirit gate was not located at its peak, but it was, in fact, only a short distance past the snow line. Mr. Kadam and the Ocean Teacher spoke animatedly about the best route to take while Kishan listened intently.

How could I possibly do this? I have to. Ren needs me. Finding this new place and object was what would help me find Ren, and nothing would keep me from doing that, not even altitude sickness or a freezing cold mountain.

The scroll was given to Mr. Kadam as well as the maps and a detailed explanation, including directions, to the spirit gate. Kishan's warm hand picked up mine.

"Kelsey, are you alright?"

"Yes. I'm just a little scared about the trip."

"Me too. But, remember, he said it requires faith."

"Do you have faith?"

Kishan considered, "Yes. I think I do. More than I did anyway. What about you?"

"I have *hope*. Is that good enough?"

"I think it is."

The Ocean Teacher shook our hands warmly, winked, and excused himself. He left flanked by his escorts. A monk led us to our room, so we could gather our belongings.

Mr. Kadam spent the rest of the day preparing for our trip. Kishan and I packed lightly, remembering the warning to take little with us. Mr. Kadam determined that we would bring no food or water, knowing that the Golden Fruit would sustain us. He told me that he had tested the limitations of the Fruit and said that it seemed to work from as far away as one hundred feet and though it could not produce water, it could make a variety of other beverages. He recommended hot herbal teas and sugar-free drinks to stay hydrated. I thanked him and wrapped it carefully in my quilt before placing the bundle in my backpack.

We debated the merits of a tent for a long time and decided on a large sleeping bag instead. They didn't feel I could carry a tent up the mountain, and I needed room in my backpack for Kishan's clothing, Fanindra, and all the weapons. Kishan would have to change to tiger form and back, so he would need the warm clothes.

The next day, we drove to the base of the mountain. After arriving, Mr. Kadam walked with us for a while and then hugged us both briefly. He told us that he would set up a camp at the base and would eagerly wait for our return.

"Be very careful, Miss Kelsey. The journey will no doubt be difficult. I've put all my notes in your bag. I hope that I've remembered everything."

"I'm sure you did. We'll be okay. Don't worry. Hopefully, we'll be back before you know it. Maybe time will stop like it did in Kishkindha. Take care of yourself. And if for some reason we don't come back, will you tell Ren—"

"You *will* come back, Miss Kelsey. Of that I am certain. Go off now, and I will see you soon."

Kishan changed into a black tiger, and we started up the mountain. Half an hour later, I turned to see how far we'd come. The Tibetan plain swept out before us as far as the eye could see. I waved at Mr. Kadam's small figure far below, then turned, climbed between two rocks, and set my feet on the path ahead.

17
spirit gate

I shivered and yanked my Gore-Tex gloves a little higher on my wrists. We'd hiked up the mountain most of the first day and set up camp near some rocks that blocked the wind. When we stopped, I gratefully shrugged off my backpack and stretched.

I searched the area for a while, gathering wood to start a fire. After a hot dinner, thanks to the Golden Fruit, I snuggled deep in my king-sized sleeping bag fully clothed.

Kishan nudged his head into the opening and crawled in after me. It was awkward at first, but after an hour I felt extremely grateful for the warm fur that stopped my shivering. I was so exhausted that, despite the noise of the wind, I was able to sleep.

The next morning, I used the Golden Fruit to wish up warm oatmeal with maple syrup and brown sugar and some steaming hot chocolate for breakfast. Kishan wanted to stay in tiger form to keep warm, so I gave him the option of a large platter full of rare venison steaks or a giant dish of the same oatmeal I ate and a large bowl of milk. He started with the meat but finished off the oatmeal and milk too, lapping it up quickly. I rolled up our belongings and stowed them in the bag before we set off on our journey again.

We settled into a routine for the next four days. Kishan led the way, I supplied meals via the Golden Fruit and built the fires, and then we slept snuggled together, tiger and human, in the large sleeping bag at night while the wind howled around us. The upward climb was challenging. If I hadn't been working out with Kishan and Mr. Kadam, I wouldn't have been prepared for it.

The ascent wasn't bad enough that I would need climbing gear, but it was no stroll through the park either. Breathing was harder the higher we went because there was less oxygen, so we stopped frequently to drink and rested often.

We hit the snow line on the fifth day. Even in the summer, there was snow on Mount Everest. Kishan was easy to see now, even from a distance. A black animal on the white snow drifts did not go undetected. He was lucky he was probably one of the biggest animals out here. If he were smaller, we'd be hunted by predators.

I wonder if polar bears live here? No, polar bears live at the poles. Hmm, maybe there are other bears out here, or possibly mountain lions. Sasquatch? The Yeti? What was the snow monster in Rudolph the Red-Nosed Reindeer *called? Ah, the Bumble.* I giggled as I imagined a puppet-like Kishan attacking the Bumble and hummed the "Misfit" song from the movie.

I followed Kishan's tiger tracks and started keeping an eye out for animal footprints. When I spied small animal tracks in the snow, I tried to figure out what they could be. Some were obviously birds, but others I thought might be rabbits or small rodents. Not seeing anything bigger and becoming bored with my game, I relaxed and let my mind drift as I followed Kishan.

The trees were becoming sparse and the terrain rocky. The snow drifts were deep, and it became increasingly difficult to breathe. I started to get nervous. I didn't really think it would take us this long to find the spirit gate.

Day seven was when we ran into the bear.

Kishan had taken off about a half hour before to search for wood and a likely place for us to camp. I was to follow his tracks and he'd circle back and sniff me out. He was actually due back soon as he never left me for longer than thirty minutes at a time.

I was trudging slowly along, stepping in his tiger prints, when I heard a rumbling bellow behind me. I figured Kishan had circled around and was trying to get my attention. I turned and stopped in my tracks, gasping in horror. A large brown bear was galloping toward me in attack mode. Its round ears were laid back against its head. Its mouth hung open revealing sharp teeth, and it was coming at me fast. It ran faster than I could.

I screamed.

The bear came to a stop five feet away, stood on its hind legs, and bawled at me again, swiping the air with its paws. Its shaggy fur was wet with snow. Tiny black eyes watched me over a long snout as it assessed my ability to fight back. The skin around the mouth pulled back as its jaw quivered, baring an impressive display of teeth that could rip me to shreds.

I quickly dropped to the ground remembering a story about mountain men surviving in the wilderness. I'd heard that the best thing to do during a bear attack is to lie on the ground, fold yourself into the fetal position, and pretend you're dead.

I rolled into a ball and covered my head with my hands. The bear dropped down on all fours and bounced up and down a bit, its paws crunching in the snow as it tried to incite me to move so it could attack. It swiped at my back, and I heard the fabric rip as it hit the backpack, tearing the outer compartment.

Being this close to the bear, I could smell its fur, which carried odors of wet grass, dirt, and lake water. Its warm breath smelled slightly fishy. I whimpered and rolled a little. The bear bit the backpack and pressed its foreleg on the back of my thigh to hold me still. The pressure was intense. I was sure my thigh bone was going to break.

It probably would have if I was on bare ground. Lucky for me, the weight of the bear's leg just pushed me deeper into the snow. I didn't know if it was defending its territory or if it wanted to eat me for lunch. Either way, I'd be dead soon.

Just then, I heard Kishan's roar. The bear looked up and hollered back, defending its dinner. It turned to face the tiger and raked its claws down the back of my thigh on one leg and across the calf of my other. I gasped in pain as Freddy Krueger claws with about six hundred pounds behind them sliced open the back of my thigh and calf. But, the good news was that the bear hadn't really intended to claw me. This was a love tap. Just a—*hey, I'll be right back, honey. I've just got take care of the intruder first before I eat you, but I'll be back before you know it*—kind of injury.

My legs burned with fiery pain, and tears rolled down my cheeks, but I stayed as quiet as I could. Kishan circled the animal for a moment then rushed in to attack. The tiger bit the bear's foreleg while the bear clawed at his back. The fighting beasts moved off enough that I chanced a peek at my legs. I couldn't really twist my head enough to see the wounds, but great drops of carmine blood reddened the snowdrift creating a macabre snow cone.

The bear stood on its hind legs and bellowed. Then it dropped to all fours, ran a couple of steps closer, and reared on its hind legs again. Kishan paced in a semicircle out of the bear's reach. The bear thrust its front paws out toward Kishan two or three times as if trying to scare him off.

Kishan moved closer, and the bear charged. Kishan met the bear standing on his hind legs. As they collided, the bear wrapped its arms around Kishan's body, tearing at his back, giving me a new perspective on the term "bear hug." They slashed at each other in a fury of teeth and claws. The bear bit Kishan's ear viciously and almost tore it off. Kishan twisted his head away, causing them to both lose balance. The animals fell and rolled a few times, a jumble of black on brown fur.

I recovered my senses enough to realize that I had a weapon of my own. What an idiot I was. *Some kind of fighter I turned out to be.* Kishan was circling around the animal now trying to confuse it and tire it out. I took advantage of the distance between them, raised my hand, and hit the bear right on the nose with a small lightning jolt. It was not enough to wound the bear, but enough to turn it away from its potential dinner. It ambled off at a fast pace, bellowing in pain and frustration.

Kishan changed to a man quickly and began to assess my leg injuries. He slid the backpack off my shoulders and donned his winter gear in a few seconds. Then he bent over my legs. The blood was already freezing in the snow. He tore a T-shirt in half and wrapped the pieces tightly around my thigh and calf.

"I'm sorry if this hurts. I have to move you. The scent of your blood could bring the bear back."

He bent over me and picked me up carefully in his arms. Despite his tenderness, my legs burned. I cried out and couldn't help squirming to try to relieve the pain. I pressed my face against his chest and gritted my teeth. Then I became oblivious to everything.

I wasn't sure if I had been sleeping or if I had passed out. It didn't really matter which. I woke up on my stomach next to a warm fire with Kishan carefully examining my wounds. He'd ripped up another shirt and was carefully cleaning my legs with some kind of smelly hot liquid he had summoned via the Golden Fruit.

I sucked in a breath. "It stings! What is that stuff?"

"It's an herbal remedy to stop pain and infection and to help your blood clot."

"It doesn't smell very good. What's in it?"

"Cinnamon, echinacea, garlic, goldenseal, yarrow, and some other things I don't know the English words for."

"It hurts!"

"I imagine it does. You need stitches."

I sucked in a breath and began asking him questions to take my mind off the pain. I gasped as he cleaned my calf. "How did you . . . know how to make it?"

"I've fought in many battles. I know a little bit about how to take care of wounds like this. The pain should lessen soon, Kells."

"You've treated wounds before?" I sucked in a breath.

"Yes."

I whimpered. "Will you . . . tell me about it? It will help me focus on something else."

"Alright." He dipped his cloth and started working on my calf. "Kadam took me out with a group of his elite infantry to stop some bandits."

"Were they like Robin Hood types?"

"Who is Robin Hood?"

"He steals from the rich to give to the poor."

"No. They were murderers. They robbed caravans, raped women, and then killed everyone. They had become notorious in a certain area where trading happened often. Their riches attracted many to join their group, and their large numbers caused great concern. I was being trained in military theory and was learning how to strategize and engage in guerilla warfare from Kadam."

"How old were you?"

"Sixteen."

"Ouch!"

"Sorry."

"It's okay," I groaned. "Please go on."

"We had a large group of them holed up in some caves and were trying to figure out a way to flush them out when we were attacked. They'd built a secret exit into their hideout and had circled around us, quietly taking out our sentries. Our men fought bravely and overcame the rabble, but several of our best soldiers had been killed and many gravely wounded. My arm had been dislocated, but Kadam popped it back in for me, and we helped as many as we could.

"That's when I learned battle triage. Those of us who were able followed the surgeon and helped him tend to the wounds of the soldiers. He taught me a bit about plants and their healing properties. My mother also was something of an herbalist and had a greenhouse full of plants, several of which were used in medicines. After that, whenever I went into battle, I carried a medicinal bag with me to give aid where I could."

"It feels a little bit better now. The throbbing is less. What about you? Are your wounds painful?"

"I've healed already."

"That's really not fair," I remarked jealously.

He responded softly, "I'd trade places with you if I could, Kells," and continued his ablutions carefully, wrapping the thigh and calf in thin strips of cloth and then securing them with ace bandages that Mr. Kadam had included in our first aid kit. Kishan gave me two aspirin tablets and angled my head to help me drink.

"I've stopped the bleeding. Only one of the wounds is deep enough to make me worry. We'll rest tonight and start back tomorrow. I'll have to carry you, Kells. I don't think you can walk. Your wounds might break open and begin to bleed again."

"But, Kishan—"

"Don't worry about it now. Rest for a while, and we'll see how you feel in the morning."

I stretched out a hand and placed it over his. "Kishan?"

He turned his golden eyes to my face and scrutinized it, assessing for pain, "Yes?"

"Thank you for taking care of me."

He squeezed my hand. "I only wish I could do more. Get some sleep."

I dozed on and off, waking as Kishan put more wood on the fire. I wasn't sure how he found wood that was dry enough to burn, but I didn't care enough to ask. He placed the pan of liquid he'd bathed my wounds with near the flames to keep it warm. I was snug in my sleeping bag lying on my stomach, and through a languid daze, I watched the flames lick the bottom of the pot. The herbal smell of the hot liquid suffused the air, and I drifted in and out.

At some point, I must have slept because I dreamed of Ren. He was lashed to a post with his hands tied over his head. I stood against a wall behind another post where Lokesh couldn't see me. He spoke in another language and tapped a whip against his hand. Ren opened his eyes and saw me. He didn't move a limb or twitch a muscle, but his eyes stirred. They brightened, and tiny, crinkly lines appeared on the sides. I smiled at him and took a step toward him. He shook his head slightly. I heard the crack of the whip and froze.

Ren gasped in pain. I burst from my hiding place, screaming, and attacked a surprised Lokesh. I grabbed the whip, but I couldn't tear it from his grasp. He was extremely strong. It was as futile a gesture as a bird attacking a tree. I thrashed and struggled and saw the unmitigated thrill of delight as he recognized me.

Fevered excitement reached his glittering black eyes. He grabbed my hands and twisted them together above my head, then brought his whip down across the back of my legs three times. I cried out in pain. A roar behind me stole his attention. I grabbed his shirt and raked my fingernails across his throat and chest. He shook me.

"Kelsey. Kelsey! Wake up!"

I woke with a start. "Kishan?"

"You were dreaming again."

He was zipped into the sleeping bag with me. He gently pried my fingers from his shirt.

I looked at his chest and throat and saw vicious, bloody scratches. I touched one gently. "Oh, *Kishan*. I'm so sorry. Does it hurt badly?"

"It's okay. They're healing as we speak."

"I didn't mean to. I was dreaming of Lokesh again. I . . . I don't want to go back, Kishan. I want to keep moving, keep looking for the spirit gate. Ren is suffering. I know it."

To my great dismay, I started weeping. I wept partly because of the pain in my legs, partly because of the stress of the journey, but the biggest reason I wept was because I knew that Ren was hurting. Kishan shifted and wrapped his arms around me.

"Shh, Kelsey. It's going to be alright."

"You don't know that. Lokesh may kill him before we find the stupid spirit gate." I cried while Kishan rubbed my back.

"Remember Durga said she'd watch over him. Don't forget about that."

I sobbed. "I know but—"

"Your safety is more important than the quest, and Ren would agree with that."

I laughed wetly. "He probably would, but—"

"No buts. We need to head back, Kells. Once you heal, we can come back and try again. Agreed?"

"I guess so."

"Good. Ren is . . . lucky to hold the heart of a woman such as you, Kelsey."

I turned on my side to look at him. The fire was still going, and I watched the flames dance in his troubled, golden eyes.

I touched his now healed neck and said softly, "And I'm lucky to have such wonderful men in my life."

He brought my hand to his lips and pressed a warm kiss on my fingers. "He wouldn't want you to suffer for him, you know."

"He wouldn't like *you* being the one to comfort me, either."

He grinned at that. "No. Indeed he wouldn't."

"But you do. Comfort me, I mean. Thank you for being here."

"There's nowhere else I'd rather be. Get some sleep, *bilauta*."

He pulled me close and nestled me against his chest. I felt guilty for feeling comforted lying in Kishan's arms, but I fell asleep quickly without further incident.

The next two days of travel were short by necessity. I tried to walk on my own, but the pain was too much so Kishan carried me. We walked back down the mountain slowly, stopping to rest from time to time, saving the last hour for Kishan to set up camp and tend to me. Most of my wounds were healing, but the deep one had started to fester.

The skin around it became ruddy, swollen, and inflamed. The wound was obviously getting worse. I began running a fever, and Kishan started to feel desperate. He cursed the fact that he could only travel with me for six hours of the day. He used every herbal remedy he could think of. Unfortunately, the Golden Fruit could not produce antibiotics.

A storm hit, and I was vaguely aware of Kishan carrying me through icy sleet. Not moving on my own made me more susceptible to the cold. I was freezing and drifted in and out, unaware of how many days had passed. At one point, the thought occurred to me that Fanindra might heal me as she did in Kishkindha, but she remained stiff and frozen. I knew the weather wasn't exactly snake friendly, but, perhaps she knew I wasn't quite at death's door yet either, despite all outward appearances.

We became lost in the storm, not knowing if we were going back to Mr. Kadam or forward to the spirit gate. Kishan was constantly worried about me falling asleep, so he talked to me as we walked. I didn't remember much of what he said. He did lecture me about survival in the wilderness and said that it was important that we stay warm, eat, and keep hydrated. He had those three things pretty much covered. When we stopped for the day, he would wrap me in the sleeping bag and crawl in next to me so his tiger body could keep me warm, and the Golden Fruit provided as much food and drink as we could handle.

I lost my appetite when I became sick. Kishan forced me to eat and drink, but I was shaky, and the fever made me feel like I was either freezing or too hot. He had to change to a man often to keep me covered with the sleeping bag because, in my fever, I constantly tried to push it off.

I was weak now and spent my time either staring at the sky or at Kishan's face as he spoke of various things. Bushman's rice was one topic I remembered because it was disgusting. He talked about how he had managed to live when he'd been the only survivor of a battle deep in enemy territory. He said that there was no food to be found, so he ate Bushman's rice, which was not rice at all but the white pupae of termites.

I grunted softly in reaction but was too sleepy to move my lips to form a comment. I wanted to ask him how he learned about Australian Bushmen back in his time, but I couldn't speak. He looked down at me worried and drew my hood closer over my face so the snow wouldn't fall directly on me.

He leaned over and whispered, "I promise I'll get you out of this, Kelsey. I won't let you die."

Die? Who said anything about dying? I had no intention of dying, but I couldn't exactly tell him that. My lips felt like they were frozen. *I can't die. I have to find the next three items and save my tigers. I have to rescue Ren from Lokesh. I have to finish school. I have to . . .* I fell asleep.

I dreamed of tracing my finger down an icy window. I had just made

a heart with a Ren + Kelsey in the middle and had drawn a second heart with *Kishan* + . . . when someone shook me awake.

"Kells. *Kells!* I thought we had turned back, but I think we found the spirit gate!"

I peeked out of my hood and looked up at an amethyst-gray sky. Painful, icy sleet pummeled us, and I had to squint to see what Kishan was pointing at. In the middle of a barren white stretch of snow stood two wooden posts about the size of telephone phones. Wrapped around each one were long ropes of material that flapped wildly in the storm like homemade kite tails. A line of colorful flags were attached at different sections of the posts. Some of the ropes were tied to the opposite pole. Some were attached to rings in the ground, and others just flapped loose in the wind.

I licked my lips and whispered, "Are you sure?"

Fortunately, his tiger hearing was extremely good. He bent over close to my ear and shouted over the wind, "It could be a monument or a memorial created by nomads, but there's just something different about this. I want to check it out."

I nodded weakly, and he set me down in the sleeping bag near one of the poles. He'd taken to carrying me in the sleeping bag to keep me warmer. I slipped into a deep sleep. When he woke me, I wasn't sure if it had been hours or seconds.

"This is the right place, Kelsey. I found a handprint. Now, should we go through it or turn back? I feel we should turn back and return later."

I reached a gloved hand out and touched his chest. I whispered, feeling the wind gobble up my words and tear them away just as they passed my lips. Fortunately, he heard them. I said, "No . . . we won't be able . . . find it . . . again . . . too hard. Ocean Teacher said . . . prove our . . . f . . . faith. It's . . . a test. We . . . must . . . tr . . . try."

"But, Kells—"

"Take me . . . the . . . handprint."

He looked at me with indecision battling in his eyes. Gently, he stretched out his gloved hand and brushed the snowflakes from my cheek.

I caught his hand in mine. "Have faith," I whispered into the wind.

He sighed deeply, then slid his arms under me and carried me to the wooden post. "Here it is. On the left of the pole, under the blue fabric."

I saw it and tried to get my glove off. Kishan stood me up, supporting all my weight on one arm. He pulled off my glove with the other hand and stuffed it into his pocket. Then he guided my hand into the cold depression carved into the bark of the wooden marker. Now that I was closer, I could see intricate carvings all over the wood that had been partially covered by the snow. If I'd felt better, I would have loved to examine them, but I couldn't even stay upright without Kishan.

I kept my hand pressed against the wood but nothing happened. I tried to summon the fire in my belly, the spark that made my hand glow, but I felt deadened.

"Kishan . . . I . . . c . . . can't. I'm too . . . c . . . cold." I felt like crying.

He took off his gloves, unzipped his jacket, tore his shirt underneath, and put my frozen hand against his bare chest, covering the back of it with his own warm hand. His chest was hot. He pressed his warm cheek against my cold one and rubbed the back of my hand with his palm for a few minutes. He spoke, but I didn't understand his words. He shifted to protect me from the wind, and I almost fell asleep as he held me in the warm cocoon he'd created. Finally, he pulled back a little and said, "There, that's better. Now, try again."

He helped me angle my hand. I felt a small spark of tingly warmth and urged it to build. The power was slow and lethargic, but it did build until the handprint glowed. The pole shook and began to glow too. Something happened to my eyes. A green sheen fell across my vision like I'd put on a pair of green-tinted sunglasses. It made the glow from my hand look bright orange, and the orange traveled from one pole across the fabric tail to the other pole.

The ground shook, and we were enveloped in a bubble of warmth. Too weak to continue, my hand slipped out, and I fell back against Kishan, who scooped me up in his arms again. A little bubble of static formed between the two poles and grew larger. Colors shifted inside the bubble, which were too vague and fuzzy to make out at first, but they grew bigger and started to come into focus. I heard a boom, and the picture snapped into place.

I saw green grass and a warm yellow sun. Herds of animals grazed lazily beneath leafy summer trees. Where we stood I could smell the scent of flowers and feel the sun warm my face, yet the wintry sleet still fell across my cheek. Kishan took a step forward, and another. He carried me into the warm paradise. My head lolled against his arm as I listened to the sound of the storm fade. The cold air grew more distant and then left with a *pop*. That's when I fainted.

18
good things

I woke near a crackling fire at dawn. Kishan was warming his hands.

I shifted and groaned, "Hey."

"Hey, yourself. How do you feel?"

"Umm . . . I'm feeling better actually."

He grunted. "You started healing as soon as we entered this place."

"How long have I been asleep?"

"About twelve hours. You healed here almost as fast as Ren and I do outside."

I stretched my legs and was relieved. The pain was bad, but an infection was worse. I had been sort of counting on Kishan's amulet to fix me, but it wasn't working like Mr. Kadam had said. Maybe Kishan's piece did something different. I'd gotten lucky.

"I'm starving. What's for breakfast?" I asked.

"What would you like?"

"Hmm . . . how about some chocolate chip pancakes with a tall glass of milk."

"Sounds good. I'll have the same thing."

Kishan asked the Golden Fruit to make our meal, and he hunkered down next to me to eat. I was still feeling weak and when he pulled me closer so I could lean against him, I didn't protest. Instead, I dug happily into my pancakes.

"So, Kishan, where are we?"

"Not sure. About a mile past the spirit gate."

"You carried me through?"

"Yes." He set down his plate and put his arm around me. "I was afraid you would die."

"Apparently my coming back from the dead is a common theme in these mythical cities."

"I hope this is the last time you come close."

"Me too. Thanks. For everything."

"You're welcome. By the way, it seems I can maintain human form here like Ren did in Kishkindha."

"Really? How does it feel?"

"Strange. I'm not used to it. I keep waiting for the tiger to take over. I can still become a tiger if I wish, but I don't have to take that form."

"The same thing happened to Ren. Well, enjoy it while it lasts. Ren changed back the minute we left Kishkindha."

He mumbled something and started going through the backpack.

"Can you hand me the prophecy and Mr. Kadam's notes?" I asked. "The first order of business is to find the omphalos stone, the navel stone, the stone of prophecy. We look into it, and it shows us where to find the tree. It looks like a football standing on end with a hole in the top."

"And what does a football look like?"

"Hmm, I guess you'd say it's oblong shaped, but more pointy on the ends." I stood up on shaky legs.

"Don't you think you should rest a little bit longer?"

"I feel pretty well rested, besides, the faster we can find the stone, the sooner we can rescue Ren."

"Alright, but we'll go slowly. It's pretty warm here. Wouldn't you like to change out of your snow gear first?"

I looked down at my ripped pants. "Right."

Kishan had removed my coat, but I was sweating in my insulated pants. He'd already changed and was now wearing jeans, hiking boots, and a black T-shirt.

"Don't you get sick of black?"

He shrugged. "It just feels right."

"Hmm."

"I'll scope out the area and see if I can find a trail for us to follow while you change." He grinned. "And don't worry. I won't be peeking."

"You'd better not."

He laughed and walked off through the grass toward the tree line. As I changed, I marveled at my torn pants. *That bear really did a number on me.* I checked my leg and calf. There was no wound. Not even a scar. The skin was healthy and pink, as if it had never been damaged.

By the time Kishan came back, I'd washed using the best thing I could come up with—a pot of warm rose tea courtesy of the Golden Fruit and a T-shirt. I poured the rest of the rose tea through my hair, brushed it out, and braided it into a long tail that hung down my back. I'd just changed into a long-sleeved T-shirt, jeans, and hiking boots to match Kishan, when he hollered out a warning and strode into the camp. He looked me up and down with masculine approval, and smiled.

"What are you grinning at?"

"You. You look much better."

"Ha. What I wouldn't give for a shower, but I do feel better."

"I found a creek that runs near the tree line with a game trail. I think that might be a good place to start. Shall we?"

I nodded while he shouldered the backpack and headed for the trees.

When we got to the creek, I marveled at how beautiful it was. Gorgeous flowers sprung up near rocks and tree trunks. I recognized narcissus growing by the creek and told Kishan the story of the handsome man from Greek mythology who fell in love with his own reflection.

He listened with rapt attention, and we were both so involved with the story that we didn't notice the animals. We were being followed by forest creatures. We stopped, and a pair of rabbits hopped up to look at us curiously. Squirrels leapt from tree to tree to get nearer, as if to listen to the story. They jumped to a branch that bent with their weight and brought them just a few feet from us. The woods were full of creatures. I saw foxes, deer, and birds of all kinds. I held out my hand, and a beautiful red cardinal flew down and perched delicately on my finger.

Kishan held out an arm and a golden eyed hawk flew from the top of the tree to balance on his forearm. I walked up to a fox that fearlessly watched my approach. Stretching out a hand, I stroked its soft, furry head.

"I feel like Snow White! This is amazing! What *is* this place?"

He laughed. "Paradise. Remember?"

We walked all day, escorted at times by a variety of animal companions. In the afternoon, we emerged from the forest to find horses grazing in a meadow full of wildflowers. I plucked stems to make a bouquet as we walked. The horses trotted over to investigate.

Kishan fed them apples from a nearby tree while I braided flowers in the mane of a beautiful white mare. They walked alongside us for a while as we continued.

In the early evening, we saw a structure of some kind at the base of a large hill. Kishan wanted to make camp for the night and explore it the next day.

That night, I lay on my side in the sleeping bag with a hand tucked under my cheek and said to Kishan, "It's like the Garden of Eden. I never imagined such a place existed."

"Ah, but if I recall, there was a snake in the garden."

"Well, if there wasn't one here before, there's one here now."

I peeked at Fanindra. Her golden coils were still hard and unmoving where she rested near my head. I looked at Kishan who was poking the fire with a stick.

"Hey, aren't you tired? We walked pretty far today. Don't you want to sleep?"

He glanced over at me. "I'll sleep soon."

"Oh. Okay. I'll save you some room."

"Kelsey, I think it would be wise for me to sleep on the other side of the fire. You should be warm enough here by yourself."

I looked at him curiously. "That's true, but there's plenty of room, and I promise not to snore."

He laughed nervously. "It's not that. I'm a man all the time now, and it would be hard for me to sleep with you and not . . . hold you. Sleeping near you as a tiger is fine, but sleeping near you as a man is different."

"Ah, I once said the same thing to Ren. You're right. I should've thought of that and not put you in an uncomfortable position."

He snorted wryly. "I wasn't worried about being *uncomfortable*. I was worried about getting a little *too* comfortable."

"Right." Now *I* was nervous. "So, umm . . . do you want to take the sleeping bag then? I can use my quilt."

"No. I'll be fine, *bilauta*."

After a few minutes, Kishan settled himself on the other side of the fire. He cushioned his hands behind his head and said, "Tell me another Greek story."

"Okay." I thought for a moment. "There was once a beautiful nymph named Chloris who cared for flowers and nurtured the spring by willing the buds of trees to blossom. Her long blonde hair smelled like roses and was always adorned with a halo of flowers. Her skin was as soft as flower petals. Her lips were puckered and pink like peonies and her cheeks—soft blushing orchids. She was beloved by all who knew her, yet she longed for a companion, a man that could appreciate her passion for flowers and who would give her life deeper meaning.

"One afternoon, she was working with the calla lilies and felt a warm breeze blow through her hair. A man stepped into her meadow and stood admiring her garden. He was handsome with dark, windswept hair and wore a purple cloak. He didn't see her at first; she watched him from a leafy bower as he walked among the flowers. The daffodils raised their heads at his approach. He cupped a rosebud between his hands to inhale its fragrance, and it unfurled its petals and bloomed in his palms. The lilies quivered delicately at his touch, and the tulips bent toward him on their long stems.

"Chloris was surprised. Her flowers usually responded only to her. The spears of lavender tried to twine themselves about his legs as he passed by. She folded her arms and frowned at them. The gladiolas all opened at once instead of taking turns like they were supposed to, and the sweet peas danced back and forth, trying to get his attention. She gasped softly when she saw the creeping phlox try to uproot itself.

"'That's enough!' she said. 'You all behave yourselves!'

"The man turned and spied her hiding among the leaves. 'Come out,' he beckoned. 'I will not harm you.'

"She sighed, pushed aside the gardenia plants, and stepped barefooted into the sunshine, pressing her toes into the grass.

"A small breeze blew through the garden as the man sucked in a soft breath. Chloris was more beautiful than any of the flowers he'd come to admire. He immediately fell in love with her and dropped to his knees before her. She beseeched him to stand. He did, and the warm wind shuffled his cloak, lifted it, and enfolded both of them in its purple billows. She laughed and offered him a silver rose blossom. Smiling he twisted off the petals, tossing them into the air.

"She was upset at first, but then he twirled his finger and the rose petals swirled around them in a tunnel of wind. She clapped her hands in delight as she watched the petals dance. 'Who are you?' she asked.

"'My name is Zephryus,' he said. 'I am the west wind.' He offered her his hand. When she placed her hand in his, he pulled her close and kissed her. Stroking her soft cheek with his fingertips, he said, 'I have traveled the world for centuries, yet you are the loveliest maiden I have ever seen. Please, tell me. What is your name?'

"Blushing, she answered, 'Chloris.'

"He folded her small hands in his and made a vow. 'I will return next spring. I wish to take you for my bride. If you'll have me.'

"Chloris nodded shyly. He kissed her again, and the purple cloak swirled around him. 'Until we meet next year then, my Flora.' The wind blew him quickly away.

"She prepared for his arrival all year. Her garden was more beautiful than it had ever been, the flowers happier. Whenever she thought of him, she felt the kiss of his breeze brush her cheek. The next spring, he returned to find his beautiful bride waiting for him, and they wed surrounded by thousands of blossoms. They had a happy marriage. She tended the gardens while her husband's west wind gently scattered the pollen every spring.

"Their gardens were the most beautiful, the most renowned, and people came from all over the world to admire them. They delighted in each other, and their love was bounteous. They had a child together named Carpus, which means 'fruit.'"

I paused. "Kishan?" I heard a light snore come from the other side of the fire. I wondered when he'd fallen asleep. I whispered softly, "Goodnight, Kishan."

The next morning, I woke to a munching sound above my head. I looked up at a tall, yellow body with black circles and hissed, "Kishan. Wake up!"

"I'm already awake and watching, Kells. Don't be afraid. It won't hurt you."

"It's a giraffe!"

"Yes. And there are some gorillas moving in the trees over there."

I quietly shifted and saw a family of gorillas pulling fruit off a tree. "Will they attack?"

"They aren't responding like normal gorillas, but there's one way to find out. Stay here."

He disappeared in the trees and emerged a moment later in tiger form. He walked up to the giraffe. It blinked long-lashed eyes at him then calmly went back to plucking leaves off the tree tops with its tongue. When he moved toward the gorillas, the same thing happened. They watched him lazily and chattered among themselves. Then they went back to their breakfast, even when he approached one of their babies.

Kishan shifted back to a man, staring thoughtfully at the animals. "Hmm. Very interesting. They're not afraid of me at all."

I started breaking camp. "You lost your hiking clothes, Mister. You're back in black."

"No, I didn't. I left them back there in the trees. I'll be back."

After breakfast, we hiked to the large structure we'd seen the day before. It was huge, made of wood, and obviously very old. A large rotting incline led up into it. As we got nearer, I exclaimed, "It's a boat!"

"I don't think so, Kells. It's too big to be a boat."

"It is, Kishan. I think it's the ark!"

"The what?"

"The ark—as in Noah's ark. Remember when Mr. Kadam talked about all the flood myths? Well, if this really is the mountain where Noah landed, then that must be what's left of his boat! Come on!"

We made our way up to the massive wooden structure and peeked inside. I wanted to climb in and look around, but Kishan cautioned me.

"Wait, Kells. The wood's rotting. Let me go first and test it out." He disappeared into the gaping maw of the edifice and emerged a few minutes later. "I think it will be safe enough if you stay right behind me."

I followed him in. It was dark, but where the wood had fallen out of the ceiling, jagged gaps let the sunshine through. I had expected to see stalls of some kind to keep the animals contained, but there were none to be found. It did have a few levels with wooden steps, but Kishan thought the stairs would be too dangerous. I pulled out a camera and snapped a few pictures for Mr. Kadam.

Later, as we left the wooden relic, I said, "Kishan . . . I have a theory. I think that Noah's ark *did* land here and the animals we've seen are descendents from those original animals. Maybe that's why they act differently. They haven't lived anywhere but here."

"Just because an animal lives in paradise doesn't mean that it doesn't have any instincts. Instincts are very powerful. The instinct to protect your territory, to hunt for food, and to . . ." he looked at me pointedly, "find a mate can be overwhelming."

I cleared my throat. "*Right*. But, food's abundant here, and I'm sure there are plenty of," I waved my hand in the air, "*mates* to go around."

He raised an eyebrow. "Perhaps. But how do you know it's always like this? Maybe the winter comes at a different time here."

"Maybe, but I don't think so. I've seen flowers growing that bloom in the spring, but I've also seen flowers that bloom in the fall. It's strange. It's almost like the best of everything. The animals are all perfect and well fed."

"Yes, but we haven't seen any predators yet."

"That's true. We'll keep an eye out."

I took out a notebook and started categorizing the things we'd seen. The place really was like a paradise, and from all appearances, Kishan and I seemed to be the only two people here. The fresh fragrance of flowers, apples, citrus, and grass hung in the air. The air was a perfect temperature—not too hot and not too cold.

It seemed like a well-kept garden. I couldn't see anything resembling a weed. It would be impossible for this type of landscape to maintain itself naturally, I thought. We found a perfect bird's nest with speckled blue eggs. The bird parents sat chirping happily, not upset at all as we came closer to inspect their eggs.

I also made a list of every animal we came in contact with. By the early afternoon, we'd seen hundreds of different animals that I knew shouldn't be living in this kind of environment—elephants, camels, and even kangaroos.

Late afternoon was when we saw our first predators—a pride of lions. Kishan had smelled them a mile from their lands, and we decided to go in for a closer look. He made me climb a tree while he investigated. Finally, he came back with a look of astonishment.

"There's a large herd of antelope near the pride but they graze right next to the cats! I saw a lioness eating something red that I assumed was meat but it turns out that it was fruit. The lions were eating apples."

I started to climb down. Kishan caught me around my waist and lowered me the rest of the way.

"Ah ha! So my theory was correct. This really is like the Garden of Eden. The animals don't hunt."

"It appears you were right. Still, just to be safe, I'd like to put some distance between us and the lions before we camp."

Later, we saw other predators—wolves, panthers, bears, and even another tiger. They made no moves against us. In fact, the wolves were as friendly as dogs and approached us to be petted.

Kishan grunted, "This is strange. It's unnerving."

"I know what you mean, but . . . I like it. I wish Ren could see this place."

Kishan didn't respond except to urge me to leave the wolf pack and move on.

At dusk, we stumbled into a clearing in the middle of a forest that was full of daffodils. We'd just started to set up camp when I heard the soft, haunting music of a flute. We both froze. It was the first evidence of people.

"What should we do?" I asked.

"Let me go look."

"I think we should both go."

He shrugged, and I trailed quickly behind him. We followed the lingering notes of the mysterious sound and found the source of the music sitting on a raised stone near a brook, playing a reed pipe. The creature held his pipes gently between two hands and blew air softly between pursed lips. As we hesitantly approached, he stopped playing and smiled at us.

His eyes were bright green and set in a handsome face. His shoulder-length silver hair hung loosely down his back. Two small, brown, velvety horns peeped out of the top of his shiny tresses, reminding me of young deer just growing antlers. He was slightly smaller than an average human, and his skin was white with a slight lilac tint. He was barefoot but wore pants that looked like they were made from doeskin. His long-sleeved shirt was the color of a pomegranate.

He hung his pipes around his neck and looked at us. "Hello."

Kishan replied warily, "Hello."

"I've been waiting for you to come. We've all been waiting."

I asked, "Who's we?"

"Well, me for one. Then there's the Silvanae and the fairies."

Puzzled, Kishan asked, "You've been expecting us?"

"Oh, yes. For a long time, in fact. You must be tired. Come with me, and we'll provide you with some refreshment."

Kishan stood rooted to the ground. I stepped around him.

"Hi. I'm Kelsey."

"Nice to meet you. My name's Faunus."

"Faunus? I've heard that name before."

"Have you?"

"Yes! You're Pan!"

"Pan? No. I'm definitely Faunus. At least, that's what my family tells me. Come along."

He stood up, hopped over a rock, and disappeared through the woods on a stone path. I turned around and took Kishan's hand. "Come on. I trust him."

"I don't."

I squeezed his hand and whispered, "It's okay. I think you could take him." Kishan tightened his grip on my hand and allowed me to lead him after our guide.

We followed Faunus through the leafy trees and soon heard the tinkling laughter of many people. As we neared the settlement, I realized that the sound was nothing I'd ever heard *people* make before. It was unearthly.

"Faunus . . . what are Silvanae?"

"They are the tree people, the tree nymphs."

"Tree nymphs?"

"Yes. You have no tree people where you come from?"

"No. We have no fairies either."

He seemed confused. "What kind of people emerge from a tree when it splits?"

"No one emerges as far as I know. In fact, I don't think I've ever seen a tree split unless lightning hit it or someone chopped it down."

He stopped in mid-stride. "Your people chop down trees?"

"In my land? Yes, they do."

He shook his head sadly. "I'm very glad I live here. Those poor trees. What would happen to all the future generations, I wonder."

I looked at Kishan, who shook his head imperceptibly before he led us on.

As darkness fell, we stepped under a wide arch full of hundreds of miniature climbing roses in all varieties of color and entered the village of the Silvanae. Lanterns hung from ropy vines that draped down from the largest trees I'd ever seen. The small lights inside the lanterns bobbed up and down in their glass houses, each one a different vivid color—pink, silver, turquoise, orange, yellow, and violet. On closer inspection, I saw the lights were living creatures. They were fairies!

"Kishan! Look! They glow like lightning bugs!"

The fairies looked like large butterflies, but their glow did not come from their bodies. The soft light emanated from their colorful wings, which opened and closed lazily as the creatures sat perched on a wooden mount.

I pointed at one. "Are those—?"

"Fairy lights? Yes. They have two-hour shifts on lantern duty in the evenings. They like to read on duty. Keeps 'em awake. If they fall asleep, their lights go out."

I mumbled, "Right. Of course."

He led us farther into the settlement. The small cottages were made of fibrous woven plants and were set in a circular fashion around a grassy space. The center area had been set for a banquet. A giant tree stood behind each hut; the towering limbs reached over and across, twining their branches together with their neighboring trees, creating a beautiful green bower overhead.

Faunus raised his pipe and blew a happy melody. Slight-framed, willowy people streamed out of their cottages and hopped down from hiding places in the foliage.

"Come. Come and meet those we have been waiting for. This is Kelsey and this is Kishan. Let us bid them welcome."

Shining faces came closer. They were all silver-haired and had green eyes like Faunus. Beautiful males and females were dressed in shimmering gossamer clothing in the bright colors of the flowers that grew everywhere.

Faunus turned to me. "Would you like to eat first or bathe first?"

Surprised, I said, "Bathe first. If that's alright."

He bowed. "Of course. Anthracia, Phiale, and Deiopea, will you take Kelsey to the women's bathing shallows?"

Three lovely Silvanae approached me shyly from the group. Two took my hands while the third led me out of the clearing and into the forest. Kishan scowled at me, obviously unhappy about our separation, but I noticed he was soon escorted away too, in a different direction.

The women were slightly smaller than Faunus, about a head shorter than me. My escorts followed a path colorfully lit by helpful fairies until we came upon a round, sunken pool fed by a small brook. The water dropped down from larger stones to smaller, and then dropped to the pool, creating a diminutive, hidden spray of water. It worked like a wide faucet that was constantly running.

They removed my backpack and disappeared while I took off the rest of my clothing and stepped into the pool. It was surprisingly warm. A long, submerged stone too convenient to be natural, ran along the arch inside the pool, serving as a stepping stone and then as a seating stone once I was in the water.

After I'd wet my hair, the three nymphs returned and brought bowls of fragrant liquids. They let me pick the fragrance I liked and handed me a mossy ball that functioned like a loofah. I scrubbed the dirt from my skin with the fragrant soap while Phiale soaped through my hair with three different products, having me rinse under the small waterfall each time.

The fairy lights glowed warmly. By the time I stepped out of the pool and the women wrapped my body and hair with soft cloth, my skin and scalp were tingling, and I felt relaxed and refreshed. Anthracia massaged perfumed lotion into my skin while Phiale worked on my hair. Deiopea disappeared briefly and returned with a beautiful celadon green gossamer dress embroidered with shimmering flowers.

I reached out to touch the dress. "It's lovely! The embroidery is so fine that the flowers look real."

She giggled. "They are real."

"They can't be! How did you sew them in?"

"We didn't sew them. We grew them in. We asked them to be a part of this dress, and they agreed."

Anthracia asked, "Do you not like it?"

"*No*. I love it! I would be very happy to wear it."

They all smiled and hummed contentedly as they worked on me. When they were finished, they brought out a silvered mirror set in an oval frame carved with looping flowers.

"What do you think, Kelsey? Is your appearance satisfactory?"

I stared at the person in the mirror. "Is that me?"

They erupted in tinkling giggles. "Yes, of course, it's you."

I stood transfixed. The barefoot woman staring back at me had large brown doe's eyes and soft creamy white skin that glowed with good health. Sparkling green eye shadow enhanced my eyes, and my lashes were long and dark. My lips shone with apple red gloss, and my cheeks were a becoming pink. The green gossamer dress was in the Grecian style, which made me look curvier than I was. It was draped over my shoulders, wrapped around my waist, and fell to the ground in long folds. My hair hung loose and wavy down my back, ending just above my waist. I hadn't realized that my hair had grown so long. It was adorned with flowers and butterfly wings.

The wings moved slightly. *Were there fairies holding my hair in wavy twists?*

"Oh! The fairies don't need to stay in my hair. I'm sure there are other things they would rather do."

Phiale shook her head. "Nonsense. They are honored to hold the tresses of one as fair as you. They say your hair is beautiful and soft, and it's like resting in a cloud. They are happiest when they serve. Please let them stay."

I smiled. "Alright, but just through the dinner."

The three Silvanae women fussed and primped over me for several more minutes and then declared me presentable. We started back to the village. Just before we reached the banquet area, Deiopea handed me a fragrant bunch of flowers to carry.

"Uh . . . I'm not getting married or anything like that, right?"

"Married? Why no."

Phiale said, "Do you want to get married?"

I waved my hand. "Oh no, I just asked because of the beautiful dress and the bouquet of flowers."

"Those are the marriage customs of your land?"

"Yes."

Deiopea tittered, "Well, if you did want to marry, your man does look very handsome."

The three ladies fell into giggles again and pointed to the banquet table where Kishan sat, obviously frustrated. They bounced to the table before disappearing into the silver-haired group. I had to admit, Deiopea was right. Kishan did look very handsome. They'd dressed him in white pants and a blue gossamer shirt made of the same material as mine. He had bathed too. I laughed out loud as he looked uneasily around at the Silvanae, obviously feeling out of place.

He must have heard me because he looked up and scanned the crowd. His eyes lit on me and flew past, still searching. Kishan didn't recognize me! I laughed again. This time, his eyes darted back to me and stayed. Slowly rising, he made his way to me. He looked me up and down with a big grin on his face and let out a whoop of laughter.

Annoyed, I asked, "What are you laughing at?"

He took both of my hands in his and looked in my eyes. "Nothing at all, Kelsey. You are the most enchanting creature I've ever seen in my life."

"Oh. Thank you. But why did you laugh?"

"I *laughed* because I'm the lucky one who gets to see you like this, to be with you in this paradise while *Ren* had to be chased by monkeys and fight needle trees. Obviously, I got the better quest."

"Undeniably you did, at least, so far. But, I forbid you to tease him about this."

"Are you kidding? I plan on taking your picture and explaining everything to him in *great* detail. In fact, stay right there." Kishan disappeared and came back with a camera.

I frowned. "*Kishan*."

"Ren would want a picture. Believe me. Now smile and hold your flowers." He took several shots then slipped the small camera in his pocket and took my hand. "You're beautiful, Kelsey."

I blushed at the compliment, but a feeling of melancholy stole over me. I thought about Ren. He would have loved this place. It was a scene right out of *Midsummer Night's Dream*. He would have been the handsome Oberon to my Titania.

Kishan touched my face. "The sadness is back again. It breaks my heart, Kells." He leaned over and kissed my cheek softly. "Will you do me the honor of accompanying me to dinner, *apsaras rajkumari*?"

I tried to snap out of it and smiled. "Yes, if you tell me what you just called me."

His golden eyes twinkled. "I called you 'princess,' 'fairy princess' to be exact."

I laughed. "Then what would you call yourself?"

"I am the handsome prince, naturally." He tucked my arm through his and helped me sit. Faunus took a chair across from us, sitting next to a lovely Silvanae.

"May I introduce our sovereign?"

"Of course," I said.

"Kelsey and Kishan, meet Dryope, titular queen of the Silvanae."

She nodded delicately and smiled, then announced, "It is time for the feasting! Enjoy!"

I didn't know where to begin. Plates of delicate lace cookies and honey cakes were placed next to fluffy lemon meringue tarts, platters of stewed fruits in sugary syrups, baby quiches, and cinnamon crepes. I scooped up a helping of dandelion salad with dried fruits and lime dressing and a portion of an apple, onion, and mushroom galette with baked stilton cheese. Other dishes of sugar plum pudding, blueberry scones, pumpkin cups with cream-cheese filling, soft rolls with creamy butter, and fruited jams and jellies were also brought out.

We drank honeyed flower nectar and watermelon spritzes. Kishan handed me a fruit appetizer. It was a tiny nutty pastry cup filled with raspberries and topped with fresh cream. All the food was small except for the final pastry—a gigantic strawberry shortcake. Red glaze dripped down the sides of the white cake, which was filled with sweet red berries and fluffy custard. It was topped with mounds of whipped cream, had a dusting of sugar on top, and was served with milk.

When we were finished, I leaned over to Kishan and said, "I had no idea vegetarians ate this well."

He laughed and scooped up another helping of the shortcake.

I dabbed my lips with my napkin. "Faunus, may I ask you a question?"

He nodded.

"We found the ruins of the ark. Do you know about Noah and the animals here?"

"Oh! Do you mean the boat? Yes, we saw the boat settle in the hills, and all manner of creatures emerged. Many of them left our realm and entered your world, including the people who were in it. Some of the creatures decided to stay. Others had generations of descendents and then returned to us. We agreed to let all of them remain if they followed the law of our land—that no one creature may hurt another."

"That's . . . amazing."

"Yes, it's wonderful to have had so many of the animals return to us. They find peace here."

"So do we. Faunus . . . we are here seeking something called the omphalos stone or the navel stone. Have you ever seen it?"

All the Silvanae shook their heads as Faunus answered, "No. I'm afraid we don't know of such a stone."

"What about a giant tree thousands of feet tall?"

He considered for a moment, and then shook his head. "No. If there is such a tree or such a stone, they reside outside of our realm."

"You mean back in my world?"

"Not necessarily. There are other parts of this world that we have no control over. As long as you walk our lands beneath our trees you are safe, but once you leave their shelter we can no longer protect you."

"I see." I sank back in disappointment.

He brightened, "However, you may find your answer if you sleep in the Grove of Dreams. It's a special place to us. If we have a difficult question that needs to be answered or if we need direction, we sleep there and can find the answer or see a dream of the future and realize the question wasn't so important after all."

"Could we please give it a try?"

"Of course! We will take you."

A group of excited Silvanae began chattering at the other end of the table.

"How momentous that you came at this time! One of the trees is splitting!" Faunus explained. "Come and see, Kelsey and Kishan. Come and see the birth of a tree nymph."

Kishan held my hand while Faunus guided us behind one of the cottages to the tree behind it. The whole town waited, humming quietly, at the base of the tree.

Faunus whispered, "These trees were here before your Noah and his boat of animals landed. They have given birth to many generations of Silvanae. Each cottage that you see is set before a family tree. This means that all who live in the cottage were born from the mother tree behind it. It's getting close to time. Look up. See how the other trees offer their support?"

I glanced up at the leafy bower overhead, and it did look as if the branches were squeezing the leafy fingers of the tree that was straining nearby. It made wooden groaning and popping sounds as the leaves trembled above us.

The tree nymphs seemed to be focused on a large, knobby mound that bulged near a low branch. The tree shuddered as the long branch quivered. After several intense moments of listening to the deep rumbles of the tree and watching the trunk expand and contract, so slowly that I wouldn't have noticed if I wasn't paying attention, the bottom branch broke off from the enormous trunk with a terrible crack.

A hush fell over the assembly. The branch hung loosely, touching the ground near us, held on by only the bark of the tree. Tucked in the space where the base of the branch met the trunk was a small silver head.

A group of Silvanae approached and cooed, speaking softly to the small being resting in the tree. They gently lifted it out and wrapped it in a blanket. One member of the group lifted the small Silvanae baby in the air and announced, "It's a boy!" They disappeared into the cottage while everyone cheered. Another group of Silvanae carefully removed the quivering limb from the tree and spread a creamy salve over the broken oval in the trunk where the branch had been.

Silvanae began to dance around the tree, and tiny fairies flew up into the top and lit up all the branches with their fluttering wings. When the celebration was over, it was late.

As Faunus walked us to the Grove of Dreams, I asked him, "So now we know where the Silvanae come from, but what about the fairies? Are they born from trees too?"

He laughed. "No. Fairies are born of roses. When the bloom is spent, we leave it to seed. A bud swells, and when the time is right, a fairy is born with wings the color of the bloom."

"Do you live forever?"

"No. We're not immortal, but we do live a long time. When a Silvanae dies, his body is laid to rest in the roots of the mother tree, and his memories become a part of future generations. Fairies die only if their rose plant does, so they can live a long time, but they are awake only in the evenings. During the day, they find a flower to rest on and

their bodies change into morning dew. At night, they turn back into fairies again. Ah, here we are, the Grove of Dreams."

He'd led us into a secluded area. It looked like a fairy honeymoon suite. Tall trees supported a leafy bed that hung from vines. Baskets of fragrant flowers hung from each corner of the grove. Gossamer pillows and bedding were embroidered with swirling vines and leaves. A group of fairies who had followed us in took their places in the lanterns.

"The four large trees that support the bower stand one in each direction—north, south, east, and west. The best dreams are had when the head points west so you wake with the sun in the east. Good luck to you and sweet dreams." He smiled and was off, taking two fairies with him.

I shifted uncomfortably. "Umm, this is a little awkward."

Kishan was staring at the bed like it was a mortal enemy. He turned to me and gallantly bowed. "Not to worry, Kelsey. I will be sleeping on the ground."

"Right. But, uh, what if you're the one who has the dream?"

"Do you think it matters if I'm in the bed or not?"

"I have no idea, but just in case, I think you better join me."

He stiffened. "Fine. But we're sleeping back to back."

"Deal."

I climbed in first and sank into the soft feather bed and pillow. The bed shifted back and forth like a hammock. Kishan muttered as he stowed the backpack. I caught snippets of phrases. There was something about *fairy princesses*, and *how does she expect me to sleep*, and *Ren better appreciate*, etc., etc. I stifled a laugh and rolled onto my side. He pulled the gossamer cover over me, and then I felt the bed sway as he lay next to me.

As a breeze softly stirred my hair, I heard Kishan sputter, "Keep your hair on your side, Kells. It tickles."

I laughed. "Sorry."

I pulled my hair over my shoulder. He muttered some more, something about *more than a man can bear* and shifted quietly. I fell asleep quickly and had vivid dreams of Ren.

In one dream, he didn't know me and turned away from me. In another he was laughing and happy. We were together again, and he held me close and whispered that he loved me. I dreamed of a long rope lit with fire and a black pearl necklace. In another dream, I was underwater swimming alongside Ren, while we were surrounded by schools of colorful fish.

Despite dreaming very clearly, there was no hint of the omphalos stone. I woke disappointed and found I was sleeping nose to nose with Kishan. He had his arm draped over me, and his head was pillowed on my hair, pinning me to the bed.

I shoved him. "Kishan. Kishan! Wake up!"

He woke only halfway and pulled me closer. "Shh, go back to sleep. It's not morning yet."

"Yes, it *is* morning." I pushed against his ribs. "Time to wake up. Come on!"

"Okay, honey, but how about a kiss first? A man needs some motivation to get out of bed."

"That kind of motivation keeps a man *in* bed. I'm not kissing you. Now get up."

He woke with a start. Confused, he groaned and rubbed his eyes. "Kelsey?"

"Yes, Kelsey. Who've you been dreaming about? Durga?"

He froze and blinked a couple of times. "That is none of your business. But, for your information, I did have a dream about the omphalos stone."

"You did? Where is it?"

"I can't really describe it. I'll have to show you."

"Okay." I hopped out of the bed and adjusted my dress.

Kishan watched me and commented, "You're prettier now than you were last night."

I laughed. "Yeah, right. I wonder why you dreamed of the omphalos stone, and I didn't."

"Perhaps you went to bed last night with different questions in your mind."

My mouth fell open. He was right. I hadn't thought about the stone at all before I slept. My thoughts were entirely focused on Ren.

He watched me curiously. "And what did *you* dream about last night, Kells?"

"That's none of your business either."

He narrowed his eyes and scowled. "Forget it. I think I can figure it out on my own."

Kishan took the lead in walking back to the Silvanae village. A short distance away, he stopped and ran back to the Grove of Dreams. "Be right back. I forgot something," he hollered over his shoulder.

When he returned, Kishan was grinning from ear to ear, but no matter how hard I tried, I couldn't get him to tell me what had made him so happy.

19 bad things

We breakfasted with the Silvanae again and were gifted with new clothing. Both of us were given lightweight shirts, khaki pants with a subtle sheen, and plush-lined boots. I asked if they were leather, and the peaceful creatures didn't know what I was talking about. When I explained, they seemed shocked and said that no animals were ever harmed in Silvanae. They said that the fairies wove all their cloth and that there was no material on Earth as fine or as soft and beautiful.

I agreed with them. They also added that, while journeying in Silvanae, if you hung fairy-made apparel on the limb of a tree at night, the fairies would clean and repair the clothes while you were sleeping. We thanked them for their gifts and enjoyed our repast. As we lounged at breakfast, Faunus appeared carrying a small infant and said, "Before you go, we would like to ask a favor. The family with the new baby wondered if you would name their child?"

I sputtered, "Are you sure? What if I name it something they don't like?"

"They would be honored by any name you give him."

Before I could mouth another word of protest, he laid the tiny infant in my arms. A small pair of green eyes looked up at me from the soft blanket. He was beautiful. I bounced him softly in my arms and cooed at him instinctively. I reached in a finger to lightly tap his nose and touch his downy, soft, silver hair. The little baby, much more active than a newborn human baby would be, reached a hand out to grab a lock of my hair and tugged.

Kishan gently removed my hair from the baby's grasp. Then he brushed the rest of my hair over my shoulder. He touched the baby's hand, which grabbed onto his finger.

Kishan laughed. "He's got a strong grip."

"He does." I looked up at Kishan. "I'd like to name him after your grandfather, Tarak, if you don't mind."

Kishan's golden eyes sparkled. "I think he'd like to have a namesake."

When I told Faunus that I wanted to name the baby Tarak, the Silvanae cheered. Tarak yawned sleepily, unimpressed with his new moniker, and started sucking his thumb.

Kishan put his arm around my shoulders and whispered, "You'll be a good mother, Kelsey."

"Right now, I'm more of an auntie. Here. Your turn."

Kishan settled the small creature in the crook of his arm and spoke quietly to it in his native language. I went off to change my clothes and braid my hair. When I came back, he was rocking the sleeping baby in his arms and staring thoughtfully at its little face.

"Ready to go?"

He looked up at me with a tender expression. "Sure. Just let me change too."

He handed off the baby to his family. Before he left, he brushed a finger across my cheek and smiled at me. His touch was hesitant and sweet. When he came back, we said our good-byes and picked up our pack, which now held my gossamer dress, several honey cakes, and a flagon of flower nectar, and started walking east.

Kishan seemed to know where he was going, so he led the way. I often caught him watching me, staring at me with a strange sort of smile on his face. After an hour or so of walking, I asked, "What's wrong with you today? You're acting differently."

"Am I?"

"Yes. Care to share?"

He hesitated for a long moment, and then sighed. "One of my dreams was about you. You were propped up in bed, tired, but happy and beautiful. You held a dark-haired newborn baby boy in your arms. You called him Anik. He was your son."

"Oh." *That explains why he was acting differently toward me.* "Was there . . . anyone else there with me?"

"There was, but I couldn't see who."

"I see."

"He looked like *us*, Kelsey. I mean . . . he's either Ren's or . . . he's *mine*."

What? Is he saying what I think he's saying? I conjured in my mind a sweet baby boy with Ren's vivid blue eyes; in a flash, the eyes changed color and became as golden as an Arizona desert. I bit my lip nervously. *This isn't good. Is it possible that Ren won't survive? That somehow I'll end up with Kishan?* I knew that Kishan had feelings for me, but I couldn't fathom any future in which I'd choose him over Ren. Maybe I wouldn't have the option. *I have to know!*

"And did you uh . . . see the baby's eyes?"

He paused and looked intently at my face before saying, "No. His eyes were closed. He was sleeping."

"Oh." I started walking ahead again.

He stopped me and touched my arm. "You once asked me if I wanted a home and a family. I didn't think that I'd ever want one without Yesubai, but seeing you like that in my dream, with that little baby . . . yeah. I want it. I want him. I want . . . *you*. I saw him, and I felt . . . possessive and proud. I want the life that I saw in my dream more than just a little, Kells. I thought you should know that."

I mutely nodded and fidgeted while he watched me.

He asked, "Is there anything you dreamed about that you'd like to share with me?"

I shook my head and played with the hem of my fairy shirt. "No, not really."

He grunted and walked ahead.

A baby? I'd always wanted to be a mom and have a family, but I'd never imagined that I'd have two men—brothers, nonetheless—vying for my attention. *If Ren, for some reason, doesn't survive . . . no. I'll stop that line of thinking right now. He will survive! I'll do everything I can to find Lokesh. If that puts me in danger, then so be it.*

We walked all afternoon, stopping for breaks along the way. I was bothered by Kishan's confession. I didn't want to deal with this, didn't want to hurt him. There were so many unresolved questions. Words formed in my mind, but I couldn't seem to find the courage to broach the subject. This was bad!

My heart screamed that it wanted Ren, but my mind reminded me that we didn't always get what we wanted. I wanted my parents back too, and that was impossible. My thoughts roiled like boiling water, but the ideas and thoughts burst into steamy nothingness when they reached the surface.

We didn't talk much except to say, "Look out for that log," or, "Watch out for the puddle." Being with Kishan felt different now, awkward. He seemed to expect something from me, something more than I could give him.

He led us to a range of hills and made for a small cave at the base of one. When we arrived, I peered into its murky depth. "Great. Another cave. I don't like caves. My experiences with them have not been good thus far."

He replied, "It'll be okay. Trust me, Kells."

"Whatever you say. Please lead on."

I heard a buzzing noise that grew louder the deeper we went. It was dark. I pulled out my flashlight and swung it around. Thin pillars of light broke through the soil above in several places, spotlighting the rocks and ground. Something brushed my face. Bees! The cave was full of bees. The walls were dripping with honeycomb. It was like we'd stepped into a giant beehive. In the middle of the cave, on a pedestal, sat a stone object with a hole on top that looked not unlike a beehive.

"The omphalos stone!"

A bee crawled down the neck of my shirt and stung me.

"Ow!" I smacked the insect with my hand.

"Shh, Kells. Keep quiet. They'll bother us less if we move slowly and quietly and get done with what we came to do."

"I'll try."

Bees swarmed angrily around us. It took all my resolve not to bat them violently away from my body. Several had landed on my clothing, but it seemed the stingers couldn't penetrate the fairy cloth. I felt a sting on my wrist and pulled my hands into my long sleeves, holding the opening closed. I approached the stone and looked inside. "What do I do?" I asked.

"Try using your power."

Kishan had been stung several times on the face; in fact, his eyebrow was swelling. I shook my hands out of my sleeves and winced as a bee took the opportunity to crawl up my arm. I put both hands on the sides of the stone and willed the heat to move up from my belly. Fiery warmth shot down my arms and into the stone.

The stone turned yellow, then orange, and then bright red. I heard a hissing sound from within and smelled gas fumes. As smoky gas began to fill the cave and the bees became sluggish, they plopped to the cave floor like fat gumdrops and slept.

"I think you might have to inhale the fumes, Kells, like those oracles Mr. Kadam talked about."

"Okay, here goes."

Leaning over, I took a big whiff. I saw shooting stars and colors. Kishan became distorted, his body twisted and elongated. Then, I was sucked into a powerful vision. When I woke, we were in the jungle again, and Kishan was dabbing my stings with a gooey substance the color of inch-worms. To say it wafted a strong odor would be an understatement. The fetor permeated my hair, my clothes, and everything around us.

"Ugh! That stuff is nasty! What is it?"

He held out a jar. "The Silvanae gave it to us when I told them we would be seeing lots of bees. They've never heard of bees that sting but they use this salve on the trees to repair damage when a limb is blown off by the wind. They believed it would help."

"When did you tell them we'd be going to a bee cave?"

"When you were changing. They said this bee cave was outside their realm."

"It smells awful."

"But how does it feel?"

"It feels . . . good. Soothing and cool."

"Then I imagine you can tolerate the smell."

"I guess."

"Were you successful then? Did you see the tree?"

"Yeah. I saw the tree and the four houses and something else too."

"What else?"

"Like you said before, there's a snake in the garden. To be specific, it's a very large snake wrapped around the base of the tree preventing anyone from accessing it."

"Is it a demon?"

I considered, "No. It's just an exceptionally large snake with a job to do. I know how to get there. Follow me, and we'll figure out what to do on the way."

"Right. Before we get underway though, would you mind?"

He held out the salve and I began smoothing the substance on his neck. He removed his shirt so I could reach the raised red stings on his upper chest and back. I quickly moved behind him to hide my red face. Though I tried not to linger, I couldn't help but notice his bronze skin was smooth and warm.

When I circled around him, he swept his hair back away from his face so I could dab the green slime over his cheeks and forehead. There was a large sting near his upper lip. I touched it lightly. "Does it hurt?"

My gaze moved from his lips up to his eyes. He was looking at me in a way that made me blush.

"Yes," he responded quietly.

It was obvious to me that he was not talking about the sting, so I said nothing. I could feel the warmth of his gaze on my face as I quickly finished his lip and chin. I stepped away as soon as possible and put the top back on the jar, keeping my back to him as he put on his shirt.

"Let's get a move on then, shall we?" I began walking, and he caught up, matching my pace.

We hiked another hour or two and made camp as the sun went down. That night, Kishan wanted another story so I told him one of the stories of Gilgamesh.

"Gilgamesh was a very clever man. So clever, in fact, that he found a way to sneak into the realm of the gods. He wore a disguise and pretended he was on an errand of great importance. Through cunning questioning, he discovered the hiding place of the plant of eternity."

"What is the plant of eternity?"

"I'm not sure. It could've been tea leaves, or something they put in their salad or food. Or, perhaps it was an herb or maybe even a drug like opium, but the point is that he stole it. For four days and nights he ran without stopping to rest so that he could escape the wrath of the gods. When the gods found out the plant had been stolen, they were angry and announced that there would be a reward for anyone who could stop Gilgamesh. On the fifth evening, Gilgamesh was so tired he had to lie down to rest, even if it was to be for only a few moments.

"While he was sleeping, a common snake on its evening hunt passed by. It came upon the fragrant plant, which Gilgamesh had placed in a small rabbit-skin bag. Thinking it was getting an easy rabbit dinner, the snake swallowed the entire bag. The next morning, all Gilgamesh found was a snake skin. This was the first time a snake had ever shed its skin. From then on, people would say that snakes have an eternal nature. When a snake sheds its skin, it dies and is born anew."

I paused. Kishan was quiet. "Did you stay awake this time?" I asked.

"Yes. I liked your story. Sleep well, *bilauta*."

"You too."

But I couldn't sleep for a long time. Thoughts of a golden-eyed baby kept me awake.

It took us two days to find what I was looking for. I knew the tree was in a large valley and that if we climbed between the twin peaks we would see it. We made it to the peaks the first day and spent almost all of the second day climbing. At a lookout spot, we finally gazed below.

We were high enough that clouds obscured the view. Wind broke up the clouds, and the valley appeared to be a dark forest. The trees were so tall that they rose as high as the mountain. In my omphalos stone vision, I saw only one tree with an enormous trunk.

Despite that things looked different in my vision, we descended into the valley. As we continued on, I was shocked to realize that what I was looking at was not a forest of trees at all—but the branches of one gigantic tree, a tree whose limbs stretched taller than the mountains. When I pointed this out to Kishan, he reminded me of Mr. Kadam's research. I fished the papers out of the backpack and read as we hiked on.

"He said it's a giant world tree with roots descending to the underworld and leaves touching heaven. It's supposed to be a thousand feet wide and thousands of feet tall. I'm guessing this is it."

Kishan replied dryly, "It appears so."

When we finally stepped onto the grassy valley floor, we trailed a giant branch back to the trunk. Because the sun could not penetrate the massive limbs overhead, it felt dark, cold, and still under the leafy roof.

The wind blew through the large leaves, which slapped against the branches like stiff clothes on a line. Eerie, strange noises assaulted our ears. Creaking and moaning, the wind found ways to blow over and through the mighty limbs making it seem as if we were walking through a haunted forest.

Kishan moved closer to me to take my hand. I accepted his gesture gratefully and tried to ignore the feeling of being watched. Kishan felt it too, and said it was as if strange creatures were studying us from above. I tried to laugh.

"Imagine the size of the tree nymphs that would be born out of this tree."

I'd meant it to be funny, but the possibility that it could be true caused both of us to look up warily.

Hours later, we finally reached the trunk. It extended like a giant wooden wall as far as we could see. The nearest limb was hundreds of feet high. It was too high for us to reach, and we had no rock climbing gear with us.

Kishan said, "I suggest we make camp here at the base and start

hiking around one side early in the morning. Maybe we can find a lower branch or a way to climb it."

"Sounds good to me. I'm exhausted."

I heard a flapping noise and was surprised to see a black raven settle on the ground near our camp. He cawed at us and stridently beat his wings as he flew away. I couldn't help but feel this might be a bad omen, but I chose not to voice my concerns to Kishan.

When he asked for a story that night, I told him one I'd read in a book that Mr. Kadam had given me.

"Odin is one of the gods of the Norse people. He has two ravens named Hugin and Munin. Ravens are notorious thieves, and these two pet ravens were sent all over the world to steal for Odin."

"What did they take?"

"Ah, that's the interesting thing. Hugin took thoughts and Munin took memories. Odin sent them out early in the morning, and they came back to him in the evening. They perched on his shoulders to whisper the thoughts and memories they had stolen into his ears. This way, he knew everything that happened and everyone's thoughts and intentions."

"They would be convenient to have during a battle. You would know what moves the enemy was planning."

"Exactly. And that is what Odin did. One day, Munin was caught by a traitor. When Hugin returned to whisper thoughts in Odin's mind, he immediately forgot them. An enemy snuck in that night and overthrew Odin. After that, the people stopped believing in the gods. Hugin flew away, and both birds disappeared. The legend of Odin's ravens is one of the reasons that seeing a raven is a bad omen."

Kishan asked, "Kells, are you afraid the raven will steal your memories?"

"My memories are the most precious things that I possess right now. I would do anything to protect them, but no, I'm not afraid of the raven."

"For a long time, I would've given anything to have my memories wiped clean. I thought that if I could forget what happened I might be able to get on with my life."

"But, you wouldn't want to forget Yesubai, just like I wouldn't want to forget Ren or my parents. It's sad to remember, but it's a part of who we are."

"Hmm. Goodnight, Kelsey."

"Goodnight, Kishan."

The next morning, as we packed up for the day, I noticed the bracelet Ren had given me was gone. Kishan and I looked everywhere, but couldn't find it.

"Kells, the camera is missing too, and all the honey cakes."

"Oh, no! What else?"

He pointedly looked at my throat.

"What? What is it?"

"The amulet is gone."

"What happened? How were we robbed in the middle of nowhere? How could I not feel someone taking things from off my body as I slept?" I cried frantically.

"I have a suspicion it was the raven."

"But it's not real! It's just a myth!"

"You said yourself that myths are often based on truths or partial truths. Maybe the raven took them. I would have known if it was a person. A bird I ignore when I sleep."

"What are we going to do now?"

"The only thing we can do. Keep going. We still have our weapons and the Golden Fruit."

"Yes, but the amulet!"

"It'll be okay, Kells. Have a little faith, remember? Like the Ocean Teacher said."

"Easy for you to say. You didn't have your only picture of Yesubai taken from you."

He looked at me silently for a moment. "The only picture I ever had of Yesubai is the one in my mind."

"I know, but—"

He slid a finger under my chin and tipped my face up. "You have a chance to get the man back. Don't worry so much about the picture."

"You're right, you're right. I know. Let's get going then."

We chose the left side of the tree trunk and began walking. The trunk was so huge that I could barely see it curve in the distance.

"What happens when we see the snake, Kells?"

"It's not a vicious snake. It simply guards the tree. At least that's the way it looked from the omphalos stone. If the snake feels that we have a legitimate reason to pass, it will allow us. If not, it will try to stop us."

"Hmm."

An hour or two later, I was trailing my finger along the bark when the trunk moved.

"Kishan! Did you see that?"

He touched the trunk. "I don't see anything."

"Put your hands on it. Feel it right . . . here. You see? The texture changes. There! It's another shift! Put your hand on top of mine. Can you feel it now?"

"Yes."

A section of the trunk about six feet wide began to move. Another segment above that shifted in the opposite direction. The patterns seemed familiar, but I couldn't put it together. It was confusing, like seeing the giant tree and mistaking it for an entire forest. Wind swirled around us like deep bellows. A giant suction of air followed by a strong wind disturbed the short grass and caused prickly goose bumps to rise on my arms.

Kishan looked up and froze. "Don't move, Kelsey."

The air began moving harder, like the bellows were pumping faster.

I hissed, "What is it, Kishan?"

A rustling noise stirred behind me. It sounded like someone was dragging a heavy bag through a pile of leaves. Twigs cracked, leaves shuddered, and branches groaned. I heard a deep, sibilant voice.

"Why isss ittt you are comminngg to my foresssttt?"

I slowly turned and looked into a giant, unblinking, horned eye. "Are you the guardian of the world tree?"

"Yessssss. Why are you presssssenttt?"

I looked up and up and up. Now I knew what I'd been looking at before. The giant snake was coiled around the tree, and the six-foot segments were the snake's body. It was perfectly camouflaged. In fact, as I watched, its body shifted color to match its environment like a chameleon. Its head was as big as Ren's Hummer, and there was no way to know just how long its body was. Kishan stepped up beside me to take my hand. I noticed he held the chakram loosely in his other hand.

"We're here to claim the airy prize that rests at the top of the tree," I declared.

"Why sssshould I let you passsssss? Why do you neeeeddd the Divine Ssssscarffff?"

"The airy prize is a scarf?"

"Yessssssssss."

"Huh. Well, we need it because it will help break the curse placed on two princes of India, and it will also help to save the people of their country."

"Who areee thesssseeee princcccccccesss?"

"This is Kishan. His brother Ren has been kidnapped."

The giant snake flicked its tongue out toward Kishan several times, who withstood the inspection bravely. I would've run in the other direction.

"I know not thesssssseee brothersssssss. You may notttt passsssssssss."

The huge head began to turn as heavy coils slid over the ground. I felt a similar movement on my arm and shouted, "Wait!"

The snake turned back toward me and lowered its head to see me better. Fanindra stretched out her coils and slid around the back of my neck. She raised her head toward the giant eye and flicked out her tongue several times.

"Whooo isssss sssssheeee?"

"Her name is Fanindra. She belongs to the goddess Durga."

"Durgaaaaa. I have heard of this godddeesssssss. Thissss ssssnakeee is hersssss?"

"Yes. Fanindra is here to help us on our quest. The goddess Durga sent us and gave us weapons."

"I sssssseeeeeeeee."

The guardian peered at Fanindra for a long moment as if pondering our fate. The snakes seemed to be communicating silently with each other.

"Youuu may crossssss. I sssseennssse your purposssssse is not maliccciousssss. Perhapssssss you will be succccesssssful. Perhapssssss it issss your dessssstiny. Who knowssssssss? You will passsss through four housssseeessss. The housssse of birdsssssss. The housssse of gourdssssss. The housssse of sssssirensssssss. And the housssse of battssssss. Beee cautiousssssss. To move on, you musssst make the besssstt of choiccccessssssss."

Kishan and I bowed. "Thank you, Guardian."

"Besssst wissssheessss."

The large snake swung its heavy body, and the great tree rumbled. The coils wrapped around the trunk moved, separating to reveal a secret passage into the trunk and a hidden stairway. Fanindra wound her body around my upper arm and settled into her dormant state.

Kishan pulled me into the passage. I had enough time to recognize the floor was covered with sawdust, when the snake moved. Its body dropped over the passage, sealing us into the black root of the giant world tree.

20

the tests of the four houses

Fanindra's emerald eyes began to glow and provided enough light that Kishan could retrieve our flashlight. Five feet beyond us was another tree trunk that appeared as solid as the one outside—a trunk within a trunk. Between the two trunks was a spiral stairway. He took my hand again before we started our climb. The stairs were wide enough that we could walk side by side and deep enough that we could stop and rest or even sleep if we needed to.

We ascended at a slow pace and rested frequently. It was hard to tell how high we'd climbed. After several hours, we came upon a door of sorts. It was yellow-orange and bumpy. A rough, woody stem was at the exact place where a knob should have been. I strung my bow and nocked an arrow while Kishan readied his chakram. He stood to the side, took the handle, and pushed the door slowly inward while I slid in my foot and scanned for attackers. No one was in sight.

The room was full of shelves that had been carved into the walls of the tree. Covering the shelves and the floors were hundreds of gourds of all shapes and sizes. Some were solid; some were hollowed out. Many of them had beautiful, elaborate designs and were lit from within by flickering candles.

Some pumpkins were depicted with carvings far beyond anything I'd ever seen on Halloween. We walked past shelf after shelf, admiring the designs. Some were painted and oiled until they shone like carved gems. Kishan reached out to touch one.

"Wait! Don't touch anything yet. This is one of the tests. We need to figure out what to do. Hold on for a second while I look at Mr. Kadam's notes."

Mr. Kadam had provided three pages of information on gourds. Kishan and I sat on the polished wood floor and read through them.

"I don't think they have anything to do with the American slave song 'Follow the Drinkin' Gourd.' I can't see how that could apply. It refers to the stars, the Big Dipper specifically, which guided American slaves to freedom as they journeyed on the Underground Railroad."

I flipped a page. "Here's a lot of stuff about where certain gourds originated and facts about how sailors sought seeds of certain types to grow them. There's a myth about gourd boats. I don't think that's it either."

Kishan laughed. "How about this one? The one about gourds and fertility? Want to give it a try, Kells? I'm willing to make the sacrifice if you are."

I skimmed through the myth and narrowed my eyes at him while he laughed. "Ha! In your dreams maybe. Definitely skipping that one." I turned to another page. "This one says to throw a gourd onto water to call up sea monsters and sea serpents. Huh, not really needing one of those."

"What about this Chinese myth? It says that a young boy coming of age must choose the gourd that would guide his life. Each one contained something different. Some were dangerous; some not. One even had the elixir of eternal youth. Maybe we'll get lucky. Perhaps we should just pick one."

"I think picking one is probably the right thing to do, but how do we know which one?"

"Not sure. I guess we just need to try. I'll go first. Keep your hand aimed at whatever comes out."

Kishan picked up a plain bell-shaped gourd. Nothing happened. He shook it, threw it in the air, and thumped it against the wall . . . still nothing.

"I'm going to try breaking it." He smashed it on the ground, and a pear rolled out.

He snatched up the fruit and took a bite before I could warn him there might be something wrong with it. When he finally paid attention to me, the fruit was almost gone. He dismissed my warning and said it tasted fine. The broken gourd dissolved and melted into the floor.

"Okay, my turn." I picked up a round gourd painted with flowers, raised it above my head, and smashed it to the floor. A black, hissing snake emerged from the broken pieces. It coiled to strike and spat at my leg. Before I could raise my hand, I heard a metallic whirring. Kishan's chakram sank into the wooden floor at my feet, severing the snake's head. The serpent's body and the broken gourd melted into the floor.

"Umm, your turn. Maybe it's a good idea to go with plain gourds."

He chose a bottle-shaped gourd, which produced something that looked like milk. I cautioned him not to drink it because it might not be what it seemed. He agreed, but we found that if we didn't drink it, the next gourd wouldn't break, and the broken one with the milk inside wouldn't dissolve. He gulped down the milk and we went on.

I chose a huge white gourd and got moonlight.

A small warty gourd produced sand.

A tall thin one made beautiful music.

A thick, gray gourd that looked like a bottle-nosed dolphin splashed seawater on Kishan's leg.

My next choice was a spoon-shaped one. When I broke it, a black mist emerged and headed for me. I darted away, but it followed and moved toward my mouth and nose. There was nothing Kishan could do. I breathed it in and began coughing. My vision blurred. I felt dizzy and staggered. Kishan caught me.

"Kelsey! You're turning pale! How do you feel?"

"Not good. I think that one was disease."

"Here. Lie down and rest. Maybe I can find a cure."

He began frantically breaking gourds while I watched. I shivered and started to sweat, a scorpion came out of the next one and he stomped on it with his boot. He found a gourd with wind, one with a fish, and one that contained a small star that glowed so brightly we had to close our eyes until the light diminished and it sunk into the floor.

Every time he found a liquid, he rushed it over to me and made me drink. I drank some fruit nectar, regular water, and some kind of bitter dark chocolate. I refused to drink one that smelled like rubbing alcohol but I dabbed it on my skin so the gourd would disappear.

The next three contained clouds, a giant tarantula, which he kicked into the corner of the room, and a ruby, which he pocketed. My vision was going black at this point, and Kishan was getting desperate. The next gourd he chose had some kind of pill. We debated if I should take it or not. I was really dizzy and weak, feverish and sweaty. Breathing was hard, and my heart was racing. I panicked, feeling sure that if we couldn't find something soon, I'd die. I chewed the pill and swallowed. It tasted like a kid's vitamin, and it didn't make me feel better.

Two more gourds contained cheese and a ring. He ate the cheese and slipped the ring on his finger. The next one had a white liquid. He was nervous. It could be a poison that killed me outright or it could be my cure or it could be the elixir of eternal youth for all we knew. I waved him over.

"I'll drink it. Help me."

He lifted my head and tilted the gourd, its contents spilling between my dry, cracked lips. The liquid trickled down my throat as I swallowed weakly. Immediately, I began to feel strength return to my limbs.

"More."

He held the gourd steady as I drank. It tasted delicious and gave

me enough strength to take the gourd from him. Wrapping both hands around the bowl shape, I gulped down the rest in two big swallows. I felt stronger than I had before we'd come into the room.

"You look much better, Kells. How do you feel?"

I stood up. "I feel good! Strong. Invincible, even."

He let out a shaky breath. "Good."

I looked around with clear sight. Almost better than clear. "Hey. What's that?"

I pushed a few gourds out of the way and grabbed the handle of a large round gourd with a long top stem. "It has a tiger carved on the outside. Try this one, Kishan."

He took it from my hands and smashed it on the floor. Inside was a folded paper.

"It's like a fortune cookie! What does it say?"

"It says—*The hidden vessel shows the way.*"

"The *hidden* vessel? Maybe it means a hidden gourd."

"Pretty easy to hide a gourd in a room full of gourds, Kells."

"Yeah. Let's look for out-of-the-way gourds that are in the back of the room or tucked in corners."

We collected a group of smaller-sized gourds. Kishan had about ten, and I had four. He opened his group first, which contained rice, a butterfly, a hot pepper, snow, a feather, a lily, a cotton ball, a mouse, another snake, which he got rid of—it could have been harmless, but better to be safe than sorry—and an earthworm.

Disappointed, we turned to my group. The first had thread, the second contained drum sounds, the third held a vanilla scent, and the fourth, shaped like a small apple, had nothing. We waited for a minute and started to get nervous thinking one of us was going to get sick again. The broken gourd disappeared like the others, so something had happened.

"Is that it? Do you see anything?"

"No. Wait. I hear something."

After a minute, I said, "Well? What is it?"

"There's something different about the room, but I can't tell what. Wait. The air! It's moving. Can you sense it?"

"No."

"Give me a minute."

Kishan crept around the room examining shelves, walls, and gourds. He placed his hand on one of the walls and leaned in closer, bumping gourds that rolled and shifted.

"There's air coming through here. I think it's a door. Help me move these gourds."

We cleared the entire section of wall, which left only bare shelves.

"I can't move this one. It's stuck."

It was a tiny gourd that seemed to be growing out of the wall. I pulled and pushed, but it wouldn't budge. Kishan stepped back to get a better look and started laughing. I was still yanking on the small gourd.

"What is it? Why are you laughing?"

"Stand back a second, Kells."

I moved out of the way, and he placed his hand on the gourd.

"I don't know what you're trying to prove. It won't move."

Kishan twisted and pushed. "It's a knob, Kelsey." He laughed and pushed open the section of wall that was now obviously a door. On the other side, we found more steps that led higher into the tree.

He held out his hand. "Shall we?"

"You know, I'm never going to look at pumpkin pie the same way again."

His laughter echoed through the tree trunk.

After a few hours of climbing, Kishan called a halt. "Let's stop and eat something, Kells. I can't keep up with you. I wonder how long your special energy drink is going to last."

I stopped about ten steps ahead of him and waited for him to catch up. "Now you know how I feel trying to keep pace with you tigers all the time."

He grunted and slung the backpack off his shoulders. We made ourselves comfortable on a large step. He unzipped the bag, took out the Golden Fruit, and rolled it between his palms. After thinking for a moment, he grinned and spoke in his native language. A large plate shimmered and solidified. The steam coming from the vegetables smelled familiar.

I wrinkled my nose. "Curry? Ugh. My turn."

I wished for scalloped potatoes, cherry glazed ham, green beans almondine, and rolls with honey butter. When my dinner appeared, Kishan eyed my plate.

"How about we share?"

"No thanks. Not a curry fan."

He finished off his meal quickly and kept trying to get me to look at imaginary monsters so he could steal bites from my plate. I ended up just giving him half.

Another hour of stairs and my power juice wore off. I felt drained. Kishan let me rest while he looked for the next house. When he returned, I was writing in my journal.

"I found the next doorway, Kells. Come on. It might be better to rest there."

The dusty circular steps inside the trunk of the world tree led us to a cottage overgrown with thick ivy and flowers. Tinkling laughter could be heard inside.

I whispered, "There are people in there. Let's be careful."

He nodded and untied the chakram from his belt while I nocked an arrow.

"Ready?"

"Ready," I whispered.

He carefully opened the door, and we were greeted by the most beautiful women I'd ever seen. They ignored our weapons and bid us welcome to their home.

A gorgeous woman with thick waves of long brown hair, green eyes, downy soft, ivory skin, and cherry lips dressed in a shimmering, blush-colored gown took Kishan's arm.

"You poor things. You must be tired after your trip. Come inside. You can bathe and rest from your travels."

"A bath sounds great to me," said an entranced Kishan.

She paid absolutely no attention to me. Her eyes were locked on Kishan. She stroked his arm and murmured to him of soft pillows, hot water, and refreshments. Another woman joined the first one. She was blonde and blue-eyed and wore a gown of sparkling silver.

"Yes, come," she said. "You will find comfort here. Please follow us."

They'd started to lead Kishan away when I protested. Kishan turned and a man approached. Six feet of tanned, muscular, bare chest, blue-eyed, blond male turned all of his attention to me.

"Hello, welcome to our humble home. My sisters and I rarely have any visitors. We would love for you stay with us for a while." He smiled at me, and I blushed furiously.

I stammered, "Umm, that's very generous of you."

Kishan frowned at the guy, but the girls turned their long-lashed fluttery charm on and distracted him again.

"Uh, Kishan, I don't think—"

Another man came out from behind a curtain. This one was even better looking than the first. He was dark-haired with dark eyes, and his mouth riveted my attention. He pouted and said, "Are you sure you can't stay with us? Just for a while. We'd love to have some company." He sighed dramatically. "The only thing we have to keep us occupied is our book collection."

"You have a book collection?"

"Yes." He smiled and offered me his arm. "Will you allow me to show it to you?"

Kishan had left with the women, and I decided to check out the book collection. I rationalized that I could always blast the guys with lightning if they tried something.

They did indeed have a book collection and happened to have many of the books that I loved. In fact, on closer inspection, I found I knew every title. They offered me refreshments.

"Here, taste one of these tarts. They are amazing. Our sisters are excellent cooks."

"Oh. Umm, no thanks. Kishan and I just ate."

"Ah then, perhaps you would like to freshen up?"

"You have a bathroom?"

"We do. It's behind the curtain over there. There's also a shower. Pull on the long vine, and water will rain down from the leaves of the tree. We will arrange some refreshment and a comfortable place for you to rest."

"Thank you."

We were obviously in the House of Sirens. Their bathroom was real, thankfully, and I took the opportunity to shower and change clothes. When I emerged, I found a long golden gown had been left hanging for me. It was similar to the gowns the two women had been wearing. My original clothes were still torn and bloody, so I put on the golden dress and hung out my fairy clothes to see if the fairies would still clean them in the world tree.

Quietly, I read through Mr. Kadam's notes on sirens. I skimmed through the sirens of the *Odyssey* and the story of Jason and the Argonauts. I already knew those tales, but he had also included information on sea nymphs, mermaids, and mermen, who were sometimes called sirens as well.

These people were probably more tree nymphs than water nymphs. They retained beauty until they died. They could ride through the air. Slip through small holes. Hmm, that's a new one. *Extremely long life . . . sometimes invisible . . . special times are noon and midnight.* Midnight should be soon. *They could be dangerous, cause madness, a stroke, dumbness, and besotted infatuation.*

A soft knock startled me from my study. "Yes?"

"Are you ready to come out, Miss?"

"Almost."

I quickly glanced through the rest of my notes and slipped the papers into my backpack. The two men were standing directly outside the door, staring at me like a pair of snakes watching a bird's nest.

"Umm, excuse me."

I slipped between them, walked to the other side of the room, and sat on what looked like a giant bean bag sofa covered in soft fur. The men sat on either side of me.

One of them nudged my shoulder. "You're too stiff. Lie back and relax. The seat molds itself to your body."

They wouldn't take no for an answer. The dark haired man pushed me back gently, but insistently.

"Yes, it is comfortable. Thank you. Umm, where's Kishan?"

"Who's Kishan?"

"The man I came here with."

"I didn't notice a man."

"It was impossible to notice anything after *you* stepped into the room," the other man said.

"Yes. I agree. You're quite lovely," said his brother.

One of the men began stroking my arm while the other started massaging my shoulders.

They indicated a table in front of us laden with treats.

"Would you like to try some candied fruit? It's delicious."

"No. Thank you. I'm not hungry quite yet."

The man massaging my shoulders began kissing the back of my neck. "You have the most delicate skin."

I tried to sit up, but he pressed me back in the chair. "Relax. We're here to please you."

The other one handed me a fluted glass with bubbling red liquid. "Sparkling elderberry juice?"

He picked up my other hand and began kissing my fingers. A foggy dimness clouded my vision. I closed my eyes for a moment, and my senses focused on lips kissing my throat and warm hands massaging my shoulders. Pleasure wound through my body, and I greedily wanted more. One of the men kissed my lips. It didn't feel right. Something was wrong.

I murmured, "No," weakly and tried to shake the men off, but they wouldn't leave me alone. Something tickled the back of my mind. Something I was trying to grab onto. Something that would help me focus. The massage on my shoulders felt so good. He moved to my neck and moved his thumb in little circles. That's when the something I was trying to remember snapped into my conscious mind.

Ren. He'd massaged my neck like that. I pictured his face. It was out of focus at first, but I started to list the things I loved about him in my mind and the picture became clearer. I thought about his hair, his eyes, how he held my hand all the time. I thought about him laying his head on my lap while I read to him, how he got jealous, his love for peanut-butter pancakes, and about how he chose the peaches-and-cream ice cream because it reminded him of me. In my mind, I heard him say, "*Mein tumse mohabbat karta hoon, iadala.*"

I whispered, "*Mujhe tumse pyarhai*, Ren."

Something popped, and I abruptly sat up. The men pouted as they tried to pull me back. They began singing softly. My vision started to shift out of focus again, so I hummed the song Ren wrote for me and recited one of his poems. I stood up. The men were now insisting that I eat something again or sip some juice. I refused. They tugged me over to a soft bed. I stood my ground while they pulled and begged and cajoled. They complimented my hair, my eyes, and my beautiful dress and cried that I'd been their only visitor in millennia and that they just wanted to spend some time in my company.

Refusing again, I insisted that we needed to be on our way. They persisted, took my hand, and pulled me toward the bed. I twisted away and grabbed my bow. Quickly, I strung it and nocked an arrow, then aimed at whichever male chest was closest, threatening them. The two men backed away and one raised his hand in a gesture of defeat. They silently communicated, and then shook their heads sadly.

"We would have made you happy. You would have forgotten all of your troubles. We would have loved you."

I shook my head. "I love another."

"You would have treasured us over time. We have the ability to take away all thoughts and replace them with only feelings of passion and pleasure."

I replied sarcastically, "I'll bet."

"We are lonely. Our last companion died several centuries ago. We loved her."

The other one interjected, "Yes, we loved her so. She never knew sorrow for even a day in her life with us."

"But we are immortal and her life was over too quickly."

"Yes. We must find a replacement."

"Well, sorry, boys, but I don't want that. I have no interest in being your," I swallowed, "love slave. And besides, I don't want to forget everything or everyone."

They studied me for a long moment. "So be it. You are free to go."

"What about Kishan?"

"He must make his own choice."

With that, they spun into a thin wisp of smoke, entered a knot on the wall of the tree, and disappeared. I went back into the bathroom to retrieve my fairy clothes and was delighted to see that they had been cleaned and repaired.

Picking up the bag, I stepped back into the room. Instead of a seductive boudoir, it was now a simple, empty room with a door. I opened it, left the house, and ended up back on the circular stairway that wound around inside the trunk of the world tree. The doorway closed behind me. I was alone on the stairs.

I changed back into the pants and shirt the fairies had woven for us and wondered when or if Kishan would exit. *That soft bed would have made a much better place to sleep than the hard wooden steps. Then again, if I had stayed in that bed, I don't think I would've been getting a lot of sleep.*

I mentally thanked Ren for saving me from the tree nymphs or man sirens or whatever they were. Completely exhausted, I curled up in the sleeping bag and fell asleep. Sometime in the middle of the night, Kishan nudged my shoulder.

"Hey."

I leaned up on an elbow and yawned, "Kishan? Took you long enough."

"Yeah. It wasn't exactly easy to shake off those women."

"I know what you mean. I had to threaten to shoot those guys to make them leave me alone. In fact, I'm surprised you got out as quickly as you did. How did you purge their influence from your mind?"

"Talk to you about it later. I'm tired, Kells."

"Okay. Here, take my quilt. I would offer to share the sleeping bag, but I've had enough of men for the moment."

"I understand completely. Thanks. Goodnight, Kells."

After we woke, ate, and packed, we continued up the steps of the world tree. Bright light shone ahead. A hole in the trunk opened, and we stepped through to the outside. I appreciated the sunshine, but the steps were no longer enclosed. I hugged the trunk, refusing to look down.

Kishan, on the other hand, was fascinated by how high we were. He couldn't see the bottom despite his super tiger vision. Giant branches extended out from the tree. They were so large we could have walked across one together side by side without any danger of falling off. Kishan ran along a couple of them from time to time to explore. I stayed as close to the trunk as possible.

After several hours at our slow pace, I stopped in front of a dark hole that led back inside the trunk. I waited for Kishan to return from his latest exploration, so we could enter the hole together. This part of the trunk was darker and moist. Water trickled down the inside, dripping and plopping from somewhere above. The walls changed from smooth to splintered and peeling. Our voices echoed. There seemed to be a large gap in the tree, like it had been hollowed out.

I said, "This part of the tree feels dead, as if it's been damaged."

"Yes. The wood under our feet is rotting. Stay as close to the trunk wall as you can."

Another few minutes passed, and the stairs stopped below a black hole just big enough to crawl through.

"There's nowhere else to go. Should we climb in?"

"It's going to be a tight fit."

"Then let me go first and look around," I volunteered. "If it's blocked ahead, there's no need for you to climb through. I'll just back out, and we'll figure out another way to the top."

He agreed and traded the flashlight for the backpack. Kishan boosted me up, and I wiggled into the hole and crawled through on my hands and knees until the passage started to narrow and become taller. At that point, the only way to proceed was to stand, turn to the side, and shimmy forward. Then the passageway lowered, and again I sunk to my knees.

The passageway felt like petrified rock. A big chunk hung down, blocking the top half of the passage. I squirmed on my stomach, wiggled under it, and found that the passage opened into a large cavern. It felt like I'd traveled a hundred feet, but it was probably more like twenty-five. I thought Kishan would fit but just barely.

I hollered back, "Give it a try."

As I waited for him, I noticed that the floor felt spongy. *Probably rotting wood.* The walls were coated with something that resembled crusty, brown deli mustard. I heard a bird flapping overhead and a soft *scree*ing. *Huh, must be a nest up there.* The sounds bounced around the inside of the tree, getting progressively louder and more violent.

"Uh, Kishan? Hurry up!"

I raised my flashlight fearfully. I couldn't see anything, but the air was definitely moving. It seemed as if flocks of birds were slapping against each other in the darkness. Something brushed past my arm and flapped away suddenly. If it was a bird, it was a big one.

"Kishan!"

"Almost there."

I could hear him sliding along on his stomach. He was almost through.

Something or a few somethings flapped toward me again. *Maybe they're giant moths.* I shut off my light to deter the flapping creatures and listened as Kishan approached.

First the backpack and then his head emerged. Over my head, something large startled me with frenzied flapping. Pinching, hooked claws curled around my shoulders and took hold. I screamed. They tightened, and with a violent beating of wings and a loud *SCREEEEEE*, I was lifted into the air.

Kishan quickly wormed his way out of the hole and grabbed for my leg, but the creature was strong and yanked me away. I heard him shout, "Kelsey!"

I shouted back, my voice echoing off the walls. I was high up, much higher than Kishan, but I could still faintly make him out below. The creature was soon surrounded by others of its kind, and I was enfolded in a screeching, fluttering, quivering mass of warm bodies. Sometimes, I felt fur brush against my skin, sometimes a leathery membrane, and, once in a while, scratching talons.

The creature slowed, hovered, and then let go. Before I could scream, I landed with a thud on my backside. I turned on the flashlight that I had somehow managed to hang onto during the sudden ride. Scared to see where I was but determined to find out, I flipped the switch and looked up.

At first, I couldn't figure out what I was looking at. All I could see were masses of brown and black bodies. Then, I realized they were *bats*. *Giant* bats. I was standing on a ledge with a drop-off of hundreds of feet. Quickly, I scooted back against the wall.

Kishan yelled my name and tried to move in my direction.

"I'm okay!" I shouted. "They haven't hurt me! I'm up here on a ledge!"

"Hang on, Kells! I'm coming!"

The bats were hanging upside down and watching Kishan's progress with blinking black eyes. The mass of bodies was constantly in motion. Some were spider-walking over their peers to a better hanging position. Some flapped their wings before tightly folding them around their bodies. Others rocked back and forth. Some slept.

They were noisy. They chattered with *clicks, pops*, and *smacks* as they hung and watched us.

Kishan progressed for a while but got stuck and had to backtrack. He tried several times to climb up to where I was, but he was always thwarted. After the sixth try, he stood near the hole and shouted up to me, "It's impossible, Kells. I can't get up there!"

I'd just opened my mouth to answer him when a giant bat spoke.

"Iiiiiimpossiiiible heeeee thiiiinks," it clicked and flapped. "Iiiitt's possiiiible, Tiiigerrr."

I spoke to the bat, "You know that he's a tiger?"

"Weeeeee seeeee hiiiiim. Heeaar hiiiiim. Heeeees speeerit eees spliittt."

"His spirit is split? What do you mean?"

"Meeean heee eeeendure grieeeeef. Heeee heeeeal hiiiis stiiiing . . . heeee reeescue youu."

"If he heals his sting, he rescues me? How can he do that?"

"Heee iiiis like weee. Heee is halfff maaan and halfff tiiigerr. Weee aree halfff bird and halfff mammalll. Halfffs neeeeeed beeeee togeeether. Heee musstt eeembracee tiiiigerrr."

"How can his two halves be together?"

"Heeee musstt leearnn."

I was about to ask another question when several of the bats dropped into the air and flew to different places in the womb-like cavern. Rhythmic smacks, which I realized was their echo sonar, beat through the air and against the walls. I could actually feel the vibrations on my skin. Soon, small stones embedded in the walls began to glow. The longer the bats kept up their noise, the brighter the lights became. When the bats stopped, the cavern was well lit.

"Theeeee lightsss wiiill failee wheeeen hiiis time isssss outtt. Heeee musstt heelpp youu beeforeeeee. Heee musstt use hiiis maaan and hiiis tiiiigerrr. Teeeell hiiiim."

"Okay." I hollered down to Kishan, "The bats say that you have to use both halves of yourself to reach me before the light turns dim again. They say you have to embrace the tiger part of you."

Now that the lights were on, the dangers of the path became obvious. A series of formations similar to stalagmites, but with flat tops, rose in the cavern. They were too far apart for a human to jump, but a tiger might be able to.

Kishan looked up and threw the chakram into the air. As it soared high, he changed into the black tiger, and leapt. He went fast. I held my breath as he quickly leapt from one thin formation to another without even stopping to balance himself. I gasped in horror knowing each leap could mean his death. When he reached the last one, he overshot slightly and gripped the spongy wood with his claws, twisting his tail around for balance.

He switched to a man, caught the chakram and threw it high. The perch was tiny, barely big enough for his feet. There was no ledge to jump to from there. Nothing was close enough, even for a tiger. He looked around for a moment, figuring out his next move. The bats blinked and stared at him wide-eyed from their upside down perches. The light started to dim. The darker it was, the more dangerous his climb would be.

I knew that Kishan could see in the dark better than I could, but the way was still very treacherous. He made a decision, crouched down, switched to the black tiger, and leapt into the air. There was nothing for him to land on.

I screamed, "Kishan! No!"

He switched to a man in midair and fell. I leaned down on my belly to peer over the edge of my small shelf and began breathing again when I saw him dangling from a long vine. He was slowly climbing up hand over hand, but he was still too far away. He caught the chakram, held the dangerous weapon in his teeth, and swung back and forth until he could grab onto a protruding piece of wood on the side of the tree. He climbed higher and rested for a minute on a tiny outcropping. After assessing his situation, he grabbed a new vine, jumped, and swung out again.

Kishan did a series of complicated acrobatic stunts. I saw the man change into tiger and back at least three times. At one point, he threw the chakram, which spun in the cavern, sliced a vine, and flew back to a tiger paw that suddenly became a hand and caught it. Chakram in his mouth again, he swung below me, across the cavern, and pushed off the other side to aim for me. He grabbed the vine he'd cut to complete the swing. As he zoomed toward me, I saw that this vine wasn't long enough and realized he would land at least ten feet away.

I wanted to close my eyes but felt I had to watch as Kishan risked his life to reach me. Kishan swung back and pushed off again. This time, when his feet touched the wall, he tossed the chakram still another time. He grabbed the vine in his teeth, quickly changed to the black tiger again, and pushed off hard with his powerful hind legs. He switched to a man again, flew out as high as the vine would take him, and then let go. Twisting in the air, he changed to a tiger. His striped, black body stretched out to my ledge. As his claws sank into the wood near my feet and he hung suspended in midair, the chakram sank into the wood a few inches from my hand. Tiger claws become hands.

"Kishan!"

I grabbed the back of his shirt and yanked as hard as I could. He rolled over onto the ledge and lay there, panting, for several minutes. The light had dimmed still more.

"Yyouu seeeee? Heee diiiid iiiitt."

His arms shook, and I brushed my tears away. "Yes. He did," I said quietly.

When Kishan sat up, I grabbed him in a fierce hug and kissed his cheek. He held me close for a minute before reluctantly letting me go. He brushed the hair away from my eyes.

"I'm sorry I couldn't bring the backpack," he said.

"It's okay. There was no way you could bring it with all you had to do."

"Weeee wiiiill geeet iiiit."

I murmured sarcastically, "Too bad they couldn't bring you up here too."

"Weeee mussstt tesssttt hiiiim. Heeee hasss succeeeeeedeedd."

One of the bats flew down to retrieve the backpack. It dropped the bag into my waiting hands.

"Thank you." I touched Kishan's arm. "Are you all right?"

"I'm fine." He grinned rakishly despite his exhaustion. "In fact, I could be convinced to do it again for a real kiss."

I punched his arm lightly. "I think one on the cheek was enough, don't you?"

He grunted noncommittally. "Where do we go from here?"

One of the bats spoke, "Weee wiiiiill takeee youu."

Two of the bats released their grip on the ceiling and fell several feet before snapping open their wings. They beat them hard, gaining altitude, and hovered above us. Then they descended slowly. Taloned feet gripped my shoulders and tightened.

I heard the admonition, "Reeeemainn stiiilll," and decided it was good advice to follow.

With frenzied flapping, the bats took off, carrying us higher and higher into the tree. It was not a fun ride, but I also recognized that this would save us several hours of climbing. I thought we'd be flying straight up vertically, but, instead, the bats circled, ascending slowly and steadily.

Eventually, I noticed our surroundings were increasingly brighter. I made out an opening, a crevice that allowed dappled orange sunlight to move across the walls. I felt a cool breeze waft over my skin and smelled fresh living tree instead of the rotting musty odor of fungus, ammonia, and burned citrus. Our winged companions flew out of the opening and, flapping loudly, carefully set us on a branch. The branches were thinner here, but they were easily strong enough for both of us to walk on.

With a final warning of, "Beeee viiiiggiiilaaant," they flew back into the tree and left us on our own.

"Hey, Kells, throw me the backpack. I want to change out of these black clothes and put some shoes on."

I threw him the backpack and turned around so he could change.

"Yeah. Too bad your fairy clothes are gone now. They've disappeared into the tiger ether. They were handy to have around. Luckily, Mr. Kadam insisted on a couple of pairs of shoes for you, just in case."

"Kells? The fairy clothes are in the bag."

"What?" I turned around to find Kishan stripped to the waist and averted my eyes. "How did that happen?"

"Not sure. Fairy magic I guess. Now turn around unless you want to watch me change."

Red-faced, I spun quickly. It was sunset, and we decided to eat and rest. I was worn out but afraid to sleep on a branch, even if it *was* double the width of a king-size mattress.

I sat dead in the middle. "I'm afraid I'll fall off."

"You're tired. You need the rest."

"I won't be able to."

"I'll hold you. You won't fall."

"What if *you* fall?"

"Cats don't fall out of trees unless they want to. Come here."

Kishan put one arm around me and cushioned my head on his other. I didn't think I'd be able to sleep, but I did.

The next morning, I yawned, rubbed my sleepy eyes, and found Kishan watching me. He had an arm wrapped around my waist, and my head was resting on his other arm.

"Didn't you sleep?"

"I catnapped."

"How long have you been awake?"

"For an hour or so."

"Why didn't you wake me?"

"You needed the rest."

"Oh. Well, thanks for making sure I didn't fall."

"Kells? I want to say something."

"What?" I tucked my fist under my cheek. "What is it?"

"You . . . you're very important to me."

"You're very important to me too."

"No. That's not what I mean. I mean . . . I *feel* . . . and I have reason to believe . . . that we could come to mean something to each other."

"You mean something to me now."

"Right, but I'm not talking about friendship."

"Kishan—"

"Is there no possibility, not even the smallest chance that you could ever let yourself love me? Don't you feel anything for me at all?"

"Of course I do. But—"

"But nothing. If Ren wasn't in the picture, would you consider being with me? Could I be someone that you could come to care about?"

I put my hand on his cheek. "Kishan, I already care about you. I already have feelings for you. I already love you."

He smiled and leaned in a little closer. Alarms started going off in my head, and I jerked back and felt like I was falling. I grabbed his arm and held on for dear life.

He steadied me and studied my face. He surely noticed my look of panic and probably recognized that it wasn't due to losing my balance. He bridled his emotions, leaned back, and said quietly, "I'd never let you fall, Kells."

I wasn't handling this well, but the best I could give him was, "I know you wouldn't."

He let me go and rose to make our breakfast.

The stairs were narrower now and wound around the outside of the tree. The trunk was much smaller too. It took us only about thirty minutes to circumnavigate it at this height. After a few frightening hours of stairs that narrowed more and more, we came across a woven rope that dangled from what looked like a tree house.

I wanted to continue up the stairs, but Kishan wanted to climb the rope. He agreed to go up the stairs with me for another half hour, and, if we didn't find anything, we'd come back to the rope. It was a moot discussion anyway because, not five minutes later, the stairs became just knobby bumps on the side of the tree trunk and then disappeared altogether.

As we started back to the rope, I said, "I don't think I have the arm strength to climb up that high."

"Don't worry about that. I've got enough arm strength for both of us."

"What exactly do you have in mind?"

"You'll see."

When we got to the rope, Kishan took the backpack from me and put it on. Then he beckoned me forward.

"What?"

He pointed at the ground in front of him.

"What are you going to make me do?"

"You're going to wrap your arms around my neck and twist your wrists into the top loop of the backpack."

"Okay, but don't try anything funny. I'm very ticklish."

He lifted my looped arms around his neck and picked me up, which brought his face very close to mine. He raised an eyebrow. "If I did try something, I can *promise* you, it wouldn't be to get a laugh."

I laughed nervously, but his face was intense, serious. "Okay. Let's go already," I mumbled.

I felt his muscles tense as he prepared to leap but he looked down at me and his gaze drifted to my lips. He ducked his head and pressed a warm, soft kiss on the side of my mouth.

"*Kishan*."

"Sorry. I couldn't resist. You were trapped and for once you couldn't turn away from me. Besides, you're very kissable. You should be happy that I restrained myself as much as I did."

"Yeah, right."

With that, he leapt in the air. I let out a squeal at his sudden move. Calmly, he started climbing the rope. He pulled us up hand over hand, stepping onto limbs when he could, sometimes keeping one hand on the rope and one on a branch for balance. Kishan was always careful not to injure me. Other than the bouncing, the swinging hundreds or maybe thousands of feet into the air, and the stomach dropping leaps from branches, I felt pretty comfortable. In fact, it was a little too comfortable being pressed up against him.

Tarzan-like men are my weakness, apparently.

When we reached the tree house door, Kishan climbed the rope a little higher and hung still while I carefully disengaged myself and jumped onto the wooden floor. Then he kicked off, swung, and landed with a flourish. Clearly, he was having fun.

"Stop showing off, for heaven's sake. Do you realize how far up we are and that you could fall to a grisly death at any moment? You are acting like this is a great, fun adventure."

He replied, "I have no idea how far up we are. And I don't care. But, yes. I'm having fun. I *like* being a man all the time. And I *like* being with you." He wrapped his hands around my waist and drew me closer.

"Hmm." I extricated myself as quickly as possible.

I couldn't blame him for the being human part and didn't know what to say about the being with me part, so I said nothing. We sat down on the wooden floor of the tree house and searched through all of Mr. Kadam's notes. We read through them twice and waited, but still nothing happened in the tree house. This was supposed to be the house of birds, but I didn't see any. Maybe we were in the wrong place. I started to get antsy.

"Hello? Is anybody here?" my voice echoed.

A flapping and hoarse croaking *rrronk* answered me. Up in the corner of the tree house, we saw a hidden nest. Two black ravens peeped over the edge to watch us. They called to each other with a thumping sound, a knocking that came from deep in their throats.

The birds left their perch and circled the tree house, performing acrobatics in the air. They did somersaults and even flew upside down. Each pass brought them closer to us. Kishan unlatched his chakram and raised it like a knife.

I put my hand on his and shook my head slightly. "Let's wait and see what they do."

"What do you want from us?" I asked.

The birds landed a few feet away. One twisted its head and stared at me with one black eye. A black tongue tasted the air from the beak's rictus as the bird moved closer.

I heard a rough, scratchy voice say, "Wantfrumus?"

"Do you understand me?"

The two birds bobbed their heads up and down, stopping occasionally to preen feathers.

"What are we doing here? Who are you?"

The birds hopped a little closer. One said, "Hughhn," and I could have sworn the other said, "Muunann."

I marveled incredulously, "You're Hugin and Munin?"

The black heads bobbed up and down again. They hopped a little closer.

"Did you steal my bracelet?"

"And the amulet?" Kishan added.

Heads bobbed.

"Well, we want everything back. You can keep the honey cakes. You probably already ate them, anyway."

The birds squawked hoarsely, snapped their beaks loudly, and flapped their wings at us. Ruffled feathers puffed up, making the birds look much bigger than they were.

I folded my arms across my chest.

"Not going to give them back, huh? We'll see about that."

The birds hesitantly danced closer, and one hopped onto my knee. Kishan was immediately concerned.

I touched his arm. "If they are Hugin and Munin, they whisper thoughts and memories into Odin's ears. They may want to sit on our shoulders and speak to us."

It appeared I was right, because the minute I tilted my head to one side, one of the birds flapped its wings and settled on my shoulder. It stuck its beak near my ear, and I waited to hear it speak. Instead, I felt a curious pulling sensation. The bird tugged gently on something in my ear, but I felt no pain.

"What are you doing?" I asked.

"Thoughtsrstuck."

"What?"

"Thoughtsrstuck."

I felt another gentle tug, a snap, and then Hugin hopped away with a filmy, web-like strand hanging from his beak.

I covered my ear with my hand. "What did you do? Did you steal part of my brain? Do I have brain damage?"

"Thoughtsrstuck!"

"What does that mean?"

The strand hanging from the beak slowly dissipated as the bird clacked its beak. I sat there, staring, mouth gaping wide in horror, and wondered what had been done to me. *Did it steal a memory?* I racked my brain trying to remember everything important. I searched for some gap, some emptiness. If the bird did steal a memory, I had no idea what it could be.

Kishan touched my hand. "Are you okay? How do you feel?"

"I feel fine. It's just—" My words fell away as something shifted in my mind. Something was happening. Something was dragging across the surface of my mind like a squeegee over soapy glass. I could feel a layer of confusion, mental clutter, and dirt, for lack of a better word, peeling away like dead skin after a sunburn. It was as if random fears, worries, and dismal thoughts had been clogging the pores of my consciousness.

For a moment, I could see everything I needed to do with perfect clarity. I knew we were almost at our goal. I knew there would be fierce protectors guarding the Scarf. I knew what the Scarf was and I knew what it could do. In that moment, I knew how we'd use it to save Ren.

Munin hopped back and forth in front of Kishan, waiting for its turn.

"It's okay, Kishan! Go ahead. Let it sit on your shoulder. It won't hurt you. Trust me."

He looked at me doubtfully, but he cocked his head to one side anyway. I watched with fascination as Munin flapped its wings and landed on Kishan's shoulder. He kept its wings open, flapping them up and down lazily as it worked on Kishan's ear.

I spoke to Hugin, "Is Munin doing the same thing to Kishan?"

The bird shook its head and shifted from foot to foot. It started preening its feathers.

"Well, what's the difference? What will it do?"

"Waitforit."

"Waitforit?"

The bird nodded.

Munin hopped down to the floor and held a wispy black strand in his mouth about the size of an earthworm. It opened its beak and swallowed it.

"Uh . . . that looked different. Kishan? What happened? Are you okay?"

He responded quietly, "I'm fine. He . . . he showed me."

"Showed you what?"

"He showed me my memories. In full detail. I saw everything that happened. I saw Yesubai and me all over again. I saw my parents, Kadam, Ren . . . all of it. But with one major difference."

I took his hand in mine. "What is it? What's the difference?"

"That black thread you saw—it's hard to explain, but it's like the bird removed a dark pair of sunglasses from my eyes. I saw everything as it really was, as it really happened. It wasn't just from my perception anymore. It was like I was an outside observer."

"Is the memory different now?"

"It's not different . . . it's clearer. I could see that Yesubai was a sweet girl who cared for me, but she was encouraged to seek me out. She didn't love me the same way I felt for her. She was afraid of her father. She obeyed him completely, but she was also desperate to leave him. In the end, it was her father who killed her. He threw her viciously—hard enough to cause her neck to break.

"How did I overlook her fear, her anxiety?" He rubbed his jaw. "She hid it well. He took advantage of my feelings for her. I should have seen what he was all along, but I was blind, infatuated. How could I not see this before?"

"Love makes you do crazy things sometimes."

"What about you? What did you see?"

"I sort of got my brain Hoovered."

"What does 'Hoovered' mean?"

"A Hoover is a vacuum. My thoughts are clear, like your memories are clear. In fact, I now know how to get the Scarf and what comes next. But first things first."

I jumped up and lifted the nest tucked into the corner of the tree house. The two birds hopped up and down, squawking in irritation. They flew over to me and flapped their wings in my face.

"I'm sorry, but it's your own fault, you know. You're the ones who cleared my mind. Besides, these belong to us. We need them."

I took the camera, my bracelet, and the amulet out of the nest. Kishan helped me attach the bracelet and the amulet chain and tucked the camera in the bag. The birds looked at me sulkily.

"Maybe we can give you something else instead as compensation for losing your prizes," I said.

Kishan hunted up a fishhook, a Glowstick, and a compass and placed them in the nest. After I put the nest back, the birds flew up to inspect their new treasures.

"Thank you both! Come on, Kishan. Follow me."

the divine weaver's scarf

After retrieving our treasures from the nest, I headed toward a simple rope that hung from the wood ceiling. When I pulled it, a rattling noise came from above the tree house and a panel opened. A ladder descended and struck the floor.

I explained to Kishan, "The next part will be the hardest. This ladder leads to the outside branches, which we have to climb until we hit the top where there's a giant bird's nest. The Scarf will be there, but so will the iron birds."

"Iron birds?"

"Yes, and we'll have to fight them to take the Scarf. Wait a second." I rifled quickly through Mr. Kadam's research and found what I was looking for. "Here. This is what we're fighting."

The picture of the mythological Stymphalian bird was frightening enough without the description he'd included.

Kishan read, "Terrible flesh-eating birds with iron beaks, bronze claws, and toxic droppings. They usually live in large colonies."

"Swell, aren't they?"

"Keep close to me, Kells. We can't be sure that you heal here."

"For that matter, we can't be sure you heal here, either," I grinned, "but I'll try not to leave you alone too long."

"Funny. After you."

We climbed the ladder and found ourselves in a cluster of branches set tightly enough together that they reminded me of a children's jungle gym. It was easy enough to climb if I didn't think about falling. Kishan insisted that I climb first so he could catch me if I slipped, which only happened once. My foot slipped on some wet wood, and Kishan caught it, shoe and all, in his palm and pushed me upward again.

After a good climb, we rested on a branch with our backs against the trunk, Kishan lower, me higher. He tossed me a canteen of sugar-free lemonade, which I accepted gratefully. As I drained it in long gulps, I noticed some damage on the limb I was seated on.

"Kishan, take a look at this."

A thick, gummy, chartreuse paste was splattered on the end of my branch and had apparently eaten through half of it.

"I think we're looking at the toxic droppings," I remarked wryly.

Kishan wrinkled his nose. "And this is old, maybe as long as two weeks ago. The smell is nasty. It's sharp and bitter." He blinked and rubbed his eyes. "It's burning my nostrils."

"I guess we'll have to watch out for toxic bombs, huh?"

Now that he had the smell of the birds, we could follow his nose to the nest. It took another hour of climbing, but we finally came upon a giant nest resting on a trio of tree limbs.

"Wow, that's huge! Much larger than Big Bird's."

"Who's Big Bird?"

"A giant yellow bird on kid's television. You think any of the birds are close?"

"I don't hear anything, but the smell is everywhere."

"Huh, lucky I have a tiger nose nearby. I can't really smell anything."

"Count your blessings. I don't think I'll ever get this smell out of my mind."

"It's only fair you get to fight nasty-smelling birds. Remember, Ren got the Kappa and immortal monkeys."

Kishan grunted and kept moving toward the giant nest. Old droppings bleached the surface of the tree branches, weakening them. If we stepped too close to one, the branch's surface crumbled into white powder and sometimes broke off altogether.

We crept closer and depended on Kishan's hearing for warning of approaching birds. The nest was the size of a large swimming pool and made of dead tree limbs the thickness of my arm all woven together like a giant Easter basket. We climbed over the top and dropped into the nest.

Five massive eggs rested in the middle. Each one would have filled a Jacuzzi. Bronze and gleaming, they reflected the sunlight into our eyes. Kishan lightly tapped on one, and we heard a hollow metallic echo.

I circled the egg and gasped. The eggs were resting on top of the most beautiful diaphanous material I'd ever seen. *The Divine Weaver's Scarf!* The cloth looked alive. Colors shifted and swirled in geometric patterns on the Scarf's surface. A kaleidoscope of pale blue shifted into hot pink and yellow, which twisted into soft green and gold, and then slid into blue-black raven billows. It was mesmerizing.

Kishan scanned the sky and assured me the coast was clear. Then he crouched down next to me to examine the Scarf.

"We'll have to roll the eggs off one by one, Kells. They're heavy."

"Alright. Let's start with this one."

We gripped a gleaming egg and rolled it carefully to the side of the nest, and then went back for the second. We found a feather near the second egg. Normal bird feathers were lightweight, hollow, and flexible. This one was longer than my arm, heavy, and metallic. Kishan could barely move it, and the edge was as sharp as a circular saw.

"Uh, this isn't good."

Kishan agreed, "We'd better hurry."

We were rolling the third egg when we heard a loud screech.

A far-off bird was making its way toward the nest. It didn't sound happy. I shaded my eyes to get a better look. It seemed small at first, but my opinion of its size quickly changed as it sped closer. Mighty wings held the creature in the air as it rode the thermals.

Thump. The sun hit the metallic body of the giant bird and reflected the light, blinding me. *Thump.* It had now come much closer and seemed to have doubled in size. It screeched out a harsh wailing call. A quieter screech echoed an answer as another joined the first bird. *Thump.*

The tree moved up and down as something landed on a nearby branch. A bird screamed at us and started making its way toward the nest. As always, Kishan stepped in front of me. We moved backward quickly, keeping the trunk behind us.

Thump. Thump. Thump. A bird flew over us. It was more monster than bird. I got a good look at it as it swooped overhead. Its head was tilted, so it could fix its eye on us. I estimated the wingspan to be around forty feet, or about half the length of Mr. Kadam's plane. I strung my bow, drew back an arrow, and shivered as its shrill, high-pitched shriek vibrated through my limbs. My hand shook, and I let the arrow go. I missed.

The body of the creature was like a giant eagle. Rows of dense, overlapping metal feathers covered the bird's torso and grew larger along its long, broad wings. Its feathers were about the size of a surfboard. The wingtips were tapered and widely separated. The iron bird beat its wings and spread its tail feathers to help it brake and swoop into the sky again.

It moved like a raptor. Powerful, muscular legs with razor sharp talons stretched out to grab us on its second pass. Kishan pushed me face-down into the nest so that the bird missed us, but only by inches. Its head looked something like a gull with a stout, longish hooked beak but there was an extra hook resting on the upper mandible of its beak, sharp on both sides like a double-edged sword.

When one of the birds came closer, it nipped at us, and I heard a metallic *shear* as the sharp edges of its beak snapped together like a pair of giant scissors.

Another came too close so I zapped it with a lightning bolt. The energy hit the bird on its chest and bounced off, scorching the nest not a foot from where Kishan was standing.

"Watch it, Kells!"

This was not looking good. I shouted, "My lightning bolts just bounce off!"

"Let me try!" He threw the chakram. It hurled through the air in a wide arc past the bird.

"Kishan! How do you miss something that big?"

"Just watch!"

As the chakram completed its arc and spun back to Kishan, it hit the bird on the return trip and sliced through a metallic wing, making a terrible sound, something like a drill on sheet metal. The bird screamed and fell thousands of feet to the ground below, tearing off branches and tree limbs as it went. The tree shook wildly as it crashed.

Three more birds circled overhead and tried to grab us with knife-like talons or beaks. I nocked another arrow and aimed for the nearest one. The arrow struck the bird right in the chest, but all it did was make it angry.

Kishan ducked between some eggs as a bird tried to shish kabob him with a talon.

"Aim for the neck or the eyes, Kelsey!"

I shot off another arrow into the neck and a third into the eye. The bird flew off and then fell, spinning like an out of control airplane before crashing to the ground. Now they were really mad.

More birds arrived. They seemed intelligent and resourceful. One nipped at Kishan, backing him to the edge of the nest. While he was busy there, a second bird reached out and grabbed him with its talons.

"Kishan!"

I raised my hand and aimed for its eye. This time, the lightning bolt worked. The iron bird shrieked and let Kishan go, dropping him with a thud into the nest. I did the same thing to the other bird, and it took off, calling madly to its flock mates.

I raced over to Kishan. "Are you alright?"

His shirt was torn and bloody. The bird's talons had raked across both sides of his chest, and he was bleeding freely.

He panted. "It's okay. It hurts. It feels like hot knives pressed against my skin, but it's healing. Don't let them get near you."

The skin around the slices was blistered and angry red.

"It looks like their talons are coated with acid too," I said sympathetically.

He sucked in a breath when I lightly touched his skin. "I'll be fine." He froze. "Listen. They are communicating with each other. They're coming back. Get ready to fight." Kishan stood to distract them while I took a position behind the remaining two eggs.

"All things considered, I'd rather have monkeys," Kishan shouted.

I shivered. "Tell you what. We'll rent *King Kong* and *The Birds*. Then you can decide."

He yelled as he ran from a swooping bird, "Are you asking me on a date? Because if you are, it will definitely give me more incentive to come out of this alive."

"Whatever works."

"You're on."

He ran across the nest, jumped off the edge, flipped over in mid-air and landed on a tree limb that jutted out. He threw the chakram, and it soared into the sky. The sun glinted off the golden disc as it whirled around the tree and sliced through the dozen or so birds circling the top.

They split off in every direction and then regrouped. I could almost see them calculating their next maneuver. All at once, they dove for us. Shrieking, the flock attacked. I'd once seen a colony of seagulls display mobbing behavior. They all pecked and harassed a man with a sandwich at the beach until he ran away screaming. They were violent, determined, and aggressive, but these birds were worse!

The birds ripped limbs off the tree to reach us. More than half of them dove for Kishan, who agilely leapt from branch to branch until he was back with me behind the eggs. Frenzied flapping around the nest blew air in every direction. I felt as if I was caught in a whirlwind.

Kishan threw his chakram again and again, cutting off the leg of one bird and slicing the belly of a second before the weapon returned to his hand. I got rid of two with arrows through the eyes and blinded two more with lightning shots.

Kishan shouted, "Can you keep them off me for a minute, Kells?"

"I think so! Why?"

"I'm going to move the last two eggs!"

"Hurry!"

I experimented and drew back an arrow, infused it with lightning power, and let loose. It hit the bird in the eye and blew its head off. The charred, smoking, headless torso landed with a boom, half on the nest and half dangling over the side. The nest cracked and tilted precariously before settling. The impact shot me into the air as if I'd been on a trampoline, and the momentum dropped me over the edge of the nest. I desperately stretched out to grab the edge as I fell.

Rough branches scraped my skin as I struggled to slow my momentum. Finally successful, I threw my arms over the side, but still slipped.

Blood trickled down my arm. Gritting my teeth in pain, I dug my fingers in and rammed my feet between the branches to get a foothold. I tore several fingernails and scratched up my legs and arms, but it was worth it. I didn't fall to a horrible death. At least, not yet.

Kishan had held on better. He righted himself quickly and headed toward me. "Hold on, Kells!"

Kishan lay on his stomach and stretched out a hand. He grabbed my hands and yanked until I landed on top of him. "Are you okay?" he asked.

"Yeah. I'm fine."

"Good." He grinned and had just wrapped his arms around me when he saw something overhead. He put a hand behind my head and another around my waist and rolled several times until we bumped against the back of the nest. We ended up with his body sprawled on top of mine.

"Look out!" I screamed.

Two of the birds were leaning in, trying to snap us in half with their metallic beaks. I picked up a broken branch nearby and shoved it into the bird's eye just before it eviscerated Kishan. Then I hit the other one with lightning.

"Thanks."

I grinned, feeling proud of my accomplishment. "Anytime."

The nest shifted. The weight of the dead bird hanging off the edge of the nest was too heavy. The bird was falling and taking the nest with it. Kishan grabbed branches on both sides of my head.

"Hold on!" he shouted.

I wrapped my arms around his neck, and clung to him as the nest tilted several feet into the air and snapped in half. Half of the nest fell with the dead bird and the other half—the half we were in—hung precariously from two almost sheared off limbs. My stomach lurched as the nest and everything around it, including the branches holding us, suddenly dropped three feet and hit with a bone-jarring *bang*. Three of the eggs fell out of the nest and broke on the branches below. We fell into what was left of the nest before rolling to a stop.

"Where's the Scarf?" I yelled.

"There!"

The Scarf had blown out of the nest and was draped loosely on a broken limb several feet below. It fluttered in the breeze and would probably blow away at any moment.

"Kells, hurry! Grab my hand. I'll lower you down so you can reach the Scarf."

"Are you sure?"

"I'm sure! Go!"

He gripped my arm and lowered me. I couldn't believe he had the strength to do it, but he wrapped his other arm around a branch and held the weight of both our bodies with one arm. It still wasn't good enough.

"I'll have to go lower! Can you hold my leg instead?"

"Yes. Come back up for a minute."

He grunted and pulled me up, throwing me into the air as if I was a sack of groceries and caught me around the waist as I began to fall. I gasped and grabbed his neck again.

"What do I do?"

"*First—*" he ducked his head and kissed me hard. "Now wrap your left leg around my waist."

I gave him a look.

"Just do it!"

I swung back and forth, then managed to hook my leg around his waist. Next, he let go of my waist and grabbed my leg. It was frightening, but I trusted that he was strong enough to hold both of us with only one arm. Compared to this, standing on Ren's shoulders in Kishkindha was child's play.

I grimaced, wondering what insane things I'd be expected to do in the next two tasks. I mentally willed the branches holding the nest to support us a little bit longer, just long enough for me to grab the Scarf. Realistically, I expected to hear them snap at any second, causing us to plummet to our deaths.

I let go of Kishan's neck and slowly turned my body upside down, holding the waistband of his pants, then his leg, and then his foot. I mumbled as he lowered me, "Why couldn't they pick a girl from Cirque du Soleil to do these tasks? Hanging upside down from a broken branch thousands of feet in the air is just too much to ask from a girl in beginner wushu!"

"Kells?"

"What?"

"Shut up and get the Scarf."

"I'm working on it!"

I stretched farther and heard Kishan groan. "Just another few inches."

His grip slipped deliberately from my calf to my ankle, causing me to swing out over the green abyss.

Frightened, I yelled Kishan's name and closed my eyes for a second, swallowed, and swung my body back toward the Scarf. The wind whipped it off the branch. It swirled in the air and shot past me. I grabbed the tail of it at the last second—hanging upside down, blood pounding in my head, the tips of my fingers desperately grasping the Scarf, with Kishan barely holding on for both of us—and had a vision.

The green canopy dizzily swinging back and forth in front of my eyes faded to white, and I heard a voice.

"Kelsey. Miss Kelsey! Can you hear me?"

"Mr. Kadam? Yes, I can hear you!"

I saw the vague outline of a tent behind him. "I can see your tent!"

"And I can see you and Kishan."

"What?" I looked behind me and saw a blurred image of Kishan clutching the leg of my upside-down limp body. The Scarf dangled precariously from a hooked finger. I heard him shouting as if from a great distance.

"Kelsey! Hold on!"

The vague outline of another person was coming into view.

Mr. Kadam instructed, "Don't say anything. Don't let him provoke you into speaking. Just pay attention to every detail—anything could help us find Ren."

"Okay."

Mr. Kadam's medallion was glowing red. I glanced at mine and saw it was bright red too. When I looked back up, the image of the other person solidified.

Lokesh. He was dressed in a business suit. His dark hair was slicked back, and I noticed that he wore several rings. His medallion was also glowing red and was much larger than ours.

His deceitful eyes glittered when he smiled.

"Ah! I've been wondering when I'd see you again." He spoke politely as if we were getting reacquainted at an afternoon tea party. "You have cost me a great deal in time and resources, my dear."

I watched him silently and flinched as he appraised me in a disturbing way.

Lokesh spoke quietly, menacingly, "We've not the time for the *niceties* of the game I would prefer, so I'll be blunt. I want the medallion you're wearing. You will bring it to me. If you do, I will let your tiger live. If you don't . . ." He took a knife out of his pocket and tested its sharpness on a thumb. "I will find you, slit your throat . . ." He looked directly into my eyes to conclude his threat, "and *take it* from your bloody neck."

Mr. Kadam countered, "Leave the young lady out of this. I will meet you and give you what you want. In exchange, you will let the tiger go free."

Lokesh turned to Mr. Kadam and smiled unpleasantly. "I do not recognize you, *my friend*. I am interested to know how you acquired the amulet. If you wish to negotiate, you may contact my business office in Mumbai."

"And which office would that be, *my friend*?"

"Find the tallest building in Mumbai; my office is the penthouse."

Mr. Kadam nodded as Lokesh continued to give instructions. As they talked, I studied the hazy scene that had appeared behind Lokesh. I memorized as many details as I could. A man was speaking to him, but Lokesh paid him no heed.

The servant behind Lokesh had black hair that was swept forward into a bun resting just above the top of his hairline. Across the length of his forehead, he had a line of black tattoos that looked like the Sanskrit words from the prophecy. Bare-chested, the man wore loops of handmade bead necklaces. His ears were pierced in several places with golden hoops. He was also pulling along another man and gestured to him.

The second man stood farther back with his head hanging down. Matted, filthy black hair hung in his face. Bleeding and bruised, he struggled against the hands of the man holding him. The servant yelled and yanked the man forward until he staggered and fell to his knees. Then he slapped him across the face and yanked his shoulders back. As the injured man looked up, his hair fell to the side, and I gazed into piercing cobalt blue eyes.

Overcome with emotion, I took a step forward and shouted, "*Ren!*"

He didn't hear me. His head drooped down to his chest. I started crying.

Someone did hear me, though—Lokesh. He narrowed his eyes and whipped around to see what I was looking at. He tried to speak to his servants, but they didn't hear him. He turned back to me and, for the first time, studied the wispy images behind *my* shoulder. Everything was already fading. I couldn't tell if Lokesh recognized Kishan or not. I froze and willed him to see only me.

Lokesh did focus his attention on me. He gestured to Ren and, with false sympathy, clucked his tongue.

"How terribly *painful* it must be for you to see him like this. You know, between you and me, he screams out for you when I torture him. Unfortunately for him, he's been quite unforthcoming as to your whereabouts." He chuckled, "He won't even tell me your first name, though I already know what it is. It's Kelsey, isn't it?"

Lokesh watched my expression carefully waiting for me to give away a clue.

He continued his mocking diatribe. "It's become something of a sticking point between us. The prince is so tight-lipped he won't even confirm your given name. I must say I expected as much. He's always been quite stubborn. More tears? How sad. He can't hold out forever, you know. The pain alone should have killed him by now.

"Fortunately, his body seems quite resilient." He watched me out of the corner of his eyes while he cleaned microscopic dirt from under his fingernails. "I have to admit, I've quite enjoyed torturing him. It's the best of both worlds seeing him suffer both as a man and as an animal. The exquisite lengths I can go to are unheard of. He heals so quickly that even I have been unable to test his limits. I assure you, though, I *am* making *every* effort."

I bit my trembling hand to stifle a sob and glanced at Mr. Kadam. He shook his head discreetly, indicating to keep quiet.

Lokesh smiled sardonically. "Perhaps if you would just confirm your name, I might give him a brief . . . *reprieve*? A simple nod would suffice. It *is* Kelsey Hayes, is it not?"

Mr. Kadam's warning raced through my thoughts. It took all my determination, but I kept my eyes focused on Ren. Tears ran down my face, but I didn't move or even look at Lokesh.

He became angry, "Certainly, if you care for him, you would spare him *some* pain, *ease* his anguish? No? Perhaps I was mistaken in your affections. I am relatively sure that I am not mistaken in *his*. He won't speak of you at all except to call out in his dreams for his beloved. Or perhaps you are not the one he begs for?" His voice started to fade.

"Ah, well. The two brothers were not always lucky in love, were they? Maybe it is time to put him out of his misery. It seems to me as if I'd be doing him a favor."

I couldn't help it. I screamed, "No!"

He raised his eyebrows and spoke again, but his words were too quiet to hear. When the three of us could no longer hear one another, Mr. Kadam turned to me. Lokesh was gesturing with his hands, but I ignored him and focused on Mr. Kadam as he faded to white. I wiped away my tears while he smiled sympathetically and then winked at me just before he disappeared.

I blinked and white turned to green. Blood pounded in my head.

Kishan was yelling at me, "Kelsey! *Kelsey!* Snap out of it!"

Fortunately, I was still holding the Scarf. I shouted, "Got it! Pull me up, Kishan!"

"Kelsey! Watch out!"

A bird screeched above us. I twisted and saw the gaping black maw of a metallic bird and got an up-close and personal view of its green, verdigris-coated, double-edged scissor beak. I shot a bolt of lightning into its beak, and it took off squawking, smoke trailing from its mouth.

With a mighty grunt, Kishan swung me upright. I grabbed his waist and held on for dear life. He let go of me, trusting I'd have the muscle to cling to him. I wrapped my arms around him, grabbed my wrists to lock my arms at his waist, and clutched the Scarf in my hands. He pulled himself over the edge of the broken nest and helped me over. His arms shook with fatigue.

Kishan sat up and inspected my limbs. "Kells, are you okay? What happened to you?"

"Another vision," I breathed. "Tell you about it later."

We ducked as a bird called out nearby. I picked up our backpack and stowed the bow and quiver, which had magically refilled with golden arrows, as well as the Scarf and chakram.

"Okay. Now what?" he said.

"Now we make our escape. Come on."

We descended until we had sufficient enough cover that the birds could no longer see us. We could still hear them circling the tree and shrieking to each other, but the farther down the tree we went, the quieter the noises became. Soon we couldn't hear them anymore.

"Kells, stop. We need to rest for a while."

"Okay."

The Golden Fruit created something quick to eat and drink, and Kishan insisted on inspecting me for injuries. He seemed fine. His cuts had healed already, but I had some wicked gashes on my arms and legs. I was healing too, but several of my nails were torn and bloody, and I had a long splinter under one that Kishan worked out carefully.

"This will hurt. Splinters and quills are the tiger's worst enemies."

"Really? Why do you say that?"

"We rub up against and scratch trees to mark territory, and we sometimes snack on porcupines. A smart tiger attacks it from the front, but occasionally they whirl on you. I've had quills stuck in my paws before, and they hurt and fester. They break off as I walk. There's no way for a tiger to get them out, so I'd have to wait until I could change into a man and pull them all out."

"Oh! I wondered why Ren was always rubbing against trees in the jungle. Don't the quills eventually work themselves out though?"

"No. They actually bend into a circle and stay in the skin. They won't dissolve either. Splinters can, but quills won't. They can stay in a tiger's body their whole lives. It's what makes some become man-eaters. With an impairment like that, they can't hunt fast prey anymore. I've even come across a couple of tigers who had died from starvation because they'd been injured by porcupines."

"Well, the common sense thing would be not to eat porcupines then."

Kishan grinned. "But they're delicious."

"Ugh." I sucked in a breath. "Ow!"

"Almost got it. There. It's out now."

"Thanks."

He cleaned the worst of my scrapes with alcohol wipes and then bandaged up what he could.

"I think you'll heal here quicker than normal, but not as fast as I do. We should rest."

"We'll rest when we get down."

He sighed and rubbed his forehead. "Kells, it took us days to get up here. It will take days to get back down."

"No it won't. I have a shortcut. When the ravens cleared my mind, I saw what the Scarf could do. We just need to walk out onto a branch."

I could tell Kishan was wary, but he followed me anyway. We made our way to the edge of a long branch.

"Now what?" he asked.

"Watch."

I held the Scarf on top of my palms and said, "A two person parachute, please."

The Scarf twisted, snapped taut and lengthened, and then folded itself over and over. From all four corners, threads pulled out and stretched. They wove and twisted together, forming belts, risers, and ropes. Finally, the Scarf stopped moving. It had become a double-harnessed large backpack.

He stared at it incredulously. "What did you do, Kelsey?"

"You'll see. Put it on."

"You said parachute. You think we're going to parachute out of here?"

"Yep."

"I don't think so."

"Ah, come on. Tigers aren't afraid of heights, are they?"

"This isn't about heights. This is about being extremely high up in a tree and hurtling our bodies into oblivion based on a strange fabric that you now claim is a parachute."

"It is, and it will work."

"*Kelsey*."

"Have faith, like the Ocean Teacher said. The Scarf does other cool stuff too. I'll tell you about it on the way back. Kishan, *trust* me."

"I trust *you*; I just don't trust the fabric."

"Well, I'm going to jump, so are you coming with me or not?"

"Did anyone ever tell you you're stubborn? Were you this stubborn with Ren?"

"Ren had to deal with stubbornness *and* sarcasm, so consider yourself lucky."

"Yeah, but at least he got some kissing for his effort."

"You got a few kisses yourself."

"Not voluntary ones."

"True, you stole them."

"Stolen kisses are better than none."

I raised my eyebrow. "Are you just starting an argument with me to chicken out?"

"No. I'm not chickening out. Fine. If you insist on doing this, please explain to me how it works."

"Easy. We strap ourselves in, jump, clear the tree, and pull the ripcord. At least I hope that's how it works," I mumbled softly.

"*Kelsey*."

"Don't worry. It's the way we're supposed to get down. I know we'll make it."

"Right."

He strapped himself in while I put our regular backpack on backward against my chest. Then I approached Kishan.

"Umm . . . you're too tall for me. Maybe I can stand on a taller branch."

I looked around for something to stand on, but Kishan wrapped his hands around my waist and picked me up. He snuggled me next to his chest while I strapped myself into the other part of the Scarf's harness.

"Er . . . thanks. Okay, so what you need to do is carry me, run, and leap off the branch. Can you manage that?"

"I'm sure I can handle it," he responded dryly. "Ready?"

"Yes."

He squeezed me close.

"One . . . two . . . three!"

Kishan ran five steps and hurled his body into the void.

22

exit

The wind screamed around us as we plummeted freefall through the sky, spinning like Dorothy's house in the tornado. Kishan was able to stabilize us in a face-down position. He took hold of my wrists and drew our arms out in an arc. Not a moment after we stabilized, we heard a screech overhead. An iron bird was on our tail.

Kishan lifted my left arm in the air, and we dramatically veered to the right and picked up speed. The bird followed. He lifted our right arms, and we swung left. The bird was on top of us.

Kishan screamed, "Hold on, Kells!"

He pulled our arms back to our sides and tilted our heads down. We burst forward like a bullet. The bird folded its wings and plummeted with us.

"I'm going to flip us! Try to hit it with a lightning bolt! Ready?"

I nodded, and Kishan flipped us over in the air. Our backs were now to the ground, and I had a great view of the bird's belly. Quickly, I shot off a succession of bolts and managed to irritate the bird enough to get rid of it. I missed its eye but hit the edge of its mouth. The bird didn't like that and flapped off, screeching angrily.

"Hold on!"

Kishan flipped us back over and steadied us once more. He pulled the ripcord, and I heard the slither of material as it was fed out into the wind. With a *snap*, the Scarf's parachute opened to catch the air. Kishan tightened his arms around my waist as it opened and slowed our descent. Then he let go to grip the toggles and direct the steering lines.

I shouted, "Aim for the pass between the two mountains!"

A terrible screech overhead meant the birds had found us. Three of them began circling, trying to grab us with talons and beaks. I tried to use my lightning power, but it was too hard to hit their eyes from this distance. Instead, I opened the backpack and retrieved my bow.

Kishan banked left, and I drew back and let an arrow fly. It whizzed right over the head of a bird. My second arrow hit its neck and, imbued with lightning power, gave the bird a shock. It fell to the ground injured. Another bird hit us with its razor-sharp wing, sending us into a spin, but I managed to irritate it enough that it soon flew off in another direction.

The third bird was wily. It circled out of my line of vision to stay behind us as much as possible. When it attacked, it ripped a large hole in the parachute with a talon. The collapsing chute dropped us into another freefall. Kishan tried to guide us, but the wind bucked the torn canopy wildly.

Suddenly, the chute began to repair itself. Threads wove in and out and up and through the material until the Scarf looked as though it had never been damaged. As it filled with air again, Kishan yanked on the toggle to head us in the right direction.

The angry bird reappeared and managed to avoid my arrows. Its loud screeches were answered by others.

"We've got to land!"

"Almost there, Kells!"

At least a dozen birds were streaking their way toward us. We'd be lucky if we survived long enough to hit the ground. The flock circled, screaming, flapping, and snapping their beaks.

We were almost there. If we could just hold out for a few more seconds! A bird came right at us. It was fast, and we didn't see it until the last moment. The creature opened its beak to snap us in two. I could almost hear the crunch of my bones as I imagined the metal bird cutting me in half.

I shot several more arrows but missed with each of them. The wind suddenly turned us, and I could do nothing from my current position. Kishan maneuvered the chute, piloting the canopy into a dangerous swoop and a hook turn. I closed my eyes and felt a jolt as our feet touched solid ground.

Kishan ran a few steps and then pushed me flat to the grass. He lay on top of me while he frantically unhooked us from the rigging.

"Keep your head down, Kells!"

The bird was right on us. It grabbed a beak full of parachute and yanked, tearing it in half. I winced listening to the horrible rip of the special material. Frustrated, the bird dropped the chute and circled around for another pass. Kishan freed himself, dug his chakram from the backpack, and threw it while I crouched down and gathered the folds of the parachute.

"Please knit back together."

Nothing happened. Kishan threw the chakram again.

"Little help here, Kells!"

I shot off a few arrows and saw the material move from the corner of my eye. It began weaving itself back together, slowly at first, and then faster and faster. It shrunk down to its original size again.

"Hold them back for a minute, Kishan. I know what to do!"

I picked up the material and said, "Gather the winds."

The patterns shifted, colors changed, and the Scarf grew. Twisting up and over itself, it swelled and stretched to create a large bag that fanned out in the breeze. A strong burst of wind hit my face and gusted into the bag. When it waned, another wind whipped around my body from behind and began filling the bag as well. Soon, winds from every direction were pummeling me. I felt buffeted from every direction and could barely contain the bagful of powerful winds.

Finally, the gusts died so that I could feel not even a wisp of a breeze, but the bag bucked violently. Kishan was surrounded by ten birds, barely holding them at bay with the chakram.

"Kishan! Get behind me!"

He drew back his arm and, with a powerful thrust, let loose the chakram. As it spun through the air, he ran to me, grabbed the bag on the other side, and caught the hurtling chakram just before it took off my head.

I raised an eyebrow while he grinned.

I yelled, "Okay, ready? One, two, three!" We opened the bag and let loose all the winds of Shangri-la in the bird's direction. Three of the birds were slammed against the mountain while the others spun off toward the world tree, trying desperately to escape the tumult.

When the winds died down, the empty bag hung limp between us. Kishan stared at me incredulously.

"*Kelsey*. How did you—" he trailed off.

"Scarf, please."

The bag shifted and twisted, turned a soft blue and gold color, and then shrunk into a Scarf again. I wrapped it around my neck and tossed the end over my shoulder.

"The answer is, I don't know. When Hugin and Munin cleared our minds, I remembered stories and myths I had learned before. I recalled things the Divine Weaver told us and also things that Mr. Kadam had speculated about. He'd told me a story of a Japanese god called Fūjin who controlled the winds and had a bag to carry them in. I also knew that this material was special, like the Golden Fruit.

"Maybe everything was in my mind all along or maybe Hugin

whispered it in my thoughts. I'm not sure. I do know that the Scarf can do something else, something that will help us save Ren, but we should get out of here before the birds come back. I'll show you then."

"Alright, but first, there's something *I* need to do."

"What's that?"

"This."

He yanked me up against his body and kissed me. Thoroughly. His mouth moved against mine passionately. The kiss was fast, turbulent, and wild. He held me tightly, one hand cradling my head while the other held me firmly at my waist. He kissed me fiercely, with an utter abandon that I could no more put a halt to than I could stop an avalanche.

When you're caught in an avalanche you have two choices: stand there and try to block it, or you can give in, roll with it, and hope you come out alive at the base. So, I rolled with Kishan's kiss. Finally, he lifted his head, spun me around, and let out a jubilant whoop of victory that echoed in the surrounding hills.

When he finally set me down, I had to catch my breath. I panted and said, "What was that for?"

"I'm just happy to be alive!"

"Okay, fine. But keep your lips to yourself next time."

He sighed. "Don't be upset, Kells."

"I'm not *upset*. I'm . . . I'm not sure what I think about it. It all happened too fast for me to even react."

A scoundrel's smile lit his face. "I promise to slow it down next time."

"What next time?"

He frowned slightly. "You don't need to make a big deal out of it. It's just a natural reaction to narrowly escaping death. It's like when soldiers come back from war and grab a girl to kiss right after they get off the boat."

I retorted wryly, "Yeah, maybe so, but the difference is, *this* girl was on the boat *with* you. Feel free to grab any girl you like when we get back to the mainland, sailor, but *this* girl is hands off."

He folded his arms across his chest. "*Really?* It felt more like your hands were *on* if you ask me."

I sputtered in outrage, "If my hands were on you at *all*, they were there to push you away!"

"Whatever you have to tell yourself to have a clear conscience at the end of the day. You just won't admit that you *liked* it."

"Hmm, let me see. You're right, Casanova. I *did* like it. After it was *over*!"

He shook his head. "You *are* stubborn. No wonder Ren had so many problems."

"How *dare* you even *mention* your brother!"

"When are you going to face facts, Kells? You like me."

"Well, I'm not liking you so much right now! Can we just head back to the spirit gate and drop this conversation?"

"Yes. But we *will* continue this discussion later."

"Maybe when Shangri-la freezes over."

He took the backpack and grinned. "I can wait for that. After you, *bilauta*."

"*Kissing Bandit*," I muttered.

He smirked wickedly and lifted an eyebrow. We hiked for several hours. Kishan kept trying to talk to me, but I stubbornly refused to acknowledge his existence.

The problem with what happened between us was . . . he wasn't wrong. I had spent more time with him now than I had with Ren, and we'd been living under the same roof for months. We'd been hiking through Shangri-la and spent day and night together for weeks.

Day to day contact like that creates a level of closeness, an . . .

intimacy between two people. Kishan was just more willing to recognize it than I was. It was not surprising that Kishan, who already admittedly had feelings for me, was beginning to feel comfortable expressing them. The thing was, it didn't bother me as much as it should have. Kishan kissing me was not like Artie or Jason or even Li.

When I kissed Li, I felt in control. It wasn't like kissing Ren either. Ren was like a fantastic jungle waterfall—sparkling and shimmering in the sunlight. He was an exotic paradise waiting to be discovered. Kishan was different. Kishan was a raging, grade six whitewater river—fast, unpredictable, and un-navigable to even the most skilled thrill-seekers. The brothers were both magnificent and fascinating and powerful, but kissing Kishan was dangerous.

Not dangerous like the man sirens; they just felt wrong. If I was being honest with myself, kissing Kishan didn't feel wrong. It actually felt good, like a wilder, fiercer version of Ren. With Kishan, it was like I'd literally caught a tiger by the tail, and he was ready to turn on me and drag me off. It wasn't an altogether unpleasant notion, and that was the part that disturbed me.

Clearly, I've been separated from my boyfriend for too long, I tried to rationalize my feelings. *Kishan's the next best thing, and I'm just missing my tiger. I'm sure that's all it is.* I let those thoughts comfort me as we walked.

Like Ren, Kishan had a knack for charming his way out of difficult problems. Before long, he made me completely forget that I had been upset with him.

As dusk turned into twilight, we decided to set up camp for the night. I was exhausted.

"You take the sleeping bag, Kells."

"Don't need it. Watch this."

I took the Scarf from around my neck and said, "A large tent, a sleeping bag, two soft pillows, and a change of clothes for each of us, please."

The Scarf shifted and moved; threads began weaving in and out. They twisted together to create thick cords, which shot out in several directions and wrapped around the strong branches of nearby trees. Once the cords were tied and secure, the Scarf created a roof, walls, and a tent floor. The tent was suspended from two lines twined about the tree overhead. Instead of a zipper, the opening flaps tied together.

I ducked my head inside, "Come on, Kishan."

He followed me into the spacious tent, and we watched as the colorful threads continued to weave a thick sleeping bag and two soft pillows. When it was finished, I had a green sleeping bag and two white king-sized pillows. A change of clothes for each of us rested on top of them. Kishan spread the old sleeping bag out next to me while I fluffed a pillow.

He asked, "How does it choose the color?"

"I think it depends on its mood or perhaps on what you ask for. The tent, sleeping bag, and pillows all look like they're supposed to. Otherwise, the Scarf shifts colors on its own. I noticed it as I walked all day."

Kishan left to change in the jungle while I put on fresh clothes and hung my fairy clothes on a branch outside. By the time he came back, I was snuggled deep into my sleeping bag and had turned on my side to avoid conversation.

He climbed into his sleeping bag, and I could feel his golden eyes staring at my back for several tense moments.

Finally, he grunted and said, "Well, goodnight, Kells."

"Goodnight, Kishan." I was exhausted and fell asleep quickly, drifting right into a new dream.

I dreamed of Ren and Lokesh, the very same scene as in my last vision. Ren was sitting in the back corner of a cage in a dark room. His hair was filthy and matted, and I almost didn't realize it was him until he opened his eyes and looked at me. I'd recognize those blue eyes anywhere.

His eyes gleamed steadily in the dark like bright sapphires. I crept closer, letting them guide me, staring at them like a desperate sailor watches a lighthouse on a stormy black night.

When I got to the cage, Ren blinked as if seeing me for the first time. His voice cracked like a man thirsty for water.

"Kells?"

I wrapped my fingers around the bars wishing I were strong enough to break them. "Yes. It's me."

"I can't see you."

For one horrible minute, I was afraid Lokesh had blinded him. I knelt in front of the cage.

"Is that better?"

"Yes." Ren slid a bit closer and wrapped his hands around mine. Clouds parted and moonlight shimmered through a tiny window, casting its soft glow on his face.

I gasped in shock and tears filled my eyes. "Oh, Ren! What did he do to you?"

Ren's face was swollen and purple. Blood trickled out of the sides of his mouth, and a deep gash ran from his forehead down to his cheek. I reached out a finger and touched his temple gently.

"He didn't get the information he wanted from you and decided to take out his anger on me."

"I'm so . . . so . . . sorry." My tears splashed his hand.

"*Priyatama*, don't cry." He pressed his hand to my cheek. I turned and kissed his palm.

"I can't bear to see you like this. We're coming for you. Please, *please*, hold on a little longer."

He lowered his gaze as if ashamed. "I don't think I can."

"Don't say that! *Never* say that! I'm coming. I know what to do. I know how to rescue you. You have to stay alive. No matter what! Ren, promise me!"

Ren sighed painfully. "He's too close, Kells. Every second Lokesh

has me you're at risk. You are his obsession. Every waking moment, he tries to extract information about you from my mind. He won't stop. He won't give up. He's . . . he's going to break me. Soon. If it was just the physical torture, I think I could endure it, but he's using dark magic. He's tricking me. Causing hallucinations. And I'm just so . . . *tired*."

My voice shook, "Then *tell* him. Tell him what he wants to know, and maybe he'll leave you alone."

"I will *never* tell him, *prema*."

I sobbed, "*Ren*. I can't lose you."

"I'm always with you. My thoughts are of you." He captured a lock of my hair and brought it to his lips. He inhaled deeply. "*All the time*."

"Don't give up! Not when we're so close!"

His eyes shifted. "There is an option I could consider."

"What is it? What option?"

"Durga," he paused, "has offered her protection, but she asks a heavy price. It's not worth it."

"Anything is worth your life! Take it! Don't think twice about it. You can trust Durga. Do it! Whatever the price is, it doesn't matter as long as you survive."

"But, *Kelsey*."

"Shh." I pressed a fingertip lightly against his swollen lips. "Do what you have to in order to survive. Okay?"

He let out a ragged breath and looked at me with bright, desperate eyes. "You must go. He might return at any time."

"I don't want to leave you."

"And I don't want you to leave. But you need to."

Resigned, I turned to leave.

"Wait, Kelsey. Before you go . . . will you kiss me?"

I put my hand through the bars and lightly touched his face. "I don't want to cause you more pain."

"It doesn't matter. *Please*. Kiss me before you go."

He knelt in front of me, gasping as he put weight on his knee, and then gently put shaking hands through the bars and drew me closer. His hands slid up to cup my cheeks, and our lips met through the bars of his cage. His kiss was warm and soft and too brief. I tasted the salt of my tears. When he drew back, he gave me a sweet, crooked smile through cracked lips. He winced as he withdrew his hands. It was then that I noticed that several of his fingers were broken.

I began crying anew. Ren wiped a tear from my cheek with his thumb and quoted a poem by Richard Lovelace.

When Love with unconfined wings
Hovers within my gates,
And my divine Althea brings
To whisper at the grates;
When I lie tangled in her hair
And fetter'd to her eye,
The birds that wanton in the air
Know no such liberty.
Stone walls do not a prison make,
Nor iron bars a cage;
Minds innocent and quiet take
That for an hermitage;
If I have freedom in my love
And in my soul am free,
Angels alone, that soar above,
Enjoy such liberty.

He pressed his forehead to the bars. "The only thing I couldn't bear is if he hurt *you*. I won't allow it. I *won't* let him find you, Kelsey. No matter what."

"What do you mean?"

He smiled. "Nothing, my sweet. Don't worry." He moved back to rest his broken body against the wall of the cage. "It's time to go, *iadala*."

I got up to leave but paused at the door when he called out, "Kelsey?"

I turned.

"No matter what happens, *please* remember that I love you, *hridaya patni*. Promise me that you'll remember."

"I'll remember. I promise. *Mujhe tumse pyarhai*, Ren."

"Go now."

He smiled weakly, and then his eyes changed. The blue leeched out, and they became gray, flat, and lifeless. Perhaps it was a trick of the light, but it almost looked as if Ren had died. I took a hesitant step back.

"Ren?"

His soft voice replied, "Please go, Kelsey. Everything will be alright."

"Ren?"

"*Good-bye, my love*."

"Ren!"

Something was happening, and it wasn't alright. I felt something snap. I gasped for air. Something was very wrong. The connection I felt between us was almost tangible, like a metal tether. The closer we'd become, the stronger the connection was. It rooted me, connected me to him like a telephone line, but something had severed the cable.

I felt the break, and sharp, jagged ends ripped and tore violently through my heart like hot knives through warm butter. I screamed and thrashed. For the first time since I'd laid eyes on my white tiger, I was alone.

Kishan shook me out of the fog of my dream.

"Kelsey! *Kelsey!* Wake up!"

I opened my eyes and began crying fresh tears that spilled onto my cheeks and followed the old trails left behind from my dream. I wrapped

my arms around Kishan's neck and sobbed. He pulled me onto his lap, pressed me close, and stroked my back, while I wept inconsolably for his brother.

I must have slept at some point because I woke tangled in my sleeping bag with Kishan's arms around me. My fist was pressed into my cheek, and my eyes were swollen shut and crusty.

Kishan whispered, "Kelsey?"

I mumbled, "I'm awake."

"Are you okay?"

My hand lifted involuntarily to the hollow, raw pit I felt in my chest, and a tear leaked out from the corner of my eye. I buried my head in the pillow and took deep breaths to calm myself.

"*No,*" I said dully. "He's . . . *gone*. Something's happened. I think . . . I think Ren may be *dead*."

"What happened? Why do you think that?"

I explained my dream and tried to describe my broken connection to Ren.

"Kelsey, it's possible that this is all just a dream, a very disturbing one, but just a dream. It's not uncommon to have violent dreams if you have recently experienced something traumatic, like the fight we had with the birds."

"*Maybe*. But I didn't dream about the birds."

"Even so, we can't be sure. Remember that Durga said she would protect him."

"I remember. But it was so *real*."

"There's no way to know for sure."

"Maybe there is."

"What are you thinking?"

"I think we should visit the Silvanae again. Maybe we can sleep in the Grove of Dreams, and I can see the future. Maybe I'll see if we can save him or not."

"Do you think it will work?"

"The Silvanae said if they had a desperate problem to work out, they went there for answers. Please, Kishan. Let's try."

Kishan wiped a tear off my cheek with his thumb. "Okay, Kells. Let's find Faunus."

"Kishan, one more thing. What does *hridaya patni* mean?"

"Where did you hear that?" he asked softly.

"In my dream. Ren said it to me before we parted."

Kishan got up and walked outside the tent. I followed and found him staring into the distance. His arm was propped up against a tree limb. Without turning around, he said, "It's a pet name our father used for our mother. It means . . . 'wife of my heart.'"

It took a long day of hiking to reach the Silvanae village. They were overjoyed to see us and wanted to have a party. I didn't feel like celebrating. When I asked if we could sleep in the Grove of Dreams again, Faunus assured me that everything they had was at our disposal. The tree nymphs brought me a small dinner and left me alone in one of their cottages until nightfall. Kishan understood that I wanted to be alone and he ate with the Silvanae.

When evening came, Kishan returned with a visitor. "I want you to meet someone, Kells." He held the hand of a small silver-haired toddler.

"Who's this?"

"Can you tell the pretty lady your name?"

"Rock," the boy replied.

"Your name is Rock?" I asked.

The sweet baby face grinned at me.

Kishan said, "Actually, his name is Tarak."

"Tarak?" I gasped. "That's impossible! He looks like he's almost two!"

Kishan shrugged. "Apparently, the Silvanae mature quickly."

"Amazing! Tarak, come here and let me take a look at you."

I held out my arms, and Kishan encouraged him forward. Tarak took a few clumsy steps toward me before falling into my lap.

"You're such a big boy now! And so handsome too. Would you like to play? Watch this."

I took the Scarf from around my neck, and we watched the kaleidoscope of colors shift and change. When the baby touched it, a tiny handprint of hot pink appeared on the fabric before disappearing in a swirl of yellow.

"Stuffed animals, please."

The fabric shifted, divided, and turned into stuffed animals of every kind. Kishan sat beside me, and we played with Tarak and the stuffed animal parade. The sting in my heart lessened as I laughed with the young Silvanae child.

When Kishan picked up the stuffed tiger and taught Tarak the proper way to growl, he looked up at me. Our eyes met, and he winked. I grabbed his hand, squeezed it, and mouthed, "Thank you."

Kishan kissed my fingers, smiled, and said, "Aunt Kelsey needs to get some sleep. It's time to take you back to your family, Little Man."

He scooped up Tarak, placed him on his shoulders, and said quietly, "I'll be right back."

I gathered the stuffed animals and told the Scarf we didn't need them anymore. Threads began spinning in the air and wove themselves back to form. Just as it finished, Kishan returned.

He crouched down, cupped my chin, and tilted my face up for his perusal. "Kelsey, you're exhausted. The Silvanae have prepared a bath for you. Go soak for a while before you sleep. I'll meet you in the Grove, okay?"

I nodded and let the same three Silvanae women lead me back to the bathing area. They were quiet this time, leaving me to my thoughts as they gently soaped my hair and rubbed scented lotion into my skin. They dressed me in a spun-silk robe before an orange-winged fairy guided me to the Grove of Dreams. Kishan was already there and had taken the liberty of creating a hammock with the Divine Scarf.

I mocked gently, "Not interested in sharing the honeymoon suite again, I see."

His back was turned toward me as he tested a knot of the hammock. "I just thought it would be better to . . ." He turned around and gave me a potent, steamy look. His golden eyes widened, and he quickly busied himself with knots again. Clearing his throat, he said, "It's definitely better for you to sleep by yourself this time, Kells. I'll be comfortable over here."

I shivered and tried to pretend Kishan's gaze hadn't affected me. "Suit yourself."

Kishan got into his hammock, laying back with his hands behind his head. He watched me as I pulled back the sheets.

I heard him say softly, "You look really . . . beautiful, by the way."

I turned toward him, lifted an arm, and ran my hand down the blue silk robe with long fairy sleeves. I knew that my hair hung down in supple waves and my pale skin gleamed from a vigorous scrubbing and the sparkling lotions of the Silvanae. Perhaps I did look beautiful, but I felt hollow, as empty as a plastic Easter egg. Colorfully, perhaps even elaborately decorated on the outside, but there was nothing in my center. I was drained to the core. "Thank you," I said mechanically as I climbed into the bed.

I lay awake staring at the stars for a long time. I could feel Kishan's eyes on me as I tucked a hand under my cheek and finally drifted to sleep.

I dreamt of nothing. Not of Ren, not of myself, not Kishan or even Mr. Kadam . . . I dreamed of emptiness. A great blackness filled my mind, a void. A space with no shape, no depth, no richness, and no *happiness*. I woke before Kishan. Without Ren, my life meant nothing. It was empty, hollow, and worthless. That was what the Grove of Dreams was trying to tell me. Too much was gone.

When my parents died, it was like two mighty trees had been uprooted. Ren had come into my life and had filled the empty landscape of my heart. My heart had healed, and the dry ground had been replaced by soft grass, lovely sandalwood trees, climbing jasmine, and roses. Right in the center of everything was a water fountain surrounded by tiger lilies, a beautiful place where I could sit and feel warmth and peace and love. Now the fountain was shattered, the lilies uprooted, the trees toppled, and there just wasn't enough soil left to grow anything else. I was barren, desolate—a desert incapable of sustaining life.

A soft breeze stirred my hair and blew strands of it across my face. I didn't bother pushing them aside. I didn't hear Kishan get up. I just felt his fingertips brush against my face as he lifted the strands from my cheek and tucked them behind an ear.

"Kelsey?"

I didn't respond. My unblinking eyes stared at the brightening dawn sky.

"Kells?"

He slid his hands under my body and picked me up. Then he sat on the bed and hugged me to his chest.

"Kelsey, please say something. Talk to me. I can't stand to see you like this."

He rocked me for a while. I could hear him and respond to him in my mind, but I felt detached from my environment, from my body.

I felt a raindrop hit my cheek, and the shock of it woke me, brought me to the surface. I lifted a hand and brushed the drop away.

"Is it raining? I didn't think it rained here."

He didn't answer. Another drop splashed on my forehead.

"Kishan?" I looked at him and realized it wasn't rain but tears.

His golden eyes were full of watery tears.

Puzzled, I lifted a hand to his cheek. "Kishan? Why are you crying?"

He smiled weakly. "I thought you were lost, Kells."

"Oh."

"Tell me. What did you see to take you so far away from me? Did you see Ren?"

"No. I saw nothing. My dreams were filled with cold blackness. I think it means he's dead."

"No. I don't think so, Kells. I saw Ren in my dreams."

Vitality surged back into my limbs. "*You saw him? Are you sure?*"

"Yes. We were arguing on a boat, actually."

"Could it be a dream from the past?"

"No. We were on a modern yacht. In fact, it's the yacht that belongs to us."

I sat up straighter. "Are you absolutely 100 percent certain that this happens in the future?"

"I'm sure."

I hugged him and kissed his cheeks and forehead. I punctuated each kiss with "Thank you! Thank you! Thank you!"

"Wait, Kells. The thing is, in the dream, we were arguing about—"

I laughed, grabbed his shirt, and shook him lightly, crazed with giddy relief. *He was alive!* "I don't care what you were arguing about. You two always argue."

"But I think I should tell you—"

I hopped off his lap and began moving quickly, gathering our things. "Tell me later. There's no time now. Let's get going. What are we waiting for? A tiger needs to be rescued. Come on. Come on!"

I darted around with crazed energy. A desperate, fevered determination filled my mind. Every minute we delayed meant more pain for the one I loved. The dream of Ren had been real. I wouldn't have thought

up new words in Hindi by myself, especially an endearment his father has used for his mother. I had been with him somehow. I had touched him, kissed him. Something had broken our connection, but he was still alive! He could be saved. In fact, he *would* be saved! Kishan had seen the future!

The Silvanae prepared a sumptuous breakfast, but we took it to go, hurried through good-byes, and headed back toward the spirit gate. It took two days of fast hiking to get to the gate following the directions the Silvanae had given us. Kishan said very little on the trip, and I was too wrapped up in thoughts of finding Ren to find out why.

Upon reaching the gate, I asked the Divine Scarf to create new winter gear for us, and after changing, I summoned my lightning power and placed my hand in the carved depression on the side of the gate. My skin glowed, becoming translucent and pink as the gateway shimmered and opened. We looked at each other, and I suddenly felt sad—as if we were saying good-bye. Kishan removed his glove and pressed a warm palm to my cheek as he studied my face soberly. I smiled and hugged him.

I'd meant it to be brief, but he wrapped his arms around me and hugged me tightly. I disentangled myself ungracefully, replaced my glove, and stepped through the gate into a sunny day on Mount Everest. My winter boots crunched on the white sparkling snow as Kishan stepped through and changed into the black tiger.

23 going home

After we passed through the gate, I turned to watch the land of Shangri-la vanish in a swirl of color. The red light that pulsed in the handprint faded, and the spirit gate returned to its former appearance—two tall wooden poles with long strings of prayer flags blowing in the breeze.

I blinked several times and rubbed my eyes lightly. Something was sticking to my lashes. I carefully peeled away a transparent green film, which had slipped off each eye like a pair of contact lenses.

Kishan appeared to be stuck in tiger form and probably would be for a while like Ren had been after Kishkindha. He blinked his eyes at me, and I could see the green film peeling away from one eye.

"Hold very still. I've got to get this out or it will bother you the whole way."

I lifted the film off one eye and then the other. It took a long time, but I was proud I could do it at all. The Ocean Teacher had said that as we exited Shangri-la the scales would fall from our eyes, and we could see the real world again. I didn't expect his words would be this literal.

I adjusted the backpack over my shoulders and began the steep descent back to Mr. Kadam's camp. The sun was shining, but it was still cold. I felt the same burning energy pushing me forward. I wouldn't stop to rest, though Kishan clearly wanted me to. I encouraged him to keep going and stopped only when it was too dark to see the landscape.

Since Hugin had helped me get my thoughts *unstuck*, my mind had become limpid, clear. I calculated and devised a plan. I knew how to save Ren. The only thing I didn't know was *where* to find him. I hoped that Mr. Kadam would know something about the culture or the whereabouts of the people we had seen in the vision.

The physical features I'd taken note of might not be enough for him to go on, but it was all we had. If anyone could figure out where to begin searching, it was Mr. Kadam. I also hoped that time had stood still, or at least slowed, while we were in Shangri-la. I was sure that Ren would be tormented every moment he was with Lokesh. It was unbearable thinking of him being in pain at all, let alone for the many days we'd spent in the world beyond the spirit gate.

I lay awake in our tent that night for a long while thinking about my strategy and analyzing it from as many angles as I could. I would not allow Lokesh to take anyone else. There would be no trades for Ren. We were going to save him and all of us would be going home.

The next morning, Kishan woke and changed to a man. I quickly had snow gear made for him, and he dressed in the tent while I got some breakfast together. He soon joined me dressed in his new clothes: a rust colored base-layer shirt that fit tightly under a black waterproof jacket, black pants with elastic cuffs, warm insulated gloves, thick wool socks, and snow boots. I appraised his appearance and congratulated myself on doing a good job.

We discovered that recovering the Scarf had given Kishan another six hours of freedom from his tiger self. We were now halfway finished with our quest. The tigers could take human form for twelve hours of the day.

Though I was in a hurry, Kishan reminded me that it would take us at least two full days to hike down the mountain. When we made camp the second night, I decided it was time to talk to him about my rescue plan and show him what else the Scarf could do.

After we'd settled in our tent, conveniently made by the Scarf, I unzipped my sleeping bag and spread it on the floor. I encouraged him to sit across from me, before I picked up the Scarf.

"Okay, the Scarf can do several things. It can become or create anything made of fabric or natural fibers. It doesn't have to reabsorb what it creates. It can, but it can also leave the thing behind, and then the creation loses the magic of the cloth. The Scarf can also be shaped to gather the winds like in the story of the Japanese god Fūjin's bag. The third thing it can be used for is . . . changing appearance."

"Changing appearance? What do you mean?"

"Umm, how do I describe it? Have you ever seen a magician pull a rabbit out of a hat or change a bird into a feather?"

"We did have magicians come to court occasionally. One of them changed a mouse to a dog."

"Yes! It's similar to that. It's an illusion. A trick done with light and mirrors, sort of."

"How does that work?"

"Remember the Divine Weaver said there was power in the weaving? It not only creates the clothes of that person, but it can make you look like him or her as well. The key is, you have to be specific and capture in your mind exactly who you want to look like. I'm going to try it. Watch and tell me if it works."

I said, "Disguise, please—Nilima."

The Scarf grew into a long piece of sparkly black fabric with colors swirling quickly through the entire piece. It glittered as if embellished with jeweled sequins that surfaced briefly and then disappeared. Light reflected and moved around the tent like thousands of prisms shooting rainbows in every direction.

I wrapped the fabric around my body and covered my entire frame, including my hair and face. My skin became warm and tingly. The swirling colors were iridescent and lit the dark small space in which I sat wrapped inside the warm blanket the Scarf had become. It was like watching my own personal laser light show. When the glow diminished, I unwrapped myself and looked at Kishan.

"Well?"

His mouth opened in shock. "*Kells*?"

"Yep."

"You . . . you even *sound* like Nilima. You're dressed like her."

I looked down and found I was wearing a powder-blue silk dress that ended at my knees. My legs were bare. "I just realized that. I'm freezing!"

Kishan wrapped his coat around me then picked up my hand and examined it. "Your skin looks like hers. You even have her long painted nails. Unbelievable!"

I shivered. "Okay, demonstration done. I am seriously freezing." I wrapped the fabric around me again and said, "Back to myself, please." The colors began swirling again and after a long minute I removed the material and returned to looking like myself. "Now you try, Kishan. I didn't have a mirror. I want to see how accurate it is."

"Okay." He took the Scarf from me and said, "Disguise—Mr. Kadam."

He wrapped it around his entire body. When he took the fabric off a minute later, I found myself sitting across from Mr. Kadam. He looked exactly like I had last seen him. I stretched out a finger and touched his short beard.

"Wow! You really look like him!" I felt the hem of his pants. "The pants feel real. It's a perfect replica!"

He touched his face and rubbed a hand over his close-cropped hair.

I said, "Wait a minute! You've even got his amulet on! Does it feel real?"

He touched the amulet and felt the chain. "It looks real, but it's not."

"What do you mean?"

"I wore an amulet for most of my life, and when I gave you mine to wear, I could feel its absence. This one doesn't feel real to me. It doesn't feel powerful. Also it's lighter in weight, and the surface is slightly different."

"Hmm, that's interesting. I don't know that I can really feel the power of mine yet."

I reached over and touched the amulet around his neck and then compared it to mine. "I think the one you are wearing is made of some kind of fabric."

"Really?" He rubbed it between his fingers. "You're right. The surface is slightly off. You really can't feel the amulet's power?"

"No."

"Well, if you wore it for as many years as I did, you would feel it."

"Maybe it's something only you tigers can feel because you're so closely associated with it."

"Maybe. We'll have to ask Mr. Kadam about it."

Kishan changed back to himself. "So what exactly is your plan, Kells?"

"Well, I haven't hammered out all the details yet, but I was thinking that maybe we could impersonate Lokesh's guards and sneak into wherever they're holding Ren."

"You don't plan to make a trade then? An amulet for Ren?"

"Not if we can avoid it. I'd like it to be a last resort. The big problem with the plan is that I don't know *where* Ren is being held. I told you I saw Ren in the vision, but I also saw a person that I'm really hoping Mr. Kadam can identify."

"Identify how?"

"His hair and tattoos were unique. I've never seen them before."

"It's a long shot, Kells. Identifying where the servant is from doesn't necessarily mean that that's where Lokesh is holding Ren."

"I know, but it's all we have to go on."

"Okay, so we have a *how*. We just need a where."

"Right."

The next day, we finally passed the snow line and continued moving quickly downhill. Kishan had slept as a tiger so he walked with me as a man for most of the day, which gave us the opportunity to talk. He said that he felt stifled being forced back into the tiger form. Like Ren, now that he'd gotten a taste of being human, he craved it desperately.

I tried to remind him that twelve hours was much better than six. He could sleep as a tiger and spend most of his waking hours as a man now, but he still complained about it.

During a lull in the conversation, I said, "Kishan?"

He grunted as he slid downhill a bit on loose gravel. "Yeah?"

"I want you to tell me everything you know about Lokesh. Where did you meet him? What is he like? Tell me about his family, his wife, his background. All that stuff."

"Okay. To start off, he didn't come from a royal bloodline."

"What do you mean? I thought he was a king."

"He was, but he didn't start off that way. The first time I met him, he was a royal advisor. He had moved up quickly to a position of authority. When the king died unexpectedly without any progeny, Lokesh stepped into the king's position."

"Huh, probably an interesting story there. I would love to hear the tale of his ascent to power. Did everyone just accept him as the new king? Were there any protests?"

"If there were, he quickly snuffed out any malcontents and went about building up a powerful army. That kingdom had always been very peaceful, and we'd never had a problem with them until Lokesh took power. Even then, he was always very careful around my family.

"Minor skirmishes broke out between our armies, which he always claimed he had no knowledge of. We now think that he was gathering intelligence because the skirmishes always occurred in key military areas. He dismissed them as minor misunderstandings and assured us that he would reprimand the survivors."

"Survivors? What do you mean?"

"The skirmishes often resulted in the deaths of his soldiers. He used his soldiers like disposable tools. He demanded their loyalty, and they gave it—even to the point of death."

"And nobody in your family ever suspected anything?"

"If anyone suspected him, it was Mr. Kadam. He was head of the military at the time, and he felt that there was more going on than soldiers *misunderstanding* their orders. Nobody else suspected Lokesh, though. Lokesh was very charming when he visited. He always assumed a humble demeanor around my father, but all the while he was coldly calculating our downfall."

"What weaknesses does Lokesh have?"

"I think he knows more of my weaknesses than I of his. I imagine he abused Yesubai. According to him, his wife had died long before we met him. Yesubai never spoke of her mother, and I never thought to ask. As far as I know, he has no family left, no posterity, unless he took another wife over the years. He craves power. That could be a weakness."

"Does he crave money? Could we offer to buy Ren's freedom?"

"No. He uses money only as a means to get more power. He couldn't care less about jewels or gold. He might say differently, but I wouldn't trust him. He's an ambitious man, Kelsey."

"Do we know anything about the other pieces of the amulet? Like where he got them from?"

"The only thing I know about the amulet is what my parents told us. They said that the amulet pieces were carried by five warlords and were handed down over the centuries. My mother's family had one piece, and my father's family had another. That's how Ren and I each got one. The one you wear was Mother's, and Kadam wears Father's. I have no idea how Lokesh acquired the other three pieces. I'd never heard of any other amulet pieces until Lokesh mentioned them. Ren and I wore our pieces under our clothing as carefully protected family heirlooms."

"Maybe Lokesh found a list of the families who had been entrusted with them?" I pondered.

"Maybe. But I've never heard of such a list."

"Did your parents know the amulets were powerful?"

"No. Not until we were changed to tigers."

"You didn't have an ancestor who lived a long time like Mr. Kadam?"

"No. Our family was prolific on both sides. There was always a young king to pass the amulet to, and in our family, tradition was to pass on the amulet when the boy turned eighteen. Our ancestors had longer lives than normal, but the life span then was considerably shorter than it is today."

"Unfortunately, none of this information gives us an inkling as to any of Lokesh's weaknesses."

"Perhaps it does."

"How so?" I asked.

"He craves power above all else. Since he is pursuing the amulet pieces at all costs, then that is his weakness."

"What do you mean?"

"We just saw the Scarf create a replica when I assumed Mr. Kadam's form. If he takes the replica version, he'll think that he's won."

"But we don't know if the replica can be removed from the person or not. Even if it could be, we don't know how long it will last."

Kishan shrugged and said, "We'll test it when we get back."

"It's a good idea."

I stumbled over a rock, and Kishan caught me. He held me for just a moment longer than necessary, smiled, and brushed the hair out of my face.

"We're almost there. Can you keep going or do you need to rest?" he asked intently.

"I can keep going."

He released me and took the backpack from my shoulders.

"Kishan, I just want to say thank you for everything you did in Shangri-la. I wouldn't have made it without you."

He threw the backpack over one shoulder and stopped, considering me for a minute. "You didn't think I'd let you go alone, did you?"

"No, but I'm grateful that I had you with me."

"Grateful is all I'm going to get, isn't it?"

"What else were you hoping for?"

"Adoration, devotion, affection, infatuation, or just plain finding me irresistible."

"Sorry, Don Juan. You'll have to live with my undying gratitude."

He sighed dramatically. "I guess that's as good a place to start as any. How about we just call it even. I never actually thanked you for convincing me to come home. I've . . . found a lot of things about being home that I like."

I smiled at him. "It's a deal."

He put his arm across my shoulders, and we continued our hike.

"I wonder if we'll come across that old bear again," Kishan mused.

"If so, I should be able to keep him away this time. I didn't think to use my power when we first ran into him. Apparently, I'm not much of a warrior."

"You fought the birds really well." He grinned. "I'd ride into battle with you any time. Let me tell you about the time I left my sword at home." He kissed my forehead and remembered happier times.

At dusk, we could see a small fire in the distance at the base of the mountain. Kishan assured me that it was Mr. Kadam's camp. He said he could smell him on the breeze. He held my hand the last half mile because he said he could see better in the dark than I could—but I suspected that wasn't the only reason. When we got closer, I could just make out Mr. Kadam's shadow inside the tent.

I approached the tent and said, "Knock. Knock. Any room in there for a couple of wandering strangers?"

The shadow moved, and the tent's zipper slid down.

"Miss Kelsey? Kishan?"

Mr. Kadam stepped outside and grabbed me in a big hug. Then he turned to clap Kishan on the back.

"You must be freezing! Come inside. I'll make some hot tea. Let me just get a kettle to put on the fire."

"Mr. Kadam, you don't have to do that. We have the Golden Fruit, remember?"

"Ah, yes, I forgot."

"And we have something else too."

I took the amethyst-colored Scarf from around my neck, which caused it to shift to turquoise. "Soft cushions please, and could you make the tent just a bit larger?" I asked.

The turquoise threads immediately shifted and stretched. Several of them wove large cushions of various colors and another piece broke off and began looping through the end of the tent. A few moments later, we were able to sit comfortably on large cushions in a tent that had doubled in size. Mr. Kadam quietly watched the busy threads, in fascination.

I struggled briefly to get out of my coat. Kishan helped and stroked my arm. I shoved his hand away, but Kishan only grinned and reclined on the cushions.

Mr. Kadam asked, "Does it work like the Golden Fruit except it creates woven things?"

I shot Kishan a warning look and replied, "Sort of, yeah."

Mr. Kadam mumbled, "'India's masses shall be robed.'"

"Huh, I guess we *could* clothe India's people with this thing."

Funny that that hadn't occurred to me before.

"Wait a minute. Didn't the prophecy say something about 'chief's disguise' too?"

Mr. Kadam rummaged through some papers and found a copy of the prophecy.

"Yes. It says here, 'Discus routs and 'chief's disguise can stave off those who would pursue'. Is that what you're referring to?"

I laughed. "Yep, that makes sense then. You see, the Divine Scarf can do a couple of other things too. I mean other than making clothes and weaving things. It can gather the winds like the god Fūjin's bag."

Mr. Kadam exclaimed, "Similar to the bag of winds Odysseus received from Aiolos? Ulysses' leather bag tied with a silver cord?"

"Yes, but it's not leather. Silver cord would work, though."

"Perhaps sent by one of the gods of wind? Vayu? Striborg? Njord? Pazuzu?"

"Don't forget Boreas and Zephyrus."

Kishan interrupted, "Could you two speak English, please?"

Mr. Kadam laughed. "Sorry. I got carried away for a minute."

"Do you want to show him now, Kishan?" I asked.

"Sure."

Mr. Kadam leaned forward. "Show me what, Miss Kelsey?"

"You'll see. Just watch."

Kishan took the Divine Scarf, mumbled, "Disguise," and twisted it around his body. It lengthened and turned black with swirling colors.

"I want to see if it will work without me saying a name out loud like the Golden Fruit does," he said from beneath the folds of fabric.

"Yes. That's a good idea," I responded.

When Kishan took the Scarf away from his face, I was unprepared for what I'd see. It was Ren. He'd taken Ren's form. He must have seen my stricken face.

"I'm sorry. I didn't want to shock Mr. Kadam by showing him his own face."

"It's okay. Just change back quickly, please."

He did, and Mr. Kadam sat there dumbfounded. I couldn't speak. Seeing Ren sitting there—even knowing it was really Kishan—was extremely difficult. I had to tamp down all the emotions that surfaced.

Kishan quickly took over for me and explained, "With the Scarf, we can take the form of other people. Kelsey changed to look like Nilima, and I became you. We need to test its range and try different forms so we can figure out the Scarf's disguise abilities and limitations."

"Simply . . . amazing!" Mr. Kadam sputtered, "Uh, Kishan, may I?"

"Sure."

He tossed the Scarf to Mr. Kadam. Its colors changed as soon as his fingers touched the fabric, first turning a brown mustard color and then changing to olive green.

I teased, "I think it likes you, Mr. Kadam."

"Yes, well . . . imagine the possibilities. The many people the Golden Fruit and this glorious fabric could help. So many people suffer from want of food and warm clothes, and not just in India. These are truly divine gifts."

I let him examine the Scarf while I had the Golden Fruit make us some chamomile tea with cream and sugar. Kishan wasn't especially fond of tea, so he got a hot chocolate with cinnamon and whipped cream instead.

I asked, "How long were we gone?"

"A bit over a week."

I quickly calculated in my mind how many days we were up on the mountain. "Good. Our time in Shangri-la didn't count."

"How long were you two in Shangri-la, Miss Kelsey?"

"I'm not sure exactly, but I think it was almost two weeks." I looked at Kishan. "Is that about right?"

He nodded silently and sipped his cocoa.

"Mr. Kadam, how soon can we get going?"

"We can leave at dawn."

"I want to get home as soon as possible. We need to get ready to save Ren."

"We can go across the border and enter India from the Sikkim province. It will be much faster than going through the Himalayas again."

"How long?"

"It depends on how fast we get through the border. If there's no trouble, perhaps a few days."

"Okay. We have so much to tell you."

Mr. Kadam sipped his tea and looked at me thoughtfully. "You have not been sleeping well, Miss Kelsey. Your eyes are tired."

He made eye contact with Kishan, and then set down his cup. "I think we should let you sleep. We have a long journey ahead and much can be discussed on the road."

"I agree," Kishan interjected. "These last few days have been hard on you. Get some rest, *bilauta*."

I finished my tea. "I guess I'm outnumbered. Fine. Let's all get some sleep then, and we can leave that much earlier in the morning."

I used the Scarf to make another bedroll and pillows for all of us. I fell asleep to the quiet sound of Mr. Kadam and Kishan speaking softly in their native language.

The next day, we began our journey home. We made it past customs and then drove about halfway home before stopping at a hotel in Gaya. We took turns driving and napping in the back. Kishan got a turn, but Mr. Kadam kept an eye on him, still smarting about the wreck with the Jeep in India.

While we drove, we told Mr. Kadam all about our journey. I started with Mount Everest and the bear. Kishan talked about carrying me through the spirit gate and hiking through paradise.

Mr. Kadam was fascinated by the Silvanae and asked dozens of questions. While I drove, he took copious notes. He wanted to keep a detailed record of our journey, and he listened carefully and wrote page after page in his refined style of penmanship. He asked many specific questions about the tests of the four houses and about the iron-bird guardians, nodding as if he had expected this or that to occur.

At the hotel, we sat around a table and showed him the pictures Kishan took of the ark of Noah, the world tree, the Silvanae, and the four houses. The visual record helped us remember more details, and Mr. Kadam pulled out his notebook again and began scribbling.

Kishan showed me the camera and asked, "What *is* that?"

I turned it different ways and laughed. "It's one of Hugin's eyes. See? There's the nest."

Kishan flipped through some more. "Why didn't you take a camera into Kishkindha?"

I shrugged but Mr. Kadam explained, "I didn't want to burden her with too many heavy objects. She needed water and food."

Kishan grunted and said, "I'm definitely getting a copy of this one, *apsaras rajkumari*."

He handed the camera to me. It was the one of me in the gossamer gown with fairies "hair clips." I looked like a princess with glowing skin and bright eyes. My hair hung in soft waves down my back, and I could just make out a pink fairy peeking around a lock of hair to see my face. Mr. Kadam looked over my shoulder.

"You look quite becoming, Miss Kelsey."

Kishan laughed. "You should have seen her in person. *Quite becoming* is an understatement."

Mr. Kadam chuckled and went to get his bag from the car.

Kishan rested a hip against the table. He cupped his hands, brought up a knee, and looked at me with a serious expression. "In fact, I'd say that I've never seen *anything* more beautiful."

I shuffled my feet nervously. "Well, it's always startling when someone gets a makeover. A fairy makeover would be all the rage at the salons."

He gently took my elbow and turned me toward him. "The *makeover* is not what made you beautiful. You are always beautiful. The makeover just accentuated what was already there." He lifted my chin with a finger, and looked into my eyes. "You are a lovely woman, Kelsey."

Kishan put his warm hands on my bare arms and rubbed them lightly. He tugged me closer. His eyes darted down to my mouth. As he lowered his lips to within inches of mine, I deliberately pressed my hands against his chest and admonished, "*Kishan.*"

"I like the way you say my name."

"Please let me go."

He lifted his head, sighed, and said softly, "*Ren* . . . is a lucky, *lucky* man."

He reluctantly slid his hands from my arms and then stepped over to the window.

I busied myself by gathering toiletries and pajamas. Kishan watched me quietly for a minute, and then announced, "I think I need a makeover too. A hot shower is calling my name."

Still nervous, I said, "Yeah. Me too. A hot shower is going to feel heavenly."

He raised an eyebrow. "Would you like to go first?"

"No, you go ahead."

His eyes twinkled as he regarded me, "It would be more heavenly if you told me you wanted to conserve water."

My mouth opened in shock. "*Kishan!*"

He winked at me. "I didn't think so. Can't blame a guy for trying."

I was saved from responding by Mr. Kadam's return.

By the second day, Mr. Kadam and I had compared notes on the vision of Lokesh. He had noticed the tattooed servant helping Lokesh too, and he thought his appearance was distinct enough to track down where the man was from. Mr. Kadam had also planned to discreetly investigate Lokesh's office in Mumbai.

The air was so muggy outside that we probably could have filled our water bottles just by hanging them out the window. We passed temples with golden cupolas and busy people working in their fields, drove over swollen rivers and through flooded roads, but all I could think about was getting back to Ren. In fact, the only thing that interrupted my thoughts of Ren was Kishan.

Something had changed between us in Shangri-la, and I didn't quite know what to do about it. Spending all those weeks with Kishan didn't help. He was moving past flirting and was starting to make serious overtures. I had hoped that he would lose interest.

Originally, I had thought that the more he got to know me, the less he would like me. But I seemed to have the opposite effect on him. I did love him, but not in the same way he felt about me. I'd learned to rely on and trust him. He'd become a good friend, but I was in love with his brother. If I had gotten to know Kishan before Ren, things might have been different. But I hadn't.

Thoughts kept nagging at me as we drove. *Was it just luck that I met Ren first? That we had the opportunity to fall in love? What if Kishan had followed me to America and not Ren? Would I have made a different choice?*

The truth was that I didn't know. Kishan was a very attractive man, both outside and in. There was something about him, something that would make a girl want to wrap her arms around him and keep him forever. He was lonely. He was searching for a home, for someone to love him, like Ren was. He needed someone to take him in and let the wandering, lost tiger rest. I could easily envision that person being me. I could see myself falling in love with him and being happy with him.

But then I thought about Ren who had the same qualities that I loved about Kishan. Ren also needed someone to love him, to quiet the restless tiger. But Ren and I fit together so much more easily, like he was made especially for me. He was everything I could possibly wish for wrapped up in a gorgeous package.

Ren and I had so much in common. I loved the way he called me little nicknames. And how he sang for me and played his guitar. I loved how he got excited about reading Shakespeare and how he liked to watch movies and cheer on the good guys. How he would never cheat, even if it was to win the girl he loved.

If I had never met Ren, if Kishan had been the one in the circus cage, I felt I could be happy with him too. But with Ren loving me and wanting to be with me, I could never be persuaded to look in Kishan's direction. Ren filled my world even when he wasn't here.

There were no shades of gray for Ren. He was the white cat and Kishan was the black, literally. The problem was that I just didn't see Kishan in the same way Ren did. Kishan was a hero too. They'd both been hurt. They'd both suffered. And Kishan really did deserve a happy ending just as much as Ren did.

Behind the wheel, Kishan glanced in the rear-view mirror from time to time, watching me.

I was biting my lip, deep in thought, when he said, "Penny for your thoughts."

I blushed and replied, "Just thinking about saving Ren." Then I deliberately turned in my seat and napped.

When the car finally pulled into the driveway, Kishan gently shook me awake. "We're home, *bilauta*."

confessions

I was so happy to be back home I could've cried. Kishan carried our bags inside and quickly disappeared. Mr. Kadam also excused himself to check with some of his contacts. Left alone, I decided to take a long, hot shower and do some laundry.

Dressed in pajamas and slippers, I padded into the laundry room and threw in a load. I wasn't sure what to do with the fairy clothes. I decided to hang them on the veranda overnight, just to see if there were any fairies in the real world. Then I walked through the house to find out what everyone else was doing.

Mr. Kadam was in the library on the phone. I heard only half of the conversation. He glanced at me and pulled out a chair so I could sit beside him.

"Yes. Of course. Contact me as soon as possible. That is correct. Send in as many as necessary. We'll be in touch." He hung up the phone and turned to me.

Playing with my wet hair, I asked, "Who was that?"

"A man of my employ who has many remarkable talents. One of which is infiltrating large organizations."

"What's he going to do for us?"

"He will begin investigating who works in the penthouse office in the tallest building of Mumbai."

"You aren't planning on going there yourself, are you? Lokesh would capture you too!"

"No. Lokesh gave away more about himself than he learned of us. Did you notice his suit?"

"His suit? It looked like a regular suit to me."

"It isn't. His suits are custom made in India. Only two businesses in the entire country specialize in expensive suits such as that one. I've sent my men to hunt down an address."

I shook my head and grinned. "Mr. Kadam, did anyone ever tell you that you are extremely observant?"

He smiled. "Perhaps once or twice."

"Well, I'm very glad that you're on our side. I'm impressed! I didn't even *think* to look at his clothes. What about the servant?"

"I have a few ideas about where he might have come from. Based on the beads, the hair, and the tattoo, I should be able to narrow it down by tomorrow. Why don't you have a snack and head to bed?"

"I took a long nap in the car, but a snack sounds good. Will you join me?"

"I believe I might."

I stood quickly. "Oh! I almost forgot! I brought something for you!"

I found my backpack at the foot of the stairs and also retrieved a couple of glasses and two small plates from the kitchen. I set out the plate and glass in front of Mr. Kadam and unzipped the backpack.

"I don't know if the pastry is still edible, but the nectar should be."

He leaned forward, curious.

Opening the Silvanae's delicious packages, I placed several dainty delicacies on his plate. Sadly, the small pack of sugar-dusted lace cookies had become a pack of crumbs. But, the other items still looked as fresh and delectable as they had been in Shangri-la.

Mr. Kadam appraised the tiny appetizers from several angles,

marveling at the artistry involved. Then he carefully tasted a mushroom galette and a tiny raspberry tart as I explained that the Silvanae were vegetarians who loved sugary things. I popped the stopper of a tall gourd and poured sweet, golden nectar into his cup. Kishan walked in and pulled up a chair next to me.

"*Hey!* Why wasn't I invited to the Silvanae tea party?" he teased.

I slid my plate to Kishan and went to get another glass. We laughed and enjoyed a peaceful respite as we savored pumpkin rolls with walnut butter and mini apple, cheese, and onion stuffed pies. We drained every drop of the nectar and were thrilled to see that the Golden Fruit could produce more.

The only thing that could have made this moment better would have been to share it with Ren. I promised myself that I would write down each delicious food we'd eaten in Shangri-la so I could taste them all again with Ren by using the Golden Fruit after he was rescued.

We stayed awake until late that night. Kishan changed into a tiger and slept at my feet as Mr. Kadam and I read books on the rural tribes of India. At about 3:00 a.m., I turned a page in the fifth book I'd picked up and found a picture of a woman with tattooing across her forehead.

"Mr. Kadam, come look at this."

He sat on the leather chair next to me. I handed him the book, so he could study the woman.

"Yes. This is one of the groups I thought of. They're called the Baiga."

"What do you know about them? Where are they?"

"They are a mostly nomadic indigenous tribe who avoid association outside of their communities. They hunt and gather food, preferring not to till the ground. They believe farming harms Mother Earth. There are two groups of them that I know of: one in Madhya Pradesh in central India and one in Jharkhand, which is in eastern India. I believe I have a book that has more details of their culture."

He scanned through several shelves until he found the right text. He sat next to me and opened the book.

"It's about the Adivasis. There should be more about the Baiga in here."

I leaned down to scratch Kishan's ear. "What are the Adivasis?"

"It's a term that classifies all of the native tribes together, but it doesn't differentiate among them. Several cultures fall under the heading Adivasis. Here, we have the Irulas, Oraon, Santals, and," he flipped another page, "the Baiga."

He found the section he was looking for and ran his finger down the page as he read important parts in a verbal shorthand.

"*They practice bewar cultivation. Slash and burn agriculture. Famous for tattooing. Depend on jungle for sustenance. Employ ancient medicines and magic. Bamboo handicrafts.* Aha! Here is exactly what we're looking for, Miss Kelsey. *Baiga men grow their hair long and wear it in a jura or bun.* The man holding Ren fits that description. Though the confusing thing is, a Baiga leaving his tribe to serve someone like Lokesh would almost never happen."

"Even if he paid the man well?"

"It wouldn't matter. Their lifestyle is centered around their tribe. There would be no reason for him to leave his people. It's not within their cultural norm. They are a simple, straightforward people. A person of the Baiga would be unlikely to join the ranks of Lokesh. Still, this warrants investigation. I will begin my study of the Baiga tribes tomorrow. For now, it's time to rest, Miss Kelsey. I insist. It's very late, and we both need fresh minds."

I nodded and replaced the books I'd taken from his library shelves. He squeezed my shoulder.

"Don't fret. All things will work out in the end. I feel it. We've made great progress. Kahlil Gibran said, 'The deeper that sorrow carves into

your being, the more joy you can contain.' I know that you've had many great sorrows, but I also feel that your life will hold many great joys, Miss Kelsey."

I smiled. "Thank you." I hugged him and whispered against his shirt, "I don't know what I'd do without you. You get some sleep too."

We said goodnight, and Mr. Kadam disappeared into his room while I climbed the stairs. Kishan padded along behind me and followed me into my room. He stood at the glass door to the veranda, waiting for me to let him out. When I slid open the door, I knelt beside him and patted him on his back.

"Thanks for keeping me company."

He hopped up on the swinging love seat and promptly fell asleep. I climbed into bed and hugged my stuffed white tiger tightly, hoping to fill the empty space inside my chest with thoughts of Ren.

I woke around 11:00 a.m. Mr. Kadam was on the phone and hung up as soon as I sat across from him.

"I think we've had a lucky break, Miss Kelsey. In my investigation of the Baiga, I've found nothing out of the ordinary regarding the tribe located in Madhya Pradesh. The tribe in eastern India, however, seems to be missing."

"What do you mean missing?"

"There are usually small villages near the Baiga tribes who deal with them from time to time. Such meetings are often due to controversies over deforestation or other various disputes. This tribe appears to have relocated recently and hasn't been found. They are nomadic and do move around, but this is the longest they have gone without contacting the locals.

"The Baiga are limited by law now and cannot move about as freely as they did in the past. I will do some more research today. I also have some connections than can take satellite photos of the area and find the tribe at its current location.

"If it warrants more attention, I will inform you and Kishan. You two have had quite an ordeal the last few weeks, so I want you to rest today. There is nothing you can do until I have more data. Go for a swim, watch a movie, or go out to eat. You two deserve a break."

"Are you sure there's nothing I can do? I can't really relax when I know Ren is suffering."

"Your worrying about him won't make him suffer less. He would want you to rest too. We will find him soon, Miss Kelsey. Don't forget that I have led soldiers into battle many times over, and if there is one thing I've learned, it's that all war-hardened troops need R&R, including you. Making time to relax is very important to the mental well being of all soldiers. Be off with you. I don't want to see you or Kishan until this evening."

I smiled at him and saluted. "Yes, General. I will convey your instructions to Kishan."

He saluted me back. "See to it."

I laughed and went in search of Kishan.

I found him in the dojo working on martial arts and sat on the bottom step to watch him for a few moments. He did a complicated set of aerial leaps and twists that would have been impossible if he didn't have tiger strength. Then he landed two feet away and faced me with a playful grin.

I laughed. "You know, if you and Ren entered the Olympics you could both win several gold medals. Gymnastics, track and field, wrestling, you name it. You'd both get millions of dollars in endorsements."

"I don't need millions of dollars."

"You'd have pretty girls fawning all over you."

He smiled rakishly. "I only need one pretty girl fawning all over

me, and she's not interested. Now what brings you down here? Want to work out?"

"No. I wondered if you wanted to go for a swim. Mr. Kadam has ordered us to relax today."

He grabbed a towel and scrubbed his face and head. "A swim, huh? It might cool me off." He peeked from around his towel. "Unless you're planning to wear a bikini."

I snorted. "I don't think so. I'm not a bikini kind of girl."

He affected a deep, dramatic sigh. "That's a pity. Alright, meet you at the pool."

I headed upstairs and changed into my red one-piece swimsuit, slipped on a robe, and stepped out onto the veranda.

Kishan had changed into a pair of board shorts and was setting up the net for water volleyball. I'd just tossed my robe onto a deck chair and tested the water with my foot when I felt something cold on my back.

"Yikes! What are you doing?"

"Hold still. You need sunscreen. Your skin is so white you'll burn."

He efficiently coated my back and neck with lotion and started on my arms when I stopped him.

"I can take it from here, thanks," I said, holding out my hand for the bottle. I squeezed out a quarter sized blob of lotion and rubbed it onto my arms and legs. It smelled like coconuts.

Kishan grinned, glanced at my legs, and winked. "Take your time."

By the time he got the ball and a couple of towels out of the storage locker, I was done.

He asked, "Care for a game of volleyball?"

"You'll beat me."

"I'll take the deep end. It'll slow me down."

"Okay, I guess we can try."

He took a step closer. "Hold on a second."

"What?"

He grinned mischievously. "You missed a spot."

"Where?"

"Right here."

He dabbed a giant blob of sunscreen on my nose and laughed.

I punched him and smiled. "You troublemaker!" I reached up to try and blend it in better.

"Here," he said. "Let me."

I let my hands drop down to my sides while his fingers lightly brushed the lotion over my nose and cheeks. The touch was friendly at first, but then his mood changed. He closed the distance between us. His golden eyes studied my face. I sucked in a deep breath and ran.

I took a few steps and cannonballed into the deep end of the pool, effectively splashing him and everything else nearby.

He laughed and dove in after me. I shrieked and swam underwater to the other side of the net. When I popped my head above water, I couldn't see him. A hand grabbed my ankle and tugged me under. After I surfaced again, coughing and pushing the hair out of my eyes, Kishan sprung up next to me, flipped his hair back with a toss of his head, and laughed as I tried to shove him.

He didn't budge, of course, so I splashed water at him instead, which turned into a water fight. It soon became painfully obvious that I was losing. His arms never seemed to tire, and when wave after wave of water drowned out my pathetic splashing, I called a time out.

He happily stopped the bombardment and, using his arms, pushed himself up and out of the pool to grab the volleyball. We started playing, and I was delighted to see that I'd finally found a game where I seemed to have an advantage.

After I spiked the ball for the third time, winning another point, Kishan asked, "Where did you learn to play? You're pretty good!"

"I've never played in the water before, but I was decent at standard volleyball in high school. I almost joined the team, but that was the year my parents died. I wasn't as interested in playing the next year, but it's still my favorite game. I did okay at basketball too, but I was never tall enough to be competitive. Did you guys play sports?"

"We didn't really have time for sports. We had competitions in archery, wrestling, and some games like Parcheesi, but no team sports."

"Still, you can see I'm barely winning against you, even though you're in the deep end and have never played before."

Kishan grabbed the ball out of the air and fell into the water. When he surfaced, he was right across from me on the other side of the net. He lifted it and swam under. My feet were barely touching the bottom of the pool, leaving only my face above water. Our heads were at about the same level. He was still a good three feet away, and I narrowed my eyes wondering what he was up to. He watched me for a moment and smiled mischievously. I prepared for another water fight by raising my arms to splashing position.

Kishan was next to me in an instant. He snaked his arms around my waist, yanked me close, grinned roguishly, and said, "What can I say? I'm very competitive." Then he kissed me.

I froze. Our lips were wet from the water. The chlorine taste was strong, and he didn't move at first, so I could have been kissing the cool tile on the side of the pool for all I knew. But, then, he squeezed my waist, slid his hands up to caress my bare back, and tilted his head.

All of a sudden, the clean, wet, bleached out, non-kiss turned into a very real kiss from a very potent man who was very much *not* Ren. Kishan's lips warmed and moved against mine in a pleasant way. Pleasant enough that I forgot that I didn't *want* to kiss him and felt myself responding. My hands stopped pushing against him, and I gripped his strong upper arms. His skin was smooth and warm from the sun.

He responded with enthusiasm, wrapping one arm around my waist to crush me against his chest, while his other hand slid up my bare back to cup the back of my head. For the briefest of moments, I let myself delight in his embrace. But then, I remembered, and instead of making me happy or blissful, as kisses should, it made me sad.

I broke off the kiss and drew slightly away. Kishan kept his arm around my waist and placed a finger under my chin, tilting my face so I'd look at him. He studied my expression quietly. My eyes filled with tears. One rolled down my cheek and dropped to his hand.

He smiled tenuously. "Not exactly the reaction I was hoping for."

He reluctantly let me go as I swam away to sit on a step of the pool.

"I never claimed to be an expert kisser, if that's what you mean."

"I'm not talking about the kiss."

"Then what are you referring to?"

He didn't say anything.

I spread my fingers and placed my hand on the surface of the water, letting it tickle my palm. Without looking at him, I asked quietly, "Have I ever given you a reason to hope for more?"

He sighed and swept his hair back ruefully. "No, but—"

"But what?"

I looked up. Big mistake.

Kishan looked vulnerable. Sort of hope*less* and hope*ful* at the same time. Wanting to believe but not daring to. He seemed angry, frustrated, and unfulfilled. His despairing golden eyes were full of longing, but they also glittered with determination.

"But . . . I just can't help thinking that maybe Ren was taken for a reason. That maybe fate intervened. That maybe you were meant to be with *me* all along."

I replied bitingly, "The only *reason* that Ren was taken was because *he* volunteered himself to save our lives. Is this how you repay him?"

I watched the sting of my words wound him. It was easy to blame

Kishan, but I was more upset with *my* reaction to him. I felt incredibly guilty about letting the kiss happen at all. My accusation was as much to me as to him. That I'd actually enjoyed his kiss made me feel even worse.

He swam to the side and rested his back against the wall of the pool. "You think I don't care, don't you? You think I don't feel anything for my brother. But I do. Despite everything that's happened, I wish I was the one who had been taken. You'd have Ren. Ren would have you. And I'd get what I deserved."

"*Kishan!*"

"I'm serious. Do you think a day goes by that I don't *hate* myself for what I've done? For what I *feel*?"

I winced.

"You think I wanted to fall for you? I stayed away from you! I gave *him* the chance to be with you! But there's another part of me that asks *what if*? *What if* you're *not* supposed to be with Ren? *What if* you were supposed to be the answer to *my* prayers? Not his!"

He watched me from the other side of the pool. Even from this far away, I could see that he was hurting.

"Kishan, I—"

"And before you say anything, I want to warn you that I don't want your sympathy. It would be better if you said nothing than if you tried to tell me you didn't like it or that you feel only friendship for me."

"That's not what I was going to say."

"Good. Then are you admitting that you *did* like it? That there *is* chemistry between us? That you *are* attracted to me?"

"Do you *need* me to admit it?"

He folded his arms across his chest. "Yes. I think I do."

I threw my hands up in the air. "Fine! I admit it. I liked it. We have chemistry. Yes! I'm attracted to you. It was nice. In fact, it was *so* nice that it actually made me forget Ren for all of about five seconds. Are you happy now?"

"Yes."

"Well, *I'm* not."

"I can see that." He assessed me from across the pool. "So all I got was five seconds, huh?"

"Honestly, it was probably more like thirty."

He grunted. His arms were still crossed over his chest, but he wore a very self-satisfied-male type of grin now.

I sighed unhappily. "Kishan, I—"

He interrupted, "Do you remember when we escaped the House of Sirens in Shangri-la?"

"Yes."

"And you said you escaped because you thought of Ren?"

I nodded.

"Well, I escaped because I thought of you. You filled my thoughts, and the spell of the sirens went away. Don't you think that means anything? Couldn't it mean that maybe *we* were meant to be together? The truth is, Kells, I've thought about you for a long time. Since I first met you, I haven't been able to get you out of my mind."

A tear fell down my cheek, and I said softly, "I'm sorry for all that's happened. I'm sorry for everything that you've been through. And I'm especially sorry for any suffering I'm causing you. I don't know what to say, Kishan. You're a wonderful guy. *Too* wonderful. If the situation were different, I'd probably still be over there kissing you."

When I put my head in my hands, he ducked under the water and swam over to me. I heard him stand and looked up at his face. Water sluiced off his bronze torso. He really was a gorgeous man. Any girl would be lucky to have a guy like him.

He held out a hand. "Then come back over here and kiss me."

I shook my head. "I'm *not* . . . I *can't*," I sighed sadly. "Look, all I know is, I *love* him. And being with you, as tempting as you are, is not something I can do. I can't turn away from him. Please don't ask me to."

I got out of the pool and wrapped a towel around my body. I heard a splash and felt his nearness as he also dried off.

Kishan turned me to face him, willing me to meet his eyes. "You need to know that this is not about me competing with him. It's not about some hidden agenda. It's not a crush." He brushed his thumbs across my cheeks and cupped the sides of my face. "I love you, Kelsey."

He took a step closer.

I placed my hand on his warm chest and said, "If you *really* love me, then don't kiss me again." I stood my ground and waited for his reply. It wasn't easy. I felt like running, escaping to my room, but we needed to settle this between us.

He stood there breathing deeply. He looked down, and I could see flashes of emotion cross his face. Then he raised his eyes to mine. He acquiesced and said, "I won't promise that I'll never kiss you again, but I will promise not to kiss you unless I'm sure that you and Ren are through."

I was about to protest when he continued.

He touched my face lightly. "I'm not the kind of man to bottle up my feelings, Kells. I don't sit up in my room pining away, writing love poems. I'm not a dreamer. I'm a fighter. I'm a man of action, and it will take *all* of my self-control not to fight for this. When something needs to be done, I do it. When I feel something, I act on it. I don't see any reason why Ren deserves to get the girl of his dreams and I don't. It doesn't seem fair that this happens to me twice."

I put my hand on his arm. "You're right. It's not fair. It's not fair that you've had to be with me night and day for the past few weeks. It's not fair to ask you to set aside your feelings. It's not fair to ask you to be my friend when you feel this way. But, the fact is, I need you. I need your help. I need your support. And, I especially need your friendship. I wouldn't have survived one day in Shangri-la without you. I don't think I can rescue Ren without you, either. It's not fair to ask, but I'm asking. *Please.* I need you to let me go."

He looked at the house, brooding for a moment, and then at me. He touched my wet hair and discontentedly said, "Alright. I'll back off, but I'm not doing it for him and definitely not doing it for me. I'm doing it for you. Remember that."

I nodded silently and watched him stalk off to the veranda. My knees buckled, and I sat down hard on the pool chair.

I spent the rest of the day in my room studying texts on the Baiga. I kept rereading sections. I felt divided, torn. I was confused. I felt like someone had asked me to pick which parent would live and which would die. Whichever choice I made, I would feel responsible for the death of the other one. It wasn't about choosing happiness; it was about choosing suffering. Which one would I make suffer?

I didn't want *either* of them to suffer. My happiness was irrelevant. This wasn't like breaking up with Li or Jason. Ren needed me, loved me. But Kishan did too. There was no easy choice, no answer that would appease both of them. I pushed the books aside, picked up one of Ren's poems and a Hindi/English dictionary. It was one of the poems he'd written after I left India. It took me a long time to translate it, but it was worth it.

Am I alive?

I can breathe
I can feel
I can taste
But the air doesn't fill my lungs
All textures are rough
All tastes are muted

Am I alive?

I can see
I can hear
I can sense
But the world is black and white
Voices sound tinny and small
What I sense is confusing and out of place

When you're with me
Air rushes into my being
Fills me with light
And happiness
I am *alive!*

The world is full of color and sound
Tastes tantalize my palate
Everything is soft and fragrant
I sense the warmth of your presence
I know who I am and what I want

I want *you.*

Ren

A giant tear fell with a splat on the paper. I quickly moved it out of teardrop range. Despite Kishan's heartfelt words and the confusion about my relationship with him, there was one thing I couldn't deny. I *loved* Ren. Wholeheartedly. The truth was, if Ren had been here, been with me, this wouldn't be an issue.

When he was with me, I *also* knew who I was and what I wanted. Even without the strong connection, I could feel my heart swell at his words. I could picture him saying them, sitting at his desk, and writing them.

If I needed an answer, it was here—in my heart. When I thought of Kishan, I felt confusion and affection, mixed with a dollop of guilt. With Ren, I felt open and light. Free and desperately happy. I *loved* Kishan, but I was *in* love with Ren. How it happened was irrelevant. The fact was, it did happen.

As Kishan had said, I'd been with him longer now than with Ren. It wasn't surprising that we'd become closer. But, Ren held my heart in his hands. It beat only because he cherished it.

I was determined to be kind to Kishan. I was familiar with heartbreak. Mr. Kadam was right that Kishan needed me too. I had to be firm with him and let him know he was my friend. That I could be anything he needed me to be with the exception of a sweetheart.

I felt better. Reading Ren's poem grounded me. The feelings he spoke of, I felt too. I tucked the poem into my journal and went downstairs for dinner with Kishan and Mr. Kadam.

Kishan raised an eyebrow when I smiled at him. He turned back to his dinner, and ignoring him, I picked up my fork.

"The fish looks delicious, Mr. Kadam. Thank you."

He waved a hand in dismissal, leaned forward, and said, "I'm glad you're here, Miss Kelsey. I have news."

Saving Ren

My mouth went dry as I swallowed the fish. I coughed, and Kishan slid a glass of water in my direction. I sipped the cold liquid, cleared my throat, and said nervously, "What news?"

"We've found the Baiga tribe, and something is wrong. The tribe is located in a jungle area far away from other villages. Farther than they've been in the last hundred years. Farther, in fact, than the law allows them to travel. But what's even more strange is that the satellite images show technology nearby."

Kishan asked, "What kind of technology?"

"They have some large vehicles parked near the settlement, and the Baiga don't use cars. A sizeable structure has been built near their village as well. It's much larger than anything the Baiga have traditionally constructed. I believe it is a military compound."

He pushed aside his plate. "Reports show that there are also guards with weapons watching the forest. It looks as if they are defending the Baiga from attack."

"But who would attack the Baiga from the jungle?" I asked.

Mr. Kadam replied, "Who indeed? There are no skirmishes happening between the Baiga and any other group. The Baiga have no warriors and own nothing of value to the outside world. There is no reason for them to fear attack. Unless they expect it to come in the form of . . ." He looked at Kishan. "A tiger."

Kishan grunted. "Sounds like you found something alright."

"But why the Baiga?" I asked. "Why not keep Ren in the city or in a regular military compound?"

Mr. Kadam pulled out some papers. "I think I may know. I placed a call to a friend who is a professor of ancient history at Bangalore University. We've had many a great discussion on the kingdoms of ancient India. He is always fascinated by my . . . *insights*. He has studied the Baiga in great detail and has shared some interesting facts with me. First, they are extremely afraid of evil spirits and witches. They believe that any bad events—sickness, a lost crop, a death—are all caused by evil spirits.

"They believe in magic and honor their *gunia*, or medicine man, above all others. If Lokesh had demonstrated magic of some kind, it is likely the people would do anything he asked. They consider themselves guardians or caretakers of the forests. It's very possible that Lokesh persuaded them to move by convincing them that the forest was in danger and that he has placed guards there to protect it. The other thing he mentioned, and what I found most interesting, is that the *gunia* of the Baiga are rumored to be able to control tigers."

I gasped, "*What*? How is that possible?"

"I'm not entirely sure, but they are somehow able to protect their villages from tiger attacks. Perhaps Lokesh has found truth in the myth."

"You think they're using some kind of magic to keep Ren there?"

"I don't know, but it surely seems it would be worth our time to investigate, or perhaps infiltrate would be a better word."

"Then what are we waiting for? Let's go!"

"I need a little time to come up with a plan, Miss Kelsey. Our goal is to get everyone out of there alive. Speaking of which, I feel I should share with you two that my informants have disappeared. The men

I've sent to investigate the penthouse office of the tallest building in Mumbai are gone. They haven't contacted me, and I fear the worst."

"Do you mean they're dead?"

He replied soberly, "They aren't the type of men to allow themselves to be taken alive. I won't allow any more men to die in this cause. From now on, we're on our own." He looked at Kishan. "We're at war with Lokesh again in a new century."

Kishan clenched his fist. "This time, we won't run away with our tails between our legs."

"Indeed."

Clearing my throat, I said, "That's great for you two, but *I'm* not a warrior. How can we possibly win? Especially when it's just the three of us against all of his men?"

Kishan put his hand over mine. "You're as fine a warrior as any I've fought with, Kells. Braver even than many I've known. Mr. Kadam has been known to come up with strategies when we've been outnumbered before that won a battle with ease."

"If there is one thing I've learned in my many years, Miss Kelsey, it's that careful planning can almost always create a positive outcome."

Kishan interjected, "And don't forget, we have many weapons at our disposal."

"So does Lokesh."

Mr. Kadam patted my hand. "We have *more*."

He pulled out a satellite photo and a red pen and began circling items of interest. Then he handed me a piece of paper and a pen. "Shall we get started?"

First, we made a column of our assets, brainstorming how each could be used. Some of the ideas were silly and some had merit. I recorded everything we came up with, not knowing what might turn out to be handy.

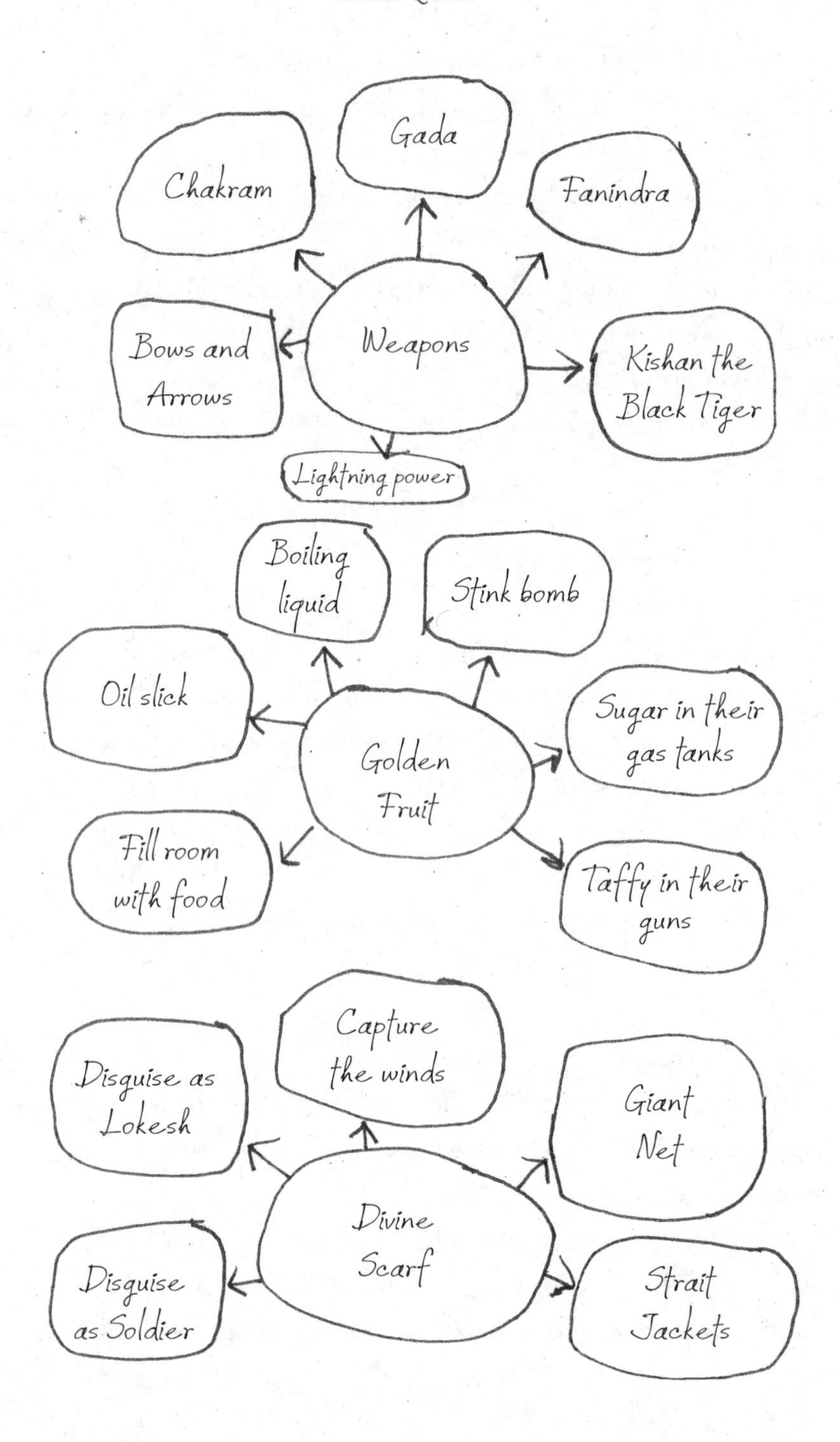
Gada
Chakram
Fanindra
Bows and Arrows
Weapons
Kishan the Black Tiger
Lightning power
Boiling liquid
Stink bomb
Oil slick
Sugar in their gas tanks
Golden Fruit
Fill room with food
Taffy in their guns
Capture the winds
Disguise as Lokesh
Giant Net
Divine Scarf
Disguise as Soldier
Strait Jackets

Mr. Kadam made a star on the map where he thought Ren might be found. He felt the simplest plans were the easiest to follow, and our plan was pretty straightforward: Sneak in. Find Ren. Get out. Even so, Mr. Kadam made sure to analyze the plan from several different viewpoints.

He prepared for every contingency. He asked dozens of *what if* questions. *What if Kishan can't enter the compound because he's a tiger? What if there are tiger traps in the jungle? What if there are more soldiers than we thought? What if we can't enter from the jungle? What if Ren isn't there?*

He made a separate plan to overcome each problem and still have a successful outcome. Then, he combined problems and drilled Kishan and me on our roles. We had to remember how our roles would switch depending on what problems came up. I felt like I was memorizing every possible ending in a *Choose Your Own Adventure* book.

Mr. Kadam also organized practice runs. We had to test the limits of the Golden Fruit and the Divine Scarf as well as several complicated moves using our weapons. He made us train most of the day in hand-to-hand combat and practice several techniques simultaneously. By the time he let us quit on the first day, I was exhausted. Every muscle hurt, my brain was tired, and I was covered in maple syrup and cotton fluff—a Fruit and Scarf combo test that backfired.

When I said goodnight, I wearily climbed the stairs, took Fanindra off my arm, and set her on the pillow. Mr. Kadam had a plan for her, but she didn't move when he'd explained it.

We didn't know if she would do anything, but I was going to bring her along anyway. She'd saved my life enough times to deserve to be in on the action, if nothing else. I watched her golden coils shift and twist until she settled in a circular position with her head resting on the top coil. Her emerald eyes gleamed for a moment and then went dark.

Something fluttered outside the window. My fairy clothes! It seemed there weren't any fairies here. The clothes still seemed solid enough, but now they just needed a spin in the washing machine. I threw them into my hamper before stepping into a hot shower. As my sore muscles relaxed, I let my thoughts dwell on trivial things, such as wondering if I should wash the fairy clothes in cold or hot water. The shower soothed me until I almost fell asleep on my feet.

Mr. Kadam drilled us for a week before he felt we were ready to seek out the Baiga village.

The three of us stood at the base of a large tree in the dark jungle. We passed around the Divine Scarf and assumed the appearance we had each been assigned to mimic.

Right before Mr. Kadam changed, he whispered, "You know what to do. Good luck."

I wrapped the Divine Scarf around his neck, tied it, and whispered, "Don't get caught in a trap."

He quietly slipped off toward the jungle.

Kishan hugged me briefly and departed as well. His steps were quiet. Soon, I was left in the dark jungle by myself. I strung my bow and slid Fanindra up my arm as I waited for the signal.

A loud roar echoed through the jungle followed by the shouts of several men. That was the signal I'd been waiting for. I made my way through the trees toward the encampment about a quarter mile away. When I neared, I pulled out the Golden Fruit and murmured directions. My assignment was to take out the two watchtowers on the outskirts of the camp and the floodlights.

Lights first. I scanned the area and recognized the various buildings. We'd studied the satellite images until all of us had the layout memorized. The Baiga huts were arranged in a semicircle closer to the edge of the jungle. They were behind the military bunkers and an assortment of M-ATVs. Mr. Kadam had said the *M* stood for MRAP, or Mine Resistant Ambush Protected, which meant that they were awfully difficult to take out.

The Baiga huts were made of woven grasses and were big enough for only one or possibly two families to live in. I didn't want to hit those. They'd go up in a ball of fire easily.

The command center had four compartments, each about the length of a semitrailer but twice as tall. They were attached in pairs and were made of some type of alloy. They looked sturdy. Two watchtowers stood, one on each side of the camp. Three guards watched the area from the top of each tower, while two men stood guard below. Next to the southern tower, I saw a tall post with a large satellite dish at the top. I counted four floodlights, not including the two spotlights attached to the watchtowers.

I was supposed to find the generator, but I didn't see it. *Maybe it is hidden in one of the Baiga huts?* I decided I'd just have to take out the lights one by one. I held up my hand and aimed. Warmth flooded down my arm until my hand glowed red in the dark. Energy shot out in a long white burst. First one and then the other three floodlights popped and exploded when my lightning power hit.

Someone got into one of the vehicles and turned on the lights. The ATV sputtered and choked. The gas had probably all been absorbed by the sponge cake I'd used the Fruit to fill the tanks with. The electricity still worked, though, and powerful headlights and spotlights scanned the trees for me. I turned my lightning power on the vehicle full blast because I knew it would be hard to destroy, sending an extra-thick pulse of energy through my palm.

My lightning hit the car with a thunderous boom that shot the ATV thirty feet into the air. It exploded in a fiery ball and slammed down on top of another one, landing with a screeching of twisted metal. I shot

another one with a blast; this time, the vehicle rolled. It flipped over three times and landed on its side against a huge tree. It only took me a few seconds to extinguish the other spotlights.

Next, I needed to take out the two towers. The towers were simply made compared to the other buildings. Four wooden supports, one level taller than the command post, were topped with a boxy structure and armed with three men and a spotlight. The only way up was a simple wooden ladder, probably created by the Baiga.

By now, soldiers had located my position. Flashlights were bobbing in my direction, seeking me out. I let loose a few golden arrows and heard a grunt and a thud as a body hit the ground. I had to move. I heard a ping as darts flew through the bushes I was hiding in. *They must have instructions to take us alive.*

I ran in the darkness. Fanindra's eyes glowed softly, giving me just enough light to reach my next location. Crouching behind a bush, I summoned my lightning power again and took out the closest tower. It exploded in a giant, fiery bomb that lit up the area. Frightened people ran in every direction.

I made my way to the other tower, running openly amidst the crowd. I hid between two buildings as a group of soldiers ran past and took out a couple of them from behind. Mr. Kadam was shouting at the people, rallying them, and asking for their aid in the battle. His theatrics made me smile briefly. I planted the *gada* where he would find it and moved on.

Back to business. I slunk around the shadowed part of a building and scoped out the other tower. I needed to destroy the satellite too. I nocked an arrow, infused it with lighting power, and let it fly. It thunked into the satellite and fizzed and crackled with electricity before it exploded. By this time, the soldiers in the second tower had figured out that I was their target. I leapt behind some boxes as they turned their

weapons on me. I heard the *thwap, thwap* of several darts plugging the area where I had just been.

My heart pounded with fear. If they hit me with a dart, I'd be done. I wouldn't be able to help Kishan or find Ren. Hearing shouts of men searching for me, I gathered my courage and nocked another arrow. The golden arrow twinkled in the moonlight and shimmered as I infused it with lightning power. This time, I was too close to my target, and as the explosion of the tower rocked the complex, the blast lifted me into the air. My head slammed against the building on the landing. Heavy wood chunks from the destroyed tower rained down and several of the flaming fragments hit me as I stood up. Gingerly I touched the back of my skull. I was bleeding.

A soldier jumped out to attack me. We rolled across the dirt. I punched him in the gut and leapt up. When he started to rise too, I jumped on his back as Ren had taught and tried to cut off his air. He struggled only briefly before twisting and slamming me against a rock. I cracked my head sharply and felt a wet trickle of blood drip from my temple down my cheek.

I lay still against the rock panting, exhausted, dizzy, and bloody. The soldier stood, grinned, and stretched out his hands to strangle me. I raised my hand, narrowed my eyes at his soot-blackened face, and shot him in the chest with a lightning bolt. He flew back several feet, hit the command center, and slumped to the ground in a sitting position, with his head drooping heavily on his chest.

Now I had to find Ren. I ran unsteadily between some huts, and when another soldier came after me, I ducked to the side, dropped and rolled. When he shot a tranquilizer, I came up on one knee and took him out with a quick jolt. The door to the main building was being guarded by two soldiers standing at battle alert. When I approached, they spoke several words in a different language. I nodded briefly, and one of them used his key to let me in. I got off easily that time. I was a familiar face, and they hadn't seen me in action.

I stepped between them and quietly slipped inside. Unfortunately, the door shut behind me and locked itself automatically. I ignored the problem, figuring I'd just zap my way out later. My head throbbed at my temple, but other than that I'd been lucky. I had several wicked scrapes and cuts on my limbs, a major bump on the head, and I would be bruised all over my body, but nothing life-threatening. I hoped that Mr. Kadam and Kishan were faring as well.

The inside of the command center was dark. I was in a storage area full of boxes and supplies. I crept through another section and found the barracks for the soldiers. An awkward moment came when I turned a corner and ran into the person I was imitating. The amazed expression quickly changed as I struck. A brief burst of light lit the room, and the individual sank to the floor.

Despite the building being sparsely furnished, I stumbled over boxes in the dark while checking room after room. Finally, Fanindra's green eyes glowed so I could see my environment more clearly. The area was lit with her special night vision, and I could make out nearly everything. I heard Lokesh and Kishan in another room. The situation there was escalating. Time was running out. According to our drills, I should have found Ren by now.

If I had taken out the generator, I could have saved time; but, instead, I had to take out the lights one by one and fight more soldiers than I'd expected. The plan needed to be modified. I needed to get to Kishan first. Luckily, Mr. Kadam had prepared us for this contingency. Reluctantly, I left off my search for Ren and went to find Kishan instead.

I made my way into the rear part of the command center and climbed several boxes until I was perched high above. It was a large room, almost as big as a warehouse. Metal shelves held weapons and supplies of every kind. A heap of soldiers' bodies indicated that Kishan had been successful in disabling Lokesh's guards. But, now, Lokesh had him cornered in his private office.

It was luxurious by military standards. Thick carpet covered the floor. An opulent desk sat in the corner, and on one wall several television monitors flashed scenes of the chaos going on outside the compound. One wall was full of electronic equipment and gadgets. It looked like the inside of a submarine. The wall was covered with switches and monitors. Several red lights were blinking quietly, which I imagined were alarms of some kind.

Three hanging lights buzzed overhead, flickering occasionally as if the compound was losing its power. A glass case near the desk held several gleaming weapons, some from every era of battle. Kishan was playing his part well. I nocked an arrow and waited for him to move back so I'd have a clear shot. Supercilious and overconfident, Lokesh kept on, trying to intimidate Kishan into doing what he wanted.

Lokesh wasn't wearing fatigues like his soldiers. He wore a black suit and a blue silk shirt. He looked younger than Mr. Kadam, but his hair was graying at the temples and was slickly combed away from his face in a modern mob-boss style. I noticed again that he wore rings on each finger that he twisted casually as he spoke. An invidious remark caught my attention.

"I can rip you apart with a mere word, but I enjoy watching people suffer. And having you here is a special treat I've been waiting for, for a long time. I can't imagine what you were trying to accomplish. There's no way for you to win. But, I must say, I'm impressed with the way you dealt with my special guards. They were highly trained."

Kishan grinned wickedly as they circled. "Not highly trained enough, it seems."

"Yes." Lokesh chuckled warmly. "Perhaps I could interest you in working for me. You are obviously resourceful, and I am a man who well rewards those who serve me. Of course, I should also warn you that I mortally punish those who defy me."

"I'm not looking for a job right now, and something tells me your employee-satisfaction rating is pretty low."

Kishan ran at Lokesh, flipped into the air, and round-house kicked him across the face.

Lokesh spat blood. He smiled as a line of crimson trickled from his mouth. Wiping it delicately with a finger, he rubbed it across his bottom lip, licked it, and laughed. He actually seemed to enjoy the pain. I shivered with revulsion.

He continued, "This has been a pleasant enough diversion, but enough of this banter. You have one amulet; I hold the power of the other three. Give it to me, and you can take the tiger and leave. Not that I'll let you get far, mind you, but I'll give you a sporting chance anyway. It will make the hunt that much more enjoyable."

"I think I'll leave with the tiger *and* the amulet. And while I'm at it, I think I'll kill you and take yours as well."

Lokesh cackled madly. "You *will* give me what I want. In fact, you'll soon regret snubbing my generous offer. In a matter of moments, you'll offer me anything I want just to stop the pain."

"If you want the amulet that badly, then why don't you come over here and try to take it? Let's see if you can fight as well as you threaten. Or, do you just leave all the fighting to other people now . . . *Old Man*?"

The smile fell away from Lokesh's mouth, and he raised his hands. Electricity sparkled between his fingers.

Kishan leapt toward Lokesh again, but he was stopped by an invisible barrier. Lokesh began muttering enchantments, opened his palms, and lifted his arms. Loose materials in the room rose in the air and began swirling in a whirlwind, moving faster and faster. Lokesh slowly brought his hands together, and the whirlwind moved closer to Kishan.

Objects revolved around him and began to hit him. A pair of scissors ripped open a gash in his forehead, but he began to heal immediately.

Lokesh saw him heal and stared at the amulet greedily. "Give it to me! It's my destiny to unite all the pieces!"

Kishan began capturing the larger items and crushing them between his palms. "Why don't you try to take it from my dead body?" he shouted.

Lokesh laughed—a terrible sound of sheer delight. "As you wish."

He clapped his hands together and rubbed them. The ground started shaking. The boxes I was sitting on swayed precariously. Kishan had fallen to the ground and was being bombarded by a hail of objects, including lethal items like staplers, scissors, and pens, as well as larger things like loose file drawers, books, and computer monitors.

I shook with fear. This man frightened me more than anything else I'd ever faced. I'd rather be running from a horde of Kappa than look into this man's eyes. Evil dripped off him in waves. It blackened everything around him. His darkness choked me. Even though he wasn't aware of me yet, I felt like black, misty fingers were making their way toward me, seeking me to strangle the life from my body.

I raised my trembling hand and shot out a bolt of lightning. It missed him by about a foot, and he was so intent on Kishan that he didn't even see the streak of light pass behind his body. He did notice the impact of it on his weapon display case and probably assumed it was his earthquake that had done it. The glass exploded outward. The pieces joined the whirlwind and began slicing Kishan. They were soon joined by a lethal barrage of weapons. Lokesh laughed in delight as he watched Kishan torn apart by sharp glass and then heal. A large piece flew into Kishan's arm. He yanked it out. Blood streamed down his arm and joined the spinning miasma of the whirlwind.

I was mortally afraid. My hands shook. *I can do this! I've got to get a grip! Kishan needs me!* I lifted the arrow and aimed for Lokesh's heart.

Meanwhile, I heard people shouting outside. I assumed it was the

villagers and things were going according to plan. If not, then Kishan and I were in for worse trouble and soon. A huge *bang* sounded, and I smiled in relief. I knew it was Mr. Kadam. Nothing could pound like the *gada*. The building shook on its foundation. Time was of the essence. If they were attacking the building that meant the soldiers had all been rounded up and taken care of. Mr. Kadam was indeed efficient. Either that or Lokesh had abused these poor people sufficiently enough that they were on the verge of rebellion already.

I shot my arrow straight at Lokesh's heart, but he turned at the last moment as he finally heard the bang of the *gada* and the arrow sunk deeply into his shoulder instead. The whirlwind surrounding Kishan suddenly halted, and all the items dropped to the floor in a treacherous shower. A heavy metal safe landed on Kishan's foot; he grunted and shoved off the bulky object. I was sure his foot was broken.

Lokesh spun with thunderous rage and found me. Electricity shot out of his fingertips, and his breath froze the air, sending an icy gust up toward me. I froze and felt the blood congeal in my body thickly. I panted, more terrified than I'd ever been in my life.

"You!"

My skin broke out in goose bumps. Spitting castigating commands in what he assumed was my language, he yanked out the bloody arrow and began chanting. The arrow suddenly flew back at me. In an unconscious move of self-preservation my inner fire warmed me enough so I could move. My hands darted up to cover my face, but the arrow stopped in midair inches from my nose. I held out my hand, and it dropped slowly into my palm. Frustrated, Lokesh clapped his hands together and rubbed them viciously to make the box I was on teeter. I tumbled to the floor, painfully hitting several sharp corners along the journey. I groaned and shoved boxes off my body. My ankle was twisted sharply and pinned under a box, and my shoulder was badly bruised.

Kishan took out his chakram, which he had hidden in his shirt, and flung it toward the overhead lights. The room sank into blackness as I heard the metallic whir of the weapon move through the room. He threw the chakram a few more times but he couldn't hit Lokesh with it because sudden winds whipped through the room, causing the disc to change direction. I crawled with difficulty to a new hiding place. Kishan caught the chakram and leapt on Lokesh. The two men fell to the floor in a mighty struggle.

Lokesh shouted to his soldiers; his voice was loud and augmented as if carried by the wind to the outside camp. I could hear it amplified as if he was speaking into a microphone, but all his soldiers were now contained. No one came to his rescue. The two men rolled toward me. Lokesh mumbled some words until a cushion of air bubbled between the men. It shoved Kishan back until Lokesh could stand again.

I stood and raised my hand. My entire arm shook as I tried to gather the courage. The fire wouldn't come. My gut felt cold, like the fire inside me had been tamped out. Lokesh flicked his head instantly when he saw my gesture. He laughed at my pathetic effort and began muttering anew. I became stiff. I couldn't move. A tear rolled down my cheek and froze.

Kishan took advantage of Lokesh's distraction and grabbed an arm, twisting it behind Lokesh's back. In an instant, he had the chakram pressed against Lokesh's throat. The gleaming blade slid into the tender flesh, releasing trickles of blood to stream down the blade and drip on Lokesh's blue silk shirt.

Lokesh grunted and muttered softly, "Do you wish him to *die*? I can kill him in an instant. I can freeze his blood so his heart stops beating."

Kishan looked at me and stopped. He could have decapitated Lokesh with the flick of a wrist, but he paused, and I saw emotions cross his face. He was holding back for my sake. Lokesh cackled in a rasping voice, breathing heavily at his exertions. A deep thump and the walls shook as Mr. Kadam and the villagers continued to beat on the building, trying to knock it off its foundation.

Lokesh threatened again, "If you don't unhand me, I *will* kill him. Choose now!" The glint of anger burned in his eyes, a smoldering fire that could never be quenched.

Kishan let him go. I groaned inwardly because I couldn't move. We had almost won. Now we were at the mercy of a monster.

Lokesh quickly murmured again, and Kishan was soon held in the same immovable grip as I was. Lokesh straightened and ceremoniously dusted off his jacket lapels. He pressed a clean white handkerchief to his bleeding throat. Then he laughed, approached Kishan, and patted his cheek fondly.

"There, now. It's always better to cooperate, isn't it? Do you see how feeble and useless it is for you to grapple with me? Perhaps I slightly underestimated you. You certainly put up a better fight than I've had in centuries. I look forward to the challenge of breaking your spirit."

He pulled a very old, wicked-looking knife from inside his jacket and waved it almost lovingly in Kishan's face. He moved closer and trailed the blunt edge down Kishan's cheek. "This blade is the same one I used so many years ago on your prince. See how I've kept it in such good condition for all of these years? You could call me a sentimental old fool, I suppose. I've been secretly hoping that I'd get to use it again and finish what I'd begun many years ago. Isn't it fitting that I should also use it on you? Perhaps it was saved for just that purpose.

"Now, where should I begin? A nice scar would make your face a bit less attractive, wouldn't it? Of course, I'll have to remove the amulet first. I've seen how it heals you. I've waited so long for this piece. You have no idea how I've yearned to feel the power it possesses. It's sad that you won't be around to appreciate what it does for me."

He pouted briefly. "Too bad I don't have time for a little experimental surgery. I would so enjoy teaching you some lessons in discipline. The only thing that would give me more pleasure than running my knife across your skin would be to disfigure you in front of your prince. Still, he will appreciate my handiwork, regardless."

I was afraid. If I wasn't already stiff, I would have been scared stiff anyway. It didn't matter how prepared I was. Fighting someone who was truly evil was not an easy thing to do. The birds, the monkeys, and the Kappa were all just doing their jobs. They protected the magical gifts, and I was okay with that. But, facing Lokesh and watching him brandish that knife against Kishan's throat was horrifying.

I tuned him out when he started speaking of dismembering Kishan piece by piece. It was nauseating. If I could have vomited, I would have. I just couldn't conceive of someone that cruel. I wished that I could have covered my ears. My poor Ren had been abused by this psychotic fiend for months. My heart broke at the thought.

Lokesh had the conniving persona of Emperor Palpatine mixed with the sadistic cruelty of Hannibal Lecter. He craved power at any price, like Lord Voldemort, and he displayed the pitiless brutality of Ming the Merciless who, like him, had killed his own daughter. My frame shook with terror. I couldn't watch him hurt Kishan. I couldn't bear it.

He gripped Kishan's chin and was just about to cut his face when I realized that, even if I couldn't move, the Golden Fruit would still work. I wished for the first thing that crossed my mind: jawbreakers. And jawbreakers I got. A storm of them. They broke monitors and one of the glass windows. The booming roar of them buffeted my eardrums as they fell in the command center. It sounded like thousands of marbles dropped in a lake of glass, and everything shattered and broke around us. Kishan and I wobbled and fell as we were pelted with a hail of the hard, round candy. My backpack was what saved me from breaking my

neck. I was sure Kishan was hurt again. Luckily, he'd heal quickly. I would be grateful if even just one of us got out of this alive.

Soon, every inch of the floor was covered with the colorful candy about a foot deep. Lokesh was pummeled and hit hard enough that he lost his balance and went down. He spat out several expletives in his language as he tried to regain his footing and figure out where the storm was coming from. Then, he realized the knife was missing and began combing through the candy to find it. Kishan and I were almost buried by that point.

The building shook and a segment of wall crashed in the partition next to us. Lokesh scrambled to his feet after finding his knife, grabbed the amulet around Kishan's neck, and yanked until the chain broke, leaving a red welt behind.

He bent over him briefly and touched Kishan's face with the knife. "We'll meet again," he smiled horribly, "soon." He trailed the knife from Kishan's cheek down to his throat, leaving a trail of blood that would terribly scar but not kill. Then with a pained noise, Lokesh wrenched himself away. He waded through the jawbreakers to a hidden button in the wall. A panel opened, and he disappeared.

A few villagers accompanied Mr. Kadam into the office, and they hurried to help us into standing positions. Kishan was already healing, but his shirt was spattered with blood. The cut had been deep. I heard the roar of an engine and a ripping sound as a vehicle tore itself from under the building and sped off on the dirt road leading away from the village. I could have used the Golden Fruit to stop up his engine, but I chose not to.

I was ashamed, but I didn't want to face him again. I *wanted* him to escape. I never wanted to see him again. I stood stiffly, berating myself for being a coward. I was weak. If I could have moved, I would have whimpered in the corner of the room, hiding. Lokesh was too powerful. We couldn't win.

The best thing we could hope for would be to avoid him. I knew Kishan and Mr. Kadam would be disappointed with me. Some warrior I turned out to be. Giant iron birds? No problem. Kappa? I had Fanindra and Ren. Monkeys? A few bites and bruises wouldn't kill me. But Lokesh? I turned tail and ran in the face of the enemy. I wished I could understand why I was reacting this way. He was a monster. That was *all*. Just another thing for me to fight. But, this monster had a human face. It seemed worse somehow.

After a few moments, the spell Lokesh had used on Kishan and me faded. We tried to rub our stiff limbs awake. When Kishan had recovered sufficiently, he waded through the jawbreakers to help me. Mr. Kadam gave the villagers instructions while Kishan supported me on my sprained ankle and helped me search for Ren. Fanindra decided to wake and help in the search. She shifted and grew.

I lowered my arm so she could slide to the floor, and she wound her way between boxes of weapons and bags of supplies. She stopped and tasted the air near a section that looked like a dead end. Smoothly, she slid under some boxes, and Kishan inspected the arrangement more closely. He found they were a fake display and shoved them aside. Behind it was a locked door. We were just in time to glimpse Fanindra's golden tail disappearing under it. Kishan struggled to pry it open. I ended up using my lightning power to blow the lock. It took me several seconds to build up the capacity to use it again. Thinking of Ren still suffering was what finally got me past my internal freeze.

The door swung open, and Kishan's nostrils widened. Inside, the dank, sweet smell of blood and human sweat permeated everything. I knew where I was. I'd been here before. It was the chamber where Lokesh had tortured Ren. Terrible tools hung on the walls and were laid out on gleaming surgical tables. I froze in horror as I looked at all the instruments and imagined the pain Lokesh had brought upon the man I loved.

Modern surgical tools were spread out upon the utility trays while the older items were stacked in corners and hung on pegs. I couldn't help myself. I reached out and touched the frayed ends of a whip. Next, I rubbed the handle of a large mallet and began to shiver as I imagined it breaking Ren's bones. Various knives of different lengths and sizes hung in a row.

I saw wood, screws, nails, pliers, ice picks, leather straps, an iron muzzle, a modern drill, nail-studded collars, a vice that could be used to crush whatever limb was placed in it, and even a blow torch. I touched the items briefly as I passed and wept bitterly. Somehow, touching them was the only thing I could do to truly empathize and try to understand what this experience must have been like for him.

Kishan gently took my arm. "Don't look at them, Kelsey. Just look at me or keep your eyes down and look at the floor. You don't have to do this. It would be better for you to wait outside."

"No. I need to be here for him. I need to do this."

"Okay. Just stay by me."

Ren's cage stood in the far corner, and I could just make out a broken form inside and a gleaming snake coiled nearby. After retrieving Fanindra and thanking her, I stood back and blew the lock off. Then I approached and swung open the door.

I called softly, "Ren?"

He didn't respond.

"Ren? Are you . . . *awake*?"

The form moved slightly, and a pale, wan face turned to me. His blue eyes narrowed. He looked at Kishan. His eyes widened, and he shifted closer to the opening. Kishan beckoned him and reached out a hand to help.

Carefully, he stretched out a shaky hand to grasp the bar on the edge of the cage. His fingers were newly broken and bloody. My eyes

filled with tears, and my vision blurred as I took a step backward to give him room. Kishan stepped forward to assist him. When Ren finally stood, I gasped. He'd recently been beaten. I'd expected that. He was already healing from his wounds, in fact.

What shocked me was that he was so *gaunt*. Lokesh had been starving him. He was likely dehydrated too. His strong frame was thin, much thinner than I'd imagined he would be. His bright blue eyes were circled with dark hollows. His cheekbones were sharp and pronounced, and his silky dark hair hung lifeless and dank. He took a step closer to me.

"Ren?" I said and held out a hand.

He narrowed his eyes at me, clenched his fist, and swung with a burst of energy I didn't expect he had. I felt a sharp pain in my jaw and then nothing as my body slumped to the ground.

Baiga

I felt movement and woke to find myself staring up at a dark green canopy. Kishan was carrying me through the jungle. He looked like himself again, which I have to admit was a relief. I'd been uncomfortable staring at him in his disguise.

"Kishan? Where are we going?"

"Shh. Relax. We're following the Baiga deeper into the jungle. We have to get as far away from the encampment as possible."

"How long have I been out?"

"About three hours. How do you feel?"

I touched my jaw lightly. "Like a bear punched me. Is he . . . *okay*?"

"He's out of it. The Baiga are carrying him on a makeshift gurney."

"He's safe though?"

"Safe enough."

He spoke softly in another language to Mr. Kadam who approached to examine my face and lift a canteen to my lips. I drank slowly, swallowing painfully as I worked my jaw as little as possible.

"Can you lower me, Kishan? I think I can walk."

"Okay, lean on me if you need to."

He carefully lowered my legs to the ground and steadied me as I swayed, trying to regain my equilibrium. I hobbled for a while on my twisted ankle, but Kishan growled and soon picked me up again. I settled back against his chest and could feel my whole body aching. Bruises covered most of my body, and I could barely move my jaw.

We were part of a long procession. The Baiga wove between the trees quietly. I couldn't even hear their footsteps. Dozens of people passed and nodded in a show of respect as they stepped around us. Even the women and children didn't make a noise, not a whisper of sound, as they moved silently like ghosts through the dark jungle.

Four large men carried a stretcher with a slumped form on top. As it passed, I craned my neck to catch a glimpse of him. Kishan fell into step behind them so I could see Ren's inert form. He adjusted his grip easily and hugged me a little tighter to his chest, his expression unreadable.

We walked for another hour. Ren slept the entire time. When we came to a clearing, an older Baiga man approached Mr. Kadam and humbly prostrated himself before him. Mr. Kadam turned to us and said that the Baiga would camp for the night. We were invited to their celebratory feast.

I wondered if it might be better for us to keep moving toward our rendez-vous point, but I decided to follow Mr. Kadam's lead. He *was* the military strategist, and if he thought it was safe, it probably was. Actually, it was refreshing to let someone else take charge for once. It also couldn't hurt to let Ren sleep a bit more before we traveled farther.

We watched the Baiga set up camp. They were extremely efficient, but they were missing most of their supplies. Mr. Kadam took pity on them and used the Divine Scarf to create sleeping quarters for each family. My attention diverted to Ren. The men carried him into a tent just as Mr. Kadam called me over.

Kishan, seeing I was torn, told me he would check on Ren, set me down carefully near Mr. Kadam, and then headed toward the tent. He mentioned that it would be better for me to stay with Mr. Kadam but didn't explain why.

After he left, Mr. Kadam asked if I would use the Golden Fruit to create a feast for the Baiga. They needed to be fed. Several of them were starving too. Lokesh had forced them to stay in camp and use their magic to keep Ren safely contained. They hadn't been able to hunt for a long time. He gave me instructions and then used the Divine Scarf to create a thick rug that the entire tribe could sit on.

I took the Golden Fruit out of my bag and began creating the dishes he'd requested. Rice with fragrant steaming mushrooms, chopped mango mixed with other local fruits that I hoped I pronounced correctly, roasted fish, wild salad greens, grilled vegetables, and for good measure, I added on a giant strawberry shortcake with fresh whipped cream and Bavarian filling, like we'd had in Shangri-la. Mr. Kadam raised an eyebrow but said nothing.

He invited the Baiga to sit and partake of the feast. Kishan soon came back and sat beside me. He whispered that the Baiga were taking good care of Ren. As everyone took their places, I tried to excuse myself to join Ren. As I struggled to stand, Kishan wrapped a hand around my arm firmly, whispered that I should stay near Mr. Kadam, and emphasized again that Ren would be fine. He seemed earnest about it, so I stayed. Mr. Kadam began speaking in their language. I waited patiently for him to finish his speech and kept looking at the tents, hoping for a glimpse of Ren.

When Mr. Kadam was finished, two young Baiga women walked the perimeter of the circle, bathing each person's hands in fragrant orange blossom water. When they'd washed the hands of every person, huge bowls of food were passed around. There were no plates or utensils. The Golden Fruit could have created them, but Mr. Kadam wanted to feast after the fashion of the Baiga. We took a few handfuls, ate, and

then passed the dish on to the next person. I wasn't very hungry, but Kishan wouldn't take the bowl until I'd had at least one bite of each type of food.

When the food made a full circle and everyone had had a portion, the bowls were passed around again. This process continued until all the food was gone. I used my canteen to clean my hands and tried to be patient as the Baiga moved on to the next ritual. When I whispered to Kishan that time was of the essence, he said that we had plenty of time and that Ren would need a while to recover.

The Baiga began celebrating in earnest. Musical instruments were brought out. They chanted and danced. Two women approached me with bowls of black liquid and spoke. Mr. Kadam translated, "They are asking if you would like a tattoo to commemorate your husband's victory over the evil one."

"Who do they think I'm married to?"

Mr. Kadam blushed. "They believe you are *my* wife."

"Don't they think I'm a little young for you?"

"It's a normal practice for very young women to marry older, wiser men in the tribe. They've seen you use the Golden Fruit and believe you are a goddess, my mate."

"I see. Well, thank them for me, but I will remember this victory fine on my own. Just out of curiosity, what, or who, do they think Kishan is?"

"They believe he is our son and that we are here to rescue our other son."

"They think I have two fully grown sons?"

"Goddesses can remain young and beautiful forever."

"I wish *that* were true."

"Show them your hand, Miss Kelsey."

"My hand?"

"The one with the henna drawing. Make it glow so they can see the marks."

I raised my hand and summoned my lightning power. My hand glowed, lit from inside. The skin became translucent, and the henna drawing surfaced—red on a white background.

Mr. Kadam quickly spoke to the two women and thankfully they bowed and left me alone.

"What did you say to them?"

"I told them I've already given you a tattoo of fire to remember this by. They believe that tattooing their women makes them more beautiful. They wouldn't have understood if I'd said I didn't want your skin to be tattooed. All Baiga men desire a wife with intricate tattooing."

The Baiga danced and celebrated. One of the men was a fire-eater. I watched his performance, impressed with his skill, but I was in pain and exhausted. I leaned on Kishan, who put his arm around me as support. I must have slept for a while because when I woke the fire-eater was done. Everyone was watching movement at the tents. I became immediately alert. Ren emerged, accompanied by a Baiga man on each side. They'd bathed his wounds and dressed him in one of their wrap-around linen skirts, leaving him bare-chested.

Ren limped, but he looked much better. Although still severe, his wounds were better than they'd been. Someone had washed Ren's hair and slicked it back. His eyes took in his surroundings and settled on the three of us. Quickly, his gaze shot past Mr. Kadam and me to fix on Kishan. A lopsided grin lit Ren's face as he moved toward Kishan, who stood to greet him and offer his support. My heart began thumping wildly. Ren hugged his brother and patted his back weakly.

"Thank you for saving me and sending in the food. I couldn't eat much yet, but I feel . . . well, better anyway."

Ren took a seat next to Kishan and began speaking in his native language. I tried to make eye contact, but he didn't appear interested in talking to me.

Finally, I cleared my throat and asked, "Would you like more to eat?"

His eyes glanced at me briefly. "Not right now, thank you," he said politely and turned back to Kishan.

Mr. Kadam patted my hand as the Baiga's *gunia* approached. He knelt in front of Mr. Kadam and spoke quickly. Then he stood and clapped his hands. A Baiga man knelt in front of Ren and bowed to the ground. He was the same man who I'd seen in my Scarf vision, the man who'd hurt Ren. Ren narrowed his eyes at the man who quickly lowered his gaze, spoke several words, and pulled a knife from his shirt.

Mr. Kadam translated, *"Please forgive me, noble one. I fought against the demon as long as I could, but he hurt my family. My wife and children are now dead. There is nothing left for me. Unless you will restore my honor, I will leave the tribe and die alone in the wilderness."*

Reaching up a hand, the man carefully unwound his jura. Long black hair fell from the top of his head and piled on his lap. With two more words, he swept the knife up and through the ties, shearing off his long, beautiful ponytail. He picked up the shorn hair reverently, bowed his head to the ground, and with open hands, offered it to Ren.

Ren looked at the man for a long time, nodded, and held out his hands, palms up, to accept the shorn hair. He spoke a few words, which Mr. Kadam translated for me again.

"I accept your offering. We have all suffered at the hands of the demon. We will punish him for his crimes, including the unforgivable act of depriving you of your family. Your actions against me are forgiven. I return your honor. Go your way with your tribe and find peace."

The man placed the hair in Ren's hands and backed away. Next, the *gunia* had two beautiful Baiga maids brought out before us. They knelt in front of Ren and Kishan. Their dainty hands lay in their laps as they looked demurely at the ground.

The women had long, beautiful, glossy black hair and fine, delicate features. Their trim waists were accented by thin belts made of polished stone. They were curvy in a way I would never be. Both had delicate tattooing running down their arms and legs, which disappeared under the hem of the thin skirts they wore, making me wonder just how much of their bodies were tattooed. I could see why the tattooing was considered attractive. This wasn't the kind you'd see in America. There were no giant eagles or "I Love Mom" in a heart.

This tattooing was tiny. Whirls, ringlets, curlicues, coils, flowers, leaves, and butterflies trailed down their limbs like the fine border of a picture frame or the scrollwork of a medieval book. The tattoos highlighted the features of the beautiful woman within its margins and accentuated her, making her into an exquisite, otherworldly creature. The *gunia* spoke, pointing first to one girl and then the other.

Ren rose awkwardly and smiled widely. I stared at him hungrily. I knew it was my disguise that had kept Ren from recognizing me and had caused him to strike out. Now all I wanted to do was wrap my arms around him and get him out of here. Sadly, we all had roles to play. He walked, limping but dignified, around both girls. Then he picked up the hand of one girl, kissed it, and smiled at her. I narrowed my eyebrows in confusion. She smiled shyly up at Ren. Kishan wore a shocked expression, while Mr. Kadam looked grim.

I whispered, "What is it? What's going on?"

"Wait just a moment, Miss Kelsey."

Kishan stood and spoke quietly to Ren. Ren folded his arms across his chest and indicated the two women again. Kishan began arguing quietly with his brother. He looked over at me and then at Mr. Kadam as if asking for help. Ren seemed more confused than angry. He asked something that sounded like a question. In response, Kishan gestured adamantly and pointed to the *gunia*. Ren laughed, touched the hair of the girl, rubbed it between his fingers, and said something to her that made her laugh.

"Are those girls planning to cut off their hair too? I asked."

Mr. Kadam frowned. "No. I don't believe so."

Kishan bowed to the *gunia* and the two women, said a few words, and then turned his back to Ren and sat down by me again. Ren smiled at the girl, shrugged his shoulders, and sat back down near Kishan.

"Mr. Kadam! What just happened?"

He cleared his throat. "Ah, yes . . . it would *appear* that the Baiga wish to offer our two sons permanent membership in the tribe."

"So they're asking them to join the Baiga club? Okay, so they join. What's the harm in that?"

"The way they join is to marry two Baiga women. These two sisters have offered themselves to our noble sons."

"*Oh*." I furrowed my brow in confusion. "Then what were Kishan and Ren arguing about?"

"They were arguing about . . . whether they should agree or not."

"Uh-huh. Then why was Ren touching that woman's hair?"

"I . . . really couldn't say." Mr. Kadam turned aside, obviously unwilling to continue the conversation.

I thought about what I had seen and then elbowed Kishan. "Kishan, if you want a Baiga wife, it's okay. I mean, if that will make you happy, then go for it," I whispered. "They're both very pretty."

He growled at me quietly, "I don't want a Baiga wife, Kells. I'll explain later."

Now I was *more* confused and slightly jealous, but I shook it off remembering that different cultures interpreted gestures in different ways. I decided to drop it and watch the festivities. By the time the celebration was over, my head was drooping sleepily on Mr. Kadam's shoulder.

Kishan shook me awake. "Kells? Come on. Time to go."

He pulled me to my feet and slid my backpack onto his own shoulders before giving Ren instructions. Ren seemed happy to do whatever Kishan told him to. Mr. Kadam said his good-byes to the Baiga, who all settled in for the night while we made our way toward our rendez-vous.

Mr. Kadam turned on a fancy military gadget. It was a watch with a video screen about the size of a deck of cards that uploaded satellite imagery as we walked. Not only did it show our current longitude and latitude, but it kept a record of how many miles or kilometers we had to go to reach our destination.

Ren changed to a tiger. Kishan said that it would help him heal faster. He trotted along behind us. I tried to walk again, but my ankle was swollen to the size of a grapefruit. Mr. Kadam wrapped it with an ace bandage before we ate, gave me some ibuprofen to reduce the swelling, and made me elevate it, but I needed ice. It still throbbed. Kishan let me walk for a little while because I was being stubborn about it but insisted I use his arm for support. Ren passed near me, but when I reached out a hand to touch his head, he growled at me softly. Kishan quickly put himself between us.

"Kishan? What's wrong with him?"

"He's . . . not himself, Kells."

"It's like he doesn't know me."

Kishan tried to comfort me by saying, "He's probably responding to you just as any injured animal does. It's a protection thing. Perfectly natural."

"But when you two were injured in the jungle before, I took care of you. Neither of you tried to hurt me or attack me. You always knew who I was."

"We don't know yet what Lokesh did to him. I'm sure he'll snap out of it as his wounds heal. For now, I want you to always stay near me or Mr. Kadam. A wounded tiger is a very dangerous creature."

"Okay," I agreed reluctantly, "I don't want to cause him any more pain than he's already in."

After indulging me in a few more painfully slow minutes of walking, Kishan picked me up. When I protested that I'd tire him, he scoffed and said he could carry me for days and not be tired. I slept in his arms as we hiked through the jungle. When we stopped, he set me down gently. I wobbled, and Kishan's arm around my shoulders was the only thing that kept me upright.

"Mr. Kadam? What is this place?"

"It's an artificial reservoir called the Maithan Dam. Our transportation should be arriving soon."

Not a moment later, we heard the drone of propellers as a small plane passed over us heading toward the lake. We hurried to the pebbly shore and watched the plane land on the smooth, moonlit water. Mr. Kadam waved a neon light and waded into the dark lake. Kishan guided me along, but I hesitated, looking at the white tiger.

"Don't worry, Kells. He can swim."

He waited for me to go first. The water was cool and actually felt good on my ankle. As the plane drifted closer to shore, I sunk down to my neck and started swimming. Mr. Kadam was already standing on the plane's water ski, holding onto the door. He leaned down and grabbed my hand, helping me in. Nilima smiled at me from the pilot's seat and patted the space next to her.

Apologizing briefly for getting her wet, I settled myself as Kishan climbed aboard and then watched the white tiger swimming through the water. When Ren approached the plane, he changed back to a man and lifted himself up, swinging into the seat next to Kishan in the back. Mr. Kadam secured the door and buckled himself in next to me.

Nilima warned, "Hold on everybody."

A surge of motion pushed us forward as the propellers revved loudly. We picked up speed, bounced on the water a few times, and then climbed into the night sky. Ren had changed back into his tiger form. He'd closed his eyes and was resting his head in Kishan's lap. Briefly, I smiled at Kishan. He returned my gaze quietly and looked out the window.

Mr. Kadam covered the two of us with a blanket. I rested my head against his wet shoulder and drifted off to the droning sound of our seaplane.

27

war stories

I woke as the plane bounced on the water of a small lake, which was apparently owned by Ren and Kishan and just adjacent to their property. Nilima cut the engines, and Kishan leapt onto the pier and tied off ropes to secure the plane. The Jeep was parked nearby.

By now, my clothes were half-dry, dirty, and very uncomfortable. Mr. Kadam offered me the opportunity to change, saying he could create new clothes with the Divine Scarf, but I declined when he mentioned that we were only ten minutes from home.

Mr. Kadam drove while the boys sat in the back and Nilima squeezed in with me in the front seat. Ren was still a tiger and seemed content only when Kishan was nearby. At home, Mr. Kadam suggested I take a hot shower and sleep, but it was dawn, and though I was exhausted, I wanted to talk with Ren.

The only thing that convinced me to leave him was the pressure both Mr. Kadam and Kishan put on me. Ren still needed time to heal, and it was better if he was a tiger for now, they reasoned. I agreed to shower, but I told them I would come right back down to see how he was doing. Kishan carried me to my room, helped me take off my shoes, and removed the ace bandage. Then he left me in the bathroom, quietly closing the door behind him.

My hands were shaky. I hobbled to the shower and turned on the hot spray. *He was here! He was safe! We'd won. We beat Lokesh and didn't lose anyone.* I felt nervous. As I stepped into the hot water, I wondered what I should say to Ren first. I had so many things to tell him. My body hurt. My shoulder stung. It had been scraped by a heavy box and was now turning purple. In fact, much of my body was turning purple.

I tried to shower faster, but every move I made was agonizing. I wasn't cut out for this stuff. Rolling around and tumbling in the dirt wasn't for me. The thought occurred to me that I should have felt pain in Kishkindha and Shangri-la. I should have been bruised pretty badly after the fight with the birds. I'd healed there. Quickly. Except for the Kappa bite, I'd healed in those magical places.

Ren seemed to be on the mend, but I knew his wounds were not just physical. He'd been through so much. I didn't know how he had survived, but I was extremely grateful he did. I'd have to thank Durga for helping him. *She definitely fulfilled her promise. She kept my tiger safe.*

Turning off the water, I stepped out of the shower and slowly dressed in my old flannel pajamas. I wanted to hurry, but even brushing my hair hurt. I hastily braided it and hobbled at a snail's pace across my room to the door. I found Kishan on the other side waiting patiently for me with his back resting against the wall and his eyes closed.

He'd showered and changed too. Without a word, he swept me up in his arms and carried me downstairs to the peacock room. He settled me in the leather chair next to Mr. Kadam before taking a seat opposite me near Nilima. Ren was still in tiger form lying at Nilima's feet as they quietly conversed.

Mr. Kadam patted my arm and said, "He hasn't changed back yet, Miss Kelsey. Perhaps he'd been a man for too long."

"Okay. It's alright. The important thing is that he's here now."

I watched my white tiger. He'd looked up briefly when I came in the room and then set his head back on his paws and closed his eyes. I couldn't help feeling disappointed that he wasn't sitting near me. Just touching his fur would have been reassuring, but then I berated myself. *I should be more worried about him than about myself. I'm not the one who's been tortured for months. The least I could do is not pressure him.*

Nilima wanted to know everything that had happened, and Mr. Kadam felt it would be a good idea for all of us to share our stories so we could hear the different parts of our adventure. Nilima agreed to prepare food and asked for my assistance. Kishan wanted to stay with Ren, who appeared to be sleeping. He said that it was best to let sleeping tigers lie for the time being.

He carried me to the kitchen and set me on a stool before returning to the other room. Nilima pulled out ingredients to make omelets and French toast and set me about the task of grating cheese and chopping onions and green peppers. We worked quietly for a while, but I noticed her watching me.

"I'm okay, Nilima, really. You don't have to worry about me. I'm not as fragile as Kishan makes me out to be."

"Oh, it's not that. I don't think you're fragile at all. In fact, I think you are a very courageous person."

"Then why are you watching me so closely?"

"You are . . . special, Miss Kelsey."

I laughed as well as my sore jaw allowed. "What do you mean?"

"You really are the center. You are what holds this family together. Grandfather was in such . . . despair before you came. You have saved him."

"I think Mr. Kadam is much more in the habit of saving me."

"No. We became a family when you became part of our lives. Though there is danger, he's never been as fulfilled or as happy as when you are around. He loves you. They all love you."

Embarrassed, I said, "What about you, Nilima? Is this crazy life what you want for yourself? Do you ever wish for a life free of espionage and intrigue?"

She smiled as she buttered the skillet and set four pieces of French toast to cook. "Grandfather needs me. How can I abandon him? I couldn't leave him alone and companionless. I have my family too, of course. My parents wonder why I haven't married yet and why I'm so focused on my career. I tell them I am happy to serve. They don't really understand it, but they accept it. They are able to live comfortably because of Grandfather's assistance."

"Do they know they're related to him?"

"No. I have kept that from them. It took him a long time to trust me with his secret. I wouldn't share it without his knowledge."

She scrambled the eggs, added cream, and began making the first omelet. There was something comforting and homey about being in the kitchen with another woman while cooking.

Nilima said, "Now that you are here, I see that he might find his rest at last. He may be able to finally set aside his worry, his great responsibility for the princes. I'm very proud to have such a selfless ancestor, and I feel humbled that I have the opportunity to know him."

"He's a very noble person. I never knew either of my grandfathers. I would have been proud to have him as mine too."

We became quiet as we finished preparing our repast. I summoned honeyed flower nectar for our beverage and sliced the melon. Nilima finished preparing the plates, placed them on a large tray, and carried it to the peacock room. Kishan returned to retrieve me, and Mr. Kadam joined us a moment later. The white tiger lifted his head and sniffed.

I set a giant plate of eggs on the floor in front of him. He began licking the plate immediately, pushing the eggs back and forth until they somehow made it into his mouth. I took a chance and patted

his head, scratching him behind his ears. He didn't growl this time and leaned into it. Then I must've hit a sore spot because his chest rumbled softly.

I tried to reassure him, "It's okay, Ren. I just wanted to say hello and give you your breakfast. I'm sorry if I hurt you."

Kishan leaned forward and said, "Kells, *please*. Move back."

"I'll be all right. He won't harm me."

My white tiger got up and moved closer to Kishan. It hurt. I couldn't help but feel betrayed, as if he was a family pet that had turned on me and snapped at my hand. I knew I was being irrational, but his actions stung. He set a paw on either side of the plate and stared at me until I lowered my eyes. Then he turned back to his breakfast.

Mr. Kadam patted my hand and said, "Perhaps we should enjoy our meal and share what happened with Nilima. I'm sure Ren would like to know as well."

I nodded and pushed my food back and forth on my plate. I suddenly didn't feel very hungry.

Kishan began. "We parachuted into a clearing a few kilometers from the Baiga camp and hiked in. An old pilot who used to work for Mr. Kadam at Flying Tiger Airlines agreed to drop us off. He flew us in on one of those old World War II troop planes that he keeps in good condition."

Nilima nodded, sipping her nectar.

Kishan rubbed his jaw. "The guy must've been at least ninety years old. I was doubtful at first that the old man still had the ability to fly, but he definitely proved his skill. The drop was smooth and effortless despite the fact that Kelsey almost didn't jump."

"It wasn't the same as in training," I interjected, defending myself.

"You jumped three times during practice and also with me in Shangri-la, and you were always fine."

"That was different. It was daytime then, and I didn't have to . . . to *drive*."

He explained, "During practice, we'd jumped in tandem." Frustrated, he raised his voice. "You knew all you had to do was ask. I would've jumped *with* you, but you stubbornly insisted you needed to do it by yourself."

"Well, if you weren't so . . . *hands on* in tandem—"

"And if you weren't so paranoid about me touching you—"

"It would've been fine!" We both spat at the same time.

My voice squeaked in panicked alarm as I glared at Kishan. "Can we please move on?"

Kishan narrowed his eyes in a look that said he'd continue the discussion later. "As I said, Kelsey almost didn't jump in time. Kadam went first, and then I had to force Kelsey out before we missed our jump window."

I muttered, "Forcing me is about right. You dragged me behind you."

He pointedly stared at me. "You gave me no *other* option."

He'd offered me another option alright. The option to drop the whole thing, forget about Ren, and run away with him instead. It was either that or leap out of an airplane by myself.

I wasn't sure if he was serious or just trying to get me to jump. I'd just opened my mouth to lecture him on maintaining an appropriate distance, when he growled angrily, grabbed my hand, and jumped out of the hatch.

He continued, "After we made it to the clearing, we assumed our disguises and went our separate ways. I took the form of Kelsey, wearing a replica of her amulet."

"I took the form of the Baiga servant," I added. It was very uncomfortable watching you be me, by the way, Kishan."

"It was equally uncomfortable *being* you. My job was to seek Lokesh and keep him busy, so I hid behind a building until I heard the signal: a tiger's roar."

Mr. Kadam interrupted, "That would have been me. I disguised myself as a tiger and ran off into the jungle to spring a few traps and draw off some of the soldiers."

"Right," Kishan said. "Kelsey began blowing stuff up, which drew off any stragglers, so I met virtually no resistance getting into the camp. Finding Lokesh was another matter. I had to take out his highly trained ring of guards. I disabled several of them with the chakram and took out the lights before they even noticed me. After that, I used my appearance to my advantage."

Suspiciously, I inquired, "How exactly did you use *my* appearance to your advantage?"

Kishan smiled widely. "I acted female. I stumbled into the room, feigned shock and fear, and asked all the big, strong men to protect me, saying that there was a crazy guy trying to kill me with a golden disc. You know, I batted my eyes and flirted. Women stuff."

I crossed my arms and stared Kishan down. "Uh-huh. Please go on."

Kishan sighed and ran a hand through his hair. "Before you get all huffy, which is your standard reaction to me, just stop, because I know what you're thinking."

I folded my arms across my chest. "Oh, really? And what am I thinking?"

"You're thinking that I'm trying to stereotype women and you in particular." He threw up his hands in exasperation. "*You're* not like that, Kells. I was just playing the hand I was given and trying to use all my assets!"

"That's fine when you're using your own *assets*, but *not* when you're using mine!"

"Fine! Next time I'll go as Nilima!"

Nilima said, "Hey! Nobody's using *my* assets *either*."

Mr. Kadam interrupted, "Perhaps we should continue the story?"

Kishan glowered and began muttering about women in a military operation and that next time he'd go by himself.

"I heard that. You would have been carved up by Lokesh without me." I smirked.

"Indeed. *Every* person was vital to our success," Mr. Kadam said. "I will move on to my part, and you can finish later, Kishan."

He sat back and folded his arms across his chest. "Fine by me."

Mr. Kadam started by telling Nilima how liberating it was to be a tiger. "The power of the tiger is beyond anything I'd imagined. We weren't sure if the Divine Scarf worked only with human disguises, so we'd tested changing into an animal. It seems we can change to either Kishan's or Ren's tiger forms, but no other animals. When we arrived, I assumed the form of Kishan's black tiger. Then Miss Kelsey wrapped the Scarf around my neck right before we parted.

"I ran through the jungle and found several baited traps. I sprung two of them, which set off alarms, and soon heard the tread of soldiers' feet chasing me. Shots were fired, but I was faster than they were. At one point, a group of them thought they had cornered me. They were about to fire when I changed to a man, the sight of which shocked them, and gave me a moment to spring the trap. I pulled on a rope attached to a haunch of meat, and the soldiers were lifted into the air in a large net. I left them dangling from the treetops and ran back to the camp for phase two of my plan.

"By the time I reached the camp, Miss Kelsey had already destroyed one of the two watchtowers. The villagers were running in every direction, frightened for their families. I stood behind a tree and changed my appearance again."

Nilima leaned forward. "What did you become this time?"

"I took on the form of a local Baiga god named Dulha Dao, who they believe helps to avert disease and accident. I rallied the people to me and told them I was here to help them overcome the stranger. They were more than happy to help me tear down the *house of the evil one*. Miss Kelsey left the *gada* in a discreet location for me to use. It's normally heavy for me, but when I wielded it as Dulha Dao, it felt light. With the villagers' help, I knocked down the wall and the people helped me to incapacitate Lokesh's men."

Nilima asked, "What did you look like?"

He blushed, so I interrupted, "Oh, Mr. Kadam as Dulha Dao was definitely nice-looking. He looked similar to the tribesmen, except taller with a much larger frame and he was handsome. His hair was long and heavy, and part of it was wrapped in a jura at the top of his head with the other part flowing down his back.

"He was muscular, and his rather nice torso and face were covered in tattoos. He was bare-chested, covered with heavy beaded necklaces, and barefoot, and he wore a wrap-around skirt. He looked very alarming, but in a good way, especially, I imagine, when he was wielding the *gada*."

When I finished my description, everyone was staring at me, and Nilima was laughing.

"*What?*" I asked, embarrassed. "Okay. So, apparently I find burly Indian men attractive. What's wrong with that?"

Kishan was frowning, Mr. Kadam seemed . . . pleased, and Nilima giggled.

"Nothing at all, Miss Kelsey. I'm sure I would have thought the same thing," she said.

Mr. Kadam cleared his throat. "Yes . . . well . . . I appreciate the flattering description, regardless. It's been a long time since a woman found me . . . burly."

I started giggling, and Nilima soon joined me.

Mr. Kadam asked, "Are you ready to continue?"

"Yes," we voiced in unison.

"As I was saying, the people rallied to me, and we tied up all the guards. Then we moved in on the command center. The doors were heavily fortified and locked. We searched the men for a key but couldn't find one. It was easier for me to knock a hole through the wall than to take down those doors. I finally broke into the complex to find Kelsey and Kishan prostrate on the floor and Lokesh nowhere in sight. The room was full of some kind of candy."

"Jawbreakers," I added.

"How did that come about?" Nilima asked.

"I had to do something, and the Golden Fruit was the only weapon I could access, so I wished for a hailstorm of jawbreakers."

"That was very clever. We never practiced that one. It seemed to work well," Mr. Kadam commented.

"It wouldn't have worked for long. Lokesh bounces back quickly. The only thing that drove him off was you. You and the Baiga saved the day."

"So Lokesh had the power to freeze you?"

"Yes."

"Did you note any of his other powers?"

"Yes."

"Good. We will discuss them later."

"Okay. I'll write down everything that happened while it's fresh."

"Very good. Continuing on, after Kishan and Kelsey found Ren, the Baiga wanted to move away from the camp as quickly as possible. They loaded everything they could carry, and filed into the jungle. We accompanied them partly because I felt responsible to get them as far away from Lokesh as I could and partly because it was in the direction we needed to go anyway. Just before we left, Ren picked up a knife and pierced the skin of his arm."

I leaned forward. "What was he doing?"

"Removing a tracking device Lokesh had put in."

I looked down at my white tiger with sympathy. His eyes were closed, but his ears were flicking back and forth. He was listening.

"We journeyed with the Baiga, had a feast with them, and left right after I signaled you, Nilima."

"You play a deity very well," I teased.

"Yes. Well, it seems they believed all four of us were deities. If I'd seen the things they had, I would believe we were deities too."

I asked, "Did they really use magic to hold Ren there?"

"When I spoke to them about it, the *gunia* claimed he *did* have power over tigers and used his magic to hold Ren there. He can create a barrier of sorts around the encampment to protect his village from tiger attacks. However, he said that about a week ago the spell was switched to *attract* tigers to the village instead. It seems the soldiers have been plagued by tiger attacks all week."

"Ah, so that's why Kishan could get in?"

"Apparently."

"Does that mean Ren could have gotten out?"

"Possibly, but Lokesh does seem to have powers of his own as well. I presume that using the Baiga to contain Ren was just a back-up plan in case Lokesh was too distracted to incapacitate Ren himself."

I spoke softly, "He's horrible. Ren was his ultimate prize, his trophy. The one he's waited for and hunted for centuries. He wouldn't have let Ren escape."

Kishan interjected, "I think he's lost interest in Ren. He's after someone else now."

Mr. Kadam shook his head discreetly.

"Who?" I asked.

He said nothing.

"It's me, isn't it?" I stated flatly.

Finally, Kishan spoke, addressing Mr. Kadam. "It's better that she knows so she can be prepared." Turning to me, he said, "Yes. He's determined to go after you, Kells."

"Why? I mean, why is he after *me*?"

"Because he knows how important you are to us. And because . . . you beat him."

"That wasn't me. That was you."

"But he doesn't know that." Kishan shot me a meaningful look.

I groaned softly and only half listened as Kishan began describing our fight with Lokesh. I offered comments only when Kishan forgot something.

Ren was watching us now and listening intently to what we were saying. I set my uneaten plate of food on the floor, hoping he might be interested. He watched me curiously, and then stood up and came a few steps closer.

He ate the eggs but pushed the pieces of French toast back and forth, unable to get them in his mouth. Cautiously, I used my fork to pick up a thick slice. He delicately pulled it off the fork, and swallowed it in one gulp. I did the same with the other one. After he licked the plate clean, he lay down near Kishan and began licking sticky syrup from his paws.

Kishan had fallen quiet, and when I looked up, I saw him watching me. His eyes crinkled at the corners with just a touch of sadness. I looked away. He frowned and started speaking again. When he got to the part where Lokesh threatened to kill me and stop my heart, I interrupted him and clarified.

"Lokesh wasn't talking about me."

"Yes, he was, Kells. He must have known who you were. He said I'll kill him, stop his heart."

"Yes, but why would *you*, disguised as *Kelsey*, be concerned about *me* in my Baiga servant disguise? He said kill *him*, not kill *her*. He merely thought I was betraying him."

"But Lokesh threatening to kill you was why I stopped."

"That may be why you let him go, but he wasn't threatening me."

"Then who was he threatening?"

I looked down at the white tiger and felt my face flame red.

"Oh," he said dully. "He was threatening *him*. I wish I would have known that at the time."

"Yes, he was threatening Ren. He knew I wouldn't do anything to harm him."

"Right. Of course you wouldn't."

"What does that mean? And what do you mean you wish you would have known that at the time? Do you mean you wouldn't have *stopped*?"

"No. Yes. Maybe. I don't know what I would have done. I can't predict how I would have reacted."

The subject of our discussion perked up the tiger's ears. He looked at me.

"Well, then I'm glad you misunderstood. Otherwise, Ren might not be here right now."

Kishan sighed. "*Kelsey*."

"*No!* It's nice to know you would have been willing to sacrifice him!"

Mr. Kadam shifted in his chair. "It would not have been an easy decision for him, Miss Kelsey. I have trained both boys that, though each individual is of great importance, sometimes sacrifices for the good of all must be made. If he had the opportunity to rid the world of Lokesh, his first reaction would have been to end the tyrant's life. The fact that he stayed his hand at all speaks to the depth of emotion he felt at the time. Don't think less of him."

Kishan leaned forward, pressed his fingertips together, and stared at the floor. "I know how much he means to you. I'm certain I would have made the same decision if I had known Lokesh was speaking of Ren and not of you."

"Are you sure about that?"

He raised his eyes to mine, and several unspoken thoughts passed between us. He knew what I was asking. There was more to my question than Mr. Kadam and Nilima were aware of. I was asking Kishan if he would knowingly let his brother die to secure the life he wanted to have. It would be easy for him to step in and fill Ren's shoes if Ren wasn't around any longer. I was asking him if that's the kind of man he was.

Kishan studied me thoughtfully for a few seconds and then, with utter sincerity, said, "I *promise* you, Kelsey, that I will protect him with my life, until the end of my days."

His golden eyes glittered and pierced mine. He meant it, and I suddenly realized that he had changed. He wasn't the same man I'd met in the forest a year before. He'd lost the cynical, sullen, woebegone attitude. He was a man fighting for his family, for a purpose. He'd never make the same mistake he'd made with Yesubai again. Looking into his eyes, I knew that no matter what happened in our future, I could rely upon him for anything.

For the first time since I met him, I saw the mantle of a prince fall about his shoulders. Here was a man who would sacrifice for others. Here was a man who would do his duty. Here was a man who acknowledged his weaknesses and worked to overcome them. Here was a man telling me that I could choose another, and that he would watch over us and protect us even if it broke his heart.

I stammered, "I . . . apologize for doubting you. Please forgive me."

He smiled sadly. "There's nothing to forgive, *bilauta*."

"Shall I pick up the story from here?" I asked softly.

"Why not?" he replied.

The first thing I told Nilima was how I used the Golden Fruit to

stop up the gas tanks with sponge cake and the guns by filling them all with beeswax. The problem was that it worked only on the guns and cars I could see. That's why Lokesh had been able to escape in his car and the men I couldn't see still had weapons that worked.

I described the jawbreaker shower, how Lokesh got away, and about how Fanindra led us to Ren. Then I talked about meeting *myself*. I told her I had disguised myself as the Baiga servant who was helping Lokesh, which was probably why Ren punched me in the jaw. I explained that the servant had been forced to work with Lokesh and how he had shorn his hair as a sign of contrition, offering it to Ren while begging for his forgiveness.

I went into great detail about the Baiga feast and told Nilima about the two women who were offered to my *sons* as wives. She rolled her eyes and commiserated with me as she sipped her nectar. I added that Kishan apparently wanted one of the sisters for a wife, but that Ren had argued with him.

Kishan scowled. "I told you that's not what happened."

"Then what *did* happen?"

I caught Mr. Kadam shaking his head discreetly again out of the corner of my eye and quickly turned to him.

"What *now*? What aren't you two telling me?"

Mr. Kadam quickly tried to reassure me, "Nothing, Miss Kelsey. It's just that," he paused uncomfortably, "it was considered very rude of us to reject the women, and the boys were trying to demonstrate their reluctance to appease the tribal leaders."

"Oh."

Mr. Kadam and Kishan locked eyes. Kishan turned away with an expression of distaste, annoyance, and impatience. I glanced at Nilima, who seemed confused. She was watching Mr. Kadam very carefully.

I said, "Something's going on here that I'm not privy to and I'm really too tired to figure out what it is, which is fine. Actually, I don't really care about the two women anyway. It's over and done with. We have Ren back, and that's all that really matters."

Nilima cleared her throat and got up, gathered the dishes, and was taking the tray to the kitchen to wash them, when Ren decided to become a man again. Everyone in the room froze. He looked at each one of us in turn, and then he smiled at Nilima. "May I help you with that?" he asked politely.

She paused and smiled, slightly nodding her head. We all stared at him expectantly, waiting for him to speak to us, but, instead, he quietly helped Nilima take everything to the kitchen. We heard him asking her if she would like some help with the dishes. She said she would take care of it and indicated that the others, meaning us, would probably like some time to talk with him. He entered the room hesitantly and evaluated the expressions of all three of us.

He sat down next to Kishan and said quietly, "Why do I feel like I'm standing before the Spanish Inquisition?"

"We just want to assure ourselves that you are indeed all right," Mr. Kadam said.

"I'm well enough."

His words hung in the air, and I imagined the rest of his sentence to be *for a man who has been tortured for months*.

I ventured, "Ren? I'm so . . . *sorry*. We shouldn't have left you there. If I had known about the fire power I have, I could've saved you. It was my fault."

Ren narrowed his eyes and studied me.

Kishan contradicted, "You had nothing to do with it, Kells. He pushed you toward me. It was all his decision. He wanted you to be safe." He nodded to Ren. "Tell her."

Ren looked at his brother as if he wasn't making sense. He said, "I don't remember it exactly the same way, but if you say so."

He let his words trail off and looked at me curiously, but not in a good way. It was as if I was a strange new creature he'd found in the jungle, and he wasn't sure if he should eat me or bat me around with his paws. As he openly considered me, he wrinkled his nose as if he smelled something distasteful and then spoke to Mr. Kadam.

"Thank you for saving me. I should have known you would have come up with a plan to liberate me."

"Actually, it was Miss Kelsey who came up with the idea for me to impersonate a deity. Without the Divine Scarf she and Kishan retrieved, we wouldn't have been able to rescue you at all. I had no idea where to find you. Only through the vision and seeing the Baiga man did we come to figure out where Lokesh was holding you. And only through the weapons given to us by Durga were we able to subdue the guards."

Ren nodded and smiled at me. "It would appear I owe you a debt of gratitude. Thank you for your efforts."

Something was wrong. He didn't seem like the Ren I knew. His demeanor toward me was cold, distant. Kishan wouldn't look at Ren.

We all sat quietly. Thick tension radiated between all of us. I suddenly found myself envying Nilima in the kitchen. There was definitely an elephant in the room, and it wasn't helping that all three men were staring at me with questions and concern in their eyes. First, I needed to talk with Ren. Then once we were okay, I'd move on to Kishan.

I raised my eyebrows meaningfully at Mr. Kadam, and he finally got my unspoken message. He cleared his throat and announced, "Kishan, would you mind helping me move something in my room? It's much too heavy for me to lift on my own."

Ren stood and said, "I don't mind helping you. Kishan can stay."

Mr. Kadam smiled. "Please sit and rest for a while longer. Kishan and I can handle it, and I believe Miss Kelsey would like some time to talk with you alone."

Kishan spoke, "I really don't think it's safe yet to—"

I locked my eyes on Ren. "It's okay, Kishan. He won't injure me."

Kishan stood and faced Ren, who nodded and said, "I won't harm her."

"Uh, Kishan? Could you?"

He sighed, and knowing what I was asking for, picked me up carefully, and settled me on the couch near Ren. Before he left, he warned, "I'll be close by. If you need me, just shout." He turned to Ren and threatened, "Do *not* hurt her. I'll be listening."

"You will *not* be listening," I said.

"I *will* be listening."

I frowned. Kishan gave me a look as they left, but I ignored him. I was finally alone with Ren. I had so many things to say to him; I didn't know how to act. His cobalt blue eyes measured me as if I was a strange bird who'd suddenly perched on his arm. I searched his handsome face and finally spoke. "If you're not too tired, I'd like to talk with you for a minute."

He shrugged. "If you like."

I tucked my leg gingerly on the cushion so I could face him. "I . . . I missed you so much." He raised an eyebrow. "There's so much to tell you, I don't even know where to start. I know you're tired and probably still in pain, so I'll be brief. I wanted to say that I know you need time to heal, and that I understand if you need some alone time. But, I'm here whenever you need me.

"I can be a good nurse even if you want to be cranky. I'll bring you chicken soup and chocolate peanut butter cookies. I'll read you Shakespeare or poems or whatever you like. We could start on the *Monte Cristo* book and go from there." I took his hand in both of mine. "Please just tell me what you need. I'll make sure you get it."

He gently extracted his hand and said, "That's very kind of you."

"Kind has nothing to do with it." I moved closer and put my hands on the sides of his face. He sucked in a breath as I said, "You're my home. I love you."

I didn't mean to push him so fast, but I needed him. We'd been apart for so long, and, at last, he was here and I could touch him. I leaned forward and kissed him. He stiffened in surprise. My lips clung to his, and I felt the wetness of tears on my cheeks. I wrapped my arms around his neck and slid nearer until I was almost sitting on his lap.

One of his arms was stretched out on the couch behind us, and his other hand rested on his thigh. He seemed distant. He wasn't holding me or kissing me back. I kissed his cheek and buried my face in his neck, inhaling the warm sandalwood scent of him.

After a moment, I pulled back and dropped my arms awkwardly into my lap. His surprised expression remained. He touched his lip and grinned. "Now that's the kind of welcome home a man likes to get."

I laughed, deliriously happy that he was back. I shrugged off my doubts and worries, realizing that he just probably needed some time to feel like a normal person before he could be part of a relationship again. He grunted in pain, and I quickly moved away to give him more room. He seemed much more comfortable after I'd moved.

"Can I ask you a question?" he said.

I took his hand in mine and kissed his palm. He watched my actions, intrigued, and then pulled his hand away.

"Of course you may," I replied.

He reached out, tugged my braid lightly, and twisted the ribbon in his fingers. "Who *are* you?"

28

worst birthday ever

With a pathetic giggle of nervous shock, I chided, "That's not funny, Ren. What do you mean *who am I*?"

"As much as I appreciated your proclamations of undying devotion, I think you may have hit your head while fighting Lokesh. I think you might have me confused with someone else."

"Confused you with someone else? No, I don't think so. You are Ren, aren't you?"

"Yes. My name is Ren."

"Right. *Ren*. The guy I'm crazy in love with."

"How can you express love for me when I've never laid eyes on you before?"

I touched his forehead. "Are you feverish? Is something wrong? Did *you* get hit in the head?"

I probed his skull with my fingers, searching for a bump. He gently removed my hands from his head. "I'm fine, um . . . Kelsey, is it? There's nothing wrong with my mind, and I don't have a fever."

"Then why don't you remember me?"

"Possibly because I've never met you before."

No. No. No. No. No. No! This can't be happening! "We've known each other for almost a year. You're my . . . my boyfriend. Lokesh must've done something! Mr. Kadam! Kishan!" I yelled.

Kishan ran into the room as if his tail was on fire. He pushed Ren away, inserting his frame between us. Quickly scooping me up, he deposited me in the chair across from Ren. "What is it, Kells? Did he hurt you?"

"No, no. Nothing like that. He doesn't *know* me! He doesn't remember me!"

Kishan looked away, guilt-ridden.

"You *knew!* You knew about this and you *hid it* from me?"

Mr. Kadam entered the room. "We both knew."

"*What?* Why didn't you tell me?"

"We didn't want to alarm you. We thought it might only be a temporary problem that would resolve itself," Mr. Kadam explained, "when he healed."

I squeezed Kishan's arm. "So with the Baiga women—"

"He wanted to take them as wives," Kishan explained.

"Of course. It all makes sense now."

Mr. Kadam sat near Ren. "You still can't remember her?"

Ren shrugged. "I've never seen the young lady until she, or I guess Kishan, stood outside my cage and rescued me."

"Right! A cage. A cage is where I first met you. Remember? You were at the circus. You were a performing tiger, and I drew your picture and read to you. I helped free you."

"I remember being at the circus, but you were never there. I recall freeing myself."

"No. You *couldn't*. If you could have freed yourself then why didn't you do it centuries before?"

He furrowed his handsome brow. "I don't know. All I remember is stepping out of the cage, calling Kadam, and then him coming back to take me home to India."

Mr. Kadam interrupted, "Do you remember going to Phet in the jungle? Arguing with me about taking Miss Kelsey with you?"

"I remember arguing with you, but not about her. I was arguing about going to see Phet. You didn't want me to waste my time, but I felt there was no other way."

Upset and emotional, I said, "What about Kishkindha? I was with you there too."

"I remember being alone."

"How can that be?" I asked. "You remember Mr. Kadam? Kishan? Nilima?"

"Yes."

"So it's just me?"

"It would seem so."

"What about the Valentine's dance, the fight with Li, chocolate peanut butter cookies, watching movies, making popcorn, Oregon, college classes, going to Tillamook? Is all of that just . . . gone?"

"Not exactly. I remember fighting with Li, eating cookies, Tillamook, movies, and Oregon, but I don't remember you."

"So you just happened to go to Oregon for no reason?"

"No. I was going to college."

"And what were you doing in your free time? Who were you with?"

He frowned as if concentrating. "No one at first, and then I was with Kishan."

"Do you remember fighting with Kishan?"

"Yes."

"What were you fighting about?"

"I can't remember. Oh wait! Cookies. We fought over cookies."

Tears filled my eyes. "This is a cruel joke. How could this have happened?"

Mr. Kadam stood and patted my back. "I'm not sure. Perhaps it is just a temporary memory loss."

"I don't think so," I snuffled angrily. "It's too specific. It's only me he doesn't remember. Lokesh did this."

"I suspect you are right, but let's not lose all hope. Let's give him enough time to recover from his injuries before we become too worried. He needs to rest, and we'll try to expose him to things that will jar his memory. Meanwhile, I will contact Phet to see if he might have an herbal remedy to help with this."

Ren held up a hand. "Before you all subject me to tests and herbs and trips down memory lane, I'd just like to have a little time to myself."

With that, he left the room. More tears came to my eyes.

I stammered, "I think I'd like a little time alone too," and hobbled away. When I made it to the stairs, after painfully slow progress, I paused. I gripped the banister hard, my vision blurred with tears. I felt a hand on my shoulder and turned to bury my wet face in Kishan's chest, sobbing. I knew it wasn't fair to seek comfort from Kishan and cry over his brother, but I couldn't help myself.

He put his arm under my knees and picked me up. Cradling me close, he carried me up the stairs. After he laid me on my bed, he went to the bathroom, came back with a box of tissues, and set it on the nightstand. Kishan murmured a few words in Hindi, smoothed the hair back from my face, pressed a kiss on my brow, and left me alone.

Late that afternoon, Nilima came to see me.

I was sitting in my room in the white chair, clutching my stuffed tiger. I'd spent the morning crying and sleeping. She hugged me and sat down on the couch.

"He doesn't know me," I whispered.

"You must give him time. Here, I've brought you a snack."

"I'm not hungry."

"You didn't eat your breakfast either."

I looked at her with watery eyes. "I just don't think I can eat."

"Alright."

She went into my bathroom and returned with my hairbrush.

"Everything will be fine, Miss Kelsey. He's back with us, and he *will* remember you."

She unbraided my hair and began brushing it out in long, smooth strokes. It comforted me and reminded me of my mother.

"You really think he will?"

"Yes. Even if he doesn't get his memory back, he is bound to fall for you again. My mother has a saying: *a deep well never runs dry*. His feelings for you are too deep to ever disappear completely, even in a dry season, such as this."

I laughed wetly. "I'd like to meet your mom sometime."

"Perhaps you shall."

She left me alone after that, and, feeling better, I headed slowly downstairs.

Kishan was pacing in the kitchen. He stopped when I entered and helped me hobble in. I wrapped the dishes of uneaten food that Nilima had brought me, placing them in the refrigerator.

"Your ankle looks better," he said after a brief inspection.

"Mr. Kadam had me ice it and elevate it all morning."

"Are you okay?" he asked.

"Yeah. I'll be fine. It's not the reunion I'd hoped for, but it's better than finding him dead."

"I'll help you. We can work with him together."

It must have killed him to say that. I knew he would, though. He wanted me to be happy, and if helping me reunite with Ren would make me happy, he'd do it.

"Thank you, I appreciate it."

I took a step closer and almost fell. He caught me and drew me hesitantly into his arms. He expected me to push him away like I had a habit of doing lately, but I put my arms around him instead and hugged him.

He stroked my back, sighed, and kissed my forehead. Right then, Ren walked into the kitchen. I stiffened as he looked at us, expecting him to react to Kishan touching me, but he dismissed us completely, grabbed a bottle of water, and left without saying a word.

Kishan lifted my chin with his finger. "He'll come around, Kells."

"Right."

"Do you want to watch a movie?"

"That sounds good."

"Okay. But something with action. None of your musical stuff."

I laughed. "Action, huh? Something tells me you'd like *Indiana Jones*."

He put an arm around my waist and helped me over to the indoor theater.

I didn't see Ren again until late that evening. He was sitting on the veranda watching the moon. I paused, wondering if he wanted to be alone; then decided if he did, he could always ask me to leave.

When I slid open the door and stepped outside, he tilted his head but didn't move.

"Am I bothering you?" I asked.

"No. Would you like to sit down?"

"Okay."

He rose and politely helped me sit down across from him. I studied Ren's face. His bruises were almost gone, and his hair had been washed and cut. He was dressed in casual designer clothes, but his feet were bare. I gasped when I saw them. They were still purple and distended, which meant they'd been terribly hurt.

"What did he do to your feet?"

His eyes followed my gaze and he shrugged. "He broke them over and over until they felt like swollen bean bags."

"Oh," I said uneasily. "May I see your hands?"

He held out his hands, and I took them gently in mine and studied them carefully. His golden skin was unmarred, and his fingers were long and straight. Nails that had been torn and bloodied earlier were now healthy and filled in. I turned his hands over and looked at the palms. Except for a gash on the inside of his arm ending at his wrist, they looked undamaged. A normal person who'd had their hands broken in so many places would likely have lost the use of them. At the very least, the repaired knuckles would have been swollen and inflexible.

Tracing the gash lightly, I asked, "What about this?"

"This is from an experiment when he tried to drain all the blood out of my body to see if I'd survive. The good news is that I did. He was rather put out about getting his clothes all bloody though."

He pulled his hands out of mine abruptly and stretched out both arms along the back of the love seat.

"Ren, I—"

He held up a hand. "You don't need to apologize to me, Kelsey. It's not your fault. Kadam explained the whole thing to me."

"He did? What did he say?"

"He told me that Lokesh was actually after you, that he wanted Kishan's amulet that you now wear, and that if I hadn't stayed behind to fight, he would have gotten all three of us."

"I see."

He leaned forward. "I'm glad that he took me instead of you. You would have been killed in a horrible way. Nobody deserves to die like that. Better me or Kishan being captured than you."

"Yes, you were very chivalrous."

He shrugged and looked at the pool lights.

"Ren, what did he . . . do to you?"

He turned back to me and lowered his gaze to my swollen ankle. "May I?"

I nodded.

He lifted my leg gently and placed it on his lap. He touched the purple bruises lightly and tucked a pillow under it.

"I'm sorry you've been injured. It's unfortunate that you don't heal quickly like we do."

"You're avoiding my question."

"Some things in this world shouldn't be uttered. It's bad enough that one person must know of them."

"It helps to talk, though."

"When I do feel ready to talk about it, I'll tell Kishan or Kadam. They're battle-hardened. They've seen many terrible things."

"I'm battle-hardened too."

He laughed. "You? No, you are far too fragile to hear of the things I've experienced."

I crossed my arms. "I'm not that fragile."

"I'm sorry. I've offended you. *Fragile* is the wrong word. You're too . . . pure, too innocent, to hear of those things. I won't contaminate your mind with thoughts of what Lokesh has done."

"But it might help."

"You've sacrificed enough for me already."

"But everything you experienced was to protect me."

"I don't remember that, but if I could remember, I'm sure I would still refuse to tell you about it."

"Probably. You can be pretty stubborn."

"Yes. Some things never change."

"Do you feel well enough to revisit some memories?"

"We can try. Where do you want to begin?"

"Why don't we start at the beginning?"

He nodded, and I told him of seeing him for the first time at the circus and working with him. How he escaped his cage and slept on the hay, and I blamed myself for not locking the door. I told him about the cat poem and about the picture I drew of him in my journal. The weird thing was that he remembered the cat poem. He even quoted it to me.

When I was finished, an hour had gone by. He'd listened attentively and nodded. He seemed the most interested in my journal.

"May I read it?" he asked.

I twitched uncomfortably. "I guess it could help. There are some of your poems in there, and it is a good record of almost everything we did. It might trigger something. Just prepare yourself for lots of girl emotions."

He raised an eyebrow. I quickly explained, "We didn't exactly get off to a smooth start romantically. I rejected you initially, then changed my mind, then rejected you again. It wasn't the best of decisions, but I thought I knew what I was doing at the time."

He smiled. "'The course of true love never did run smooth.'"

"When did you read *Midsummer Night's Dream*?"

"I haven't. I studied a book of famous Shakespeare quotes in school."

"You never told me that."

"Ah, at last something I know that you don't." He sighed. "This situation is very confusing for me. I apologize if I've hurt you. It isn't my intention. Mr. Kadam told me your parents are gone. Is that right?"

I nodded.

"Imagine if you couldn't remember your real parents. You've heard stories of this man and woman, but they were strangers to you. They had memories of you doing things that you couldn't remember, and they had expectations of you. They had dreams for your future, different dreams than what you might imagine for yourself."

"It would be very hard. I might even doubt what I was being told."

"Exactly. Especially if you had been mentally and physically tortured for several months."

"I understand."

I stood, my heart breaking all over again. Ren touched my hand as I passed.

"I don't mean to hurt your feelings. There are a lot of worse things I can imagine than being told I have a sweet, kind girlfriend that I can't remember. I just need time to wrap my mind around this."

"Ren? Do you think? I mean, is there any possibility? Could you learn to . . . to *love* me again?"

He looked at me thoughtfully for a moment and said, "I'll try."

I nodded mutely. He dropped my hand, and I shut myself in my room.

He'll try.

A week went by with little to no improvement. He couldn't remember anything about me despite the efforts of Kishan, Mr. Kadam, and Nilima. He began to lose patience with everyone except Nilima, who he liked to visit. I figured she bothered him much less about it. She didn't know me as well as the others and spoke of things both of them remembered.

I made him every dish he'd liked while in Oregon, including my chocolate peanut butter cookies. The first time he ate them he seemed to enjoy them, but then I explained the significance of the cookies, and the second time he was less enthusiastic. He didn't want me to be disappointed when eating them didn't trigger his memory. Kishan took advantage of his reluctance and single-handedly polished off every batch I made. I stopped cooking soon after that.

I came to dinner one night and found everyone staring eagerly at me from the dining room, which had been decorated with peach and ivory streamers. A large layer cake rested in the center of a beautifully decorated table.

"Happy Birthday, Miss Kelsey!" Mr. Kadam exclaimed.

"My birthday? I totally forgot!"

"How old are you now, Kells?" asked Kishan.

"Umm . . . nineteen."

"Well, she's still a baby. Eh, Ren?"

Ren nodded and smiled politely.

Kishan grabbed me in a hug. "Here. Have a seat while I get your presents."

Kishan helped me sit, and then left to gather the gifts. Mr. Kadam had used the Golden Fruit to summon my favorite dinner: a cheeseburger, French fries, and a chocolate malt. Everyone else got to pick their favorite meals as well, and we all laughed and remarked on our neighbors' selections. It was the first time I'd laughed in quite a while.

After we finished dinner, Kishan announced it was present time. I opened Nilima's gift first. She gave me an expensive bottle of French perfume, which I passed around.

Kishan smelled it and grunted. "Her natural scent is much better."

When it got to Ren, he smiled at Nilima, and said, "I like it."

The easy smile slipped off my face.

Next was Mr. Kadam's present. He pushed an envelope across the table. He winked at me as I slipped my finger under the edge to open it. Inside was a picture of a car.

I held it up. "What's this?"

"It's a new car."

"I don't need a new car. I have the Boxster at home."

He shook his head sadly. "It's gone. I've sold it and the house through another organization. Lokesh knew about it and could have traced it to us, so I've covered our tracks."

I waved the picture around and grinned. "And what type of car did you decide I needed this time?"

"It's nothing really. Just something to get you from here to there."

"What's it called?"

"It's a McLaren SLR 722 Roadster."

"How big is it?"

"It's a convertible."

"Will a tiger fit?"

"No. It seats only two, but the boys are men half the day now."

"Is it more than $30,000?"

He squirmed and hedged, "Yes, but—"

"How much more?"

"Much more."

"*How* much more?"

"About $400,000 more."

My mouth dropped open. "Mr. Kadam!"

"Miss Kelsey, I know it's extravagant, but when you drive it, you will see it's worth every cent."

I folded my hands across my chest. "I won't drive it."

He looked offended. "That car was meant to be driven."

"Then you drive it. I'll drive the Jeep."

He looked tempted. "If it will appease you, perhaps we can share it."

Kishan clapped his hands. "I can't wait."

Mr. Kadam wagged a finger at him. "Oh, no! Not you. We'll get *you* a nice sedan. *Used*."

"I'm a good driver!" Kishan protested.

"You need more training."

I stopped them, laughing. "Okay. When the car arrives, we'll talk about it some more."

"The car is already here, Miss Kelsey. It's in the garage as we speak. Perhaps we can go for a drive later." His eyes twinkled with excitement.

"All right, just you and me. Thank you for my wonderfully extravagant, over-the-top present."

He nodded happily.

"Okay." I smiled. "I'm ready for my next present."

"That's me," Kishan said. He handed me a large white box wrapped with a blue velvet ribbon. I opened it, brushed aside the delicate tissue, and touched silky blue material. I stood up and took the soft gift from the box.

"Oh, Kishan! It's lovely!"

"I had it specially made to match the robe you wore in the Grove of Dreams. Obviously the Scarf couldn't replicate the real flowers woven through the material, but it embroidered flowers instead."

Delicate blue cornflowers with soft green stems and leaves ran around the hem and up the side of the robe to the waist, then continued on the other side to the shoulder. Purple and orange winged fairies perched jauntily on the leaves.

"Thank you! I love it!"

I hugged him and pecked him on the cheek, and his golden eyes sparkled with pleasure.

"Thank you everyone!"

"Uh, there's still my gift. It's definitely not as interesting as any of those." Ren pushed a hastily wrapped gift toward me and missed my shy smile when he stared at his hands.

The package held something soft and squishy. "What is it? Let me guess. A new cashmere hat and gloves? No, I wouldn't need that in India. Ah, I know, a silk scarf?"

Nilima said, "Open it so we can see."

I tore open the present and blinked my eyes a few times.

Mr. Kadam leaned forward. "What is it, Miss Kelsey?"

A tear plopped onto my cheek. I quickly dashed it away with the back of my hand and smiled.

"It's a very lovely pair of socks."

I turned to Ren. "Thank you. You must have known I needed a new pair."

Ren nodded and pushed some uneaten food around on his plate. Nilima sensed something was wrong, squeezed my arm, and then said, "Who's ready for cake?"

I smiled brightly, trying to lighten the mood.

Nilima cut the cake while Mr. Kadam added giant scoops of ice cream. I thanked them and took a bite of my cake.

"It's peach! I've never had peach cake before. Who made it? The Golden Fruit?"

Mr. Kadam was busy making the next perfect scoop. "Actually, Nilima and I made it," he said.

"The ice cream," I grinned, "it's peaches and cream too?"

Mr. Kadam laughed. "Yes. It's actually from that dairy you love. Tillamook, I believe it is."

I took another bite of cake. "I knew I recognized the taste. It is my favorite brand of ice cream. Thank you for thinking of me."

Mr. Kadam sat down to enjoy his piece and said, "Oh, well, it wasn't me at all. This is something that was all planned a long—" his words trailed off as he realized his error. He coughed uncomfortably and stammered, "Well, suffice it to say, it wasn't my idea."

"*Oh*."

He went on awkwardly, trying to distract me from figuring out that my old Ren had planned a peaches and cream birthday party for me months in advance. Mr. Kadam started telling me about how the peach was a symbol of long life in China and that it was good luck.

I tuned him out. The cake suddenly stuck in my throat. I sipped some water to clear it.

Ren pushed the peach ice cream around on his plate. "Do we have any of that chocolate peanut butter ice cream left? I'm not a big fan of the peaches and cream."

I raised my head and looked at him with shock and disappointment.

I heard Mr. Kadam tell him it was in the freezer. Ren pushed aside his peach dessert and headed out of the room. I sat immobile. My fork was raised halfway to my mouth when I'd paused.

I waited. Soon, I felt the overwhelming wave of hurt rush through me. In the midst of what should have been heaven, surrounded by the people I loved, celebrating the day of my birth, I was experiencing my own private hell. My eyes welled with tears. I excused myself, stood, and turned away quickly. Kishan got up also, confused.

Trying vainly to infuse my voice with enthusiasm, I asked Mr. Kadam if we could take that drive tomorrow.

"Of course," he said quietly.

As I went upstairs, I heard Kishan threatening Ren. Suspiciously, he asked, "What did you *do*?"

I heard Ren's soft reply, "I don't *know*."

EPILOGUE

unloved

The next day, I woke determined to try to make the best of things. It wasn't Ren's fault. He didn't know what he did or why it hurt so much. He didn't remember about the socks, or how I smelled, or about choosing peaches and cream ice cream instead of peanut butter chocolate. *It's just stupid ice cream! Who cares?*

No one remembered those things. No one knew now. Except me. I went for a ride in the fancy new convertible with Mr. Kadam and tried to be happy as he went over its features. I went through the motions, but I was numb inside. I despaired. I felt like I was interacting with a stunt-double Ren. He looked like my Ren and could even talk like him, but there was a spark missing. Something was off.

I'd planned to work out with Kishan when we got home, so I changed and headed through the laundry room and down the stairs to the dojo, stopping when I heard voices arguing. I didn't mean to eavesdrop, but I heard my name mentioned and couldn't leave.

"You're hurting her," Kishan said.

"You think I don't know that? I don't want to hurt her, but I won't be coerced into feeling something that I don't."

"Can't you at least try?"

"I have been."

"I've seen you give more attention to ice cream than you do to her."

Ren let out an exasperated sigh. "Look, there's something . . . off-putting about her."

"What do you mean?"

"I can't really describe it. It's just that when I'm near her . . . I can't wait to get away. It's a relief when she's not around."

"How can you *say* that? You *loved* her! You were more passionate about her than you've ever been about anything in your entire life!"

Ren spoke softly. "I can't imagine feeling that for her. She's nice and cute, but she's a bit young. Too bad it wasn't Nilima I was in love with."

Kishan responded with outrage, "*Nilima*! She's like a sister to us! You've never expressed any feelings for her before!"

"She's easier to be around," Ren replied quietly. "She doesn't look at me with big brown eyes full of hurt."

Both brothers were silent for a minute. I'd bitten my lip deeply and tasted blood, but the pain didn't affect me.

Kishan spoke intently, "*Kelsey* is all that a man could ask for. She's perfect for you. She loves poetry and sits endlessly content while listening to you sing and play your guitar. She waited months for you to come after her, and she has risked her life repeatedly to save your mangy white hide. She's sweet and loving and warm and beautiful and would make you immeasurably happy."

There was a pause. Then I heard Ren say incredulously, "You *love* her."

Kishan didn't answer right away, but then said softly, almost so I couldn't hear it, "No man in his right mind wouldn't, which proves you *aren't* in your right mind."

Ren said thoughtfully, "Maybe I was grateful to her and allowed her to believe I loved her once, but I don't feel that way about her now."

"Believe me. *Gratitude* was not the emotion you felt for her. You pined for her for months. You paced in your room until you wore a hole in the carpet. You wrote thousands of love poems describing her beauty and of how miserable you were when she was gone. If you don't believe me, go up to your room and read them for yourself."

"I *have* read them."

"Then what's your problem? I have never seen you happier in your miserable excuse for an existence than when you were with her. You loved her, and it was real."

"I don't know! Maybe it was being tortured over and over again that did this. Maybe Lokesh planted something in my brain that ruined her forever in my mind. When I hear her name or her voice, I cringe. I expect pain. I don't want that. It's not fair to either of us. She doesn't deserve to be lied to. Even if I could learn to love her, the torture is still there in the back of my mind. Every time I look at her, I see Lokesh questioning, always questioning. Hurting me because of a girl I didn't know. I can't do it, Kishan."

"Then . . . you don't deserve her."

There was a long pause.

"No, I guess I don't."

I bit my hand to hold back a sob and gasped. They heard me.

"Kells?" Kishan said.

I ran up the steps.

"Kells! Wait!"

I heard Kishan following me and ran up the stairs as fast as I could. I knew if I didn't hurry, one of them would catch me. Slamming the laundry room door behind me, I ran up the other flight of stairs, into my bathroom, and locked the door. I crawled into the dry tub and pulled my knees to my chest. An assortment of knocks fell upon the door—some gentle, some insistent and harsh, some barely audible. Everyone seemed to take a turn. Even Ren. Eventually, they left me alone.

I clutched my heart. The connection between us was gone. The beautiful bouquet of tiger lilies that I'd nourished and cared for since Ren's absence dried up. My heart was devastated by merciless drought. One by one, the soft, fragrant petals turned brown and fell off the stem.

No amount of coaxing, trimming, watering, or cutting was going to save them. It was winter. The stems shriveled. The blooms were spent. Old, broken petals were crushed into dust and were blown away by a stiff, hot wind. All that remained were a few brown stumps—a sad memoriam to a once precious and priceless arrangement.

Late that night, I emerged from my room, put on sneakers, and grabbed the keys to my new car. Unnoticed, I quietly left the house and slipped into the smooth leather seat. Speeding down the road with the top down, I drove until I found myself at a viewing point atop a hill overlooking the wide forested valley below. Reclining the seat, I lay back, looked up at the stars, and thought about constellations.

My dad had once told me about the North Star. He had said that mariners could always rely on it. It never deviated. It was always there, always dependable. *What was its other name? Ah, Polaris.* I searched for the Big Dipper but I couldn't see it. I remembered Dad said it was only visible in the northern hemisphere. He said there was no other constellation like it in the southern hemisphere. It was a unique celestial phenomenon.

Ren had said once that he was as constant as the North Star. He had been my Polaris. Now, I had no center. No guide. I felt despair sneaking through me again. Then a tiny voice inside me, with a similar sarcastic wit to my mother's, reminded me, *Just because you can't see the star doesn't mean it's not there. It might be hidden from view for a while, but you can rest assured that it still shines brightly somewhere.*

Maybe someday that spark will be found again. Maybe I'd waste my life seeking it. I was adrift on an ocean of loneliness. A mariner without

a star to follow. Could I be happy without him? I didn't even want to consider it.

I'd experienced loss. My parents were gone. Ren was . . . gone. But *I* was still here. I still had things to accomplish. I had a job to do. I'd done this before, and I could do it again. Push through the pain and move on with life. If I could find love with someone along the way, then so be it. If I couldn't, then I would do my best to be happy by myself. I'd suffered when Ren was gone before, and I'd suffer now, but I'd survive.

I reasoned, *There's no denying that I loved him and still do, but there are lots of things to be happy about. The Ocean Teacher said that the purpose of life is to be happy. The Divine Weaver told me not to become disheartened when the pattern doesn't suit. She said I should wait and watch and be patient and devoted.*

The threads of my life are all tangled and jumbled up. I don't know if I'll ever get them straightened out. The fabric of my existence is pretty ugly right now. All I can do is hold onto my faith, believing that someday I'll see the light of that bright star again.

I once told Ren that our story wasn't over.

And it's not.

Not yet.

ACKNOWLEDGMENTS

As always, I'd like to thank my early reading group. My family—Kathy, Bill, Wendy, Jerry, Heidi, Linda, Shara, Tonnie, Megan, Jared, and Suki. And my friends—Rachelle, Cindy, Josh, Nancy, Heidi Jo, Alyssa, and Linda.

A warm expression of gratitude for my editor/adviser/counselor from India, Sudha Seshadri, who has also become my friend and who I think loves my tigers as much as I do.

I am eternally thankful for my husband, who has faithfully read each chapter out loud as I write them. Without his punctuation edits, no one else would understand the material. He's always eager to read the next chapter and even admits to liking the kissing scenes. He's my biggest fan and my biggest critic, which is usually how the best marriages go.

A special thanks to my brother Jared and his wife, Suki, who patiently described, and even demonstrated, all the martial arts moves so I would have better fight scenes.

I would also like to express appreciation for Tsultrim Dorjee, assistant at The Office of His Holiness the Dalai Lama for allowing me to use quotes from the Dalai Lamas.

Thanks to my first team of editors at Booksurge, Rhadamanthus and Gail Cato, for their hard work and a hearty thank you to all the people at Booksurge without whose services, my tigers might never have seen the printed page.

Please send many kind thoughts to my agent, Alex, for his efforts in my behalf. His expertise was sorely needed and is deeply appreciated.

A huge thank you and the warmest of wishes to Team Tiger at

Sterling, especially Judi Powers, and a round of applause for my fabulous editors and friends Cindy Loh and Mary Hern who made the book the best it could be.

Lastly, thanks to all my fans who read and reread tirelessly, obsessing to the point that your moms have to hide the books from you. You know who you are. You are all crazy and wonderful! Thanks for all your lovely e-mails and letters of support and encouragement.

tiger's voyage

NOVEMBER 2011

"I won't let you be alone ever again. I love you, too, Kishan."

I leaned forward and pressed my lips to his. He shifted to hold me against him and kissed me back, gentle, soft and sweet. But then, I felt a crack, a splinter, and a pull.

My heart jerked wildly and a fire burned suddenly within me. It blazed with a heat I hadn't felt in a long time. It was consuming and powerful. My heart opened. My connection was back. My frame shook from the intensity of it. I was whole again. Time seemed to stop.

Something huge hit the deck behind us and several candles extinguished in a sudden warm wind. My body vibrated from the impact and the shock of it made me topple. *What was that? A dragon? A meteor?* Thoughts of various possible disasters raced through my mind.

Kishan looked at me in confusion and we froze as an enraged, intractable voice in the dark threatened, *"Let. Her. Go."*

COLLEEN HOUCK's debut novel, *Tiger's Curse*, is a *New York Times* and *Publishers Weekly* bestseller. *Tiger's Quest* is the second volume in her popular *Tiger's Curse* series. Colleen lives in Salem, Oregon, with her husband and a white stuffed tiger.

To find out more, visit **www.tigerscursebook.com**.

GO MOBILE!

To access bonus content for the TIGER'S CURSE series, download Microsoft's free Tag Reader on your smartphone at **www.gettag.mobi**. Then use your phone to take a picture of the bar code below to get exclusive extras about Kelsey, Ren, Kishan, Mr. Kadam, and other characters from the TIGER'S CURSE series, as well as more information about the books and author Colleen Houck.

1. Download the free tag reader at: **www.gettag.mobi**

2. Take a photo of the bar code using your smartphone camera

3. Discover the spellbinding world of the TIGER'S CURSE series!

SPLINTER

An imprint of Sterling Publishing Co., Inc.

New York

www.sterlingpublishing.com

774
Multnomah Falls
Greetings from
OREGON
Mt. Hood
Pacific Ocean